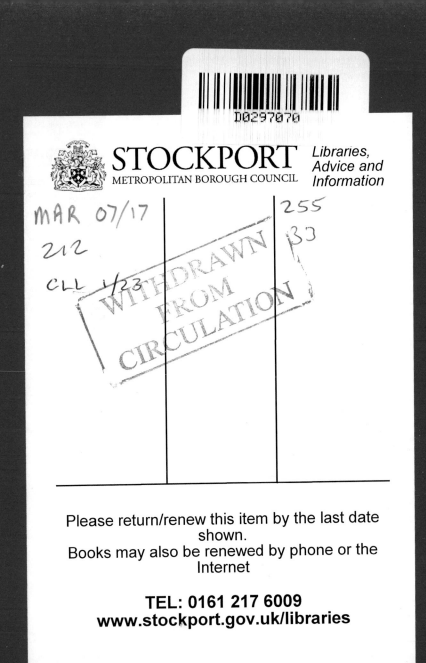

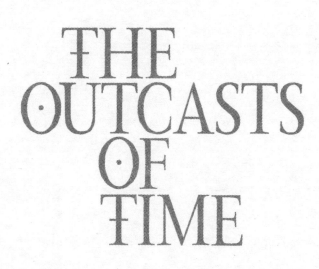

THE OUTCASTS OF TIME

IAN MORTIMER

THE OUTCASTS OF TIME

**SIMON &
SCHUSTER**

London · New York · Sydney · Toronto · New Delhi

A CBS COMPANY

First published in Great Britain by Simon & Schuster UK Ltd, 2017
A CBS COMPANY

1 3 5 7 9 10 8 6 4 2

Simon & Schuster UK Ltd
1st Floor
222 Gray's Inn Road
London WC1X 8HB

Simon & Schuster Australia, Sydney
Simon & Schuster India, New Delhi

www.simonandschuster.co.uk
www.simonandschuster.com.au
www.simonandschuster.co.in

A CIP catalogue record for this book
is available from the British Library

Hardback ISBN: 978-1-4711-4655-8
Trade Paperback ISBN: 978-1-4711-4656-5
eBook ISBN: 978-1-4711-4657-2

Typeset in the UK by M Rules
Printed and bound by CPI Group (UK) Ltd, Croydon, CR0 4YY

Simon & Schuster UK Ltd are committed to sourcing paper that is made from
wood grown in sustainable forests and support the Forest Stewardship Council,
the leading international forest certification organisation. Our books
displaying the FSC logo are printed on FSC certified paper.

This book is dedicated to my son,
Alexander Mortimer

Home is not a place but a time

Acknowledgements

How this novel came to be written and published would make a story in itself. Those who helped with the publishing side include my editors, Clare Hey, Jo Dickinson and Carla Josephson, and my agent, Georgina Capel: I owe all of them many thanks for their patience, advice and confidence in the idea. Those who contributed to the writing include my brothers, Robert and David Mortimer; the Revd Simon Franklin (who nobly struggled through the whole script when all the medieval dialogue was in Devon dialect); John Allan; Andy Gardner; Poppy Burgess; Mike Grady; Ian and Pam Mercer; Nicky Hodges; James Kidner; and Stuart Williams – plus a host of people with whom I discussed the narrative over the period of ten or twelve years. Sorry, all of you, if I've forgotten exactly what you said, or what I said, or what your names were, or what your order was at the bar. My apologies also if I spoiled it for you by telling you the ending. There have been times when my enthusiasm for this story has got the better of me. But just as the whole process has been one of passion, so too it has been one of gratitude to the people around me, and I am deeply grateful for your support.

I would particularly like to thank my wife Sophie, without whom this book would still be a pub conversation. Just by being here, she gives me the companionship I need to venture away from my own time and imagine being in that most inhospitable place, the distant past.

Ian Mortimer

Moretonhampstead, 25 November 2016

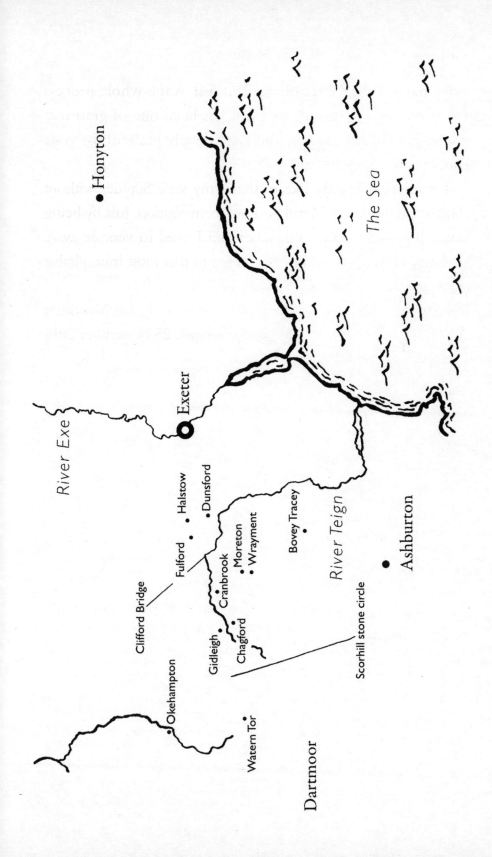

Chapter One

Tuesday, 16 December 1348

The first thing you need to understand is what it means to sell your soul. It is not a matter of shaking hands with a shadowy figure, or bartering promises with a burning bush. What do you have to sell? You don't know. To whom are you going to sell it? Again, you don't know. All you know is that your very desire to offer it up is accompanied by the most overwhelming urge to scream. You want to scream so much that you will empty your bones of time.

This is what I feel now – and have felt every day since I first saw the deadly work of the plague. When I look along the road into the distance and see no one, the desire to yell burns within me. When I look up towards the hills where once there was peace and tranquillity, I think of a horrific silence: abandoned farms and cottages, the carcasses of animals and the bodies of children and their parents. The absence of kindness. An eye without life. Now, as we approach the leafless oak on the edge of Honyton, and the inn beside it, the urge to cry out is overwhelming.

There were musicians playing when I was last here, three days before Michaelmas. That was just eleven weeks ago. I stop and let my travelling sack fall to the ground, and put my face in the hollow of my cupped hands; I whisper the names of my dead mother and father. My brother William turns and tells me to hurry, and makes a joke about me being slower than the dead. I take my hands away from my face, and stare at him, then pick up my sack and start walking again. But inside I am still yelling. I can do nothing to tell the world how I feel because everything is dying around us. And dying inside us.

I glance back at the leafless oak and remember the scene that day: the music and the gaiety. We were travellers passing through the town, watching the women and girls dance with the men, their hair let down, naturally flowing. They all had their favourites: you could see their loves in their eyes as they skipped past them. They were smiling at us too, as if they understood that we strangers, by watching their smiles, knew the secrets of their hearts. I remember slopping my ale cup and singing lustily, even though William and I had been intending to leave earlier, on our journey to Salisbury. Now, looking at that tree, I wonder how many of those women are dead. It seems that winter has twice fallen. Firstly, it has come upon us with the chill of December: in the bare branches stark against the sky, and the short days and the frozen puddles in the ruts of the roads. And secondly it is here in the crow-cry of cold despair, and the feeling that, unlike any previous year, there never will be another spring. Winter is a point of reckoning now, not a pause.

Time there was when the marketplace in Honyton was all colour and movement. On market days you'd see the russets, browns, greys and reds of tunics, and a whole gamut of hoods and hats. If you blurred your eyes for a moment, you'd see it like the movement of a hive, as if all the little twitches of the crowd were bees. There'd always be a still point in the human storm: a crier calling the news or a black-cassocked friar haranguing a group of youths about their souls' struggle to reach Heaven. Today there are no criers, friars or tormented souls. There are no market traders either – no nodding hoods as a butcher or piemaker passes over his wares and holds out a hand for the silver pennies, turning immediately to greet the next customer. Dead leaves blow across the mud and gravel of the square. A broken trestle from a stall lies on its side, commemorating the last market to be held here. It looks like an old tilted grave marker where someone who has already been forgotten lies buried.

William and I continue along the street through the town. It's still early, the third hour after prime, but both of us are tired after a restless night under the dripping trees. House after house has its shutters closed, as if the townspeople are still in bed.

'How many corpses do you think we'll see today?' asks William, adjusting the travelling sack on his shoulder. 'I'll hold you, it'll be more than yesterday. What do you say, John, more than six? A kiss of Elizabeth Tapper's honeyed lips and a jug of her best ale, for he who counts the most this side of Whymple.'

I look at my brother but I do not reply. I see the gold ring with the garnet that he always wears, his most prized possession. He seems to think that, apart from the unfortunate victims, life is the same as ever.

'Oh, come now, brother,' he says, 'I pray, speak! You're not dead yet. The heaviness of your mood is such that anyone might mistake you for Noah on his Ark, in the moment of realising that he's forgotten the cows.'

'Jest not, William. This *is* a second Flood. God is clearing the land. Not with water but with pestilence. Can you not see it?'

'Don't be a cut farthing, John. What I see is what you see. No more, no less. But your mind is closed. This pestilence is no work of God's. We've seen young children, babes even, lying by the road with black blotches on their necks, arms and thighs. Why would God be punishing them? They cannot have sinned. This is no divine clearance of iniquity. This is the work of the Devil, and I'll not be awestruck by it.'

I take a deep breath. 'William, the Devil is God's vassal, and the Devil shall do what the Lord Almighty commands him to do. If God wills the land be cleared of sinners, then the Devil shall do the clearing. Those who fail to attend church are . . .'

But William, looking ahead, raises his hand.

The body is that of a grey-bearded man in his fifties, lying face down on the hard earth and stones of the highway, with his head turned to one side. There is a sagging black swelling on the lower side of his neck, the size of two fists clasped together, clutching at his throat. His mouth is open slightly;

the whiteness of his teeth only draws attention to the fact that at least two are missing. William presses his foot against the man's cloak: it is frozen stiff. One knee is dirty where he fell. His purse has already been cut from his belt and the moistness of his eyes has frozen, glazing his expression into an opaque whiteness.

Normally, on finding a dead man, we would go to the constable. But today we remain quiet.

'He's nothing of beauty, that's for sure,' says William, turning away.

'He was one of the lucky ones,' I reply as we walk on. I scratch an itch under my arm.

'Lucky? Listen, brother, if that man's fate be fair good fortune, my horse speaks Latin. By what token was he lucky?'

'He fell face down. He did not spend days suffering, sweating and frenzied. He was able to walk until finally he collapsed. He used a cuttlefish to whiten his teeth; therefore he must have been a man of some prosperity. As for his cloak, even you would be proud of such a garment. Last, look at where his purse was. Clearly, the man who cut it from his belt opened it and saw not one or two coins but many – enough that he decided to take the risk and cut the whole purse, even though it might be carrying the infection. So, brother of mine, I say to you that this wealthy man, suddenly taken ill with the disease, choking on his pain and stumbling to a quick death, was most fortunate.'

William shakes his head. 'You should not attend so closely to the death throes of every stranger, John. Let some of the dead suffer on their own account.'

What can I say to that? This dead man was one of the few
for whom I have *not* felt sorry. It is the living who tear the
scream out of me, for whom I weep. I thought that the last
mass grave that I would ever see would be on the battlefields
of France – so many rigid arms and legs covered in dried
blood and flies in the pit. But death is all around us here too. I
see it in the windows whose shutters remain open when dusk
comes, and in the shutters that remain closed of a morning. I
see it also in the unguided progress of a boat that floats down
a river with its occupant slumped over the side, bumping
into banks and quays. Passing a church in Somerset, where a
father and a mother were burying their child, I even heard the
sound of death. It rang out in the silence of the bells that did
not acknowledge the dead boy. Even the tolling of a funeral
bell is an act of life. Today, our private thoughts are the only
chimes that send the dead on their way. And then we move
on, and leave them – and even the silent bells of our thoughts
cease to toll.

Six miles on from Honyton we stop to have a dinner of
hard bread and cheese. We eat in silence. I notice a second
dead man, about fifty yards from the road. He is wearing a
russet tunic and lying crumpled in a fallow field. His figure
blends in with the earth so that at first neither of us notices
him. It is only when a crow lands on his torso that I pay
attention to the lump on the soil, and glimpse the flesh of his
lower leg and the shape of his shoulder.

William wipes his face and lifts his bag. 'Coming?'

I watch the crow fly away. The landscape of cold red earth,
grey sky and corpse make me wonder whether this man's fate

will be ours too. After all, who will eventually bury that man when the plague comes to an end? His corpse will lie there, slowly soaking back into the soil as the rains fall and the wild pigs and other beasts find the bones and gnaw on them. If a fox carries away the skull, the next farmer to till the ground might look at the scattered remains and be uncertain whether they belonged to a man or a beast.

I pick up my sack and join William.

Who *was* that man in the field? Nothing but a nameless object. I feel as if my head is in my hands – except that it is not my hands on which my cheeks are resting but two weeks of constant fear. Maybe I am not in my right mind. But how could anyone these days be in their *right* mind? The only way I can control myself is by thinking that I must not let my wife, Catherine, see me like this. I tell myself that I must walk faster, and breathe in the air that God has given me, and return to her.

In Salisbury there was another stone carver called John – John of Combe. He was one of the first in the city to catch the plague. He was very talkative before he fell ill, always spinning his chisel in his hand and catching it. But a week or so before they called a halt to the repairs, he failed to show up for work. When he did come back, two days later, he was sombre and distracted. He would strike his chisel three or four times, and then stare at the stone. One day, working on the same pinnacle as him, I saw him gazing into nothingness. I asked him what was bothering him. After a while he told me that, several days earlier, he had felt a painful swelling beneath his right arm, which he knew was the pestilence.

Straight away he had left the cathedral and walked north to the Giant's Circle. When he arrived it was almost dark. He walked around the stones and prayed to God or the Devil or anyone who was listening to save him. And as he stood there he suddenly felt a powerful figure seize him from behind and put his hand over his mouth to stop him crying out, and he heard a deep voice whisper in his ear, asking him would he offer his eternal soul in return for his mortal recovery, and live many years yet? Or would he prefer to die on the road-side on his return that night to Salisbury? John said he would offer his soul. And he felt the figure release its grip. Two days after our conversation, he slipped on the wet wooden scaf-folding and fell eighty feet. I myself saw the accident from the ground. His flailing body hit the poles twice on the way down and he struck the ground heavily. I was sure that the impact had killed him but he only broke his right arm and a rib. The bonesetter said he could do nothing about John's rib but that it would not threaten his life. As for his arm, that would recover quickly, for it was a clean break. Everyone said it was a miracle that he was alive.

William, who is still ahead of me, turns and calls back. 'Let's call on Elizabeth Tapper anyway. A taste of her posset will be most welcome.'

My eyes follow the movement of his shoulders, his beard and his purposeful I'll-do-what-I-want gait. I'm not keen to see the woman. She has two children yet has never had a husband, and they say that sinners are more likely to be infected with the pestilence. I am sure William is as kind to her as he is to every woman. To be fair to him, he is generous to everyone, not only women. But I don't understand why he gives in to his wickedness, and invites damnation into our lives.

Oh, I know, I know. William will say that *that* is the difference between us: he believes men choose the laws, not God, and that it is no sin in the eyes of God to break the law of mankind, for the law is an earthly, earthy thing. He says even the Bible was written by men and is interpreted by men, and that to break the law laid down therein is no crime against God. And in the Old Testament it is written that many great and holy men had many wives. He says that the sinner who knows he has done wrong believes he will go to Hell, and the hell is in the believing; the man who accidentally sins but whose intentions are pure will have no stain on his soul.

I cannot agree. I believe that God created the world to be as He wanted it, and if a man pollutes God's world through sin, then it stands polluted, whether or not the sinner meant to deviate from the path of righteousness. I can see that Elizabeth Tapper is still an attractive woman, even though she must be more than thirty years old now. But if God preserves her thus, it is for the husband that He intends her to embrace, not the travellers who pass this way with a few coins in their purses. An honest man should be caring for her and her children, not a string of ragrowsterers.

But I say nothing. I am not innocent myself. A few years ago, when I was working on the cathedral parapet, William came into Exeter and took me to the Bear Inn near the South Gate. What followed that night was much ale drinking and, afterwards, in the hall by candlelight, an act of shallow physical love that I have always regretted. For me, that night was like a flower of time. It grew from green innocence to a bud of desire and fulfilment in a few hours, and then quickly withered into a decrepit past that stank and disgusted me.

The truth is that I want nothing more than to be at home with my Catherine, by our hearth, talking together in the firelight. I want to tell her of what I feel when I see the world in the grip of the plague, and share it with her. I want to hear her tell me what she feels. I want our wounded hearts to comfort one another, to embrace. I want to face our greatest challenge together, not apart.

Elizabeth Tapper's cottage is a furlong off the highway and built in the old style: two crucks leaning together at either end. As you approach you can see the rot at the base of the walls, where the timbers go into the soil. The whitewash needs renewing too. In places the thatch has sunk inwards; in others, moss has grown across it. I am sure that the building leaks. Most people in this part of Devon would have pulled it down by now and started again, with a square timber framework and cob infill set on a stone plinth. But Elizabeth has no money and the bailiff no kindness. The very reason why she is here, on the extreme edge of the manor, is that she is not wanted in the village.

I will say this for her, though: she has a neatly tended garden, with many cabbages, leeks and the dead stalks of onions and beans. It is a safeguard we all must undertake in these times, when harvests might dwindle rapidly at the end of summer and winters can be so hard. Gardens can be the saving of a family.

William enters the house ahead of me. I pause to look at the garden, and hear him cry out.

It has been many months since I have heard him utter a sound like that – not since he found the corpse of a friend after our victory at Crécy. He is the sort of man who does not want anyone – least of all his younger brother – to know he is in pain.

I cross myself and go into the cottage. Inside, it is dark and smells of smoke, old ale, onions and bacon – and dried lavender, which has been used to scent the floor rushes. When my eyes adjust I see the wicker partition at one end of the hall, with a doorway leading to the inner chamber. William is standing there, quite still. There is a woman beside him, almost the same height. I do not recall Elizabeth being so tall. But then I see that she is not moving. She is utterly motionless, with her hands by her sides and her head at an angle to her shoulders.

Her feet are four inches off the ground. Four inches. The width of a hand is the gulf between life and death.

My first thought is that she has been set upon, raped or robbed, and killed by being strung up over the beam of her own home. But she had precious little to steal and was a common woman, and so no one would have needed to kill her. And then I ask myself: where are her children?

I walk closer. Her eyes are open, staring at eternity, which is here in the house with her. I cross myself again and say a prayer for her soul, and then one more for the safety of my own wife and children.

A gust of wind catches the door: it creaks and partially

closes, and a broom leaning against the wall falls over. I turn and go to the door, prop up the broom and place a block of wood to hold the door open, allowing in the light.

William is almost as still as the corpse. As I go back to him, I pass the hearth in the middle of the hall floor and bend down to feel the ashes: they are still vaguely warm. I hear him say, *'Benedicat vos omnipotens Deus Pater et Filius et Spiritus Sanctus.'* Those are the words that we were taught by the priest in our parish. William crosses himself. I do likewise, and join with him in saying, 'Amen.'

For the first time in days, I feel we are together. We might be on the edge of a cliff at night, staring at the same eternal darkness that Elizabeth Tapper now sees, but we are together.

He moves away from the doorway to the inner chamber. There I see her two children, who are about five and seven, lying side by side on an old straw mattress. The chinks in the shutter allow in enough light to reveal that their faces are blotched, their eyes closed. Their limbs have been straightened by the mother, who obviously stayed with them until the end and then took her own life. There is a pot of oaten broth, half-eaten, still beside the mattress.

I withdraw to the fresher air of the hall. My thoughts run to my own family, still more than a day's walk away. What will I find when I open the door to my own house? Will Catherine be hanging from a beam, like poor Elizabeth here? Her white neck pulled long by the rope, her hands, eyes and heart utterly empty? In my mind's eye, I see her body hanging in mid-air, like a sack of flesh. Will I find my sons, William, John and James, lying with blotched faces, dead in their beds? I imagine their hair, their eyes, and recall their voices, one by one. If they are dead will I too not take a rope and end my own life?

My attention is only snatched away from this thought by the sight of William moving a bench. He stands on it and unhooks a hefty flitch of bacon hanging from a beam. He steps back down and puts it into his travelling sack.

'In God's name, William, have you no respect?'

'Someone else'll have it if I don't,' he says. 'Good food is for the living, not thieves or worms.' He fastens his travelling sack again and places it beside the door. 'Besides, if you think me disrespectful, what about the pestilence? What respect did God show Elizabeth and her children? Is not God more disrespectful?'

'That's blasphemy.'

'Cease your pious moaning, John. I'm sick of it. Help me lift her down.'

From the way he looks at her, I realise that he did not care for her because she was a whore. He cared for her *despite* that fact.

I go over and place my arms around her corpse and lift it while William unhitches the noose. It is a sad weight. Her limbs are stiff and her skin unyielding, like cold wax. As William steps down from the bench I lower her to the floor; then we carry her through to the inner chamber, her hair cascading over my arms. We place her on the floor beside her children, and stand side by side at the foot of the mattress, saying our quiet prayers.

After a while he says, 'It'll be dark in less than three hours. There's another six miles to Exeter.'

I stare at the corpses, my mind numbed by death.

'John, I'd bury all three of them, if I could. But ...'

I know. In Christ's name, I know.

I leave the house and stand outside, breathing the air. He comes out after me. I look up at the sky, and speak my mind. 'We want to do the right thing. But. But. BUT. That short, unfinished expression says everything. Life shall carry on – *but*. The pure man has nothing to fear – *but* ... You shall not steal, *but* ... You shall honour your father and mother *unless* they be dying of plague. You shall bury the dead with honour – but not if they've black swellings erupting from their armpits and necks, or be self-drowned or hanged because their children are dead of plague.'

I feel tears welling up. Angry with myself, I wipe my face with alternate sweeps of my sleeves.

'It is good to let the grief flow out, brother.'

I take a deep breath, and look away. 'I met a mariner once. He told me that he'd been on a ship that was swept out to sea in a storm, beyond sight of land. The ship had lost her mast. For three weeks she was drifting. One by one the crew fell away. He told me that what killed them was not starvation or the waves but an idea: the thought that they'd never see land again. It fastened on them, and sank its teeth in, and it gradually sucked the will to live out of them. It loosened their grip on life. That's how I feel now.'

William puts his arms around my shoulders and rests his forehead against mine. 'Do you remember our father, on his deathbed?'

I nod. I was young at the time, perhaps only twelve, but I

can still see him there, coughing and rattling in the chamber of the mill house at Cranbrook, which our older brother now inhabits. His final act, after the priest had administered the last rites, was to push off his bedclothes and declare he was going for a walk. He started laughing, and then fell back, dead.

'Sometimes I find myself saying things as if I be doiled or crazed. Like asking how many corpses we'll see. We put those things we cannot face into the basket of madness. It's like his final laughter.'

I dwell on this, and lay the thought carefully to rest.

'Come,' he says, picking up his travelling sack again. 'She does not need us any more.'

Two hours later, the air turns colder, presaging rain. The light is beginning to fail. But a late gleam is breaking through the clouds too, creating small patches of brightness shifting across the darkening landscape. Momentarily it shines on the stones of a nearby grass-covered earth bank, and highlights two more dead bodies.

The man lying by the side of the road looks as though he was kneeling until the moment of his death. He is wearing a fur-trimmed black robe and black fur-edged cap. The red tunic beneath his robe is not dyed with plain madder root such as we common folk use but with some type of brighter red. His hosen too are expensive: true black, not dark grey. I wonder why he was on his knees, doing obeisance to every passer-by.

His young wife's body is curled against the bank, about

ten feet away. Her white tunic with green and gold braid, her blonde hair and her black travelling cloak all strike the eye with their quality and cleanness, contrasting so strongly with the dark swellings and red streaks of blood vessels in her pale skin. In her last moments she must have thrown her head back, offering her neck to the sky and the crows. I marvel that someone so beautiful could be so marked with such hideous disfigurements. Her mouth is open; her eyes have not yet frozen. There is something in the emptiness of her expression that makes me think of a woman in ecstasy. Such is her beauty that I think I should try to remember her, to use her face in my carving. But why did she die at the same place as her husband? Why did she not walk on? Or, if she died first, why did he stay here?

Not far from her hand is a silver crucifix attached to a necklace of amber rosary beads. There is a small book too, its long leather thread still attached to her belt.

I am searching for answers when I see her arm move.

I jump back, repulsed. This woman is as dead as anyone suffused by the plague. I glance at William but he looks at me, not understanding.

That is when we hear the baby cry.

Now I understand. The merchant, hunched over his knees, must have known that his dead body would be mute, and that only his final posture would speak for him. So he died kneeling, begging for help from future travellers – not for himself or even for his wife but for his infant. The woman died near to her husband because she had not sought to leave him. Quite the opposite. She too had known she was dying and all she hoped for at the end was that their two forms would draw attention to the child, which I now realise is beneath her arm, kept warm by her dying body.

I use a stick to pull back the edge of the dead woman's cloak. The child is dark-haired like its father, about three months old, and strapped to a swaddling board and engulfed in yards of white linen. It is hungry, moving its head, searching at its mother's clothed breast for milk.

'Leave it!' shouts William. His face is angry and frightened at once. I have seen him look like this before; it was when the captains lost control of the army and we broke into Caen, in a mad struggle with the frantic citizens. 'Leave it be.'

I feel strangely calm, despite the child's screaming and my brother's anxiety. 'It's innocent, William. It will die if we leave it.'

'Yes, it shall die!' he shouts. 'And if you touch it, you too shall die, as surely as its mother and father are dead.'

I shake my head. 'William, no.'

'In Christ's name, John, you saw the pits in Salisbury. Piles of bodies flung into the earth – so many they were uncountable. You've smelled the overwhelming stink of decay. These folk will be like that in two days, their bodies rotting like discarded meat. Do you want to resemble them?'

'You would leave it?' I say, searching my brother's face. 'You would let another Christian soul die on the highway? An innocent child. What kind of man are you? How can you stand there and judge the weak?'

The wind rises in the branches. William says nothing.

'Where is the pikeman who fought with the king in France?' I ask him. 'That man – I was proud to call him my brother. But now . . . Look at yourself: what courage do you have, in the face of this disease?'

As I speak I hear the screams of the child again. 'In sweet Jesus's name, William, folk used to care for one another in their darkest hour. Now they run from their fellow mortal souls.'

William points to the child under its dead mother's arm. 'Touch that and I'll be your brother in name only.'

'Damn your hypocrisy, William. You and I both handled Elizabeth Tapper's corpse. You took her flitch. You and I let her down from her hanging place together.'

'She hanged herself. She wasn't infected.'

'How do you know? She'd nursed her sons – and they *were* infected. She may have been as sickly as her children when she died. Or maybe she was as clean as you think, and this child is too. All I know is that she saw nothing in the world to live for. But this child has a chance. You and me – *we* are that chance. If you are cold-hearted now, this child will die – and we will have been his killers.'

I look back towards the woman's body. I decide. I step closer and reach out for the crying infant.

'No, John! Leave it!'

I ignore him. I take hold of the swaddling board with both hands and carefully draw it and the baby away from its mother. Her corpse slumps down on the grass, as if relieved to be freed from the responsibility. Bound against the board, all the child can do is move its head and cry. It is aching for food and warmth and yet, at the same time, it implores kind-ness. That sound is exactly what I want to offer. This noise, not words, is the true sound of humanity – as native to us as a song is to a bird. I remember the cries of my own children at birth – the two that died young as well as the three who, God willing, are still alive, and I rejoice in the sound of the cry. I look into this child's deep eyes. It is squinting through its tears at the world. I know that if I put it down now I will be setting aside everything that makes me believe in myself as a father, and as a man.

Still holding the child, I walk away from the dead mother, giving it as much warmth as I can with my own body.

'You are a curse on me, John,' says my brother.

For a short while there is silence. The only sounds are those of the wind and the child's urgent crying – a regular rasping followed by a choking, and then a more urgent cry, forced out to express his intense hunger and pain.

'In Christ's name, John. This is madness. But maybe you are mad. Our elder brother inherited our father's land. I inherited his strength, his sense of humour and his mercery skill. You know me: I never overpay for anything, whether it be a fleece or a mug of ale. But you – what did you inherit? Nothing. You are soft-limbed and soft-witted, peevish, and altogether too trusting in God. These rich dead city folk, they would not have given a farthing for your soul in life; why risk your neck for their child? God made them rich. He did not make you rich. All he gave you was the skill to knock stones into divine shapes with your chisel. Now the pestilence is here, there'll be no more work on the cathedral. Nor on the church in Salisbury. As for me, no one needs wool-fells now. Or wool. We'll be nothing but two hungry bodies amid the bones. You are willing to stuff your mouth with contagion and embrace a mortal fever. I cannot risk being near you.'

The child is still crying, stopping only momentarily to search for milk in the warmth of my chest before opening its soul again. My brother shakes his head and turns away. He takes a few steps along the road before suddenly turning to say something else. But I speak first. 'Has it not occurred to you how little you've done to earn the reward of Heaven? Even now you are preoccupied with money, with what things are worth. Is that your true understanding? For my part, I wonder what you are worth as a man. What good act have you done to gain eternal bliss? I've worshipped God through my chisels. I've done my best as a husband and as a father, and to be a good brother to you and Simon. But in the Gospels it says that Jesus went among the sick and the dying – not just the healthy. He was not afraid.'

'*He* was the Son of God.'

'He was a man too, was He not? And He came to set us an example, did He not?' I gesture back at the dead couple. 'Imagine this man and woman were Joseph and the Blessed Virgin Mary, on their way to Egypt, and this was their infant. Would you still say that we should leave their child to die?'

'If Joseph and Mary were lying here in front of us, which they are not, still I would say yes. Leave the babe be.'

'You would rather kill Christ, and deny all the hundreds of thousands of innocents a path to Heaven, than risk your own neck? How miserable and cowardly is that! How contemptible in the eyes of the Lord! And yet you've the nerve to say to me that I've inherited nothing from our father? In God's name, I know this. I inherited his goodness. When he sired me I got his moral courage and his love of his fellow countrymen. I'd not exchange such virtues for all your business sense, all your fleeces, all your fond widows. And more, if you were holding this child, and not me, I would not shy away from you as you do now from me. I would say, "William, I understand your vocation. I might not be able to hear your calling but I will help you answer it." And I *would* help you too, to the ends of the Earth – not because I want you to help me now but because you are my brother. And you will always be my brother.'

I start to walk. After about twenty steps I hear him call my name. I walk on.

He calls again. Still I continue on my way.

He comes after me, still calling.

Eventually, after several hundred yards, I give in. I turn back and watch him as he strides up to me, with his travelling sack in one hand and something else in the other.

'The child is heir to his father's money,' says William. 'You may as well take it too. The child will need it.' William hands me the man's purse, together with the woman's book and the crucifix and rosary beads. 'If this plague is the will of God, John, then God bless you. You have worked the stones of God's house; your prayers have a stronger moral power than mine. But I cannot believe God will spare this child, and I fear for you. It's not that I don't love you as my brother.'

I nod my thanks.

'Maybe one day the child will read it,' he adds, looking at the book. 'I could help him.'

'That would be good.'

'And the book is valuable anyway. In Oxford, you would pay five shillings for one like that.'

Five shillings – sixty pence – that would take me ten days to earn when paid at my very best rate. And statuary work does not come along that often; most of the time it is plain masonry or vaulting, at fourpence a day. I set the babe on the ground, open my travelling bag, and place the purse, the crucifix and the book inside. Then I draw the ties tight and lift it over my shoulder again, and pick up the infant.

I glance at the darkening grey sky. 'Where do we find a wetnurse?' I ask, trying to soothe the child by putting my finger in its mouth. It sucks for a few moments and then starts to wail in its cycle of compulsive sobs.

'Susannah, the daughter of Richard the blacksmith, in the parish of Saint Bartholomew. She lives not far from the priory. But I know not whether she and her son are still alive, after these two months.'

The cries of the child grow more intense. 'Will you come with me?'

'It would be foolish.'

'Does God spare the wise? The dead folk we've seen today – were they all fools?'

'Who knows?' William closes his eyes, throws his head back, and shouts, looking at the sky. 'Christ, be my guide!'

'If you are in doubt, William, and you cannot find the right way in your own mind, you should not ask Christ what you should do, you should do what you believe He would do.'

He looks at me. And we start walking.

I marvel at the child's determination to keep crying, and at how it makes me feel sympathetic, so desperate to find some food. But I can no longer keep referring to 'it' in that way. He or she is not an 'it'. I decide it is a boy, and wonder what name would suit him. Immediately I hear the word *Lazarus* in my mind, for this child has been lifted out of the arms of death. And today is the eve of the feast of Saint Lazarus. But little Lazarus is still repeating his cycle of forcing his rasping scream into the world, then choking on it and swallowing and forcing through the next scream. How I wish I could soothe him.

When my eldest son cried desperately, Catherine gave him pieces of bread soaked in warm cow's milk to satiate his appetite. Although I have no milk, I decide to try the same. I stop on the side of the road and set the baby down, leaning the board against the trunk of an oak. I take some bread from my travelling bag and break some fragments into the palm of my hand. Carefully I tip ale from my flask into my hand and wet the bread. I then push this into Lazarus's mouth – but he sucks on air, and does not swallow it, and cries even more desperately when it fails to satisfy him.

'More is coming out than going in,' observes William, looking over my shoulder.

'Do you have a better plan?'

'No. Between the two of us, you are definitely the more expert in the matter of children.'

A final attempt to push food into Lazarus's mouth only makes him scream with greater desperation, and more hoarsely. Even offering more ale does not help. Clearly Lazarus needs milk and there is none here – not without knocking on a stranger's door, and no stranger will welcome a man with a baby. I lift him up again, set the board back on my hip, and start walking.

'Well, at least you tried,' says William. 'I do not know if it is a curse or a blessing but truly you do not recognise your own limitations. What other man would try to feed a screaming baby?'

The undulating fields stretch away on each side of the road, their different strips and furlongs noticeable by the various shades of the stubble. In a few areas the crops lie unharvested, crumpled and black, but in most places the disease struck after the grain was taken in. Less reassuringly, the fields are empty, devoid of workers. The handful of travellers we see step off the road to avoid us. Nearer to the city, we see a family on the move: the wife aboard a pony-drawn cart with two chests of possessions and a baby. The eldest boy is leading the pony by hand and four other children are walking behind: there is no sign of the father. As we approach, the eldest boy barks a warning at the children and they all cover their faces. The mother sees Lazarus and makes the sign of the cross.

At dusk we are still a mile from Exeter. More travellers approach – dark characters in ones and twos, shielding their faces with their hoods. A couple more carts come towards us. All these people are like shadows fleeing the city: wraiths of traders and merchants. But none of them are what you would call the naked poor, travelling on foot. The impoverished are staying behind – either to loot the houses of the rich or because they have nowhere else to go.

'The child's screams are like a war cry for the plague,' mutters William.

'We'll find a wetnurse soon.'

'The gates will be closed. We'd be better off staying else-where tonight. Either that or leaving the child somewhere while we arrange our accommodation.'

'In this cold? William, no.'

'Then what's our story? We cannot walk up to the gates and plainly ask to be let in with it squealing like a pig being bled.'

'We'll say that my wife died on the highway.'

'Do you think the city gatekeepers are fools?'

At that moment Lazarus's crying subsides. The instinctive choking on his own screams has exhausted his tiny frame, and within a minute he is silent, asleep.

'Is it dead?' asks William.

I am about to reply but I look ahead in the gloom and see several carts parked near what appears to be an enormously long pit beside the road. It is about four hundred feet long and ten feet wide. It looks like the foundation trench for a new cathedral.

'That is even bigger than the one in Salisbury. It could bury a thousand,' I declare.

'Three thousand, if they bury them three deep, as they did in Salisbury.'

Then the stench rises, like the smell of a stagnant pond that has dried out with the deaths of the plants, weeds and many of the fish, frogs, eels and smaller creatures that lived within its waters. But this is worse. This is the most terrible stink there is: the decaying flesh of a thousand men, women and children – a rotting smell that rides on the blended air of their sore-crusted bodies, of their excrement and urine, of their unclean clothes and of their death–sweat.

In the dimness the pit labourers look like ghosts. Their faces are swathed, their hands wrapped in old cloth. Each cart that arrives is laden with ten or twelve victims. Two men climb up and stand unsteadily on the lower corpses as they lift down the topmost ones to the waiting men on the ground. These men then drag them to the pit, where they pass them down to those arranging them in rows. For a moment I am touched by the neatness with which they lay out the dead – but then I remember why. After the blood-letting at Caen, we had to arrange the corpses carefully because we did not have time to dig a larger pit. The care has nothing to do with respect for the dead.

No one speaks to us or comes near. I feel sick with the insistence of the smell of decay, yet I cannot look away as bodies are laid on bodies. I see a naked young woman passed from the cart to the awaiting burial party and hear the men make some lewd comments about her. And I wonder where her father lies, and if he is in the pit too, and if she will be laid beside him or on top of some stranger. The next corpse is purposefully dropped on the ground while one of the men tries to remove a ring. He draws a knife, cuts the finger and snaps the joint, then pulls the ring off and tosses the finger into the pit. Who is buried with whom does not matter here. The wishes we express in life – such as asking that our bodies be buried in the corner of our parish churchyard, where our ancestors are all laid out – are like leaves in a great wind.

William and I move on in silence. It is nearly dark now. We come to the crossroads at Saint Sativola's, outside the East Gate of the city. The temperature has fallen further. Ice is forming in the cold air. Ahead, the silhouettes of the gatehouse crenellations are visible against the dark blue of the sky, and just before them, the city gallows. It is chilling to see them empty: normally we would see at least one thief left hanging as a warning to others. At the same time, there is a welcoming familiarity in the stench rising from the city ditch. Things that had once been nauseating are now comforting vestiges of normality.

'Give me your fardel,' says William. 'And cover the stubble on your face with your hood. It's dark enough. I'll pretend that you are my wife.'

'Damn your muxy breeches, William; I'll be doing no such thing.'

'We have to persuade a gatekeeper to admit us. You'll not persuade anyone that I am *your* wife. So this is your choice: either you accept my plan or you find a woman willing to play the role for you. Good luck in that, outside the city walls, in the cold, at dusk. Near a plague pit.'

I pass him my travelling sack, and take the long liripipe of my hood and wrap it around my face, covering my rough chin.

At the gate, William hammers heavily and shouts, 'Open, master gatekeeper, open!' No answer comes. He keeps hammering and calling. 'Open, if you are not deaf to the world, you cloth-headed, nun-nuzzling jade! Open this damned gate!'

'Whoever you are, you will not gain admittance here. The mayor has given orders. Citizens may only go out and re-enter by the North Gate.'

'I thank you, my good man,' calls William back a moment later. 'May the Lord in His infinite mercy spare you. Goodnight.'

William and I set off in the darkness around the city walls. We hear our footsteps crunching on the frozen ground, the whiffling and intermittent cries of the half-sleeping baby, and the hooting of the occasional owl. At moments, however, another sound can be heard: an eerie lament inside the city. At the North Gate too we hear souls breaking with grief over the dead bodies of family members.

'What's that noise?' I whisper.

'Keening. A city grieving.'

'If our bones could sing, that is the noise they would make.'

The baby wakes and renews its cries.

'Shush, Lazarus,' I say.

'You have given the child a name?' hisses William.

'After Saint Lazarus, who was raised from the dead. It is his feast day tomorrow.'

'Why did you do that?'

'It seemed the right thing to do.'

'In Christ's love, John. The right thing would have been to leave the child, and let God decide its fate.'

William again draws his knife and bashes with the hilt on the solid oak. 'Good gateman, please, for the love of God, I am a mercer who has often done good business in Exeter. Now I'm on foot with my wife . . . Johanna . . . and my son Lazarus. We've walked from Salisbury, my horse having fallen lame since I departed the city. Please open up, for pity's sake.'

We wait for an answer. 'Why are we seeking entry to this godforsaken gaol of souls?' he asks in a low voice. 'If it weren't for the child, I'd press on for home, walk through the night.' But then he calls out again. 'Good gateman! I hope to stay at the house of Richard the blacksmith, close to the priory of Saint Nicholas—'

'All right, I hear you,' comes the reply. 'I'm coming, damn your eyes. And stop that child from bawling so.'

A door to the side of the main gate swings open to reveal a scrawny, half-bald man. He is holding a flaming torch that has mostly burned itself out. Red embers are falling to the ground. 'What did you say your name was?'

'William Beard, a mercer, from Moreton. You'd recognise my face if you were to shine a light on it.'

The gateman pushes his torch to William's features. A cursory wave of the light in my direction, together with the sound of Lazarus's cries, reassures him.

'My orders are to admit only freemen of the city and their kinsmen. No journeymen, medicine traders, knife-grinders, tinkers, strollers, scullions, vagabonds, scoundrels, beggars or farriers.'

'Do I look like a vagabond?' William replies. 'My wife and I set out before Michaelmas with four horses and a cart of wool-fells; now we find ourselves returning on foot with nothing. I was forced to sell my cart and horses for pennies at the market in Salisbury. Then my own mount fell lame . . .'

'Where's your lantern? Good men carry a lantern after dark.'

William shakes his head. He sets down the travelling bags and faces me. To my surprise, he opens the ties of my fardel and removes Lazarus's purse. He feels inside and holds up a gold coin between his thumb and forefinger, in the light of the torch.

'This is my lantern,' he says.

The gatekeeper leans forward to look at it. I too stare. I have never seen a gold coin before.

'Are you offering that to me?'

'Are you offering to let us in?'

'Your light shines brighter than mine, good sir,' the gate-keeper replies, taking the coin. 'I'm sorry to have delayed you. I'm sure the beadles of the watch will give you no prob-lem. Go in peace, and may the Lord save us all.'

We climb the thoroughfare that leads from North Gate up into the heart of the city and turn right along a narrow lane towards Saint Bartholomew's parish. We feel our way, stumbling through the muddy drains and scattered gravel of the alleys. Every so often, when Lazarus's screams for food subside, we hear the keening as fathers and mothers come to terms with their loss. Occasionally an anguished scream breaks out. Or a cat fight ends in yowling.

Then it begins to rain.

I can barely see the rooflines of the houses against the dark sky. The raindrops splatter and splash into barrels left out to collect water for the houses in this impoverished quarter. Lazarus's sobs are croaked and harsh now, after so much crying. He intermittently drifts in and out of sleep. The weight of the swaddling board is growing too heavy, and I ache to set it down. I long too for warmth and rest – in the way that Lazarus longs for a woman's milk.

I slip in the mud of the road. Cold water enters my boots.

'Here,' says William in a low voice. He hammers on the door of what is, as far as I can make out, a low-roofed, single-storey house. 'Richard,' he calls, 'it's William Beard, from Moreton. I need to speak to you.'

No answer comes.

Several times William knocks and calls until the door is opened a fraction. The low arch is illuminated by a candle held to the crack, which gutters and splutters in the draught, shedding a little light on the black-bearded man within.

'What brings you here after curfew?' says the blacksmith.

'This is my brother, John, from Wrayment, near Moreton. He and his wife, Catherine, and I were travelling with their newborn babe back from Salisbury when Catherine fell grievously ill. She died yesterday. We've walked day and night hoping that your Susannah is with milk and able to help feed the little one. He'll surely die without help.'

'Tell me truly, William Beard. Was it the plague?'

William looks his friend in the eye. 'No, Richard. I assure you. Catherine did not die of plague.'

The blacksmith shuffles slightly, still holding the door.

'Please,' I say, feeling exhausted and frozen. 'We've come so far. There's precious little godliness in the world these days.'

Cold water drips down my neck and runs down my back.

'We'll pay your daughter for nursing the child,' says William. He searches for another gold coin. 'A *fiorino d'oro*, from Florence,' he says, holding it out. 'In London and Bristol they're called florins.'

Richard takes the coin and holds it in the light, staring at the design. 'What's it worth?'

'About forty pence.'

He lets us in and closes the heavy wooden door.

The hall in which we find ourselves is one part of an old merchant's house. Smoke is rising from a blazing fire in the centre of the room and fumbling its way into the dark roof space. Around the fire are three stools and a bench. Richard's candle throws light on a doorway, which I presume leads to a chamber. He hobbles over to it and shouts into the darkness, 'Susannah!' Then he picks up a stick, comes back towards us, and sits. He gestures to the stools with the stick. 'Sit yourselves down.'

'How do things fare in Exeter?' asks William, warming his hands over the fire. 'We saw the great grave by Saint Sativola's.'

Richard grunts, resting his hands on his stick. 'They're digging another, beyond the walls, near the place on Crulditch where they used to hold the Lammas Fair. Your brother's right. There is precious little godliness left in the world.' He leans forward and pushes a log into the flames with his stick.

'No one in this city goes to church these days. All the priests have departed, seeking refuge on their country manors. The markets are almost empty as no one wants to bring their grain to the city. Each morning those that've died overnight are left out in the streets to be collected by the carters. That is the last you see of your loved ones: their bodies lying in the street, flies crawling over them, waiting for the muxy gravediggers to haul them away.'

Susannah comes in. She is a plump young woman with hair that looks black in this light. Her dark tunic makes her flesh seem very white. I wonder where her husband is. These days it seems best not to ask questions of those left behind.

'He's asleep, at long last,' she says to her father.

'Good,' says Richard. 'This here infant is hungry. William has paid me in the hope that you can provide him with milk.'

'Will I be seeing any of this money?' she demands.

'You shall, my flower. But it is a gold coin, worth forty pence. I'll have it changed and give you a goodly portion.'

'A goodly portion?' she asks, looking at me and then at Lazarus.

'Tenpence,' says Richard.

'Thief.'

'Twenty,' he says.

She nods. 'Is it a boy or a girl?' she asks me.

I hesitate. 'Lazarus is his name,' I reply over the sound of his crying.

'He needs more than milk,' she says, taking him from me, and uncovering her breast. 'When did you last change his swaddling?'

'This morning, in Honyton.' Lazarus sucks on her – but not as hungrily as I thought he would. 'There was a wetnurse at the inn where we stayed.' I look at William but he is staring into the fire, avoiding catching my eye. Richard, however, is looking at me suspiciously.

'When did you say your wife died?' he asks.

'Yesterday morning,' I say.

'And you are travelling alone with the child? With only William to help you?'

'What choice do I have? The Good Lord in His wisdom has left me in this plight.'

There is a long silence. Still William does not look at me.

'It's only half a day to Moreton,' says Susannah, looking down on the child, who is alternately feeding and breaking off to cry. 'He'll have a good feed now and another when he wakes, and another before you leave in the morning, and I dare say he'll be asleep all the way. Your motion will be like a lullaby.'

I nod gratefully. She answers with a smile. Her generosity to the child is uplifting.

'Richard!' William exclaims suddenly, turning to our host. 'In times past you had a barrel of ale on the go continually. Don't tell me that fine tradition has fallen victim to the plague too?'

Richard pushes himself up with his stick. 'You should understand, we're saving our barley for bread. But I can offer you good cider. Apples from my own trees, outside the walls.'

'I'll be honoured.'

Richard lifts a ladle from the cider barrel in a dark corner of the hall and carefully fills a large, two-handled wooden cup. I listen as he pours the liquid slowly. As he comes back to the fire he says, 'A woman nearby lost her husband a year ago and gave the trees to me in return for making a pair of new locks for her house. She was worried, being there all alone. When I saw the orchard, there were rotting apples ripe for pressing all around.' He takes a swig of the cider, passes William the cup, and sits down. 'If I was not a cautious man, I could make a small fortune from making locks these days.'

'And breaking them?' I ask. 'What about those who die in locked houses, who've no one to place their body in the street?'

Richard says nothing.

William hands the cup to me without a word and resumes looking into the fire. I take it, lift the cider to my mouth and taste its sweetness. I offer it to Susannah, who is still trying to feed the child. 'When I've got him settled,' she says to me, and lifts up the swaddling board and starts to unwrap the bands.

'No doubt you are hungry too,' says Richard. 'There's the rest of some pottage.'

'We've got some bacon to add to the supper,' William says. 'And a little . . .'

But before he can utter another word, Susannah lets forth a terrifying scream. One moment she is holding Lazarus; the next, she throws him down and her hands move to her mouth, and she is staring at him in his tumble of swaddling bands. She glares at William and me. 'How could you? Damn you! Damn you!'

As she turns to me I am still looking down at Lazarus, who is screaming again, and at the excrement-soaked bands and the black blotches on the thighs and arms. I try to get up but before I can, a blow from Susannah strikes me across the face. The candle suddenly goes out and there is only the glow of the fire by which to see. The next thing I know, a stick hits my skull. Then, to my horror, I see the sudden blaze as the swaddling bands catch alight. Susannah has kicked Lazarus into the fire. With shouts and screams filling my ears, I reach for the child and burn my hands, tearing away the flaming linen to see the boiling ruptures of his skin and the fat seeping from his scorched thighs. A hard object strikes me across the back and I stumble forward, only narrowly avoiding the fire myself. I turn and roll out of the way, and take refuge in a corner of the hall.

'Get out! Get out now!' shouts Richard. 'Get out, both of you!'

'Richard,' pleads William, 'there has been a terrible . . .'

'Get out!' screams Susannah. 'You heard my father – get out now, or I shall kill you both.'

Richard has stopped. He is not shouting. He is standing still, torn apart by the realisation that he let his daughter put a plague-infected child to her breast. And in that moment I am filled with remorse. I do not even pick up my travelling sack. I reach for the door, fumble for the drawbar, yank it open, and run out into the rain and the darkness.

I cannot see where I am going, and trip on the uneven surface. I kneel in the pouring rain as the water soaks my face and my hair. The smells of the streets – the dung and the mud – rise up to choke me. I should go now, and throw myself into the plague pit with the dead, and wait for God's judgement.

The thought of my wife and children makes me raise my face. I spit out the grime that I taste on my lips and kneel there, as the rain pours on to my soaked back and through my hair. I get to my feet and start stumbling again, with no idea where I am in the darkness. My cloak is soon soaked through, and my tunic and shirt too. I see the lanterns of the city watchmen and stand still waiting for them to see me, but with the rain keeping their heads down, they do not.

In the street leading to the South Gate, not far from the Bear Inn, I stop beneath the overhanging gate of a large mansion. I am so alone. All I want is to see a friendly face – but the only ones in this city now are those I carved myself.

There is a high stone wall around the cathedral. It runs along one side of the cathedral precinct: you can climb up on to the parapet, down by South Gate, where the cottages are built right against the old walls. All you need to do is find a barrel to reach the roof of one of the cottages, and you can climb over the wooden shingles and from there to the wall. Once up on the parapet you can follow it around and jump down into the grounds of the bishop's palace.

It takes me ages to find the way. By the time I have reached the west front of the cathedral, it has stopped raining. I walk up to the screen of sculptures and reach forward to touch the lowest tier of angels, one by one, in the darkness. I run my hands over the wet stones, remembering when I carved this

arm and that face. William Joy was my master then. He told
me that my sculptures would be better if I loved them. 'Let
the figures themselves do the work,' he would say. 'Let them
smile, if they want. Let them embrace; let them dance; let
them have their own secrets.' I cannot see them now yet I
know they are there, still dancing, still whispering. I step up
on to the plinth and reach up to feel the lower parts of the Old
Testament kings that I carved above the angels: I cling to their
legs – like a condemned man in the time of the Bible must
have clung to the ankles of real kings, begging for mercy. The
figure on the buttress to the right of the great west door was
modelled on a drawing of King Henry the Third. Beneath
him I carved an angel with her wing outstretched, protecting
the columns on which the king stood. Another figure, higher
up, I based on the old canon treasurer: he always said hello to
us as we chipped away at the stones in the cathedral yard. One
of the corbels is modelled on my father. It was so high up I
thought no one would see it. No one, that is, except God. All
of the masons created a part of the cathedral in the image of
a loved one. If you were to pull it apart and examine it stone
by stone you'd see the whole edifice is constructed out of our
daily needs and aspirations – the loves of a hundred ordinary
men. So it is with every great church. From the outside it
appears huge, impersonal, dignified and mighty, but come up
close enough to hear the heartbeat of the past and you realise
it is made up of a thousand faces of lovers, mothers, fathers
and friends – the little miracles we dream of while we work.

I step down from the plinth and walk back to the north
end of the screen, where years ago we made handholds to

ascend the west front without having to rely on the scaffolding. I climb again as easily as ever I did: the act of curling
my fingers around this figure's shoulder or that sculpted leg
invites my memory to come closer. Soon I am on top of the
screen, running my hands over the shapes of the pinnacles.
'Sculpture should be listened to,' said William Joy. 'If you
listen to a beautifully produced figure, it fills your mind with
beauty.' Now I am listening. Whatever grief I have brought
into the world, my work reassures me that my intentions are
pure, and have good consequences too.

But what next? Here I sit, in the freezing cold and damp
air, unable to see anything. There is no sound except for the
occasional distraught cry. I have difficulty believing Lazarus
is dead. I begin to rock to and fro, and start to sing softly to
myself. *'Merry it is while summer lasts . . .'*

I remember my mother used to sing this to me when I was
a boy. And that brings back a good memory. When Simon,
William and I were young, being catechised one Sunday, the
rector – a bullying man called Philip de Vautort, may the
Devil never loosen his grip on him – told us that the psalms
of David were the most beautiful music in the world. Simon
asked how could he be so sure? And the priest said it was
because he had knowledge and experience of these things.
But when he sang, his voice was like a notched and rusty
blade, and we didn't understand any of the words, which were
in Latin. So I raised my hand and told him that his psalms
were not as beautiful as our mother singing *'Merry it is'*. For
this I was beaten with a rod on my hands. I cried dreadfully
and winced every time the rod rapped on my knuckles. I

blurted out, 'Why do you punish me for telling the truth?'
For this I was beaten again. But as soon as we were outside
the church, my brothers slapped me on my back and shouted
three cheers for me in the market square. As we approached
Cranbrook they lifted me on their shoulders – our father
saw them carrying me home. He was wiping his hands with
a cloth after greasing the crank of the millwheel with fat.
When they told him what I had said, he replied, 'John, you're
a good lad. Never forget that the Lord Himself made your
mother's voice as sweet and pure as it is but God does not
make priests, he merely makes men. Some are good and some
are bad – and the only way to tell the difference is to speak
the truth to them. You may carve the meat today at dinner
as your reward.'

I am snapped out of my memory by a scraping sound in
the darkness nearby. Alarmed, I hold my breath and I hear it
again.

Someone else is up here on top of the stone screen, near
me.

I move away, holding my arm out in case he approaches
and is dangerous. But he makes no attempt to conceal his
presence. I hear him rub his hands together for warmth, and
then cough. A few moments later, he starts to sing.

> *Merry it is while summer lasts*
> *with birds' song,*
> *but now draws near the winter's blast*
> *and weather strong . . .*

It chills my blood. 'Who's there? Who are you?'

The voice is not unlike my own. 'You know me, John.'

'Who are you?'

'John is what they call me.'

'How did you find the way up here? Are you one of the masons?'

'You know I am.'

'You are John of Coombe? The man who worked with me at Salisbury and went to the Giant's Circle?'

'No. I was born at Cranbrook. I live now at Wrayment, in the manor of Wray.'

I am dumbfounded. 'No! That is me. You are an impostor.'

'No, I am you.'

'Get away!' I yell. And I hear the echo of my voice against the stone. Sounds of grief in turn come at me from the rooftops around the cathedral. I move further along the parapet.

'You cannot get away from me,' says the voice. I hear whispers of men and women from inside the cathedral, as if there are ten thousand ghosts in there, and their desperation is seeping out through the stones.

'Where is my brother?'

'I left him at the house of Richard the blacksmith, as you know well.'

'And where is he now?'

'I do not know because you do not know.'

'You do not speak like me.'

'Nor do I suffer from that bite that ails you, beneath your right arm.'

Now the voice is on both sides of me. I kick out suddenly with my right foot but feel only air and the slipperiness of the wet lead.

'Jesus Christ, help me now,' I mutter.

'Our mother sings more beautifully than the priest,' taunts the voice.

'Stop!' I shout. But the voice starts singing again, *'Merry it is while summer lasts.'* I lash out again and strike nothing, only the stone parapet.

I kneel and place my forehead on the cold lead, and pray in a whisper. 'Oh Mary, Mother of God, and Saint Lazarus, of whose feast day this is the eve, and Saint Peter, who protects this church, save me from this madness.'

'I am your conscience, John.'

I am lost, like the sailors on the drifting ship. I am falling back into the darkest sea. 'I believe in the One God, the Father Almighty, Maker of Heaven and Earth ...' But as I speak the words, I hear the voice repeating them, as if it is a chorus to my lead. 'I believe in the One God, the Father Almighty, Maker of Heaven and Earth ...'

'Stop! Stop it!' I shout, hitting the parapet, and striking the lead with my knuckles so that it hurts as much as it did that day when the priest punished me.

I feel the presence near me, waiting. Whispers escape from the stones.

'You shall not have my soul,' I say. 'You shall not have my soul.'

'Do you not realise how little you have done to deserve the reward of Heaven?'

'I . . . I tried to save the child.'

'It was because of you that the infant died in the flames,' replies the voice. 'The blacksmith shall die now, and so too shall his daughter and her child.'

'I am truly sorry. Truly, truly.'

'What will you do to set things right?'

'How can I? There is so much wrong in the world. How can I unspill all the spilled bowls in the city, mend all the broken smiles, and unbruise all the hurt hearts and stricken tongues? How can I seek to improve upon God's Creation if He cannot?'

There is silence.

'Why do you suppose that God seeks only perfection?' asks the voice. 'If you believe that the Lord created everything in Heaven and on Earth, do you not believe He also created sin? Failure? Regret? Who do you think created damnation?'

'I believe in the goodness of the Lord . . .'

'Do you not believe,' continues the voice, 'that if God desired the perfection of the whole of Creation it would not happen in the sweetest and most sudden instant? How could there be goodness if there were no sin?'

'How might I atone for what I have done?'

The voice is silent. Only after a long time do I hear it. 'You have seven days to save your soul. If you will obey me.'

'Obey you? How?'

'Go to Scorhill, to the circle of stones.'

I wait to hear something more but there is no sound. No whispers, no song, no voice.

I do not hear it depart. I do not see anything. I am just

alone on the roof of the screen of the cathedral, in the darkness, shivering.

In truth, I do not know whether I have been urged by an angel to save my soul or asked by a demon to sell it. Can the fate of a man really depend on such whispered words in the night? I do not know. But I do know that either God or the Devil has asked me a question, and the only way to find out which is by going to Scorhill.

Chapter Two

I do not sleep until dawn. But hardly have my eyes fallen than I am awake again. I see seagulls swooping over the cathedral and the precinct walls, crying their raucous curses on the people below. They perch on the roof of the church that stands to the west of the cathedral and cast a cold eye on the suffering city. The wind buffets my hood as I stare at them with an equally cold heart. It is the feast day of Saint Lazarus. I bite my lip, remembering the poor child. Yet now I see that his soul is just one of so many lost in the night. People are carrying out their dead and leaving their bodies for the carters — and staring in shock at the corpses that were, until the previous evening, much-loved sons and daughters.

'John! John, are you up there?'

I crawl forward and look over the edge of the parapet, jittery and shivering. William is looking up. He is dishevelled, holding my fardel in one hand and his own in the other.

'Richard has gone to fetch the city beadles. He says that you knowingly brought the child into his house, to kill him. He is going to ask them to hang you.'

I recall the voice in the night. Do I tell William?

'Are you coming down? I've got your things.'

All the events of the previous day stream through my mind, from seeing the leafless oak at Honyton to the fight at the blacksmith's house. I don't want to believe my memories but they are like deep wounds: they are so painful they cannot be ignored. I see a priest in a cassock walking across the cathedral yard. He notices two men coming towards him and steps aside, and walks through a patch of mud. Even here, on holy soil, men are avoiding each other. And yet, who truly wants to be alone?

The disease not only causes suffering, it makes us inhuman.

'Now! For the love of God, John!' shouts William.

I climb down from the top of the screen. He holds my travelling sack out to me, at arm's length. I wonder, is he too cautious of my presence? He sees my expression and leans forward and embraces me. Then he turns and we set off towards the North Gate.

There are bodies in the lanes to either side, awaiting collection. In North Street I see a dishevelled blonde woman with an upturned face and closed eyes, crouching over a child's body; she does not leave it but moans constantly. Then suddenly a masked man grabs the body by a leg and flings it into the dead cart and she screams in raw anguish, and drags her nails over the wall of her house, and beats her fists on it. We watch that solitary cart as it is led down North Street: at the top of the road it had four corpses; but by the time it reaches the gate, it holds eight.

The gatekeeper is nowhere to be seen, the gate ajar.

Outside the city walls, and glad of the fact, we hasten down to the great bridge which stretches from the city's West Gate to the suburb of Cowick on the other side of the river. As we cross I watch the rats scampering along the marshy bank, amid all the detritus thrown down there by the citizens – the sweepings of butchers' stalls, contents of slop pails, trimmings of vegetables and a dead dog. The street in Cowick is deserted, half the shutters closed. A mile further on, heading up Dunsford Hill, which is a steep climb over loose stones in the deep ruts of frozen mud and leaves, the sun breaks out. I turn and look back at the cathedral, dominating the city behind us. How often I saw it from here in the old days: it was my soul's salvation as well as my daily craft. Now its spire-topped towers stand like two final vestiges of hope, and I am walking in the other direction. What awaits me at home? And at Scorhill? These times are surely as terrible as anything in the Bible – the Flood, the destruction of Sodom and Gomorrah, and the Exodus from Egypt. Has there ever been anything like this pestilence since then?

At the top of the hill we find another corpse. It is that of a boy, about twelve years of age, lying beneath a leafless tree a few feet from the road. He has sprawled across the mass of fallen leaves of brown, ochre, grey and yellow, as if he is a fallen leaf himself. There is a pool of vomit on the leaves near where his head stares at the earth. I look at his brown hair and his young face, marred though it is by the blotches and livid marks. I note the green dust on the back of his tunic. He must have leaned against the tree, or sat with his back to it. I do not doubt that he died alone, poor lad. No mother or father to hold his head. Not that they would have come near him if he had been at home. Perhaps it was a blessing for him to die here – and not be there to see himself deserted in his hour of greatest need by a parent.

I think back to the voice on the cathedral screen. Even now it is haunting me. I cannot stop thinking that I have seven days to save my soul.

'William, last night . . .'

'I do not want to talk about last night.'

'You were right.'

'I was right. So what? Now I am cold and tired. I feel weak. I just want to get home.'

'I know. I am sorry. But I feel I must do something good. To make up for the ill I have done. I know now it is not enough just to mean well. I must do good works. To earn my place in Heaven.'

He looks at me. 'And what does that mean? What miracles are you going to do? Are you going to found a monastery? With what? Are you going to fight a crusade? Good luck. You are not a soldier of Christ, John, nor are you a saint. You are an out-of-work mason, nothing more. And if you make another attempt at a good work, like picking up orphans dying of the plague, it may well be the death of us both.'

I stare at the leaves turning to mulch on the muddy road. Beech leaves still with tinges of green; some oak, now dark brown; others looking as if they have a crescent of orange. I kick them. What makes some plants lose their leaves? I wonder. There has to be some reason why some trees and plants lose their leaves and others, such as holly, do not. Perhaps it is God's punishment on the plant for poisoning people and animals? But then, the chestnut loses its leaves even though its fruit is good to eat. As for the holly: its berries are noxious and its prickles cause pain – and yet it does not lose its leaves. And the yew, which poisons everything – birds and plants, so that nothing grows or even survives in its shade – lives forever.

Seven days to save my soul.

Do plants have souls? Can they go to Heaven? If not, surely they cannot commit sin, for they cannot be punished for it in the afterlife.

Seven days to save my soul.

Do our feelings grow in us like plants, with roots in our hearts and flowering in our minds? They flower in our smiles, and wilt in our frowns. And if so, do they return every year? Is one feeling of gladness the same as another, if it had a different cause?

Seven days.

What have I done to save my soul? I have worked hard, I have looked after my family, I have prayed and I have carved in praise of God. I would have thought that I had done more than most. Or, rather, I have sinned less than most. But perhaps absence of sin is not enough. Perhaps even the man who is entirely without sin still cannot enter the Kingdom of Heaven if he has done no good works. Perhaps, in God's eyes, it is not the sin we do not commit but our acts of faith that matter.

But what can I do now, in the next seven days, which will earn me the rewards of Heaven? For that surely was no angel on the cathedral screen. It coughed, for Heaven's sake, and pretended to be me, and said it was my conscience. Angels don't need to clear their throats. They don't dissemble.

But then how did it know about my mother's singing being more beautiful than the priest's? Did I imagine that?

When the whole world is living through a nightmare, why should not I be faced with my own?

Seven days.

I imagine walking down the hill towards Moreton, looking across the town and its old church and marketplace, with the great moor, Dartmoor, beyond it. To the northwest I will see the hills of Butterdon and the earth ramparts of the old fort on the hill above Cranbrook; near that fort is the mill where Simon, William and I grew up, and where Simon now lives with his two children. To the south of the town lies Wrayment, where Catherine and my sons, William, John and James, will have risen and be setting about the day's tasks. Catherine and Mary from Storryge might be cleaning the house or beating the clothes clean at the Wraybrook. William, old enough now to make himself useful, might have taken some of the grain in the barn to the mill, and then be going into town to see the baker. John and James will no doubt be playing in the mud, breaking ice puddles with stones.

What good can I do for them – or anyone else – in the next seven days?

I could show the children the rudiments of carving. I could tell them of the dangers of sin. I could take in a poor child, to be a servant. And what good would any of these things do? I could turn around and walk back into Exeter, and embrace the lepers in the Magdalene hospital as saints used to do in the old days, to show they were neither afraid of God's judgement nor judging of His damnation on our fellow men. But no one would care. Who cares for lepers when the plague is in the city?

Truly, what is a good act in this age? How can one consciously do something worthy of a Heavenly reward?

I think of the stories I used to hear in church of all the saintly people: men and women who gave their lives for their faith, saints who performed miracles. William was right, I am not one of them. This is my lot: to leave my house for weeks on end and go to a cathedral or a church where they need masons, and to chisel, carve, mould, shape and bring forth liveliness from the grain of natural stone. I let faces, hands, arms, crowns and clothes emerge from God's uncut materials. It pays little. Catherine has to work hard on our four acres. They say that rich men are further from Heaven but I do not believe that is true. Rich men can give up their wealth and thereby earn eternal salvation; poor men cannot. Christ might have been poor but I have never heard a priest speak of Him trying to eke out a few pennies or sweating over His four acres. A man performing his trade for a meagre sum cannot go to Heaven – not if simply avoiding doing wrong is insufficient.

Near the village of Dunsford, the appalling stench of death hits our nostrils. We turn a corner in the hedgerow-bounded lane and see a horse-drawn sledge. It is by an ivy-clad tree, half in the ditch, at an angle. Two bodies remain on it; four others have fallen into the ditch. An open mouth and pair of hollow eye sockets stare into the ditch water. The horse that dragged them to this point has been cut from its harness but the man who led it here lies not far away, where he fell on his side, his face contorted in a grimace.

The dead leading the dead.

'Jesus have mercy,' exclaims William. 'Hell could not seem closer.'

I cover my face as I did leaving Exeter. When we are on the far side of the stink, I take the cloth away.

'Every city, every town, every village. There's no end to it.'

The village of Dunsford is empty. It seems frozen: a scattering of low, thatched houses – some built of cob, some of granite – to the south of the church. I look up at the hills beyond, thickly wooded with winter-bare trees. This is where the long climb up on to the great moor begins.

We cross the River Teign at the ford. After the recent rain the water is about thigh-deep and fast-flowing. Dead leaves and sticks have caught in the shallows at the edge. I take extra care with my travelling sack, remembering the book that it contains, whose vellum pages will be ruined if they get wet. I resolve to donate it to the church in Moreton, in memory of Lazarus.

My limbs feel tired when I step on to the solid earth, ahead of William. The weariness slows me down as we follow the path up into the woods. After a mile of trudging, I find myself exhausted and sweating. I look back at William, who is having an even harder time than me. He might be the size of an ox but he is less used to carrying his weight, being a man who normally rides. I wait for him, catching my breath, and slap him on the back when he reaches me.

'We're doing well, brother.'

He pants. 'I forget how steep this hill is. We should have gone by Clifford.'

We press on, with alder, ash, willow and beech on either side. Some twisted oaks remain, like craggy witches from long ago. The willows have been coppiced to create the wattles for houses and fences. The alder and ash too have been coppiced, for roofing and charcoal burning. A mile from the river, I pause again, sweating heavily despite the cold. On the hills above there are traces of snow in areas shaded by rocks. I glance up at the sun, which is weak but welcome. About three hours have passed since we left Exeter.

I turn and look back to William. He is slower even than before. In fact, he is stumbling. He leans against a tree. He wipes a sleeve across his brow. Concerned, I walk back towards him, and I see him vomit – a stream of yellow splatters on the leaves. He looks up as I approach. There is a streak of sick in his beard. 'Stay away from me,' he rasps, his face blotched and red. 'Stay away.'

'William?'

'I'm sweating like a hot pig. I've a pain under my arm. And I've been sick. What do you make of these things?'

In that beat of my heart, I know death is with us.

'The pestilence has entered me, John. Already it's corrupting my body.'

I open my mouth to speak but I cannot find a word to say. I know now why I am sweating so much, and why I feel so weak. My limbs ache not with fatigue or lack of hunger but with some insidiousness seeping through them.

'But I had seven days,' I say.

'What?' says William, still bending over, with his arms against the tree, grimacing. 'What did you say?'

'Nothing. I . . .' I look down at the sticks on the path, and at the rotting leaves. Quietly I search my right armpit with my left hand, and then I search my left. There is a sharp bruise there. I freeze, and the nausea within me rises. I look at my hand, which is shaking. I wipe the sweat from my forehead and look at William, tears in my eyes.

William vomits a second time. He spits and glares at me. 'What are you looking at?'

'I did what I believed was right . . .'

'Damn you, John. You have killed me. You and your bloody piety. In all the years we were together, I never hurt you, despite your tedious moralising. Now you've killed me.'

'I am sorry.'

He wipes his face. 'I don't care how sorry you are. Oh Christ, damn you! I hate your damn religion. It doesn't help things. If God wants to make a man suffer, then being all holy is no shield. God doesn't care for holiness.'

'I feel it too. Within me.'

'What?'

'The plague.'

He straightens himself up and breathes deeply. Sweat

trickles down his face and into his beard. He shakes his head. 'What a world this is.'

He starts to walk. 'I despise the thought of being one of the corpses in the road. The last thing I want is for some tatchy merchant to come along here and count me among the nameless dead.'

I say nothing. Between brothers, wordlessness is sometimes more meaningful than conversation.

I think of Catherine. I remember when I first saw her, in the marketplace in Moreton, when she was a child. Her father, Roger of Wrayment, had brought her along with him. She was five years younger than me, turning cartwheels on a patch of grass in the square. When she caught sight of me watching her, she asked, 'Can you do cartwheels?' before demonstrating another one. 'I like your belt,' she added, and I had looked down with no small pride at the pewter buckle I had fashioned from an old pilgrim badge that I'd found on the highway. The following Sunday she smiled at me coming out of church – and when anyone saw her smile, they could not help but smile too. After that, we would exchange a few words every week, on market day, or after church. Later that year I went to Exeter to learn to carve properly, and then I would only see her occasionally, when I came home. After her mother died, her father kept her at home and would not let her marry, even though several men wanted her, including Walter Parleben, the son of John Parleben, one of the richest men in Moreton. And so the years passed. Then one day, as I was working on the screen of the cathedral, she came into Exeter with a kinsman. The foreman shouted up to where I was fitting a corbel. I came down from the scaffolding. Catherine looked very anxious. Her father was dead, she told me; the cottage and its four acres were now in her hands but the bailiff had told her she had to marry. If she did not choose a husband herself, he had added, he would find one for her. 'Please,' she said to me, 'I've no wish to leave my house and you've no place of your own – why do you not come to live with me.' 'Why me?' I had asked, astonished. And she had said simply, 'Because you make me feel happy.' Two weeks later we married at the church door in Moreton.

I will not be able to speak to her again. Even if she is alive, I cannot go to see her and risk spreading the disease to our children. Better that I should go to the churchyard and dig my own grave now. It is the only way I will lie in consecrated ground.

William does not speak as we make our way up Cossick Hill. Instead he looks up at the rocks, as if he has decided they are to be his place of reckoning with God. I think of my mother's baked apples in honey; Catherine's peaceful face as she sleeps; showing my sons how to shear our few sheep. I remember brewing ale for the church, and supping so much of it that I started singing. I remember watching the young of the town carolling in the square on a summer evening, dancing hand in hand to the fiddle and pipe. I look back on the fairs in Moreton, when the whole square was filled with stalls and the borough meadows and the lord's field were packed with the colourful tents of merchants and traders, and the alehouses bursting with music and laughter.

All these memories are about to become unremembered.

We leave the road at Cossick and stumble along the rough path, over the rocks of Hingston, through the gorse and heather. A few moments of struggling to contain myself prove futile and I am sick on the dead bracken. Weak, shivering with cold and sweating, I slump down on a large stone. The sour taste of vomit in my mouth makes me spit – and I see blood in my spittle where it lands on the grass.

William shivers violently. 'How long does it take?' He sits down on a rock.

'It can be quick. Or it can be days. A few people in Salisbury lingered for three or four, one lived for six.'

'Jesus.' He puts his hands over his face and falls silent. When he removes them, he stares to our left, along the ridge, for a long time. 'You remember Christine of Luwedon?'

'I do. She had long dark hair and a kind smile – and haunches like a cow.'

'She was my first,' he says. 'Her husband was out hunting one day, up on the moor. She saw me on the road and called out to me to help her, for she was having difficulty with an angry ram. She led me up through the woods above Luwedon, not saying a word, and then – all of a sudden – she turned and put her hands to my cheeks, and held my face, and kissed me. It was such a kiss as I'd not had before and, by Saint Faith, I'll never forget it. After a minute she pushed me down on the ground and knelt astride me, hoiking up her skirts around her waist. In truth, she took me as surely as ever I took a wench in France. Do you think that that counts as a sin?'

'There were others, afterwards, weren't there?' I wince with the pain.

'More than I can count.'

'If you can't count them, then that is indeed sinful. You should at least have remembered their names.'

'I wasn't interested in their names . . .'

We fall silent again.

'I envy you, John,' he gasps suddenly, clutching his belly and grimacing. 'At least you will leave something behind.'

'What's that?'

'Your children. Your sculptures. Who'll remember William Beard? The priests won't pray for me. The portreeve will find another man to whom to rent my house. At least you will not disappear without trace.'

'Folk will still see your face,' I reply.

'No. I'll be as dust on the sea.'

'They'll see you in the cathedral. Your face is on the altarpiece in the chapel of Saint Edmund.'

He pauses to think. 'Did you do that?'

'Of course. Your face also appears in the chapel of Saint Andrew and Saint Catherine. You are in the west cloister too, though that isn't such a good likeness.'

'Why not?'

'Your ears are too big – the dean took down the scaffolding before I could amend them.'

'You are a good brother,' says William, clutching his chest, and rocking to and fro. 'Even though . . . this. Just before Christmas.'

Christmas. I won't see my sons' faces light up any more at

the sight of so much beef and mutton. I won't see our house with ivy around the doorframe and holly and mistletoe in the eaves. I will not see the glow of Catherine's smile as she watches our boys.

I look across to the moor in the distance. 'How far is it from here to Scorhill?'

'Eh?'

'The stone circle on the moor where we went that day with John Parleben and William Kena and the other tinners. How far is it from here?'

'About eight or nine miles. Why?'

'I need to go there. To save my soul.'

'What? Are you mad?'

'No, I . . . I need to go there.'

William retches again, and spits. 'You have the child's purse. Give the money to the church. The priests will pray for you.'

'It isn't mine to give. Not since the poor infant burned.'

'What's Scorhill to do with it?'

'I heard a voice last night. At the cathedral.'

'You heard a voice?'

'I did.'

'You *are* mad.'

'Maybe. But the voice told me to go to Scorhill to save my soul. And it would be madness to pretend I didn't hear it. And think, Jesus went into the wilderness, which must surely have been like the moor. The Church Fathers, they too went into the wilderness – to build the first monasteries. Isaiah prophesied that the messenger of the Lord would be a voice crying aloud in the wilderness. And John the Baptist was that man, baptising the penitent not in a church but in the wilderness, in the pure waters of Creation. The wilderness is God's Creation unchanged.'

William looks down. 'You were a lucky man while you were alive. I'd have given much to have a wife like Catherine. But now, here we are, reduced to spitting, vomiting, shaking wrecks. And you've lost your mind.'

'How can a man lose his mind? If his mind is his own, he cannot lose it.'

'Pigs' bollocks. You think that crying aloud in the wilderness is a sign of sanity? No, brother. It means only that no one need endure your wailing.'

I look up at the vast grey cloud-filled sky. 'I'm going there.'

'In Jesus's name, John, why?'

'That voice I heard, it knew things about me, about us growing up. It knew about that day when I told the priest about our mother's singing. It knows what is happening to me now. If I go to Scorhill, perhaps it will speak to me again.'

'And this voice, was it that of an angel?'

'I don't know. It sounded a bit like me. How are we to know the true voice of Heaven?'

'I doubt that the true voice of Heaven sounds anything like you. Are you sure it was not the Devil?'

'By what token can you tell the difference? A voice by itself does not have cloven feet.'

The breeze cuts cold across our faces. I lurch to one side and retch, my stomach empty except for some bile, and I look down at the string of it still on my lips. Yesterday I spoke of us being brothers until the end of time, blithely assuming that time was our empire. But we were already dying.

'Perhaps it is only seven miles to Scorhill,' he says.

'Will you come?'

He shrugs.

'You do not think it madness?'

'Don't be a cut farthing, John. Of course it's madness, chasing voices. But the madness would be greater if you were travelling alone. Or returning to your wife and children. You can't go back home now.'

I look at William. He speaks the truth. Who could I get to take a message to Catherine? William too has the plague. And there's no one else.

The world seems suddenly an empty place.

Winter has fallen a third time.

The way to Scorhill is an ordeal, a swirling together of pain and blotched glimpses of the world as our senses fail and our limbs weaken. The knowledge that we are dying is the one steady thing in our minds: it sinks into us like a knife slicing deeper through raw meat. William is no longer a wool merchant; he will never attend a fair again with a wagon of fleeces. He won't slap anyone on the back and stand them a mazer of ale and make small talk or exchange jokes with the others gathering in the marketplace. The very fact I was a carver is now just an echo of something that was once true.

At Easton Cross I look up to the top of the hill. On the far side lies Cranbrook. As children, William and I spent much of our time with our brother Simon in the woods up there, cutting staffs with which we would attack or defend the ramparts of the old fort. I remember, on the day that William and I were told by the constable of the hundred that we would be sent to fight in France, we went searching for a stout staff each to help us on our way. I remember thinking that it was a virtuous thing to fight for King Edward and for England because I was fighting also for these woods and hills, and my homeland. But now, who is the enemy? Whom do I fight? The enemy is inside me, my own blood.

I set my sack down by a rock, shivering and sweating, and slowly take off my cloak, my tunic and belt. Wearing only my shirt, I draw my knife.

'What are you doing?' asks William.

'Bleeding myself . . .'

I pull up the left sleeve of my shirt, lift my arm and smell my own stale sweat. There is the angry swelling. But it is not all black like the huge swelling around the neck of the dead man in Honyton. My swelling is yellowish, surrounded by black patches and angry blood-filled blotches. It looks like a fungus growing on me. I hate it – but I hesitate to cut it. It is only a symptom. Instead I push my right sleeve up and, taking my knife in my left hand, aim the point at the inner side of my lower right arm. It is easy to see the place: the scars of old bloodlettings show. The pain I feel as I slice is sharp, chillingly so, but it feels healthy. The blood is not flowing from me but from the disease. I have stabbed it behind its armour. I feel light-headed and relieved. When I have let out enough, I raise my arm and twist my shirt sleeve, using the tightened linen to staunch the flow. I feel faint, as often happens when letting blood, and steady myself on a low rock.

'You should have been a surgeon,' says William.

'Cutting stone is easier.' I stand up straight and find I am still a little dizzy. I retch again but my stomach is empty. I pick up my tunic, and struggle to pull it over my head. After several attempts, I manage it, fasten my belt and draw on my cloak. It feels so much heavier.

'We'll be going now,' I say, swaying on my feet, looking up at the darkening sky.

'Bleed me too,' William commands.

For a moment there is silence, broken only by the evening birdsong. I see blood marks in his neck and the part of his cheek not covered by his beard. I shake my head. 'I've never yet bled anyone else. Only myself, I know where to make the—'

'John, what happened yesterday happened – there's no pushing back the sun. But I've still faith in you. You were moved by God. Do to me what you did just now to yourself.'

'I don't know.'

'What's the worst that can happen?'

William lets his travelling cloak slip from his shoulders and, with difficulty, pulls his overtunic over his head. I am shivering as I watch him roll up his shirt sleeve. He holds his arm out.

'I cannot see the mark.'

'In Christ's name, John, make the cut, where you think best.'

I slice into his skin. The red blood seeps swiftly to the

surface and runs down his arm. 'Let it flow,' I say, wiping the freezing sweat from my brow. When enough has run out, I lift his arm. 'Hold it there,' I say, and I staunch the bleeding in the same way I did my own. 'Bend over, let the good blood reach your head.'

William does as I instruct, and breathes heavily.

'I feel that my life has started to pass before my eyes,' he says.

'Tell me when you see your greatest happiness.'

'That was my first time with Christine of Luwedon.'

'Your *first* time with her?'

'Her husband often went hunting.'

When William has recovered, we walk on up the hill, moving slowly through the trees. It is much darker under their boughs, even though they are leafless. It takes hours. We stumble into ruts. I twist my right ankle. Many times I step into a puddle, and feel the cold water seeping through my boot. Occasionally, the rising moon shines through a break in the clouds and casts a silver gleam across the inter-locking branches above us, giving the impression of walking beneath the intricate ribcage of the wood.

It is dark when William gasps, 'Enough.'

I reach out and find him lying on the path. I put my arm under his. 'Get to your feet, William. If you stay here, you will be dead by morning.'

'I can go no further. My legs'll not do it. I am so dizzy, I do not know which way is up. And there's no feeling left in my fingers. You may as well tell me to carry a horse.'

I try to pull him up. But he is too heavy.

'Come on, where's the lion of old? Imagine there's a beautiful woman up on the moor, just as God made her.'

'The most beautiful woman I ever saw,' he says, 'was in a lane in London. She was very young, and with her father. I stood and watched her pass, and then I saw her enter a church, as if I was in a trance.'

'Then imagine she is up on the moor waiting for you. And her father is nowhere near.'

'No. She was unmarried.'

'What's wrong with that? You are unmarried yourself.'

'Married women make better lovers. They know what they want.'

'Then she's married. And her husband is hunting.'

'No. It's over. There is no desire left in my body.'

'William, I'll not let you stop here. It must be less than a mile to the open moor.'

'I feel like I'm . . .' He coughs and spits, and coughs again.

'For Christ's sake, William!' I shout. 'Please! I cannot walk away and leave you. But nor can I lay myself down and wait for death. That we've got this far is due to there being two of us. The lonely corpses we've seen on the road had no one to help them. We'll not have a Christian burial, I know that, but just to lie down here to die . . .' I wipe the sweat from my face. 'If we accept this, our father and mother in Heaven will be ashamed of us. So, for them, if not for me, get up.'

I reach out for him again, and put my hand under his arm. He grabs my sleeve, and makes to rise, and this time he struggles to his feet. He puts his weight on me, breathing heavily. The swelling under my left arm hurts all the more as

I am carrying my travelling sack over that shoulder. William, I realise, is no longer carrying his. The smell of the cold earth rises to our nostrils. Above us the wind is picking up; it whistles in the leafless branches, which rattle against each other in the dark.

Eventually we walk out on to the bare moor. Here the wind is gusting across the grass, gorse, dead bracken and heather. It howls in our ears and freezes our faces and makes us even more unsteady on our feet. Looking up, the swift-moving clouds allow brief glimpses of the moon. I see the faint line of the horizon. We stumble across tussocks, rocks and gullies up to the first ridge and then descend through wet patches of bog that suck and soak our already sodden boots. Gradually we come down the side of Scorhill.

I scratch my torn hosen against a gorse bush yet again. In places the clouds are thinner, passing swiftly across the face of the moon. And then a darker, larger cloud blocks out the light altogether.

William puts his arm around my shoulder. 'Be quiet.'

I listen. When the gust of the wind dies down, I can hear the sound of water tumbling through rocks.

We come to the stream and walk along the bank. As the wind buffets my ears I think I can hear sounds of lamenting voices coming across the moor. I remember the keening in Exeter. I am so tired, and every step through this wet marshy ground is an effort. There are shapes of dark colour in the night, and brighter patterns too, as if I had pressed my fingers against my eyelids. I see orange and blue squares in the sky, and, at one point, a lake of red water.

We cannot find the circle.

'Let's return to the woods,' says William. I can barely hear him over the sound of the wind. 'We'll shelter under the trees.'

I am too weary to answer. My whole body is burdened with pain. I do not care where we lie down. But after stumbling in the darkness for some distance, William stops. He takes my hand and places it on cold, wet granite, at chest height. The clouds part again and I see the ghostly shapes of two dozen standing stones, in a wide circle. A little way outside the perimeter, slightly higher up the hill, is another stone, fallen now, which reflects a little sparkle of moonlight.

We have arrived.

William walks into the middle of the circle. I stumble forward to join him. A cloud covers the moon again. We are once more in total darkness, listening to the wind howling around us.

'What now?' William asks.

'We should pray.'

I get down on my knees and press my forehead to the ground, shielding my chilled face from the wind.

'What's that light in the rock over there?' asks William.

'A reflection of the moon.'

'It can't be. The clouds are covering the moon.'

I look up. The same light is still there, as if it were a star set in the rock.

I hear a lamenting voice from far across the moor as the wind buffets my ears. William starts to say the Lord's Prayer. This is a fear-filled place. Yet what lies beyond those stones, out there in the windswept darkness, is more troubling still. And it is from out there that the woman's voice is coming, no longer lamenting but singing, very slowly.

> *Merry it is while summer lasts*
> *with birds' song,*
> *but now draws near the winter's blast*
> *and weather strong.*
> *Ei! Alas!*
> *This night is long.*
> *And I, most unjustly wronged,*
> *sorrow and mourn fast.*

A moment passes, with only the wind to be heard.

'That was our mother's voice,' says William.

'Maybe her spirit can help us.'

'Is that why we are here? To seek her guidance?'

'You are here because you do not wish to die,' says the voice that I heard at the cathedral.

'Did you hear that?' says William.

The voice continues. 'What you ask I cannot give. It is not for me to grant any soul a longer life. After this night, you have but six days more to live. Nothing can alter that. But as you surely trusted me by coming here, John of Wrayment, so I will trust you. You will see what no living man has seen.'

'In Christ's name,' asks William, 'who is that?'

'The choice is yours, John,' says the voice. 'You may stay here and return to your house, and spend the last six days with your wife and children. Or you may put yourself in my hands now. I will wipe the scars from your face and the swellings from your body. I will extinguish your fever. I will let you live your last six days in the distance of the future. Ninety-nine years shall pass before you will return to live the first of your remaining days. Another ninety-nine years will pass before the second. Five hundred and ninety-five years will pass before your sixth and final day, when I will come for you.'

Time suddenly seems an unnecessary thing. A whole lifetime is like a single rosebud on a bush. I see many lives blossoming, and their petals unfurling and falling. And it doesn't matter how fast they come and go, whether suddenly or slowly. All that matters is that they are there.

'I'll remain here,' says William. 'I do not fear my fate. I will die here, where I belong.'

'Six days,' I say, unable to think of anything but Catherine and my sons. 'Six days and if I return home I will take this disease with me.' Slowly I get to my feet, still shivering. 'Goodbye, William,' I say, reaching out and touching him. I kneel down and embrace him. I hold him tight, not just as a brother but as the last friend I will ever know. I feel sick with sorrow as well as the plague. The tears running down my cheeks are cold in the wind.

'Ah, by the Lord's balls and breeches, I cannot do it,' says William. 'I'll not be parted from you. I'll go with you, John.'

I let go of him. The wind dies down. There is starlight above us, just two or three clouds visible in the night sky.

'Where's the moon?' I ask.

'It must have set.'

'So suddenly?'

'How do you feel?'

I rub my hands along my sleeves. 'My clothes are drenched and my feet are cold but I no longer feel feverish.'

'So, what just happened?'

'There was a voice. It called me by name.'

'Do you think that we are still—'

'Suffering the disease? I don't know.'

There is a long pause.

'Do you think that was truly our mother's voice, the singing?' William asks.

'It sounded like her.'

'Perhaps her spirit came to save us.'

'Or to lure us in. The voice that spoke to us sounded like my own.'

'That's strange,' replies William. 'I thought it sounded like mine.'

'Let us go.'

I find my travelling sack still propped against the stone where I left it, and we return the way we came.

At Easton we turn off the road and walk up through the lane to Cranbrook, and creep into one of Simon's barns at the mill. Before I go to sleep on the hay, I think back to the voice at the stones. I feel no sense of ease about what happened there. I know I am more in need of redemption than ever. But what form that redemption might take, I do not know. Nor do I know what will happen if I fail to find it. My last thought as I lie there in the darkness is a very simple question.

What do I really know about Hell?

Chapter Three

With the first light that creeps through the corners of the barn roof, I know that something is wrong. From boyhood I have known the rotten section in the great beam that spans the building. I only need to think of this place and I see the cobwebs that hang down thickly from it, sprinkled with wood dust from the decaying part. My father said that, although it looks as though it is going to collapse, the oak in the middle of the beam is still as hard as rock, and that it'll be another fifty years before it needs replacement. But even in this light I can see that a wholly new beam now supports the roof.

I shake William awake. He stops snoring, opens his eyes and looks up.

'Where, between the Scots and the Devil, are we?'

'In the barn at Cranbrook.'

'It has changed.'

We hear the bark of a dog outside. There is a voice too,

which I do not recognise. It is certainly not our brother. 'What is it, you drabbity beast? What's pritched 'ee and made 'ee so fussocky? 'Tis in the barn, is it?'

A moment later the door swings wide open and light floods in. A stout man with receding grey hair stands there. He is wearing long breeches around his legs and a thigh-length jerkin across his upper body. It is secured over his chest with wooden fasteners that pierce the cloth and hold the two sides of the garment together. On his head he is not wearing a hood but a hat like a cap, except looser. His belt is thick leather, with his eating knife tucked in one side.

'In the name of the Lord,' he exclaims, 'what pilgarlics have we here?'

I look him up and down – but he is looking at us as if *we* are the ones who are strangely dressed. My boots are worn. My grey hosen are ripped – you can see the hair and skin of my legs in half a dozen places. The bottom of my brown tunic is torn. My russet cloak is covered in mud. William's clothes look equally torn and muddy. The folded hood he usually wears with such panache has collapsed with dampness. He has lost his silver chain. Only his belt buckle and garnet ring separate him from those who have nothing of value to their name.

'We are the brothers of Simon of Cranbrook,' I explain. 'Our late father was Simon the miller, and our mother, Mary, was the daughter of William the miller, who ran the mill here before him.'

'You're no kin of ours,' the man replies. 'I'm Simon the miller, and my father was Simon before us. And I take no delight in vagrants lodging themselves in my barn.'

'We should thank this good man for his hospitality and leave him in peace,' says William, climbing down from the pile of hay. 'Simon the miller is dead. Long live Simon the miller.' He bows to the man, who has just noticed his gold ring and silver belt buckle. 'We thank you, good miller, for giving us shelter. My name is William Beard, and this is my brother, John of Wrayment. If there is any favour we can offer you by way of exchange for your service, let it be known to us and it shall be performed.'

William bows again and walks out of the barn. I nod to the miller, and follow him.

Outside it is a crisp, cold morning. We keep walking. The millpond to our right is covered with ice and the grass ahead of us is frosted. The puddles in the path are also frozen. There is a mild breeze and birdsong as fulsome as ever. But all the land beyond the millpond, which once was open, with no fences or walls but arranged for the crops to grow in furlongs, is now streaked with walls, ditches, wooden fences and gates. The hills seem to have been divided up into small enclosed fields.

'Where are we?' I say.

'Do you not remember? The voice told us.'

'You believe that ninety-nine years have passed?'

William looks around again. 'Do you have another explanation? This is what Cranbrook looks like ninety-nine years after the seventeenth of December in the twenty-second year of the reign of King Edward the Third, may God have mercy on his soul.'

May God have mercy . . . I am surpised to hear William refer to good King Edward as dead. But I suppose he must be, if we have shifted ninety-nine years ahead of our own time.

'I wonder what year we are in now,' I say.

William shrugs. 'Depends who is king.'

'Even Edward of Woodstock will be dead by now.'

William points ahead to some low walls, partially obscured by bracken. 'What happened here?'

'You know what happened,' I reply. 'The plague. You were there.'

We come to a rough square of rubble stone walls no more than four feet high. This used to be Butterdon. Ivy has partly covered the ruins; a beech tree has grown through a corner. Dead leaves, brown bracken and fallen branches now inhabit the house. It smells like the earthiness that you notice in a wood after overnight rain.

'Ilbert and Richard lived here,' says William.

I say nothing. I wonder if my own house at Wrayment is in the same state.

We walk on, across the frosted grass of pastureland. Clearly, few people take this path nowadays. Lost in our private thoughts, we say little to each other until we are almost in Moreton. There we see the old church. On the west end now stands a huge grey granite tower of four stages in height proudly lording it over the locality.

'That wasn't there yesterday,' says William.

'Why did they build a new tower and not a new church? It looks as ungainly as a man in armour riding a pony.'

'It's a sign to Chagford,' William replies. 'Our tower is higher than their tower.'

The road into Moreton now has three large thatched houses on either side. As we pass, the distant church bell rings, and then a whole peal of five bells breaks the silence with a bronze song. A single bell used to call people to Mass in our day.

'There's your answer. They built the tower to hold the bells,' says William.

Everything seems to have changed in the centre of town. In the square there are wooden houses where market stalls used to stand. Most of the buildings around the outside have been rebuilt in granite with painted shutters and wide oak doors. People are dressed in the strangest clothes. I see a woman with her hair fashioned in such a way that it sticks up like a pair of horns, draped in a fine white cloth. William and I cannot help but stare: is that any way to attend church, looking like the Devil's sister? Several of the men look just as strange, wearing short tunics that do not reach down as far as the knee. Some of the younger ones have tunics that barely cover their buttocks. An older, portly gentleman with white hair and beard strides across the square in a long black robe and with a hood folded a little like William used to fold his in our day. But even he has sleeves that hang down to his knees, so he has to walk with his hands crossed over his chest to stop himself from treading on them.

'Do you want to go to worship, truly?' William asks.

'No,' I reply. 'Everything is too much like a bad dream. Maybe later.'

More people enter the square, and stare at us. We walk among them, squinting in the bright light, self-conscious. Married women in their wimples and brightly dyed long dresses glance at us disapprovingly. Unmarried girls with their hair flowing, wearing long skirts and bodice-like short tunics, laugh at us surreptitiously. Fathers wearing strangely pointed hats lower the brims. One young woman in a group is wearing a quite plain long gown, shaped around her breasts, with long sleeves, and neat, pointed leather shoes. It is only because she is walking alone behind the rest of the family that I see that she is actually a servant. But even she sneers a dislike of our appearance.

'Have you seen a single pauper?' murmurs William.

'Not unless paupers have taken to wearing clothes trimmed with rabbit or fox.'

We walk out of the town on the lane that leads down into the Wray Valley. The bridge over the Wraybrook has been rebuilt, and the fields on either side have been given over to pasture. We pass more people hastening towards the church. Some are clearly country workers – their clothes less shaped to their bodies than those we saw in the square – but even these are of fine cloth. No one looks poor, except us. Our appearance is dishevelled, abandoned and uncared for – like the ruined building up at Butterdon.

In the valley, the farm at Storryge has changed almost beyond recognition, with many more outbuildings and a linney. Whoever lives there now has thrown out some old crumbs for the birds; a thrush is feeding, and a robin cheekily joins in. From here a lane leads towards my house. Trees have grown up where there were none before, and brambles choke a pathway down to the brook.

As I walk I am full of anticipation. But when we draw near

to the place, my hope crumples. Everything is overgrown, engulfed by the lord's beech woods. When I finally see the walls, they are partly covered in ivy. They stand a little higher than those of the ruin up at Butterdon but only to head height. The large granite lintel above the doorway has been stolen, and the roots of a tree have split the back wall in two, so that part of it has fallen outwards. It is like a rocky outcrop emerging from a sea of dead leaves and beech mast.

I put down my travelling sack and enter this place of ruined stone, rooks and roots. One window aperture is still intact, gazing into the leaves of a bush. Many times I have walked over to that of a morning, and pushed open the shutter, letting the first light into the house, and then turned to the middle of the hall to raise the heat from last night's ashes. I look at a decayed fallen branch that now lies where my fire burned, and where I would sit with Catherine after the children were asleep, drinking the ale she brewed. Maybe she survived and left this place. Did the bailiff force her to remarry? The ruins speak of abandonment and death. Clearly none of our children inherited this house and our four acres.

Even if Catherine and the boys outlived me by a few years, they are all dead now. William, John, even little James. All their bones are rotting in the graveyard. A breeze rustles the ivy. I close my eyes and know that, truly, I too am dead. I slowly walk across the floor of what was my home, feeling the sodden ground beneath my feet. Am I a ghost? Are the people in the town who are looking at us so strangely seeing ghosts? What good can a ghost do to save his soul?

I press my hand against a wall. It feels cold. My hand

feels mortal. I cannot pass through walls. If I lift something it rises. I can hear birdsong. When I spoke to the miller at Cranbrook, he heard me. I am no ghost.

'Come on,' says William gently. 'There's nothing here now but sorrow.'

'Where shall we go?'

'I thought you were hoping to do some good works?'

'Damn it, William. In six days? What can we do in that time? I am beginning to think we do not deserve to go to Paradise. It is not a matter of what we've done, it is because of what we are.'

I gesture to the walls. 'This was my home. Catherine and I lived here happily, and our boys . . .'

'At least you had a home. At least you had a family. You were blessed. Did you see where my house stood, when we were in the square? A new building has taken its place. You'll find no trace of me in Moreton. But if we were to go to Exeter now, we would surely see your carvings. If we were to go to Salisbury or Taunton, we would see them in those places too. Pinnacles and portraits, kings and prophets. The grace of your soul will move folk forever.'

I say nothing, feeling the chill of the air. The harsh cry of a crow momentarily fills the valley.

'Listen,' he continues, 'we all have regrets. I regret the moment you picked up that child. But a regret changes nothing. Maybe we already had the plague beforehand – maybe we were carrying it in our clothes all the way from Salisbury. I don't know. But I do know this: no loss is absolute. There is always something left to live for.'

I look across the valley at the trees on the top of the hill. 'When one of my sons was upset after dark, I used to lift him up and come out here and tell him to look up. I'd tell him, when you look up into a tree, even at night, you can see some vague outline of its branches. It's never truly dark.'

'Exactly. Is that not an embodiment of hope, and something worth clinging to? We've only each other now. But that is something. And we are not the only folk in the world. Truly, John, a man can find love in a woman's arms, and in her smile and in her laughter, even though he has spent no more than an hour in her company. You do not even need to touch her – just to see her move and hear her speak can make the troubles of the world seem like nothing. Does that not make your heart feel lighter?'

I say nothing.

William sighs. 'John, I do not know what to say. So let me just say this. When we live our days, one after the other, and nothing changes, we think that each one is like a pebble in the path, as if it's nothing special. We are shocked when we hear the rattle of death in our own chests, and we realise that that ordinary-looking pebble in the path is the last such stone that we will ever see. It seems less ordinary then. But in truth, you and I have been blessed. We've been allowed to see that every day – every *moment* of every day – is a gift. Do you not think that, with but a few days left to live, the world is a wonderful place? Is this tree here not a miracle, returning with new shoots each spring, not flinching from the forester's axe but yielding up its timber for fences and gates? Are you not happy to spend a few more moments of life smelling the damp earth from which all things grow? Are you not content to see a girl's long hair as it cascades around her shoulders? Are you not proud to notice a young lad's concentration as he aims with his bow? Do you not feel honoured to be a man when you see a mother attending to her children? There's so much beauty in the world, don't close your eyes to it just because you've lost your own small patch of happiness.'

'I am lucky to have you as a brother. I should have been here alone, by rights. I have not forgotten how you chose to be here with me.'

'Life in our time would have been unbearable without you.'

'But you wanted to stay.'

William looks away. 'It was different for me. In the circle. I did not hear the same things that you heard.'

'Why? What did you hear?'

'I cannot tell you. Not now. But I will. Later.'

We walk back to the bridge over the Wraybrook and I empty my fardel on to a flat-topped boulder nearby. There are the things we took from the merchant and his wife – the purse, book and rosary beads with the silver crucifix. And there are my own things: a spare pair of hosen, a dirty old tunic, two dirty shirts, a stoneworker's leather apron, seven chisels of varying sizes, a whetstone, an old wooden mallet, an almost-new mallet, two candles, a piece of flint, and my own purse containing five shillings, sixpence and three far-things. Those were my savings from nigh on two months' work in Salisbury. I was intending to give that money to Catherine, to see the family through the winter.

William picks up the merchant's purse and tips the coins into the grimy palm of his hand. There are about thirty and he sets them on the stone, one by one. Half are gold. Apart from these, there are two English groats and three pennies, which I recognise; the rest are foreign silver coins. I examine one of them: it has a picture of a man in a mitre holding a cross on one side, and on the other it shows a cross with what looks like petals or flames coming out of it. There is writing around the edge but it means nothing to me.

'What's this?' I ask, handing it to William.

'That's the Pope,' he says. He gauges the weight. 'Each one's worth about a shilling.'

'So, if all those gold coins are florins and these are worth a shilling each ... That's more than three pounds.'

'And that does not include your own money, or mine ...' He reaches for the purse on his belt. 'Curses, I put it in my fardel yesterday. I had twenty-seven shillings.'

'It does not matter. How much can we spend in six days, anyway? Methinks we should donate Lazarus's money to the church.'

There is the cry of the crow again – but an agitated call this time, repeated twice.

Silence follows.

We look at each other. The bird does not cry out again.

'I have the feeling we are being watched,' says William, looking around.

I catch a glimpse of a red tunic moving through the trees on the side of the valley. A moment later I see a man running, and hear more shouting. I tap William and point.

We quickly put the coins back in the purse, which I replace in my fardel. Up in the woods, someone cries out. It sounds like a child. We hasten back along the road towards my house and take an overgrown path up the hillside. It is steep but the lichen-covered boughs and thick trunks provide good cover for us as we ascend. Further up, we spy the thatch of a cottage. A large fallen trunk gives us a hiding place, from which we can look and listen.

'Why are we moving towards the danger?' asks William in a whisper.

'You heard the cry. Someone needs our help.'

'Another one of your good works?'

I gesture for him to be quiet as we hear the child – a boy – cry out again. 'No, no! Don't!'

'Just string him up by his hands,' says a man with a deep voice.

I look at William. 'You know what I think? We could spend the rest of our short lives seeking safety, running from one shelter to another. Or we could just do what is right, wherever we go.'

'You sound like an Arthurian knight.'

'No, just an out-of-work mason, nothing more, as you said—'

Before I can finish the sentence we hear a girl's scream, which is immediately stifled. I creep around the side of the fallen trunk and continue up the slope to a track, moving between the cover of the bare trees. I hear William following. In front of the cottage there is a muddy clearing. A pig pen and a small sheep enclosure are just off to one side. I see five horses tethered to the fence, their breath clouding in the cold air. One of them is a fine black courser, fit for a lord. Two men, both middle-aged and well built, with swords at their sides, are struggling with a dark-haired boy of about eleven years of age; he is frantically trying to untie the rope they have put around his wrists. Two other men are watching, one dressed in a grey and pale-blue tunic, the other in a leather jerkin with a red surcoat on top. The surcoat carries the design of a white chevron on the breast: the arms of the Fulford family.

The Fulfords' seat is across the river, near Dunsford. In our day they were always causing trouble in Moreton, breaking down fences, hunting other people's deer and stealing cattle – all done in the company of that archvillain, the rector of Moreton, Philip de Vautort. There were no other gentlemen in the area to stop them. The lords of the neighbouring manors lived elsewhere and sent their bailiffs to administer their lands and collect the rents, leaving the Fulfords and de Vautort free to do what they pleased together.

One of the men throws the boy to the ground. 'Teach him a lesson, Walt,' he says in the same deep voice we heard earlier. He looks like a friar, in his late thirties, except that he is wearing a livery badge on his brown tunic: this one shows a white chevron on a red background.

He stamps on the boy's chest.

Walt, who has a scrunched-up face, drags the boy along by the rope, over the frozen muddy ruts, first one way and then back, tossing the end of the rope on his return to the nearly bald man, who flings it over a bough and hauls the boy up into the air. The boy hangs by his hands, kicking, struggling and gasping.

The man in the grey and blue tunic, who is smaller and fair-haired, laughs. He too has the badge of the Fulfords on his breast.

The man in the red surcoat picks up a stone and tosses it, hitting the boy in the face. 'A hit!' he exclaims.

The cottage door opens. A stocky man dressed in the richest black clothes comes out. He walks over to the hanging boy and pushes him, setting him swinging. When he speaks, his voice has a roughness to it. 'Now your sister has satisfied me, it is your turn. Where is your father's money?'

The boy says nothing as he swings.

The man steps forward and puts his hand on the shoulder of the nearly bald retainer. 'Your turn next, John,' he says. 'But don't hurt her this time. I like her smooth skin.'

'Fulford,' I whisper.

'Ninety-nine years have done nothing to end that family's villainies,' William replies.

Fulford approaches the boy. He rests his hand on the hilt of his sword. 'I am sure you think me a tyrant, and that this is all unnecessary. And you would be right. I am a tyrant – and all this is indeed unnecessary. So tell me where your father hides his money, and then, when we have all had a bit of fun with your sister, we will set you on the ground again, and leave you alone.'

I cannot stop myself. I could perhaps have resisted the anger rising in me about the treatment of the boy. Maybe I could have resisted responding to the abuse of the girl. But not the two together. I step forward straight into the clearing, my heart beating like that of a man in battle. I don't even think to hide my fardel. 'Leave him be!' I bellow. 'You have no right to hurt these people.'

Fulford turns to face me. 'And what have we here? A warrior of God? A rescuer of children? Or one who carries a torch for the girl? Just wait in line. There'll be some left for you when we've done. Even if you do look like you've slept under a dungheap.'

'Let him down,' I say.

'Do NOT tell me what to do, churl.'

'Let him down – or this might be the last day that ever you see.'

'And what are you going to kill me with, eh? Are you going to draw your knife and hold me down and stick me like a pig while my men stand by and watch? Or are you going to fart so much I choke on your wind? If you're going to threaten me, there needs to be more than one of you, and you should come prepared for a fight.'

'I am ready to fight,' I say.

'With what?'

'With the sure knowledge, promised me last night by the Devil himself, at Scorhill, that I will not die today.'

I watch Fulford's frown as he tries to read my expression, unsure whether to laugh or guard against the evil eye. His attention shifts to something behind me.

'He is not alone,' says William, striding towards the horses tethered at the fence. 'Today, he has the Devil on his side and

I have God on mine.' He unties the great black horse. 'Life is full of surprises,' he adds, as he grabs the reins and climbs into the saddle. 'If you want this beast back, you'll have to catch me.' And with that he rides off down the path.

'Get him!' yells Fulford, and the men all rush to the other horses. Alerted by the noise, John comes out of the cottage tying the drawstring on his hosen. 'No, John, Tom, you two hold back, leave it to Rob and Walt,' orders Fulford. He shouts to them as they ride away, 'And make sure you drag him back here on his bloody knees.' Then he turns back to me. 'As for you, if the Devil is on your side, then he has met his match.'

'What does the boy's father owe you?' I say. 'Tell me, and I will pay.'

'We owe him nothing,' pleads the boy, hanging from his wrists.

'Then that is what I will pay you,' I say.

Fulford draws his sword and turns to the boy. He stabs both of the boy's legs, which are bare below the tunic. The lad screams with the pain, repeatedly, until he just sobs, swinging slightly. Blood trickles down into his boots; drops fall from the soles to the ground.

Fulford turns the point of the sword to me.

'You'll give me whatever you've got,' he says, stepping towards me rapidly. 'Your friend has abandoned you. If you weren't alone before, you are now. It's three against one.'

I back away, gathering my fardel ready to parry the sword thrust. I look around for some assistance but see nothing and no one.

A dark-haired girl of about fourteen appears in the doorway to the cottage. She supports herself there, gazing at us. I hope she will do something to distract Fulford. I look from her to the sword's point and back. She does not move. I continue retreating. The other men watch: John standing near the boy, Tom by the horses. They both seem amused.

Fulford lunges forward and I shift to my right. I glance around again, looking for a weapon. I feel for my knife and draw it, but it is no defence against a man with a sword. Fulford lunges for my right arm, and I dive to my left. He does the same again, with something like a smile. I stumble backwards, and struggle to keep to my feet. His eyes light up. Like a fox watching rabbits, he knows his victory is just a matter of time.

His next lunge is one of deadly intent. He jabs straight at my face and instinctively I raise my fardel to parry the blow but it is heavy, and he quickly withdraws the blade and stabs again low, aiming for my gut. Only by jumping backwards and falling to my right do I avoid the cut. On the ground I roll away as quickly as I can, abandoning my fardel, but the downward blow I fear does not come. I hear what sounds like two stones hitting each other and see Fulford turn sharply.

Tom in the red surcoat crashes to the ground. William is there: I see him tossing away the rock with which he has just struck Tom's skull and reaching to draw the sword from the man's belt. Fulford and John both run at him but William is quick, and Fulford falters, suddenly staring at a sword-point himself. John too draws back. William moves to my side.

The riders who went in pursuit of William return with

their lord's horse, and dismount silently, surprised at the scene they find. They tie up their mounts to a bough near where the bleeding boy is swinging.

Fulford and his men are on one side of the clearing, William and I are on the other. They all now have their swords drawn.

'Tom!' shouts Fulford. But the fallen man does not stir.

'See if he is dead.'

John goes across to the body on the ground and puts his ear to his mouth.

'He lives.'

'Go now, Fulford, and take your wounded man, and I will spare you all,' shouts William. 'But stay here and I promise you no mercy.' He adds to me, in a whisper, 'Get ready to run. Go up through the woods. I will meet you at Hingston Rocks.'

Fulford looks from us to the girl in the cottage doorway. He sees the boy still hanging by his hands and his own man still unconscious. 'You think you are a bold hero,' he shouts. 'But how bold, I wonder.' He points at William. 'I'll give five pounds to the man who brings me his head. Twenty shillings for that of his scrawny companion. And I want that sack too.'

William and I do not hesitate. We turn and run straight up through the trees.

The ground is firm with the cold but our feet sink into the piles of fallen leaves. I find myself searching for roots to step on as we climb the steep slope, ducking under boughs and pulling ourselves up on low branches. It seems stupid that a moment ago I declared that our last few days are guaranteed by fate.

'Go that way, right,' shouts William, and he runs to his left. I dart to my right and glance over my shoulder. The man in the grey and blue tunic is following me. But I am still a good enough runner to outstrip most men in their prime, even though I am still carrying my fardel. I know the lie of the land even if the paths have moved. My pursuer cannot keep up. Before long, I am running alone through the woodland, southwards, along the crest of the hill, away from Hingston.

I turn again and run down to the road, and climb up the far side of the valley. Here I recover my breath and walk through the trees, heading back north. After half an hour I see Fulford and his men on the road again. Tom must have recovered, as all five of them are riding. But they have taken the girl; she is on the horse with John. I descend and follow them at a safe distance, to make sure they are returning to Fulford.

William is sitting on a rock when I arrive up at Hingston. He seems unhurt.

'You outran him?' he asks.

'I did.'

'I had to stand and fight both of mine. I disarmed the bald one, and then he and his ugly friend ran away. I bet they've never been in a battle. I have a present for you.'

He passes me John's sword.

I notice a few notches in the blade. 'Call this a present? Where's the scabbard? Don't tell me you forgot the scabbard?'

William smiles. 'I've been looking at the moor. Always thought of it as a bleak place before. But you called it "God's

Creation unchanged". I like that. Although I dare say it has changed a bit over the ages. Just ninety-nine years have seen all the land around here laced with walls and fences.'

'The moor itself doesn't look any different.'

'But it does. We are gazing on it with the fondness of two dying men.'

'We are not in the churchyard yet.'

'No, not quite. Which is just my point.'

I look down at the church. No one alive knows where my wife and children lie buried. If Catherine married again, perhaps she is with her second husband. But I know that that is where they are.

'I want to go down there,' I say.

'You're stubborn,' William says. 'You never learn. The world does not care for your good works. While I was waiting, I thought about that cottage we just visited. The girl – she did not want us to help her. I could see tears on her face when she stood in the doorway – she was not happy to be ravished – but she said and did nothing. She did not try to run. It was as if this has happened before, and will happen again, and the best thing to do is just accept it. Then we blunder in, antagonise Fulford and his men, and the peasant children pay the penalty.'

'They took her with them. I saw them on the road.'

'And when their father gets back home . . . Sweet Jesus.'

I sigh. 'I am going to give Lazarus's book to the church. Are you coming?'

William gets to his feet. 'Yes – if only to find out what can go wrong this time.'

*

An hour later we are walking across the Sanctuary Field beside the church when I hear a voice behind us.

'You two look as though you've been dragged through the parish backsivore. Pray, what is your business in visiting our town?'

The speaker is a tall, lean man. He wears a flowing black cassock and white surplice with a black hood lying flat over his shoulders, and a high rope belt. His clothes look exactly like those that Philip de Vautort used to wear in our day. Also, his head is tonsured like a priest's, with all the top shaved. But his manner is one I cannot quite determine. His voice is clipped and authoritative but his words are not threatening. His face is narrow and his brown eyes search us for answers.

William responds. 'My brother and I were both born in this parish, Father, but we've been travelling more years than you would believe. The town has changed almost beyond our knowing. When we left, there was no campanile attached to this church. Houses stood proud that now lie in ruins. There were stalls in the centre of the square. Folk dressed differently.'

'Then you must have been travelling for most of your lives. That bell tower was built nigh on thirty years ago, in the sixth year of the reign of our most holy king, Henry the Fifth. But you've not answered my question. Are you beggars?'

'No, Father,' I say. 'We've returned to make a donation to the church where we were baptised.' I open my travelling sack, reach inside, and feel the book. 'It's my wish to present this book of devotion to the church.'

The priest takes the book reverently, opens it, and casts his eyes over several of the folios. Amid the innumerable black minims, I see a flash of gold leaf. And letters in red.

'Who gave you this?' he asks.

'An unfortunate child,' I reply. 'His father was from Exeter.'

The priest looks at us. 'Well, what a strange pair you are. I was expecting to have to chase off a couple of vagrant rapscallions; instead you place in my hands a Book of Hours. Let me share this with our rector, Canon Precentor Walter Colles. He is visiting us today, from Exeter. Come.'

Without waiting for an answer, the priest turns and starts walking back to the church, the black skirts of his cassock billowing around his legs. William and I follow.

Inside the church, I look up. The near half of the building is much as we know it, with the painted walls and barrel-vault over the nave. On the north side, however, another aisle has been built. There are large windows there, filled with brightly coloured glass – quite unlike the narrow arched windows of the old church, which are a plain, greenish colour. There is a new altar set at the east end of this new aisle, with a carved altarpiece in alabaster, depicting Saint Margaret as a shepherdess. In the chancel, which is reserved for the burial of the rector, there is a single chest tomb.

'There lies good Father Philip de Vautort.'

I turn around. The speaker is an older priest, in a red cassock and white surplice, whose face is ample and ruddy. He has a thick neck, like a bull. His tonsured hair is very short and white so that he appears almost entirely bald. With him is a shorter, fat priest in a black cassock.

'For fifty-three years de Vautort served as the rector of this church,' says the priest in red. 'And now he has lain here even more years than that, watching over the flock of this poor parish in death as he did in life. What a blessing.'

The echo of his voice dies away. This priest has the blue eyes and the precise mannerisms of a royal judge. As he looks at me and William, he pulls out a pair of tiny glass-filled wooden frames, like two round windows, which he raises and holds on the bridge of his nose. He inspects us through these. Then he puts the eye-windows away.

'Tell me your names.'

'They call me Jean de Wrayment.' It seems fitting to give the French form of my name when speaking to a man of high status. 'This is my brother, whom they call Guillan Beard.'

'Different surnames,' says the priest in red, 'even though you are brothers? Did you have a different father from him?'

He looks from me to William, as if expecting an explanation. Surely it is obvious that our different names have nothing to do with our paternity and everything to do with the hair on William's chin? Nevertheless, I answer patiently. 'His name is Beard on account of his beard. Mine is due to my place of residence. So, now that you know our names, let us know yours.'

'I am Canon Walter Colles, Precentor of Exeter Cathedral and servant of the Earl of Devon. I have been rector of this church for the last nine years. This man' – and he gestures to the tall priest – 'is Master Richard Ley, the resident vicar, who has special care of souls here, and this is Stephen Parleben, clerk of the chapel of Saint Margaret.'

I hear the name Parleben and scrutinise the man's face. I see a similarity with those I knew of the same name.

Father Colles holds up the book, which Master Ley has given him. 'This is a most unusual volume. Where did you find it?'

'I did not find it, Father. I was given it by a boy called Lazarus. He died, and left it to me.'

'I notice that it carries the coat of arms of the Keu family of Exeter. I presume that you also are familiar with Alderman Simon Keu?'

'Well no, Father, I—'

'Did that boy, Lazarus, know Alderman Keu?'

I shake my head. 'As I said, Father, he died.'

'Could this Lazarus read?'

'No, Father.'

'Can you?'

'No, Father. But I can assure you that that book was not stolen.'

The priest pauses, scrutinising my face. 'Well, I am glad. I shall be taking it back with me to Exeter, and I shall ask Alderman Keu if his chaplain is missing a Book of Hours. And if all is well, then, I shall happily accept your donation. If not, I shall return it to its rightful owner.'

His words are still echoing away when William speaks. 'Father Colles, we are travellers, not thieves. My brother here is strangely moved to do good works and that is why we've returned to the parish of our birth. It's plain to see that this church, although it's blessed with a fine new bell tower, is small and dark in itself, especially this nave. I believe my brother was considering donating some money as well as that book to help with the rebuilding of the church.'

The canon precentor looks at each of his fellow priests and then turns to me. 'Well, your timing is excellent. The very reason for my being here is to discuss how we might fund the rebuilding of the remainder of the church. As you can see, it is no longer adequate, even for such a remote and backward parish as this. May I ask how much?'

'I was hoping you would accept a donation of forty shillings, Father,' I say.

Father Parleben replies. 'A generous sum for a man who looks as though he has come begging for a crust.'

I hold his gaze for a moment. Then I turn to my sack, bend down and take out the purse. I count out a dozen gold coins and hand them to the tall priest, Master Richard Ley.

William ruefully watches the gold change hands. 'We would not turn down the offer of a good meal, Reverend Fathers. We've been on the road many days.'

'But how did you come by these coins?' asks Master Ley.

'When travelling we mostly carry gold,' says William. 'It saves us from the carriage of so many silver pennies.'

'But why not use English gold coins?' asks Father Parleben. 'Nobles and half nobles. Are not English coins fine enough?'

William spreads his arms. 'Good sirs, regard us. Does it appear to you that we would disdain the form of any English coin? The truth is that my last wool-fells were sold to an Italian merchant in the port of Southampton, and he paid me in florins.'

'Then he overpaid you,' says the canon precentor coldly. 'Those are old Venetian ducats.'

Master Ley breaks the awkward silence that follows. 'I have a suggestion, Reverend Father. There is meat enough for all of us at my house, and wine too. I have something of a feast in preparation, in honour of your visit. So let us repair to my table board and these men can tell us about their travels.'

At Master Ley's house, a servant takes my bag and our swords. We pass into a lofty wooden hall with whitewashed stone walls. Fine timbers support a long roof and there are carvings on the lower beams. A fire is burning on the hearth in the centre of the hall. The shutters are open and the air enters freely, sending the smoke in all different directions. There is meadowsweet scattered over the floor in the rushes, giving the room a scent to counter the smoke. A black-bearded man in a long, dark-blue robe is waiting: Master Ley introduces him as Peter Veysi, the portreeve of the town. He greets us politely but is clearly unimpressed by our dirtiness.

The servant reappears with a boy; they carry a ewer and basin between them, each with a towel over his left arm. The canon precentor washes his hands in the warm water. Our host does the same, and then Father Parleben, the portreeve and us. We are directed to the table: I have my back to the window and sunlight casts my shadow on the linen tablecloth before me. William sits opposite and gazes longingly at the trencher of thick brown bread set before him. Master Ley sits to my left and the canon precentor next to him, then the portreeve; Father Parleben is next to William. The canon precentor says grace, and then we follow him in taking our napkins.

The conversations naturally fall in pairs, leaving Master Ley to talk to me. Although his tone of voice is abrupt, and gives the impression of enormous strictness, his temperament is quite genial. He has a dry sense of humour, and clearly likes his wine: he announces the first sort as Rhenish and the second as from a Gascon barrel. His servants bring out a first course of two dishes suitable for the season, it being Advent: a pottage of herbs and salt fish, and roast pike in galantine sauce.

I quickly grow to like Master Ley. He speaks and he eats, then stops to think, and when he does this, his eyes look up into the smoke-filled shadows of the roof, as if he is trying to find inspiration up there. Then, suddenly, he turns back to me, smiles, and continues talking. I understand that he is beholden to the canon precentor, who is both his second cousin and his employer, but I also sense that he is not entirely happy with the arrangement. No matter how hard he works, he does not get paid a penny more than his stipend by the canon precentor, who takes the tithes of the parish. Master Ley even has to pay rent for this house, as the canon precentor does not permit him to live at the rectory. He tells me all these things in a low voice so the canon precentor, who is speaking to the portreeve in serious tones, does not overhear. Later, the portreeve asks the canon precentor whether this is the fifth or sixth time that he has visited Moreton since he became rector. 'The fifth,' the canon precentor affirms. I am shocked that a clergyman can do so little for his flock. At least

Philip de Vautort lived here. 'But I did serve as the constable of Bordeaux for three years,' adds the canon precentor, glancing at William and me.

I turn back to Master Ley and ask him about recent events in Moreton.

'Oh, doubtless, the singular piece of excitement here in recent years has been the commission set up to bring Baldwin Fulford to account. You remember Fulford, of course?'

'I do.'

'He is still a headache to people around here but he is not half the force he was. His gang, the "Satellites of Satan", have largely deserted him. They were at their worst several years ago. If anyone dared say a word, they'd go into the man's house, drink his ale, eat his meat and bread, and ravish his wife or daughter in front of him.'

'Did no one try to stop him?' I ask.

'Who would dare? If the constable acted, he would find himself the next victim. Truth is, there are just two sorts of men around these parts: those that served Baldwin Fulford and those that kept their mouths shut.'

'But what about the Earl of Devon?'

Master Ley lowers his voice. 'Baldwin Fulford and the earl are close friends. As a matter of fact, it was their friendship that proved to be Fulford's undoing. But no doubt you've heard that story. The case went all the way to the King's Bench.'

'I know nothing about it.'

'It began with Margaret Gybbys. You might remember her? A pretty young woman. Her husband was a good, hard-working man, Thomas Gybbys. One of Fulford's rogues, a man called John of Storryge, decided to try his luck with young Margaret. One day he waited for Thomas Gybbys to leave his house and then he broke in. He found Margaret alone in the hall and forced himself upon her. Of course Margaret, being still very young and dutiful, did not speak to her husband about what had happened, for she feared that he would seek revenge on Storryge and be killed by Baldwin Fulford and his smiling cutthroats. So she did nothing. John of Storryge took this as encouragement to do the same again. Eventually Gybbys found out. He was so angry to be the last to know that none of Margaret's tearful imploring made the slightest difference to him. He went to seek revenge. Sadly, God was looking the other way that day, for in the ensuing fight, the seducer smashed Gybbys over the head with an iron crock and broke his skull. And that . . .' Master Ley shakes his head. 'That was just the beginning of young Margaret's troubles.'

The servants place before us three piles of fish on three large silver dishes. One is a roast salmon, another a large dish of baked lampreys and the third is a very large white fish. The servants also lay three steaming bowls of sauces before us: one is a mustard sauce, the other two are unfamiliar. Master Ley gestures to one of the servants. 'Philip, would you be so kind as to break the fish? Now, where was I?'

'John of Storryge killed Gybbys with a blow of an iron crock.'

'Ah yes. Poor Margaret's woes. She decided that the best thing for her was to marry a man from a distant town and leave Moreton. So she went to Ashburton—'

'Could she do that? Did not the bailiff direct the portreeve to find her a new husband?'

'Oh, that sort of thing does not happen any more. No, Margaret decided to marry a prosperous fellow called William Dolbear. The banns were read three Sundays in each parish church, Moreton and Ashburton, according to the tradition. But when John of Storryge, on a rare visit to Moreton Church, heard them read aloud, he grew angry. He went to Baldwin Fulford and asked for his help in putting a stop to the marriage. When Fulford learned they were to wed in Passion Week, he declared, "We'll be showing her some passion then." The day before the wedding, Margaret travelled the thirteen miles to Ashburton with her mother and friends, and stayed at an inn there. After dark, Fulford and his gang rode into town, torches blazing. His sworn men told him where the bride could be found and he forced his way into the inn. The gang found her already in bed. I heard that Fulford himself was the first to defile her, declaring it no sin as she was not yet married. After he had finished, his men all took turns. One was instructed to go around the town and find more men – to the number of eighty – who would come and shamefully use her. Not one of the good men of Ashburton would consent to do such a foul deed, however. They said that they would not hurt the betrothed bride, as Dolbear was a much-respected and wealthy man. So Fulford, angered by their refusal, went to Dolbear's house. He broke in and beat Dolbear within half an inch of his life. He then pillaged the house and burned it to the ground. And he took Margaret back to Fulford. But that was a great mistake. Sir

William Bonville hated the Earl of Devon and persuaded the king to set up a commission to inquire into the stealing away of Margaret. That's the only way to get justice in these parts – to play powerful men off against each other.'

'I fear the girl he has taken back there today has no such powerful friends,' I say.

'He's still at it then, is he?'

'We saw him, at the cottage in the woods on the west side of the Wray Valley, above the ruins of Wrayment. Just this morning, didn't we, William?'

'We did,' William replies, with a mouth full of fish. 'While her father was in church. It is appalling. An abomination.'

'That's Mark the shepherd's house,' says the portreeve. 'This was his daughter, Alice?'

'They also hanged a boy by his hands,' I say. 'They abused the girl in her own house until we disturbed them, but they were stronger than us, and took her away.'

'He should not have left them unattended,' says Father Parleben. 'It's the father's fault.'

'Assuredly,' says the canon precentor, 'but not from negligence. Why would a God-fearing man leave his daughter unattended and not take her to church? Precisely so such a man as Fulford could help himself to her. As he was attending Mass, he could claim he was not to blame. It's a common way among the peasants of paying their debts.'

William licks some sauce off his fingers. 'A man can never be sure he has done enough to safeguard his daughters, eh father? John, you are lucky you only had sons.'

'I am. Very.'

'The problem is the girls themselves,' adds William. 'Some of them don't want to be quite as safe as their fathers would like them to be. When John and I were heading off to embark with the king's men in France—'

'William, I don't think—' I begin. But Master Ley cuts me off.

'You were in the French wars?' says Master Ley. 'Were you at Agincourt?'

'Where?' William replies.

Master Ley looks at him very curiously. 'You jest, surely?'

William shakes his head. 'No, I do not lie. Not where women are concerned. Unless I am speaking to their husbands, of course.'

'Cousin Walter,' says Master Ley, 'this man has never heard of Agincourt. Can you believe it? Is there really a man in England who does not know of King Henry's most famous battle?'

'Did we win?' asks William, spiking a large piece of lamprey on his knife, dipping it in the sweet sauce and lifting it straight into his mouth.

'That touches on treason,' mutters Father Parleben to the portreeve.

William looks at me and shrugs.

'I guessed from their appearance that they were wastrels,' says the portreeve.

'I wager that that ring on his finger is stolen,' adds Father Parleben.

The canon precentor looks sternly from William to me. 'Normally I would blame the moral corruptibility of the young. But you are not young. You should know better. God showed his judgement on Henry, our blessed king. He favoured all England that day. That you have already forgotten is truly lamentable.'

'Father Canon Precentor,' begins William, finishing his mouthful, 'my brother John and I fought in France. You may have served as constable of Bordeaux but what did that amount to? Receiving written instructions from the king and giving orders. I repeat: John and I *fought*. We shot men in the face with our bows. We stabbed men though the breast and felt their bones breaking under our blades. We both suffered the cuts of swords and the blows of maces. When a battle was done, it fell to us to go among the dying, cutting their throats and gathering up their surcoats for the king's heralds to count. Have you ever cut a man's throat? It is so soft and tender – and yet there is no harder part to cut because you know you are taking a man's life, and making orphans of his children. And yet, after you've cut ten, and felt the warm blood shoot over your hands, your spirit is so sore from so much killing that you think of it only as so much meat. After twenty throats, it is no more trouble than milking cows. After thirty, you start to enjoy it. Then you stop, and reflect on what you've done. And you stare at the last corpse – and that is when the dead speak to you in their terrible silence. Their lack of words resonates in your own conscience. And your conscience rings with their accusations so that, for your own piece of mind, you end up having to cut the throat of your conscience too. And then you are less than a man, and your only true company is other men who have debased themselves. As we endured the unending cold boredom of a siege, waiting outside the walls of Calais, while the French hesitated over whether or not to ride against—'

The canon precentor slams down his fist on the table and with it his smeared linen napkin. 'You are a liar as well as a thief. I have read my chronicles. The siege of Calais took place precisely one hundred years ago, in the year of Our Lord one thousand three hundred and forty-seven. Do you truly expect me to believe you were there? It would be ridiculous!'

William wipes his mouth on the edge of his napkin. 'The siege took place, if I remember rightly, in the twentieth and twenty-first years of the reign of our most excellent king, Edward, the third of that name since the Conquest. The manner of that other date is not something I recognise.'

'But it is the year of Our Lord,' says Father Parleben. 'The number of years since Jesus Christ was born.'

'You have heard of Our Saviour, I presume,' adds the canon precentor, 'or have you been consorting with godless Mohammedans on your journeys? In fact, where have you been, to take you so far from fraternising with honest English householders?'

I try to calm the tension. 'If we were to tell you, you'd not believe us. We've seen the dog-headed men on the far side of India. And the Sciopods south of the great desert. We've shared bread with the pagans of Lithuania and the Seres of China . . .'

Master Ley leans towards me and says in a low voice, 'I think you should know that the Lithuanians were converted some years ago. Our good king, Henry the Fourth of blessed memory, the grandfather of the present king, himself played a conspicuous role in their subjection to the Cross.'

'How do you know when Christ was born?' says William.

'Enough of your ignorance!' shouts the canon precentor.

William leans forward and spears another piece of lamprey. He points his knife at me with the eel stuck on the end, wobbling and dripping sauce on the tablecloth. 'What is the year of Our Lord now?' he asks.

'It's one thousand four hundred and forty-seven,' answers Father Ley.

William takes another swig of wine. 'But how do you know? You weren't there when He died, let alone when He was born, and how many men truly know when they were born?'

The canon precentor looks at me. 'Tell me, John, if you are not such a fool as your brother, were you in the company of Duke Humphrey of Gloucester?'

'Who is Duke Humphrey?' says William.

I can see William has had too much to drink. 'Brother, you are busky-eyed.'

My brother holds up his knife. He leans forward and skewers another piece of lamprey. He puts the fish in his mouth, chews, swallows, and then speaks.

'Have you ever seen a *chevauchée*?' he asks.

'I know perfectly well what a *chevauchée* is,' replies the canon precentor.

'That was not my question. What I asked was, have you ever *seen* one? Have you seen a force of fifteen thousand men spread out, so it covers all the country for eight or ten miles on either side of the vanguard, marching forward across the land? Every house to which we come is set alight. Likewise every barn, granary, henhouse and pigsty. The animals are all slaughtered. The people run away for the most part. If any choose to make a stand, every man and boy over the age of fourteen is killed, and every woman and girl over the age of twelve is given to the men for their pleasure – even the oldest and ugliest – and not only one or two men but dozens, like a piece of meat thrown between dogs. Only the churches are saved. And do you know why that is?'

'Because they are God's holy property,' suggests the portreeve.

William shakes his head. 'Because they've got high towers from which the commanders can see all the land burning for miles around.'

Everyone stops eating. The moment of quiet weighs on us like a lead coat.

'That was what the war in France was like, oh great constable of Bordeaux.'

The canon precentor has a cold fury in his eyes. 'Agincourt was different,' he says. 'King Henry was a godly prince.'

'And you would know, would you? Were you present?'

'No. But I have read the *Gesta Henrici Quinti*.'

'And to judge from the Latin name, that's a book written by a clerk – and if I recall rightly, clerks do not fight battles. Husbandmen and labourers, bakers and smiths, wool merchants and stonemasons – men like us do – alongside knights, kings and noblemen.' William glares at the canon precentor.

'If you take pride in a battle then you should recognise the truth of it. And the truth of any battle is in the fighting. King Edward – the greatest warrior our kingdom has ever seen – led many *chevauchées* to lure the French king's army to attack us. To send all his thousands of knights, counts and bannerets charging at us on their destriers. The king's fine notion was that, at the last moment, when all the French knights were within two hundred feet of our front lines, we would shoot them. With our bows.'

William looks from one man to the other. He holds up a finger and speaks very slowly. 'Have you any idea what it is like to stand and watch the greatest army in Christendom charging towards you, with all their banners flying and their weapons drawn, their lances sharpened? The ground shakes so much beneath the hooves of twenty thousand charging horses that you can barely stand up. The sound is deafening. And then you see all that sharpened steel aimed at your throat. Only at a hundred yards can you hope to pierce their armour and visors with an arrow. At that range, you have time left to loose just two more arrows. Both have to hit – or you are dead. But I tell you all, frightening though it was for us at Crécy, it was worse for those French knights, hardly able to see through the narrow eyeslits of their visors. Some reached our lines – you could see the resolve in their raised shoulders and arms. All the time there came the explosions of the cannon, ribalds and other machines called *gonnes*. They were deafening so that even our own horses reared up and came crashing down on the archers. This was the war that John and I saw. Not pushing about pieces of vellum with numbers on them. Not receiving and passing on orders. So, do not tell us that we should feel ashamed for not knowing the name of some battle that this other king fought. War is a sanctified and glorified terror in which frightened men cause death and tragedy to other frightened men and women. And I say again, the truth of it lies in the fighting, and the suffering of it – not in the proud boasts of clergymen who were not there.'

There is silence.

Master Ley clears his throat. 'Well, this is all most interesting. On reflection I suspect I might have been a little rash in inviting the two of you here to share this celebratory dinner. For it is said that it is the height of bad manners—'

'Be quiet, Master Ley,' snaps the canon precentor. 'These men are leaving.'

'Father Colles,' replies Master Ley, 'I was about to say that, although it is the height of bad manners to demand anything from a guest—'

'Either ask them to leave or I will send for the constable,' says the canon precentor firmly.

But Master Ley raises his own voice, continuing what he was saying. 'However, out of respect to our rector, my munificent and kindly employer, and on top of the respect we all owe to his station in this world, I must demand the truth of you two, despite you being my guests. On your oaths, where do you come from and where have you been?'

'Do you truly want to know?' I ask.

'Very much so,' replies Master Ley.

'Master Ley,' says the canon precentor, 'I want to see these thieves swinging from the gallows.'

I turn to Master Ley and address him alone, although everyone else listens. I tell the story of the terrible plague of our time, and of finding the couple dead on the highway and their baby screaming, and my trying to save the child. I mention the voice I heard on the cathedral screen that night, and the warning that I had but six days to save my soul. I explain that I did not understand this at the time, and that William and I embarked on our homeward journey in ignorance of our own infection, but when we discovered the truth, we prayed hard. I do not mention that we went to Scorhill but I say that our prayers were answered by an angel, who told us we would live one day of the six remaining to us every ninety-nine years. I conclude by saying, 'So the answer to your question as to where we come from is that we were born in this parish. But in truth, although this is our home, we are not at home. Home is not a place but a time.'

Master Ley looks from me to William and back, most solemnly. The portreeve is looking down at the straw on the floor. The canon precentor stares down the hall, ignoring me as if I were one of the Satellites of Satan. Father Parleben looks stern. 'Have you finally finished your blithering?' he asks. 'I'll call the constable myself.'

But Master Ley is not happy to see us treated thus. 'No, Father Parleben. I will not have it, not at all. This may be a miracle.'

'Pah! Miracles!' snaps the canon precentor. 'Country credulousness.'

Master Ley replies calmly, 'You may have your doubts, Cousin Walter, but there are many marvels in this world that are beyond our comprehension. We read about them in the Bible and in the pages of the works of our most learned men. Surely as an educated man you've delved into the works of Roger Bacon? He writes of the possibility of building machines with wings that can beat the air and propel a man in flight as birds do, and of protective suits of armour that allow a man to traverse the seabed with no danger of drowning, and of bridges that can cross great chasms without anything to support them. If these things are possible, as Friar Bacon says they are, then why should not men traverse periods of time? Friar Bacon also wrote of chariots that could move at the most incredible speeds without a single draught animal, and ships of vast scale that likewise could cross the world's seas in a few days, with just a single man to steer them. One might declare that these are the fictions of an old friar too fond of fathoming the future, but this was the same friar who described such previously unimagined marvels as your spectacles, without which you would be less sure of many things.'

The canon precentor turns from Master Ley to address William. 'Tell us, if you were here at the time of the Great Plague, what was the name of the rector then?'

William is now eating a baked apple, the sauce running down his fingers. 'He was a stinking pig called Philip de Vautort. He was fat and he spoke French, and we all hated him. And now, as I hope, he is burning in the hottest of all the pits in Hell.'

The canon precentor snaps his fingers at one of Ley's house servants. 'Fetch the constable. We want two vagrant plague-ridden thieves removed from here to the gaol in Exeter.'

'The plague?' I ask, astonished to think that even here, in this remote time, it is still killing people.

'Alas, we yet walk through the valley of the shadow of death,' replies Master Ley.

'Do not encourage them,' snaps the canon precentor.

'Every seven or eight years it returns. We are still at war with France too. And still suffering the depredations of brigands. Not much has changed since the time you describe as your own.'

'No, Father Ley! How can you say that? Everything has changed,' I protest, looking straight at him. 'Who were the leading men of the town in our day? I'll tell you: John Parleben, Reginald Veysi, William Kena, William Carnsleigh, William Corvyset, John White, William Tozer and Warin Bailiff. Where are they now? Dead, of course. You do not know what they looked like, or what clothes they wore – and that is so even though these two men here carry their names.'

'This is unsupportable,' declares the canon precentor, who throws down his napkin and rises to his feet.

I continue. 'Who can imagine the tenderness of a great-grandmother? Or the fears of a great-great-grandfather? But you should not think for a moment that your ignorance of the past means that nothing has changed. I am sure that the canon precentor is proud of the cathedral in Exeter, but I doubt that he knows the name of a single mason that built it. Well, I can tell you many of the names, and one of them was John of Wrayment.'

The portreeve and Father Parleben also stand. Colles

strides across the room and stops to address Father Ley from the middle of the hall.

'Master Ley, I find your attempts to humour these two men tedious and insulting. If you need me, I shall be at my rectory.' He goes to the door and opens it – not waiting for a servant to do it for him – and leaves the house. Father Parleben follows him.

Peter Veysi pauses to address Master Ley. 'I thank you for this dinner, Master Ley. It was a most excellent spread. I am sorry it has ended in such contumely. I have no choice but to go with the canon precentor. As you know, we need him to agree to the rebuilding of the chancel.' He bows to Master Ley and departs.

Master Ley looks down at his trencher, and seems almost to be smiling. 'You must excuse the canon precentor,' he says, reaching out for his wine goblet and lifting it to his lips. 'It can be no pleasure for him to come all the way out here on such a trivial matter as the rebuilding of our church. I am sure he will calm down in due course.'

He sets down his wine. 'I assume you're not actually carrying the plague. You both look well enough. Certainly your appetite, William, suggests no lasting sickness.'

'Master Ley,' I say, 'let me ask you something. What does a man need to do to secure safe passage to Heaven? Will the donation of that money and the book be sufficient in my case?'

'Now *there's* a change of subject. Why do you ask?'

'We have but a little time to live. Methinks that you, being a man of the cloth, well, you should know.'

'It's a difficult business. Our masters in Rome tell us that through the purchase of indulgences we can clear our souls of the taint of sin and thereby secure redemption. The canon precentor will tell you much the same thing. However, some of us are less certain. For instance, if you were one of the Satellites of Satan, I would say to you that no gift could redeem your soul. But that does not mean that your soul would be irredeemable. You could, for example, make a pilgrimage to Jerusalem and wash your sins away through repentence at the Holy Sepulchre.'

Master Ley wipes the edge of his mouth with a napkin. 'Imagine that you are that rare thing, a man without sin. Why should you give a penny for your soul's redemption? It is already perfect. So how can you be rightfully *charged* for the redemption of your soul? After all, who among us can truly judge another man's sin? That is a matter for God alone. If you were a sinless man, an indulgence would be as useless as a shield of straw. Therefore, in answer to your question, I do not believe that anything is now changed by your gift. I am sorry if that comes as a disappointment to you.'

'Is there nothing I can do? Nothing at all?'

'Your predicament, as I see it, is that your principal motive in wanting to perform a good work is the benefit it will bring to your soul, not the good work in itself. If you saw a good woman being attacked by Baldwin Fulford, and you stepped forward to save her, that would be a good act. However, if you were to rescue her purely so your soul would go to Heaven, the good of the act would be secondary to your self-interest. You would be benefiting from her plight. There is no virtue in that.'

A chill breeze enters by the window. Master Ley gestures to one of his servants to close it. William has drained Father Parleben's wine mazer and is finishing the canon precentor's too. I wipe the sweet red sauce off one of the platters with my finger and lick it when there is a knock at the door. Master Ley pays it no attention. But the servant who has just closed the window goes to answer it. A burly man comes in, wearing a great leather mantle over his clothes that reaches down to his knees. He sweeps one part of it aside and reaches up to remove his black hat.

'Master Ley, I am informed that your house is beset by plague-sufferers, liars and thieves.'

'I thank you for taking the trouble to attend, Constable Carnsleigh, but I am afraid you have been misinformed. There was a small altercation between the rector and my guests here over the matter of the late king's wars. As you can see, they are not suffering from the plague. If they are telling lies then I must admit their untruths be more delightful to me than many a hard fact I have heard of late. I wish you a good afternoon.'

'Seeing as that is the case, Master Ley, I am very sorry to have bothered you. Do send for me again if there are any further altercations.'

'I will indeed, Constable,' says Master Ley as the servant shows the man out.

'Well,' he says, turning to us, 'I have no further subtleties with which to entice you. It is up to you what you wish to do. You no doubt have some other places to go to and things to attend to.'

William and I look at each other. 'Truth be told, Master Ley,' I say, 'we've nowhere else to go. And it'll be dusk in a couple of hours. If it would please you, I'd happily work the rest of the day in your house, perhaps in your kitchen, to earn a place before your fire tonight.'

'By my heart, you are the strangest folk. You give me money for the church, you tell stories that are either brilliant lies or shards of miracles. And after being treated to a proper dinner, you ask to wash the dishes.'

'It's John that's doing the asking, mind,' says William.

Master Ley gets to his feet. 'You are my guests. John, if you want to work, you can help my cook, Will, in the kitchen. Your work will be a blessing upon us all.'

So we take advantage of the good clerk's hospitality. William sits by the fire, while I go through to the kitchen, which is a separate granite-built building on the other side of the courtyard. This is open to the rafters but the hearth is set against a wall, not in the middle of the room, and it has a chamber called a smoke box above it, to restrict the drifting fumes. Will the Cook is a bright young man with curly fair hair and a pleasant smile. I help draw water from the well in the courtyard and heat it over the fire in a cauldron on a swinging metal bracket, the like of which I have not seen before. When the water is hot, I help Will and the other servants put the leftovers to one side for the pigs who live in a small rough garden called the backside, and then help scour the blackened iron pots with handfuls of coarse straw and potash. The light is fading by the time we finish; we set up rushlights on metal stands by which to see in the gloom. Will feeds the fire well – the servants in this house are probably warmer in the winter months than their master – and then we set about weighing all manner of roots and seeds on the scales. Some of these I have heard of – saffron and pepper, for example, although Catherine and I could never afford them – but others are wholly new to me. Will shows me a pot of aromatic brown seeds that he calls cumins and others called caraways and cloves. In other pots he has sweet dried fruit called dates, and thick yellow sticks of a root called ginger. Pieces of scented bark, called cinnamon, are in one box; in another are large seeds called nutmegs. For a moment, in the warm, fire-lit darkness, surrounded by all these wonderful spices and smells, I have a glimpse of true wealth.

'Where does he obtain such exotic things?' I ask, as Will starts chopping almonds. 'Does he send to London for them?'

'We stock up when the fairs are held here – in Bovey, Okehampton and Chagford as well as Moreton – and the grocers in Exeter keep stocks of spices. If I buy eight ounces of nutmegs for the master they'll last all year. Even at the rate that he consumes them. He likes a little ground nutmeg in his wine with sugar.'

'Sugar? You have sugar? Never have I tasted it.'

'It was in the red sauce that accompanied the roasted turbot.' He reaches a brown cake down from a shelf and shows it to me. 'You can buy it in all different forms: pot sugar, red flat sugar, white flat sugar, Cyprus sugar, sugar candy, syrup, and so forth.' He cuts a small piece off the brown cake with a large knife and passes it to me.

It tastes as if God had made it simply to make us smile. The sweetness fills my jaw so much that I cannot help but grin. I want to share this sublime taste with Catherine, and that loss swells into a regret. This wonderful new taste makes me think of my whole life. Tears come to my eye. I keep the sugar in my mouth as long as possible, and feel it dissolve. But even then the taste lingers.

In this way the rest of the day passes. We weigh spices and we grind them, we talk about food and we sup ale with honey and herbs. Later, one of the servants comes through and says that Master Ley would like a small supper to be served to him and my brother. Will prepares a dish of oysters simmered in wine with their own broth, with milk from blanched almonds, powdered dried ginger, sugar, maces, and something called flour of rice.

'But how does Master Ley afford such luxuries?' I ask. 'He told me he has but a modicum of the income from the rectory – a modest stipend.'

'The master is no fool. When the canon precentor first came here and took a view of the glebe, his flock amounted to twenty-four sheep. That flock is still twenty-four sheep strong. Master Ley, however, has acquired a flock of more than three hundred. When men go off streaming for tin on the moor, Master Ley takes on their leases for the land they no longer use, including their meadows and their rights to pasture their animals on the common. That is why so many of the woolsacks around here are filled with his wool. He is a local man through and through. That's why the parishioners are all on his side and against the canon precentor, whom they see as a thieving foreigner.'

When supper is served, I note that Will and the two servants eat in the hall with Master Ley. The shutters are now closed, and the fire burning merrily. Four or five rushlights illuminate our tables, and, as we eat, our movements cast huge shadows on to the walls behind us. After the meal our host serves us caudled wine with nutmeg, sugar and cinnamon. William and I tell stories, and after a while Master Ley himself joins in. He tells us jokes about stupid men cuckolded by their shrewd wives, and pretty young women seduced by lustful men who promise to marry them with rings of clay and straw, which of course fall apart, and foolish monks deceived into parting with their abbot's money on account of their ungodly ambition.

At the end of the evening, we are provided with straw mattresses to sleep on, blankets to keep us warm, and a log each on which to rest our heads. I prefer to rest mine on my fardel. Will and the servants depart to sleep in the kitchen. All but two of the rushlights have burned out.

'I suppose there's a very good chance I will not see you in the morning,' Master Ley says, before he leaves the hall. 'I have enjoyed discussing things other than over-prized sheep and lost souls – or over-prized souls and lost sheep.' He pauses. 'John, if I were you, I'd not worry too much about trying to save your soul. The thing you seek to do can only come from you naturally. You cannot make it happen. No matter how many days the Lord has given you to live, they will be enough. Goodnight, and may God's blessing be upon you both now and always, in your travels, and in your eventual homecoming.'

I settle on my mattress and hear him climb the ladder to his chamber above the buttery. I shuffle a little, trying to make myself comfortable, and hear the rustling straw beneath me as I do so.

'What are you thinking?' whispers William.

'Why could we not have had a priest like Master Ley in our day, instead of de Vautort?'

Only one rushlight is now burning and that is nearing its end.

'What do you think tomorrow holds?'

'Another freezing seventeenth of December. But this time in a different year. The canon precentor said that the siege of Calais was in the year of Our Lord one thousand three hundred and forty-seven. We caught the plague the following year, and ninety-nine years have passed, so we should wake up on the seventeenth of December one thousand five hundred and forty-six.'

'Do you think it will be any different from today?'

'Yes. Undoubtedly.'

'Perhaps they'll eat more lamb. What with all these sheep.'

'Not in December they won't. It'll still be Advent.'

'Curses. Why could we not be spending our last days in July?'

The last rushlight goes out and now there is only the glow of the fire to light the hall. I roll on to my side and stare into the redness of the burning logs. A few sparks drift off. The hall is silent.

'I think you should not tell people the truth about where we come from,' says William. 'They do not recall the reign of King Edward the Third. It is incomprehensible to them. And men do not like what they do not understand.'

'I agree.'

'Say that we are travellers from places where no one has ever been. Like India. Or Muscovy.'

I lie there for a few slow minutes, on my side, looking into the fire.

I wonder if any of my children lived long enough to taste sugar.

Chapter Four

My eyes are not yet open but I am awake, my leg pressed bruisingly hard up against a heavy piece of furniture. It is dark; there is no sign of light at the window. Nor is there any trace of heat from the fire by which I went to sleep.

I hear a snuffle and the rasp of a snore.

'William?'

Another snore.

I think back to the previous morning. That miller at Cranbrook used words I did not understand. He said his dog was *fussocky*. What does that mean? Can our way of speaking change that much in ninety-nine years so that I can hear things in my own home town that I do not understand? If houses are so different, and the clothes and the food so altered in quality, what else might change? How should William and I stop ourselves looking out of place and avoid questions about where we were born?

The snoring stops.

'The sound of your thinking is so loud,' says William, 'it has awoken me. What is on your mind?'

'New raiment, brother. The further we are from our own time, the stranger we'll appear, and the more questions we'll be asked.'

'We need a tailor.'

'If we were to order new sets of clothes, how long would it take to make them? At best, a tailor would say, "Come back and collect them tomorrow," which would be no good for us, as by then we'd be another ninety-nine years further on in time.'

'What then?'

'We need someone to sell us some old clothes. Perhaps the owner of this house? At least, he might know of a local man who has died recently, so that his widow might part with his unwanted garments.'

There is a thump in the darkness, as if someone had struck one of the beams of the hall roof. I hear the sound of footsteps on floorboards, directly above us.

'I was wondering,' William says, 'whether we are ghosts.'

'The thought has occurred to me too.'

'I've decided that we are not. The living are afraid of ghosts. But we are afraid of the living.'

'Maybe they are the ghosts then,' I say. 'Everything that we see and hear is the ghost world and we are the only living folk in it.'

'That, John, is a grievous thought.'

I get to my feet, placing my travelling sack on the table. I wonder what happened to my sword – and then remember leaving it in the passageway. I remember the whitewashed stone walls of Master Ley's hall and move in the direction of where the door stood but I bump into a wooden cupboard of some sort, sending a metal plate clattering to the floor.

'You are keen to meet our hosts, then,' says William.

The embers of a fire are glowing faintly on the side of the hall. I step closer, and bend down, hoping to find a poker with which to rake the ashes. My searching hand touches nothing suitable. So I stand up again and, as I do so, I bash my head on a piece of overhanging stone. I curse, and rub the lump.

'There's a fireplace here,' I tell William.

'The new master no doubt wants to save his fine clothes from the smoke. I don't blame him.'

I move to the right, towards where Master Ley's great window was. The wall between the fireplace and the window is not stone but smoother, like plasterwork. I feel a recess and boards, which are shutters over the inside of the window. I can just see chinks of grey light through the cracks.

I move further to my right, feeling my way. On the far side of the window there is a tall piece of wooden furniture – about the same height as me. It has a pattern carved on the front. Beyond that I feel more wood. It seems to be a huge piece of furniture, taller than me, carved in large square panels, with patterns of ribbing down the middle of each one. Then I realise, from its solidity and size, that it is not a piece of furniture at all but a wall covering. The whole wall is covered in panels of wood.

The next thing I feel is a thigh-height piece of furniture.

It is overlaid with a very thick woollen fabric, far thicker and heavier than something you would wear. Underneath is a chest of some sort, with a lock at the front. Beyond that I feel a door in the panelling, with a latch, then more wood panelling, and, at the corner of the room, something that feels like a stiffened blanket hanging down. My fingers note the patches of smoothness on its rough surface. It is a painted cloth. It runs the full length of the hall, except for where it is cut around a doorway, halfway along.

I move back to the table in the middle of the room. There is stirring elsewhere in the house. 'We'd better be setting off,' I say. But no sooner have I spoken the words than I hear footsteps on the flagstones outside the door.

A girl enters, carrying a candle. I remain motionless beside the table. She does not immediately see either of us but goes to the shutters, unlatches a large metal bar on the inside and swings them open. She blows out her candle.

Outside, I can see the roofs of tall dark houses. I can see too that this room is not a hall open to the rafters any longer; it has a plastered ceiling, only a couple of feet above my head. There is clear glass in the window: a line of four lights, divided by three carved granite mullions, filled with diamond-shaped quarrels of glass. I never would have imagined a house in Moreton could have glazed windows. Indeed, I am so amazed that I forget where I am and take a step closer to make sure my eyes are not deceiving me.

The girl screams. At first it is an inarticulate yell of shock but then, as William jumps to his feet and I start to move towards her to reassure her that we mean no harm, she starts shouting.

'Master Hodge! Master Hodge! There are foreigners in the parlour!'

'How do we get out of here?' William says, picking up my old travelling sack and thrusting it into my hands.

We are too late. A door in the panelling at the far end of the room opens suddenly and a squat, muscular man enters, carrying another candle. He has dark, bushy eyebrows and is clean-shaven, wearing a soft-looking black cap. His wide shoulders are made to look even broader by the padded shoulder pieces of the tunic he is wearing under his mantle. His hosen are of fine white cloth. The knife sheath at his belt is gilt and has a jewel set in it.

'By God's wounds, what do you call this? Dolbear! Dolbear, send for the constables. Bowden! Scott! Bring all the men down.' As he speaks he sets the candle on the table and strides across to the fireplace. He pulls down a long weapon from the wall above it that looks like a combination of an axe and a spear. There is another such weapon mounted there but I dare not move towards it. He holds it threateningly. There is the sound of people descending a staircase hurriedly. Four more men appear: two hold thin-bladed swords, one a bow with an arrow loosely notched in it; the fourth what seems to be a long hollow stick with metal pieces attached to it at one end. That too must be a weapon of some sort – he is holding it in a threatening way.

Then I realise. It is a *gonne*.

William raises his hands. 'We mean no harm. We've taken nothing.'

I set my bag down and raise my hands also.

'Search them,' commands the householder.

One man goes behind me and pushes me up against the wall with my arm behind my back, forcing it upwards past my shoulder blade. Another starts feeling my clothes. After they have satisfied themselves that there is nothing concealed about my person except my eating knife, they search William. One picks up my sack and empties its contents on the stone floor. He is an unpleasant-looking fellow, with a jutting, unshaven chin and a cut on the side of his face, just below his eye. Solemnly, he pulls the silver crucifix with the amber rosary out of the pile of my possessions, and holds it up for all to see.

'Where did you obtain that?' demands the householder.

I turn to see what he means, keeping my hands high. 'I was given it. By the mother of a boy whom I helped when he was ill.' Their faces disturb me, so I add, 'We observe the law of the Holy Father in Rome.'

'Where are you from?'

'Exeter. I am a mason.'

'There's money here, and chisels and other tools,' confirms the unpleasant-looking man, standing up and placing the crucifix on the table and lifting up my purse.

'Master Hodge,' says William. 'We were only looking for shelter.'

'How did you enter this house?'

'Master Ley let us in,' William replies.

'I have never heard the name. You've no right to be here. Neither had anyone the right to admit you.'

'Sire, this is a misunderstanding,' I say. 'We've money of

our own. Regard our coins – they are from a distant land. I know we appear shabby, and in old clothes, but we are travellers. Pray, let us take our possessions and be on our way.'

'It does not matter that you've taken nothing. You would have stolen in due course. You were stopped in time. And if not, then why are you here? Spying on our worship?'

'We did not housebreak,' William pleads. 'And we are not spies.'

'Look over the building,' I say. 'See if there is a window broken or a lock forced. Is there a drawbar on the front door? Then if it has been withdrawn this morning, it was by your men, not by us. Check every piece of glass.'

'If this were so, it would be witchcraft, would it not?' says one of the men bearing a sword.

Master Hodge raises his hand. 'Bowden and Scott, search the house. Check every door and casement.'

The two men leave the room. I hear the timbers creak as they walk around the house.

One of the men who remains says, 'I fear they are guilty witches, Master Hodge. They are wearing strange clothes. And their voices are strange too, like none from around these parts. Surely they are here through witchcraft.'

All the men are staring at me as if I have two heads. 'I've never heard of folk using sorcery to break into a house,' I say. 'I know that men will go to a sorcerer or a wise woman if they've lost something, like a ring or a seal. But appearing out of thin air in someone's house? That is beyond witchcraft.'

Master Hodge is still holding the long weapon. He raises

the sharp point towards my face. 'Do you not know the king's law? All those guilty of sorcery should be hanged.'

'It cannot be evil to use magic to find things,' I repeat. 'If you lose something of your own, and then you find it, what could be evil about that? It's no more evil than believing in the Holy Catholic Church.' I lower my hands, step forward, and pick up the crucifix from the table. 'Is this evil? God can work miracles: are you going to hang Him?'

'You are bold, Roman,' says Master Hodge, withdrawing his long-handled weapon. 'There are houses in England where you would hang for what you have just said.'

Something has given me a sudden respectability. I say nothing, hearing the returning footsteps of Hodge's men who have been checking the house.

'There's no sign of any break-in,' one of them says.

Master Hodge hands his weapon to one of his men. He steps closer and looks me in the eye. 'I do not know whether you are conjurers or not, but I do not want my house cursed. Nor do I want it searched for those who cling to the old religion. I do not know who let you in. But if I send you to trial in Exeter, I have no doubt that you will use the same magic as you used to get in here to evade justice. So go, leave this town quickly, and never return.'

There is a strange silence as everyone watches me gathering up my possessions and replacing them in my old sack. I sling it over my shoulder and we walk towards the door. As we step outside into the light of a misty morning, it feels as if we have escaped from a prison.

We do not speak as we walk past the new houses in the

market square. We avoid the gaze of people outside in the street. Only when we get to the church does William speak. 'They rebuilt it then.'

The church indeed has been rebuilt. I wonder briefly if Master Ley paid for it himself or whether the canon precentor and the parishioners helped him.

I look up at Hingston Rocks, partly shrouded in mist. 'Why do you think he let us go?'

'His manner changed when you held that crucifix aloft.'

'He said men would hang in some houses in England for saying what I said.'

'And he called it the *old* religion ... Do you think that Englishmen are no longer Christians?'

'Look at the church,' I reply. 'That new work tells me that the word of the Lord is as strong as ever in these parts. Besides, if he had been a Mohammedan, he surely would have slaughtered us when he saw the cross.'

William looks back at the town. 'In Christ's name, this is a truly disquieting time, when we do not know what people believe. We don't know what the law says either. Apparently there's now a law against asking sorcerers to help find things. What else is unlawful? Drinking ale? Eating beef? Kissing women?'

'We need food and new clothing,' I say. 'We should walk to Chagford.'

'Is it market day there?'

'No. Thursday is market day in Chagford.'

'How do you know it isn't Thursday today?'

'Our last day was a Sunday. Every year that passes has three hundred and sixty-five days in it, not counting leap years. If there were only three hundred and sixty-four days in a year, the first day every year would fall on the same day. But as things are, and saving leap years for the present, each year starts one day later, so if the first year starts on a Monday, the second'll be on a Tuesday, and so forth. Thus the ninety-ninth year will start ninety-nine days later, or rather one day, as ninety-eight is divisible by seven . . .'

'You've lost me already.'

'Trust me.'

'I do.'

'Let us go to Chagford.'

Walking down the rough muddy lane, we come up behind a countryman riding a fine horse. He seems very much at ease with himself, sitting astride the beast with his chest out, wearing his cap at a jaunty angle, his shoulders broad to the morning. I cannot help noticing, however, that he is riding very slowly even though, at fourteen hands or so, his horse is taller than most of the warhorses of our day.

'Friend, good day,' I say. 'Is she ill, your mount?'

'Good day, good fellows. No, she's not ill. It's that I'm in no hurry, that's all.' He glances down at us. 'What brings you to Moretonhampstead?'

'Moreton what?'

'Moretonhampstead,' he repeats.

'Since when has it been called that?'

'As long as I remember. I suppose you're Master Periam's men?'

'No. Just travellers. And you?

'Tom Brimblecombe, at your service.'

'Are you going to Chagford?'

'Taking this horse to Plymouth. She's off to join the Duke of Norfolk's men, in Boulogne.'

'The war in France?'

'If you call it a war. Apart from Boulogne, there's only Calais left to us. Not worth Henry styling himself "King of France" if you ask me. Still, it won't be for long. They say he's dying.'

'You do not like the king?'

Tom gives a hollow laugh. 'What do you think?'

I look at William. 'I think he is the king. It is not for me to judge him.'

'Then you are a fool,' replies Tom. 'Henry the Eighth is without a doubt the greatest tyrant England has ever known. Boiling women alive for poisoning – that's nothing but cruel. Hanging the travellers that call themselves Egyptians for roaming the countryside and begging – that's nothing but unjust. Prohibiting pilgrimages and destroying all the relics – that's surely unholy. But stealing all the lands of the monasteries and closing them, and pulling them down – that is plain wrong. And he calls himself the Defender of the Faith. Pah! No one has ever so damaged the Faith as he.'

I look at William. 'Perhaps we should try to undo such damage?'

Tom laughs. 'Don't even think of it. You'll end up like Robert Aske.'

'Robert who?' I ask.

'Aske. You remember – he led the rebellion in the North,

oh, eight or nine years ago. The king persuaded him to nego-tiate, agreed to his terms, and then when Aske's army had disbanded, the king hanged him and hundreds of other good men. How can a man parley with a king who will go back on his promises?'

'Moreton seems to be thriving,' I say. 'There's wealth here – better houses, finer clothes . . .'

'For some, maybe,' replies Tom. 'For others, it is just longer hours and higher prices. You may well see fine houses up and down the streets, but my dwelling place is an attic over a stable.'

'We've not even got a stable,' says William.

Tom looks at him. 'Then I pity you. And may I say, miser-able wretches though we are, yet still our names are inscribed in ledgers and registers. Where is the reason in that?'

I look at William, and he shrugs.

'It's all taxes, taxes, taxes,' says Tom, looking down the road. 'Taxes and writing go hand in hand. Words are the spells they cast on us common folk, and taxes the curses they bring down on our shoulders. They write your name down when you are baptised. Fail to pay your dues and the king's officers will come looking for you – and they *know* where you are living, and where your kin are, because they've got lists of all the folk who reside in every parish. May all clerks go to Hell in boats of paper on a great ocean of black ink.'

'But if all these things are written down, whence come all the clerks?'

'Barely a month passes without us receiving word of some newly founded school. Folk are teaching themselves to read the Bible. Even women.'

'Lord, have mercy upon us!' exclaims William. 'Why do women want to read? Words are no good to them. They cannot understand the meaning of things.'

'They learn to read so they *can* understand,' I reply, 'just as you taught yourself – so you could keep tallies and accounts. But imagine how the world would be different if women could read.'

William laughs. 'Nothing would ever be cleaned or stitched. Women would sit around discussing Moses and Noah while their husbands toiled away to earn a crust. If the women were then so bold as to speak to their husbands about religion, the men would up sticks and head off to a distant town, never to be seen again. Then where will all that reading of books have got them?'

'I am not so sure,' I reply. 'A word of wisdom from a kindly wife might stay the hand of a hard-hearted justice. If the king thinks ungodly acts, might he not take his wife's advice more to heart if he knows she can read books of wisdom and holiness?'

'God's teeth, John. Let's not even think of such things. Your sons would be all soft-hearted if your wife were to read to them in your absence.'

Then a strange thought comes to my mind. 'What if she could write too?'

'There are those who can,' says Tom. 'Mistress Charles in Moretonhampstead for one. Mistress Whiddon of Whiddon House for another. And *her* husband, Master John Whiddon, is a judge.'

'I understand why he practises the law,' says William.

'But if he were to do her wrong,' I say, 'she could reprimand him in public – by writing to all those of their acquaintance.'

We come to Easton Cross. I look up at the hills and the leafless trees on the ridge between us and our native Cranbrook. Every time I see it I feel a pang of lost life.

The church bell in Chagford rings out nine times.

'Nine of the clock,' remarks Tom, scratching himself. 'Two hours yet to get to Jurston.'

'What is "the clock"?' I ask.

He looks at me. 'How can you not know what a clock is? It is a machine for telling the time. With weights and cogs and things like that. Surely you've heard one?'

'My brother is very ignorant,' says William. 'Please excuse him.'

'Thank you, brother.'

'They're proud of their clock in Chagford,' Tom continues. 'All the folk there live by its chimes. But those from the town are constantly saying "sorry, sorry" for all their lateness – and why? Because their clock tells them so. If they didn't have a clock, they would never be late. No one would know.'

I am still mystified. How do you get a machine to tell the hour? Time is reckoned by the motion of the Sun around the Earth, which is down to the will of God, so how do you make a machine that tells the will of God?

'You should hear the complaints when the clock stops,' Tom continues. 'Oh, the cog has broken, or the escapement is at fault, they'll say, pretending to understand these things. But I say to them, if you are so knowledgeable about clocks, why do you not mend it? That silences them good and proper.'

We say farewell to Tom Brimblecombe at the edge of the town and walk up to the church. This building too, like its counterpart in Moreton, has been rebuilt. Immediately my heart is chilled by the thought that maybe the cathedral in Exeter has also been knocked down and reconstructed in a new fashion. Perhaps new walls and sculptures now stand there, where once mine stood.

There are times in life when the cycle of the ages and the destruction of one generation's work by the next is an uplifting thing, for it promises the young so much. And there are times, later in life, when you realise that it means that your work too will be swept away. Honestly, the only way to secure everlasting fame is to produce such a fine work that no age will ever rival it. I doubt that anyone will look at my hand and rate it so highly.

The mist has now lifted over the moor and there is an uninterrupted view of the hills around us and the high ground beyond. As for the town, all the houses are now two-storey structures, no longer hall houses. The place looks every bit as prosperous as Moreton. And there are many people busying themselves in the streets. Servants are holding horses, waiting while their masters conduct their business. Most cottages have their front doors open as well as their shutters, to allow in as much light as possible, and I see women working thread on wooden machines with large, swift-moving wheels. There are many of these machines, which seem to perform much the same task as the spindle and distaff in our day. It seems the whole country around here is driven by cogs, kept to time by a clock, and kept prosperous by these wooden wheels.

Although it is not market day, there are many people standing around in the square. Men are chatting to one another, sporting their soft caps and their fine clothes. Several teams of packhorses wait patiently with bundles and boxes on their backs. Farmers are setting about their daily tasks in earnest: one leads a herd of cows up the hill; another is driving a small flock of sheep from one field to another. The clock rings out ten times as we pass among them. To the west of the church they are building a new house amid wooden scaffolding poles and planks. I reflect that, in our time, there used to be a small building in the middle of the square here, where the important tinners would meet to discuss business and have their ingots of tin assayed and marked by the stannary officials. Now in its place there is a great open house of timber, with a gathering area below for the assaying and the bargaining with merchants, and a high room above, which is presumably for the meetings of the stannary court.

William and I make our way into the covered area. We find ourselves amid the hubbub of a dozen conversations. I look from face to face, searching for someone who might be approachable and who might be able to suggest where we could buy clothes. Here a man is leaning on the low wall while someone talks to him about an idea for a waterwheel. Nearby a man in a long jerkin is listening to someone else speak at length, tapping the toe of his leather boot against the flagstones. But suddenly my view is interrupted by a large figure who stands before us. He has a blue padded tunic tucked into a thick leather belt fastened with a silver buckle. His jaw is clean-shaven and his cap is as black as dyed cloth can get.

'You have business here?' he asks.

'We hope to find someone who'll sell us clothes, new or old,' I say.

'This hall is only for those on the tinners' business. Or looking for work in one of the beams or blowing houses. You must step outside if you have no business here.'

'We're looking for work,' says William suddenly.

The man who has confronted us looks from William to me and back, weighing us up. 'You've worked on a beam before?'

I cannot think of what he can mean except a beam of wood, such as the scaffolding we erect around the cathedrals when we work on them. So I reply, 'Many times.'

'What's in the sack?'

'Chisels and mallets, and some old clothes.'

'Upstairs with you then,' says the man, gesturing towards the corner of the building. 'Alderman Periam's looking for new workers.'

We do as he says. On the upper floor there are about twenty men of various ages. A clerk asks our names and we tell him, 'William Beard and John de Wrayment.' He scrawls with his pen in an uncertain fashion, leaning on the table and frequently dipping his quill in the ink. He speaks our names very slowly as he writes, 'W-il-li-am-Bea-ard. Jo-hn-Dr-ay-man'.

A well-dressed man of about thirty is speaking on the far side of the chamber. '. . . and with that in mind, I pray that you listen to the master of the operation, my father, Alderman William Periam.'

I see an old man seated in a wooden chair. He has one

of these soft black caps like so many other people, but his is blacker than anyone else's. He has white hair and an equally white beard. He does not stand to speak, but his voice is loud, rough and clear.

'This is the fortieth year that I've been managing beams on the moor. In all that time my hearing has got worse and my voice louder. But the business has grown. That is why you are here; you all want to be wealthy. Now, in these days, most of the richest lodes are already claimed. So how might you do it? I have the answer. We'll work and enrich ourselves together. I want to share with you a portion of the wealth that I enjoy.'

As William Periam speaks he looks around the room. 'I was not born a rich man. My father was a solid, God-fearing husbandman from the east of the county: a farmer who sweated over the few acres he held from the lord of the manor. But he wanted something better for me. So he sent me to learn the trade of a capper, in Exeter. Now, a capper is a worthy manufacturer, don't mistake my meaning; many cappers are good, upstanding men. But none of them is what you would call wealthy. I knew I'd never be truly admirable in my father's eyes unless I could exceed – *exceed* – his expectations. It would never have been enough merely to meet them.'

The old man lifts his hand from the arm of the chair and holds up a finger.

'I noticed that men wanted badges in their caps but there was insufficient tin, and silver was too expensive. All the tin was being taken for export, or for the casting of bronze guns. And when I asked, "Why do we not dig more tin out of the ground?" I was told that it was because it takes a lot of time. You need to remember that in those days some tinners still made their coin by following the streams after heavy rainfall and looking for tiny nuggets. Well, I thought, if there is tin enough in the streams when it rains, there must be much more underground – it does not fall from the sky. So why wait for the rain? I claimed my first patch of land, in the Ashburton quarter, and set to work with hired men from Widecombe. I soon learned that the hills of Dartmoor are threaded through with tin ore, and only scraps are washed to the surface in wet weather. Within ten years I was one of the richest men in Exeter. Within twenty, I was *the* richest. Within thirty, I was not only an alderman of the city but I had been elected mayor too, and had land in many parishes. I had silk-covered cushions on the benches in my hall, gilt candlesticks and red velvet altar dressings in my chapel, and tapestries in my parlour. Now, after forty years of tinning, I've nothing else to spend my money on but the future. On good men like my son John here. And men like you.

'What sort of men am I looking for? Strong men, you'll be thinking. You would not be wrong. But I want more besides. I want *good* men – those of a generous and hospitable disposition. I want men who are to their fellows what Job was to those among whom he lived: a pair of eyes to the blind, legs and feet to the lame, and a steady rock to those who find themselves swept away by despair. Many of you, I know, still cling to the old religion. I understand that a man's truth is a man's truth, and there's no dislodging it. So I want men who are both strong and forgiving. Tolerant men. For this I know well: there is no creature on God's earth more damnable in his fellow's eyes than man himself. *Homo homini daemon* – man is a devil to man – as they say. I would rather have a weak man working my beams than an aggressive and selfish one, or one who seeks to put his faith before his fellow workers.'

When William Periam finishes his speech, his son steps forward. 'The moor can be a tough place, especially in winter. You've all heard the tale of Childe the Hunter, I am sure. For those who haven't, suffice to say that Childe was a rich landowner long ago who regularly hunted on the moor. One day the mist and snow came down and a gale began to howl and he was separated from his men. Then the snow started to fall even harder. When his horse crumpled beneath him, he took his knife and killed the beast. He slit the belly open, pulled out its entrails, and crept into the warm cavity. But not even that was enough to save him. When the snows cleared the monks of Tavistock found his frozen body, still wrapped in the corpse of his horse. So take that as a lesson.'

'That is true,' adds his old father. 'The weather up on the moor can be cruel hard, and can change viciously, and without warning.'

'There's another thing to be mindful of,' says John Periam, 'and that's the mires. They're not like bogs – you don't just sink into them – they suck you down, as if the earth were hungry for your flesh and bones. Every movement makes the mire suck you down more. If you fall into one, the only way out is to lie flat and roll to the side. But if that happens, you had better be quick: I've seen a horse go down in less time than I could tie a noose in a rope to try and save her. So, when you are on the moor, trust the ponies. The horses might fall straight into a mire but the ponies are born and bred on the moor and they'll not put a foot near danger. And if you have no pony with you, take care not to step off the path.'

A stern-looking, narrow-faced foreman separates the men in the room into two groups. He allocates William and me to a group of nine men heading north to a tinworks at Watern Tor. After a few further words of blessing from our employers, and the news that we will earn fourpence a day for our labours, plus meals, we are ushered back downstairs.

The men stamp their feet trying to keep warm. We all look at one other. They are mostly bearded. Their breath billows around their faces. One man extracts a small wooden comb from a pocket and starts dragging it through his hair, tugging at the knots, and wiping off the lice on his sleeve.

As the church bell starts chiming again – eleven times – I catch the eye of one of our group. He is tall, with thick dark hair and beard, and is wearing a thigh-length leather jerkin, leather cap, loose long breeches and rough leather boots. His lip almost curls as he looks at me. 'Why are you wearing women's kirtles?' he asks William and me. 'Are you going to give us some entertainment?'

This meets with a few laughs.

William pulls himself up to his full height and looks the man up and down. Even he is not as tall as this tinner. He touches the man's leather jerkin. 'I see that you feel the cold terribly. Already you've killed your mount and crept inside. I'll call you Childe.'

The tall man smiles. 'Friend, where are you from? Your voice sounds strange.'

'Salisbury,' William replies.

I turn to the team of pack animals that will be travelling with us: two horses and ten ponies waiting patiently on the north of the square, each with a halter roped to the beast in front. They all carry wooden frames with high sides on their backs, in place of the saddle. A few of the ponies bear panniers stacked high with wicker cases of bread, meat, eggs and cheese; they are covered with canvas sheets bound with ropes. There are wooden cages containing hens tied on top of these high-packed loads. The horses and the rest of the ponies bear pickaxes, saws, heavy hammers and metal chisels; there are more folded sheets of canvas, wooden poles and planks, barrels of nails, sacks of leather ties and a couple of pairs of stout boots. One horse is laden with two huge sets of leather bellows, a good four feet in length, not including the handles. As far as I can see, there is nothing in the way of spare clothes.

The foreman who selected us suddenly appears, wearing a leather jerkin and cap like the man who referred to our garments as 'women's kirtles'. He walks briskly around to the front of the packhorse team. 'We'll be setting out now, down to the blowing house at Outer Down, and then up to Teigncombe, over the bridge at Teignever and up to Watern Tor to the workings there. Follow the horses, and if the mist comes down and you get lost, follow the River Teign downstream: it'll bring you back here to Chagford.'

'What were you thinking in putting us forward to work

tin?' I ask William as we set off, walking at the back of the men.

'I was thinking of you. How can you hope to do good works and save your soul if you are in a town? We know nothing, and can do nothing. We are like children – having to be shown how to dress and speak, and what spices are hot to taste and so forth. At least if we head out on to the moor, it'll be like a levelling of things. Surely if you are ever going to be able to help a soul, it will be out there.'

I walk on. Behind me, William tries to strike up a conversation with a taciturn man called George Beddoes, whose clothes look almost as rough as our own. He gives one-word answers to William. I understand that he is from Exeter and has not previously been on the moor, but has a wife and until recently had three daughters. One died. Her death has clearly caused him great pain.

The crags rising above us look challenging. On the crest of a hill, we feel the cold wind blow harder – so much it begins to draw tears from the corners of my eyes. The colours of nature ahead of us are drawn roughly. Beneath blocks of grey sky and scudding clouds there is the grey-green strip of the high moor, half obscured by the still-drifting mist, where the grass is intermingled with blocks of granite. Nearer, there is a thick strip of red-brown, which I know is the huge swathes of dead bracken up on the moor. Nearer still is the green and brown of the trees and field grass, and the moss-covered granite posts and walls of the fields.

The tall man wearing leather who referred to us wearing 'women's kirtles' drops back and starts talking to me.

His name is Richard Townsend. I learn that he too is from Exeter.

'Your first trip out on to the moor?' I ask.

'No, I've been following Alderman Periam's expeditions up here for many years,' he tells me. 'But soon I'll be doing it on my own account.'

'You have a plan?'

'I'll make a claim at the stannary court and start to work my own beam. Our lad needs schooling, in Exeter, so he can read and write.'

'You want him to enter the Church then?

'There's no money to be made in the Church. Unless you're one of those rich folk who can buy the old monastery lands. But every man of substance has need of writing men nowadays.'

'You're the second man today that has spoken to me of the monasteries.'

'They've all gone now. One morning the monks were singing their prayers for the souls of the dear departed and the next the king's officers were banging on the door, telling them all to leave within an hour, never to return, and demanding that they hand over all their gilt, silver, precious reliquaries, ornaments and croziers. Tavistock, Buckland, Torre – all have been sold to enrich the royal purse. Many of us think it the greatest act of theft ever committed in the whole history of the world.'

'And the priory in Exeter?'

'A mercer nowadays uses it for his house.'

'No! What about the cathedral?'

'That still stands as a place of holiness. But I fear it too will go the way of the priories if the zealots get their way. They want to ban everything – religious vestments, rosaries, wedding rings, sculptures, paintings . . .'

'Why sculptures?'

'Why anything? Those that would reform the Church have this notion of wanting to return to the religion of the Bible, and the Bible says nothing about tithes and bishops and wedding rings. So they say that those things must go. As for sculptures, they say that the Good Book says you should not make graven images.'

'But sculpture is pure worship – it needs no words.'

'Be proper careful to whom you say that,' he warns.

I can hear a booming noise coming up the valley. It sounds as if the stone hammers of the furies in the underworld are beating out a steady rhythm on a huge drum. The birds are still singing in the trees, so they are used to the sound. But to my ears it sounds unearthly.

'What's that thundering?' I ask, looking around at the other men.

'The blowing house,' Richard explains. 'It's where we break up the ore. Two hammers, driven by a waterwheel, smash it all into crumble. That's so the ore can be put in the furnace and smelted.'

Within a few steps the sound of the hammers drowns out the birdsong from the nearby trees. A group of men is tending to the turf-covered charcoal fires which are burning beside the path. Ahead is a thatched building set into the side of a hill. To one side, there is a large waterwheel, fed by a leat running from the river. William and I and several other new men move forward to see this marvel of thunderous noise which stops us from speaking to one another.

The wooden door is open and we step inside. The whole building seems to be shaking with the repeated sound of crashing metal. It is smoky, dimly lit by two small empty windows, and very hot and humid. As my eyes become accustomed to the darkness I see a furnace set against the wall directly opposite me. Two men with long-handled ladles stand near, lifting the white-yellow molten metal from where it is seeping out from a stone spout into a trough to let it set. I know that metal runs like a thick pottage when it gets very hot – I have seen lead melted to seal the joins of the sheets on church roofs – but I have never seen tin dished up in a ladle. When one man sets his ladle aside and starts pumping the bellows to fire the furnace again, I see the sweat on the other man's forearms gleam in the glowing heat.

To the right of the furnace is an open doorway and it is from here the great crashing sound is coming. In there two men are shovelling ore on to granite mortar stones to be pounded by two massive hammers. As the water-wheel rotates it drives a shaft that lifts and then drops each hammer in turn, crushing the ore to gravel and dust. I have seen fulling mills before, which employ similar water-driven heavy hammers to thump the woollen cloth, but this is something altogether more overwhelming. I wonder at the resilience of the men working with that infernal noise all the time, and the dust rising from the smashed ore choking them.

Outside the air is cold and strangely dull. I can no longer hear the birdsong but only the crash of the hammers.

'I'll be going to take a piss upstream,' says William, as we stand there, numb from the noise. 'Those hammers will soon start beating double time.'

As William goes off to relieve himself I walk back to the packhorses. I look up to the sky above the moor, roiling with dark-grey clouds. It is growing cold – cold enough to snow.

We start back on the road up to the high moor. The road narrows, and we see we are approaching a sharp descent. The foreman stops the packhorses and unties them from one another, and almost loses his cap in the wind. We then lead the horses and ponies down the steep slope individually, lest one should fall or slip on the loose stones and send the whole team hurtling into the valley below. When all are safely down, they are roped together and resume plodding along the rocky path back up the next hillside of wind-tugged heather, gorse, grass and dead bracken.

I try to speak to George Beddoes but he is as taciturn with me as he was with William, and so I give up and speak to a man called Stephen Waller, who comes from the east of the county. I ask him why he wants to be working for the Periams.

'I've no choice,' he replies, 'not since the lord of the manor took my land.'

'What did he do that for?'

'In my grandfather's day we held eighteen acres in the great fields – all well-drained strips. In addition, we had ten acres of pasture and ten of meadow, and my grandfather had the rights to graze three cows and twenty sheep upon the common. Then the price of wool rose, and the lord took the common rights away, paying a pittance to all of us commoners in compensation.'

'Why did you agree to sell them?' I ask.

'If we'd not given up the common rights, would the lord's steward have granted us new leases on our acres in the great fields?' he says over the gusts of the wind. 'No. So I had to let them go. But still I had my eighteen acres, and we got by, did my wife and I. Until the lord's steward said he was buying the whole of both fields in which my land lay. "No," I told him, "we countryfolk have a need to look after our acres. We've already manured them for the forthcoming year. Besides, it is unlawful to run a tenant off the land." Two days later, as I came home from market, I saw all my tools, table, benches, kitchen stuff and bedding in the lane, and straw from the thatch of our house strewn in piles, and the lord's men pulling our house down with ropes and horses. They said that, if we are no longer resident, the lord can take our land away at will. The steward gave me six shillings and eightpence compensation for the house and told us to clear off. My wife and children were in tears, and I was precious close to crying myself, but that was what we had to do. So we made our way to Exeter, and I came out here with the Periams.'

'It seems to me that ordinary people are paying a heavy price for all the wealth in the country.'

A gust of wind blows us back, battering our ears with its force. Stephen Waller pauses until it subsides and he can be heard. 'Speak to any of these men and they'll tell you the same thing. We're all banished from life in some way or other.'

We walk in silence across the stony path beneath the vast dominion of the weather, in which all we see is the light brown of the clumps of marsh grasses, the dark brown of the peaty mud and the hard grey of the rock. I notice we are still following the line of the River Teign, although it is little more than a stream at this point. The wind here is deafening while only a mile or so downstream, at the blowhouse, it was hardly noticeable. Yet down there, this little stream is so mighty it powers those huge hammers. The elements seem to be vying for power, each showing how it can reign supreme in the right place.

I speak to no one for the last mile up to Watern Tor. The men's faces are sullen. And well they might be, for when we finally make it up to the works, I realise the full meaning of Alderman Periam's words. These men are truly digging for tin – straight through the rock of the hill. There is a great grey-brown gash running through the green ridge ahead of us, where half a dozen men are wielding pickaxes and three others are breaking up large pieces of rock with heavy lump hammers, making them small enough to be put in a wheel-barrow and transported over the crest of the hill.

Once I was a mason, delicately shaping stone into beautiful forms for the glory of God. Now I find myself on a windswept ridge, expected to smash stone for feeding into a stone-breaking machine, for the profit of Alderman Periam. I have more than half a wish to return to the stones we saw at Scorhill and ask to go back to my own time and die there, where people knew and respected me. But then I think of Lazarus, and Richard the blacksmith and his daughter. It seems to me that I might have been brought here for a reason.

The horses and ponies are led up to the top of the ridge, where the wind is so strong we can barely stand. There is another blowing house down in the valley on the far side, and the thunderous crashes from its hammers can be heard ringing out from up here, despite the wind. I look over the barren moor. Apart from the blowing house below us, and another stone building near it, there are no other houses to be seen. It is desolate waste land, good for nothing but rough grazing. William was right: it is a leveller. But it does not raise people to a level, it brings them all down.

We lead the pack animals down the slope to the blowing house where we unpack their bundles and let them graze for a while on the rough grass of the moor. The second building is a house in which the men live when they are not working, and it is here we stack the provisions. Our next task is to load the tin ingots that have been cast at the blowing house: these slabs each weigh just over a hundredweight and we carry them singlehandedly. It is heavy work. When it is done, the crew who were smashing stone on our arrival depart; they have the job of guiding the ponies back to Chagford, where the ingots will be weighed and assayed. From now until dark we have the task of digging ore and smashing it, and wheeling it in wooden barrows down to the thunderous hammers and smelting furnace.

We speak to one another only occasionally, because of the

heavy work and the wind in our ears. When I do snatch some conversation at the blowing house or when working alongside another man in the lee of the wind, I realise how desperate some of them are. Edward Bowden is a religious outcast from his parish because he refused to swear an oath of loyalty to the king as Head of the Church. But this is not because he maintains the supremacy of the Pope: he is one of those zealots they call a Protestant. He believes that anything that is not in the Bible is not the true faith but merely an aberration – man's false interpretation of faith. Men and women of his belief suffer terribly. One, called Anne Askew, was tortured in the Tower of London just six months earlier by having her arms and legs pulled from their sockets on a machine called a rack. After that, she was burned at the stake. The crime which merited this terrible punishment was reading from the Bible and not accepting that any man had the right to tell her its true meaning. Clearly, the importance of women's understanding of words goes far beyond William's prediction that no cleaning would get done if women could read.

As the daylight fades, we light torches soaked in pitch and try to smash stones by their guttering light, but the wind is too strong and they burn too quickly, so the foreman calls off the work for the day. The crashing hammers are lifted and jammed in place with wedges; the leat to the waterwheel is diverted to let the water splash down the stream freely; the furnace is raked out ready for the morning's fire and ore. Those of us who remain go to the house – which is little more than a long stone hut – and eat a supper of bread, cold beef and cheese by the light of rushlights on brackets in the walls. We drink a strange sort of drink that the men call 'beer' – like the ale of our own time but cleaner and stronger. As the wind whistles around the house and under the eaves, men start telling tales of fortunes made and lost from tin. They remain cautious of one another, however. There is a mutual distrust in the air. When anyone mentions a great find, he is careful not to disclose its location.

Listening to their voices and the wind whistling through the eaves and rattling the door, I think to myself how much worse things would be if this were not a house but a ship out at sea. And that reminds me of the mariner whose shipmates died for despair that they would ever see dry land again. In a way, these men are out at sea, washed far from the society to which they once belonged. Do they believe they will ever return? I look at the faces. The man thrown off his land, and the man who is fleeing for his religion – they are still clinging on, they still have faith. The man who has lost his land hopes to build a new home for his children. The Protestant believer trusts that God is only temporarily putting him to the test. Others believe that tinning will make them rich, and that all they have to do is earn enough to start their own team and they will be like Alderman Periam and his son. I see in their various hopes something that starkly contrasts with the society I knew in my youth. We were far more united and accepting of God's will. In this new century, people are all divided and unsatisfied, hoping that God will smile on them personally.

I sit on the earthen floor near to the door, and have to move every time a man gets up to answer a call of nature. When the door opens a blast of cold air hits me until it is latched again; once or twice the latch does not fasten and the door swings open, and I have to get up to secure it.

'This was a mistake,' whispers William, sitting beside me, as the large figure of Richard Townsend steps over to the door and leaves the house. 'I should've known better.'

'There's penance in undertaking the work,' I reply.

'But we both know there are better forms of redemption.'

'Perhaps,' I say, as George Beddoes makes his way past us and opens the door, letting in another icy blast of air.

'There are more comfortable places to sleep too. I wonder how the current king's palace appears at Westminster?'

'Much the same as any fine palace,' I reply. 'With tapestries and chests filled with gold and silver, and huge kitchens with cooks and clerks and serving boys, and a chapel with coloured glass and walls, and a chamber with a great curtained bed and feather mattress.'

'Then life is changing only for the poor, not for the king and his court.'

'Maybe the king has a clock that chimes the hour,' I suggest, at a loss to think how the rich have seen their lives change. 'A king's ambitions must change all the time: to attack this kingdom, support this crusade, arrest this renegade lord and so on. But in how he lives his life, there is no variation. He wears a crown, he sits on a throne, he eats roast meat and drinks wine. Time stands still in the palaces of kings. But for these tinners, everything has changed.'

We fall silent, listening to the wind whistling about the house. A rushlight splutters and goes out, so the foreman lights another from a still-burning one on the other side of the room.

There are indistinct murmurs of private conversations among
the men there. And then someone says aloud, for all to hear,
'Who of us has travelled the furthest? He who has travelled
furthest, he must tell his tale.'

Everyone turns to us. 'The men in kirtles – they've been to
Cathay,' says a tall man who has not spoken to me.

I look at William questioningly. He nods to me, con-
firming that that is what he told him.

'Speak, speak, speak,' one man starts chanting, and soon a
number of them have joined in.

William holds up his hand. 'Very well. But I tell you,
you'll not believe half of what we've seen.'

'With whom did you sail?' said one man.

William shakes his head. 'Friends, we didn't *sail* to Cathay.
Sailing is for the soft-limbed sorts. No. We set off from Dover
and crossed to Calais in the nineteenth year of the reign of
our monarch, and I sold a goodly pile of wool-fells at the
market there. It was our full intention to return to English
shores forthwith but, as luck would have it, we fell in with a
Lombard merchant called Niccolinus who told us that, if we
were to venture eastward with him, and invest our money in
Chinese spices and silks, we would be rich beyond our wildest
dreams. So that changed our minds.

'All the way to Venice we bartered and sold cloth, and so
by the time we were in Lombardy, we were richer than ever
before. When we arrived in Venice I was feeling like a prince
in a fur-trimmed robe, and John here was making lavish
donations to the holy bones in every church. Niccolinus enter-
tained us in his fine house, which was by the water's edge,

overshadowed by the mountains, and the parkland all round was filled with running deer. And there we met his beautiful wife, Fiesca, who had dark hair and brown eyes and a smile on her lips. She poured wine for us into silver goblets as we dined in his hall, with his servants watching. And there Niccolinus had a great chessboard of ivory, ebony and gold. He challenged me to a game and I, not wanting to disappoint him, agreed. He suggested a wager, and I, again, not wishing to disappoint him, said, "Name your stake." He replied, "All the wealth you've brought with you from France." I was dumbstruck. I couldn't withdraw my offer and so I agreed. But I said to him, "You must bet a similar treasure, of like value, and since you named *my* stake, I should name yours." "Say it, and I will match your stake happily," quoth he. So I replied, "A night in bed with your wife." I said this in her hearing. And I added, "For she is truly the most beautiful woman I've seen. Outside Devon, that is.'"

Several laughs greet his quip. William has the attention of the whole house now. So I stay silent.

'Niccolinus proudly said he had nothing to fear for he had the wit both to win my money and to save his wife's virtue. But he did not know women. Ah! He didn't even know his own wife! I saw how she received the message that he cared so little about her honour that he was happy to chance it. And she saw me prize her so highly that I deemed a night with her equal in value to all my wealth. At the game of chess, he was a master – it was not long before he had taken four of my pieces – but at the game of life, I already had his queen in check. When she poured our wine again, she poured him some dark, strong liquor that he loved, and he complimented her on producing it. Into my glass, however, she poured drink from a similar-looking pitcher – and it was nothing but water. She was a cunning one, that Fiesca. I took a long time over every move. Often I would drain my goblet and say, "Niccolinus, this is the most excellent wine, I do thank you for being so liberal with it." Sure enough, Niccolinus was soon drinking as freely as me, and in no time he was as drunk as a monastery butler. He made a mistake that made him angry, and he shouted at me for being so slow, but by then the damage was done. I took even more time over my moves. His eyelids were starting to droop, and he fell asleep with his head and arms on the table, in a sprawled manner, scattering the pieces. When that happened, Fiesca took up his wine goblet and drained it herself. Then she refilled it and said to the servants watching, "You all are wit- nesses. I am honour-bound to be this man's prize for tonight. And the reason is that my husband has a scandalous lack of care for my matronly honour, in his sloppy drunkenness." So she and I went to bed. And, by God's boots, she was a bonny wench under the sheets, I'll tell you. We didn't sleep at all that night, and she gave me such pleasure that I said to her that I'd happily have given all the money I'd made in France for such a night of passion. But she laughed and said that that was not the wager, and that I had rewarded her by shaming her too-proud husband in front of his servants. In the morning she urged me to be up and gone early, before he awoke, and as I departed she pressed into my hands a purse with ducats in it, to speed me on my way. And if you do not believe me . . .' William gives me a nudge and holds his hand out for me to pass my travelling sack. He opens it and takes out the purse. 'Here are the last of those ducats,' he declares, holding out a few gold coins for all the tinners to see.

Several men lean forward to view the coins, as if they were proof of his story. Others simply laugh.

'Where are Richard Townsend and the quiet man?' asks Edward Bowden. 'They've been gone a long time.'

We are silent. There is just the wind in the thatch and the rattle of the door.

The foreman points to three of us, myself and two men I don't know. 'John, Robert, Richard, you all come with me. We'll check the blowing house.'

We light the torch-heads of pitch-soaked cloth, and threads of black smoke wend their way across the room before we unlatch the door. When it opens, a gust of wind rips at our torches. I hang back as the others head down to the blowing house, guessing that Beddoes and Townsend will not have gone far. I look further along the side of the building: the ground is uneven here, with piles of dropped and discarded rocks and tufts of grass between slippery turns of mud and damp soil. Such is the harshness of the gale that my light flickers too much to be able to see any part of the ground for more than a moment. But then I see a hand. I bend down and put my torch close to the man's face. It is Richard Townsend. His brown hair is being tugged like grass in the wind. There is no pulse, his wrist is barely warm. The ground around him is bloodstained. His mouth is open. So are his eyes, staring upwards, as if his last thought was astonishment.

I stand up, and look further with my torch, sweeping over

the ground nearby. There is no sign of anyone else. Beddoes must have run.

I call to those at the blowing house but they cannot hear me. So I pick my way back across the slippery ground to the path that leads down there, and call again. Then I see the light of a torch as they leave the building.

'Richard Townsend's dead. Up by the house,' I shout to them as their lights approach mine.

'Richard dead?' shouts the foreman.

'The quiet one hardly seemed big enough,' says another man.

'He was stabbed from behind,' I explain. 'In this wind he'd not have heard anyone.'

We climb back up to where the corpse lies. The foreman shuts Richard's eyes and straightens his legs, and crosses his arms. Several of us make the sign of the cross over him before we return to the house.

Back inside, the foreman stands in the centre of the room and looks about. 'Richard's been murdered. Is there anything anyone wants to say?'

'God rest his soul,' one man says.

Several chorus this with 'Amen'.

'He was a good man,' says another.

'I had my suspicions of Beddoes,' says Edward Bowden. 'He didn't seem right for this job. I reckon that he only came out here to kill Richard.'

'But why?'

'That we will never know,' says another man.

'Should we not chase after him?' I ask.

'Chances are you'd leave the path and fall into a mire,' replies the foreman. 'You'd be up to your neck in sucking slime before you knew it. No one would hear you cry for help, and no one would see you. If there is any justice in the world, then that is exactly what will have happened to Beddoes by now.'

'Will we bury the body?' asks Bowden.

The foreman looks at him. 'We're in the forest of Dartmoor here, all of which lies in the parish of Lydford. Even if you know the way, the church is a whole day's journey from here. So to take him to church burial, I'll need to spare an experienced man and a stout pony. Then a day coming back. And payment for the digging of the grave, which'll be another sixpence. A few of you knew Richard; I'll not tell you what you should and should not do. But does anyone who knows the way to Lydford want to spend two days unpaid taking him to burial?'

No one speaks.

'Then that is settled.'

'Do we just leave him there?' I ask.

'We'll throw his body in the mire up the valley with a block of granite roped to his leg. First thing tomorrow. Before anyone else comes out here.'

'What then of his clothes?' asks William.

'By custom, the clothes of a dead man go to the one that found the body. John can have them.'

'They'll be too big for him,' says someone.

'But not for my brother,' I reply.

'Give them to whoever you want,' says the foreman. 'Any

money in his purse is to be shared out evenly, between us all.'

William and I get up and relight one of the torches. No one says anything as we leave, fastening the door carefully. When we come to the corpse, William holds the guttering torch while I pull off his clothes, cap, belt, knife, purse and boots. I put rocks on the pile as it grows, to hold it down in the wind.

Before we return inside, I kneel and say a prayer for the dead man's soul. It will probably be the only prayer said for him. His family will never know he was stabbed in the back, or that his body was dumped in a mire on the moor.

'If you are poor,' I say to William, 'you cannot help others. You are too busy trying to help yourself.'

'What did you say?' he shouts back.

I look at his face in the flickering torchlight, and shake my head. Picking up the clothes, I head inside, with him following me.

No one speaks much after that. Eventually, we all lie down to sleep – William wearing the dead man's leather cloak, and spreading his own clothes over the top. He gives me his old mantle to help keep me warm. And then there is silence – but for the howling of the wind around the house.

As I lie there, I try to acknowledge the meaning of this death in some way. It will not be written down in any books. In ten years' time, few people will remember there ever was a man called Richard Townsend or what he looked like. In ninety-nine years, no one will remember him at all. Even the murder of a man can be a small thing. The word *murder* has such grandness in our minds but truly, all deaths are matters of slight importance, except perhaps the king's. In four days' time, when it is my turn to die, no one will care for a man who was called John of Wrayment, or John de Wrayment, or John Drayman. My wife and children won't know a thing about it; they have already long since gone.

In truth, I no longer fear death. I only fear not joining them.

Chapter Five

I cannot breathe. Trapped in freezing darkness, I do not know which way is up. I start to feel I am about to die. Not yet, I tell myself, I have four days left. But the need to breathe is overwhelming. I push forward, struggling as if I were trapped underwater. I move my arms and legs frantically. All of a sudden, I find air on my face. I gulp it in, unable to see anything.

I am embedded in ice and snow. It is night – but I can see no stars.

'William!' I shout into the darkness.

My voice falls strangely dead.

'William!' I shout again.

I struggle to my feet. There is no wind, no noise.

I stand there, shivering. There is nothing to hear but my own voice.

Two hundred and ninety-seven years have passed since my

own time, so the year must be sixteen hundred and forty-five, by the canon precentor's reckoning. I remind myself that today is the seventeenth of December, and I work out that it must be a Wednesday. But these things are all I know. I cannot even hear the running water of the stream that once drove the blowing-house waterwheel. The only sense left to me is feeling – and my feet are numb with cold, my hands chilled to the bone.

'William!' I shout. 'William!'

I remember my travelling sack, which I was using as a pillow when I went to sleep. Reaching down into the dark-ness, I feel for it. I shovel piles of snow to one side with my palm, and eventually find the ties, and lift it, and hold it, feeling the shapes of the metal chisels and the crucifix, and the bundle of soaked clothes.

What if there were to be no dawn? What if, in these days of the sixteen hundreds, the sun no longer rises? What if the whole world is caked in this silent covering? Despite all the things I have heard about the fires of Hell, I cannot imagine that anything could be worse than to be stranded in a light-less world of deep snow, unable to see or hear anything. An eternal winter. Worst of all, I am alone. Truly, the sinner who burns in the company of others is blessed by comparison with the soul who freezes alone.

There is a rustling nearby, and I rejoice in the noise – even if it is only a fox making his way across the snow.

'God's bloody wounds!' I hear William exclaim.

'Thank the Lord!'

'Have I gone blind or is it dark?'

'If you are blind then so am I.'

'Are you as cold as me?'

'God's grave, William, of course I am. I'm soaked to the skin. There's ice all around us.'

'I wish we'd never come out here.'

'It was your idea. You said we should work for the tinners.'

'My idea? It was you who said that we should go into the wilderness. "The wilderness is God's Creation unchanged," you said. Well, put your balls and breeches to that. The wilderness is where we are right now – and I am not hearing choirs of angels.'

'William, you are altering things. It was you who said that we know nothing, and can do nothing, and are like children. "Coming out to the moor will be like a levelling of things," you said.'

'Damn you, John. Would we be here if you had not picked up the infected baby?'

I have no answer to that.

Even God would find this a cold, dismal place. Besides, what need is there for Him here? The place for God is in the cities and the towns – in all the places where, as Alderman Periam said, man is a devil to man, *homo homini daemon*. God should be in those places to soften hard men's hearts and to stiffen weak men's resolve.

'Where shall we go?' he asks.

'Towards that patch of darkness over there.'

'What?'

'How in God's name should I know? We cannot move without danger of falling down a gully or into a ravine – or worse, into a mire.'

'You chuckle-headed fool. Can you hear the gushing of a stream? No. Why not, I wonder? Perhaps some evil spirit has whisked it away in the last ninety-nine years. Or perhaps it has simply frozen over. You could go skating across all the mires of the moor right now, John.' He pauses. 'Look, we can set out by following the line of the hill. I slept in the middle of the house last night, so the door must've been on the far side of you from me.'

I hear him step towards me and feel his hand on my arm. Together we find the low ruined wall of the house and clamber through a four-foot-deep drift before turning along what we believe to be the path.

The heavy snow is difficult to walk through and it takes us an age to reach the top of the ridge. By the time we are there the sky is beginning to lighten around us. But still we can see nothing. Everywhere the snow and ice drifts into the greyness, so that the eye has nothing on which to fix. There are no trees, only ridges and slopes of ice.

We breathe heavily as we make our way across eastwards. Before us, the snow stretches away. And a slight strengthening of light behind the clouds illuminates a view that is serene, perfect and inhuman.

'What are you thinking about?' he asks.

'Richard Townsend hoped to make enough money to teach his son to read and write. That son'll be dead by now. Townsend's family would have been left destitute.'

'That's the passing of time for you.'

'It's more than that. I could not save the man – no more than I could save those children at the cottage in the woods the previous day. I could not do a good deed even when it needed to be done.'

'Maybe this is God's gentle way of warning you that you are not cut out for eternal bliss?'

'Why are we here then, if our lot is to shuffle along a path and simply tip over into Hell?'

'I'm cold,' replies William. 'I'm wet and hungry too. And there are no women. A place is desolate if it has no women.'

'And that, you think, is the meaning of our lives? To stay dry and warm – and feed ourselves and fornicate?'

'Yes.'

'Nothing else?'

'John, this world is the right place for me, I know.'

We walk on, regularly looking back to check the line of our footsteps in the snow, to make sure we keep heading eastwards. After two or perhaps three hours, we see a circle of stones, some fallen, some standing – on the side of a hill.

'You know what that is,' says William.

Scorhill. Only one of the stones still stands to its full height. I recall my earlier desire to return here, and ask to die in my own time. Now there is no thought of that in my mind. Instead, we walk on, gladdened to know where we are. We are even happier when the sun breaks through the clouds and shines across the snows before us, dazzling our eyes. We trudge up over the hill and down the far side – and there the first trees come into sight. Their leafless boughs are crested with snow and they are all ringed with beauty and frail light. Somewhere nearby there are birds singing. Here too we see the first snow-capped drystone walls of enclosures.

A few minutes later, we come across a short, squat fellow wearing a leather hat, a canvas smock and heavy leather boots. He carries a pitchfork that is longer than he is tall. The beard on the side of his face is cut away from his chin but covers his jowl on either side, as an extension of his sideburns. He has been strewing hay across a nearby snowbound field where a pair of grey nags are now feeding.

'Are you for Parliament or for the king?' he shouts at us, lowering his pitchfork in what is clearly intended to be a threatening manner.

William turns to me. 'The king or Parliament. Whose side are we on, John?'

'We've no wish to be disloyal to either, being but travellers,' I shout back.

The fellow in the hat looks at me quizzically. 'What's that? Why do you talk in such a strange fashion? You're Royalist spies, I'll warrant.' He pushes the points of the pitchfork towards us. 'Let's be going; you can account for yourselves to Mister Parlebone.'

'Mister?' William asks me. 'What sort of name is that?'

'I suspect it is a title, like "Master",' I reply.

'Hands up,' shouts the man, thrusting his pitchfork forward.

We walk past a fine house of granite. Icicles seven or eight feet long hang down from the edges of its thatch, gleaming and dripping in the sunlight. I can smell a wood fire, and look up to see smoke rising from its chimney. But this is not the house to which the man is leading us. The 'Mister' must live in an even grander one. And about a quarter of a mile further on down the snowy lane, we see it.

Mister Parlebone's mansion house is also built of granite but much higher and wider, and the stones are carefully shaped ashlar blocks of the sort you would use for building the base of a cathedral pillar, which has to be exactly level. It has wide, well-carved mullion windows of four lights on the upper floor and, to the left of the porch, six spaces of glass, to allow light into what I imagine is the great hall. The porch has an arch over the outer door: this ends in carvings of sun motifs, one of which has been damaged. No icicles hang from the thatch of this house: lead guttering runs around the eaves and feeds through lead drainpipes. In front is a cobbled yard with a stable building. On the near side of this yard is a fence and a gate leading through to a farmyard, around which are barns, byres, henhouses and a sty.

As I look across this farmyard, a number of chickens strut across the snow to where some grain has been scattered for them. Among them are three much larger, round birds: they have humped backs, black feathers, blueish faces and bare heads flecked with what looks like blood. Two more similar birds come across the snow, pecking at the corn.

'What in the Devil's name are those?' says William.

'Turkey fowl,' responds the farmer, wiping his nose on his sleeve.

'Where do they come from?' I ask.

'From over there, behind the barn,' he replies.

Before I can explain that that was not what I meant, a woman appears in the porch of the house. She is in her mid-thirties and wearing a long blue robe which has a sort of white apron pinned before it and a white collar around her shoulders. Her hips and backside are padded – they must be, for I do not believe any woman in any age can have a figure so curved. She has a basket looped over one arm and her hands are folded across her middle. But the most eye-catching thing about her is her hair: it is reddish-brown and falls in waves down either side of her face. In our day, only an umarried woman would show off her tresses out of the house in such a manner. But she is clearly of an age and a beauty to be married.

She watches us approach.

'Whose men are these, Caleb?' she asks, looking from me to William and back.

'They're Royalist spies, Mistress Parlebone,' replies our captor. 'I found them searching round the top field.'

'Studying our fine horses, no doubt.' She looks at me. 'Colonel Fairfax has already taken all our decent mounts.' She looks at William. 'Come, tell me, if you have tongues. What brings you to Gidleigh?'

William replies. 'We have come to admire your beauty, my lady. For those locks surely frame the face of an angel; your skin is as dazzling white as the snow on the moor; and your lips look like the curved bows of cherubs guarding all the sweet delights of Heaven.'

'I doubt there are many spies who can make such a pretty speech. Even if it be a pile of dung for the truth.'

'We're not spies, Mistress Parlebone,' I say. 'We're travellers who have got lost. Very lost. It is not that we don't know where we are – we do – but that that is the only thing we know. I do not know how we got here, nor where we should be going, nor how to get to wherever that might be. What's more, I don't know how we'll be received when we arrive, or when that'll happen. In fact, I don't know why we're going there in the first place. That's how lost we are.'

Mistress Parlebone smiles. A tabby cat slips through the half-open door behind her and skips across the snow, and the man called Caleb raises his pitchfork to bend down and attract the animal, clicking his fingers so that it comes close. He strokes it.

'Caleb, if you believe these men are spies, your priority should be them, not the kitten.' She turns to us. 'What are your names?'

'I'm John Drayman,' I say, using the form in which I heard my name repeated in Chagford. 'And this is my brother, William.'

'Are you hungry? Is that it?' She looks from William to me.

I am indeed ravenous. But to admit it would reduce us to the level of beggars. I shake my head.

'We are starving,' William says. 'I could eat a horse.'

Mistress Parlebone speaks to the farmer. 'Caleb, you need not worry about these men. Go back to your work.' Then she says to us, 'Come and warm yourselves by the fire in the hall. As for food, we are a good Protestant family and will happily share what we have for our dinner.'

I touch the damaged carving of a sun on the right hand side of the porch. Mistress Parlebone sees my interest. 'It was blasted by the king's men on their way back through here, after the fighting in Blackaton Mead.'

'You mean – by a *gonne*?' I ask.

'That's right. A musket, to be precise.'

I inspect the smashed stone. Had we enough time, I could have offered to carve her a replacement. But it would be a good day's work, to re-create one of these sun carvings. Granite is an unyielding stone, which crumbles too easily.

William and I follow her inside. The inner door, which is a solid-looking barrier of many thick oak planks, is defended by a drawbar. This seems odd to me: on the one hand this house has huge windows of glass, which would easily be broken by anyone choosing to attack, and on the other they have a front door that is nigh on impregnable.

Inside we go along a dark passage, and enter a great hall. The floor is flagstones, the walls covered with oak panelling. At the far end there is a huge fireplace, and the good fire burning there makes the air in the room noticeably warmer. I hear it crackle. On one side of it is a curved bench large enough for three people to sit, with a high back to keep the heat in. Immediately before us is a long table covered with a white cloth, with a bench on each side, a chair at both ends, and six places arranged around the table – each one with a napkin, silver spoon and silver platter. Four have glass goblets.

'Wait here,' says Mistress Parlebone. 'I will go and find Carnsleigh, and ask him to attend to your needs.'

William and I look around. The windows have green velvet curtains on either side. In one corner is a painted table with a very deep top: like a coffin on wooden legs. Bowls of blue and white pottery of an extraordinary fineness stand on this, in the same way that silverware was displayed on an aumbry in our day. On the wall directly opposite the window are several paintings in gilt frames. One illustrates a battle, with many men in armour and horses rearing up in panic. Another shows a man resting his hand on a black-draped table. He looks rich. His long hair is folded back from his forehead. His upper tunic has padded shoulders but is tailored very close to his waist, so his chest is compressed into a tapering tube; it then expands in an embroidered short skirt, and his breeches are decorated with the same patterns and colours. White hosen cover his lower legs, and he wears black shoes with tassels on the front. From his belt hangs what looks like the hilt of a very thin sword.

William plucks a note on a musical instrument hanging on the wall. It has a teardrop-shaped body and six courses of strings, and a head that is at ninety degrees to the neck.

'What sort of music do you think they play nowadays?' I say to him as I walk over and place my travelling sack on the curved bench by the fire, and hold out my hands to warm myself.

'Joyful music,' he replies. 'The master of this house has everything he could desire – glazed windows, a fireplace, cushions, paintings, music, food, silverware – and a beautiful wife.'

'She said there's a war in progress.'

'It appears not to bother her unduly.'

We hear footsteps and Mistress Parlebone appears in the doorway with a young dark-haired lad. 'Carnsleigh here will take you to change into some dry attire,' she announces. 'He will bring you back to the hall for lunch.'

'By "lunch" do you mean "dinner"?' enquires William.

'Indeed. Cook informs me that we will be having a venison pie, with vegetables.'

The very thought of venison, a prince among meats – one
that is reserved for only the wealthy – melts on my tongue
and swells my appetite.

'This is Heaven. I could stay here forever,' murmurs
William.

'I thought you did not care for Heaven any more,' I reply,
as Carnsleigh leads us out of the hall.

'I've changed my mind, now I've seen what it'll be like.'

Carnsleigh is tall, about sixteen years old. We follow him
to a staircase which is the grandest I have ever seen in a house.
It is all carved of wood, with banisters and a banister rail,
rising in stages around a large square stairwell, so that light
pours down from a window.

Upstairs, we follow him along a corridor to a panelled
door. The chamber within is whitewashed. There is a plasterwork frieze above the fireplace, which depicts dogs and
hunters pursuing a stag in full flight. A fine bed frame stands
opposite, with wooden posts showing semi-clad women
beneath strange trees in an exotic land; it has an unmade-up
mattress with pillows stacked on it. Against two walls are
chests. But what catches my eye is an object on a table to the
right of the fireplace. I see it reflect the light of the window. I
stop, and walk closer. I lower my face towards it, and see the
light disappear and an image move in the glass. I am looking
at a narrow face, which is looking at my face, which is looking at it.

I turn away, startled. Then I look again at what I realise is a reflection – but not like a normal reflection in a puddle of water. This is as clear as seeing myself in the flesh.

'William, look at this!'

I lift the reflecting object and take another look at my face. It is gaunt. I stare at it, seeing the lines around the eyes, the scars and marks on the cheeks, the griminess of the ears, and the stubble on the chin. I look at the dark hair, which is long and dirty. It is my hair. I turn the glass, and look at myself from an angle – and see that the nose on my face is not at all how I imagined it to be. But most of all I look at the eyes.

'You are not beautiful enough to warrant gazing at yourself for so long,' says William, and takes the object from me. He alters the angle, then looks up at Carnsleigh. 'Does this glass ever lie?'

'No. It is a looking glass,' says the lad, bemused at our interest in it. 'It reflects whatever is held before it.'

'You mean, it always shows the truth?' asks William.

'Yes, but in reverse. If you close your left eye, it will appear in the looking glass that your right is closed.'

William performs this experiment. And stares at himself. 'So that is what other folk see when they regard me.'

I take the looking glass back from him. I turn it so that I can see William's face.

William points at the mirror. It looks like he is pointing at me. He says, 'Just think of all the people who have lived over the years not knowing how they appeared to the world. Even Jesus did not know what He truly looked like.'

Carnsleigh lifts down a chest from where it rests on top

of another. 'The mistress says to try these.' He opens the lid. Inside are piles of clothes.

I stare at them. This is the answer to our prayer. 'We should wash first, before dressing in such fine garments.'

'They are all old,' Carnsleigh replies. 'It will not matter to Mister Parlebone. I do not think he will want them back after you have worn them.'

'I'd prefer it if we were clean.'

William agrees. 'If we are going to Heaven, then the least we can do is not trample mud in through the front door.'

Carnsleigh bows. 'I'll fetch you some fresh water.'

I turn to look through the chest of clothes. Remembering the painting I saw in the hall, I select a pair of reddish-brown breeches and white hosen for my legs, and a tightly fitting tunic of a similar reddish-brown hue for my upper body. This will be the first time I have worn a garment with these fasteners at the front. I look through my bag and choose the least filthy shirt, and, although it is wet, I decide that that will do. It will dry out with my body heat. My boots look out of keeping with this new attire and I search for some newer ones. I find a pair of black shoes but they have great wedges underneath the heel. I can barely walk in them; I certainly could not run. I put my old flat-soled boots back on my feet.

William is still staring at himself in the looking glass. 'Why do you think Mistress Parlebone is being so kind to us?'

'Perhaps she has a weakness for beards.'

'In truth, John.'

'Maybe those who are so rich have nothing to spend their money on but doing good works.'

'Do you believe that?'

I shrug. 'This is the third day we've visited away from our own time – and it's the strangest yet. If I asked you, "Are you loyal to the king?" you'd say, "Of course." And if you were to ask me if I obey the laws agreed by Parliament, I'd say the same, for Parliament sits in the king's name. But now the law-makers and the king are fighting one another. I do not know what to make of it.'

Carnsleigh enters holding a brass basin of water. An older man follows him, holding another, which is steaming, with several white linen towels draped over his arm. This older man bows his greetings to us. Both basins are set on the table where the looking glass previously stood.

'The cold water is for your washing,' says Carnsleigh, 'and the warm for your hair.' He puts down an earthenware flask beside the latter, and two ivory combs. 'Here are lye, combs, and towels. Dinner will be served in half an hour.'

After both servants have gone, William sets the looking glass down. He selects a bright-red tunic, holds it across his chest, and picks up the looking glass again. 'Does the colour suit my complexion?'

'Since when has that ever been a concern to you?'

'I bet that the last man to wear this had not a single louse on his body.'

'Everyone has lice. Always has done, always will. Folk will always need clothes and shoes, sleep, water and food. And lice will always need folk.'

I strip off and wash my body, and rinse my hair in the hot water.

'Use the lye,' says William.

'How?'

'Rub it into your scalp. It kills the fleas and lice and loosens the dirt. And then you can comb the filth out of it.'

'How come you know these things?'

'I knew some women in our own time who were very particular about their hair.'

The lye irritates my scalp. I lean over the basin but some water trickles down my neck. I find the whole washing process very vexing. But worse comes when I look up, for water gets into my eyes, and it stings. I rub them.

William is combing his hair in the looking glass, pulling at the snags. 'Do you think that Mistress Parlebone will have me now?'

'What did you say?'

'Do you think Mistress Parlebone will welcome a kiss or two?'

'She's a married woman.'

'But she has a loving side to her. If you were to distract her husband in some way, it would allow me to charm her. You would not deny a man his last request, would you? Your own brother too, who has been so forgiving.'

'William, you may be my brother but sometimes you are the Devil incarnate. Can you not leave women alone? Especially one who is married, and who is our hostess – and even more especially when you are on the verge of meeting your Maker.'

'That's cruel hard of you, John. You are right and moral, I know. But you could have some pity. You have so many joys to help you along; I have few. My life is a swift-moving river of loneliness. Women are the stepping stones I need to avoid getting swept away.'

'So you need to tread on them? To feel that you are not alone? Can you not be content to . . . to talk with them?'

'That is like picking at the pastry and not tasting the meat. A man like me needs to *feel*. Feeling is the truest of the senses, no? We trust our eyes and our ears, but when we want to test the truth of something, we reach out and touch it.'

'She is married, and that's that. She'll not have you.'

'I've never yet known a woman who would only say no.'

'That's a lie.'

'But it is true that I want to love them all, and many women want to be loved.'

I finish putting on my new clothes and look at myself in the glass. To see myself the first time was strange enough but now I am almost a stranger to myself. William, on the other hand, looks almost comfortable in his red suit. He holds up his ring over his chest, as if to see how the gold-set garnet goes with his new attire.

Carnsleigh returns, looks at us without a word, and bids us follow him. As I descend the stairs, I hear the notes of a musical instrument. I smell cooked meat. Entering the hall, I see a small gathering near the fire: Mistress Parlebone is there with three men and a boy of about six years of age. At the painted table, which I thought looked like a coffin on legs, all the blue and white pottery and bowls have been taken away and the top lifted up and propped at an angle. A girl of about thirteen sits there pressing ivory keys down to make the sweet

notes of a lively tune – she is playing several parts simultan-
eously with astonishing dexterity. There are now eight places
laid at the table.

'So these are our strange travellers,' says a clean-shaven
man with short fair hair, in his mid-forties. I notice his belt
is a wide leather strap, with the fastenings for a sword. 'I have
to say,' he continues, 'those faces of yours do not seem to suit
those clothes. Could you not have chosen others?'

'It is not our fault,' I reply. 'When we were at the market,
looking for faces, our elder brother had first pick, William
here had the second, and I had the third.'

'Thank the Lord you did not have a younger brother,'
says the elder of the two other men, who is grey-haired and
bearded.

'Nay, thank the Lord they did not have a sister,' says the
third man. He has longer, dark hair, which hangs down to his
shoulders, and his face is shaved. He has a bandage around his
right arm, which looks recently tied, and his topmost garment
is hung over that shoulder, the sleeve hanging empty.

'Good, good,' says our host. 'You are welcome, the pair of
you. Forgive my vulgar jest. I am Charles Parlebone, master
of this house, and these two gentlemen are my friends.'

The younger-looking man seems jovial, and nods a greet-
ing. The older one withdraws his right hand from his glove
and extends it to me. He grasps my right hand very tightly,
and shakes it, and then does the same with William. 'It's a
bitterly cold winter, is it not?' he says. 'All the better for being
in Mister Parlebone's warm hall.'

The master invites us to take a seat at the table and Mistress

Parlebone points to two places next to each other. Mister Parlebone sits at the head and his two guests sit opposite us. Mistress Parlebone sits at the foot. The girl who was playing the musical instrument finishes and takes the seat on my right. She bows to us and introduces herself as Sarah. Her little brother, Thomas, sits opposite her.

'Friends, please be silent,' says Mister Parlebone. He utters a short prayer. As he gives thanks for the food, I notice that no one but me crosses themselves when the Lord is mentioned. Not even when Mister Parlebone says the name of Christ. From the corner of my eye I look towards Mistress Parlebone's hands, which are palms-together in prayer. She is not wearing a wedding ring.

I remember her saying 'we are a good Protestant family'. Does this mean they abhor sculpted images? Then I remember what we are about to eat – venison – despite the fact that it is still Advent. I feel nervous and unsteady. When I spoke of us not knowing how people behave now, I never realised it would entail failing to observe the most important fast of the year.

Mister Parlebone says 'Amen' and nods to the door. Carnsleigh and the older servant are there; they enter bearing two large silver bowls. My pulse is racing, my fingers wavering. Everything is so wrong I want to leave. My hunger has suddenly diminished. But these people have been so kind in allowing us new clothes, warmth and food, I cannot refuse. I look in the bowls: the one nearest me contains bulbous white lumps. They look like solid fat. The next has yellow roots in it.

'Have you not seen carrots before?' says Mister Parlebone,

as Carnsleigh pours a modicum of translucent wine into the glass before me.

I point at the bulbous lumps. 'These are carrots?' I ask.

'Those are cauliflowers,' says Sarah. '*Those* are carrots.'

Had you dragged me through all the countries of Africa, I could not have felt further from home. Yet I was born only two parishes away.

I watch as the servants bring in another silver dish topped with pastry. It is steaming and smells of meat.

'Mister Parlebone,' I begin, nervously. 'Am I correct in saying that this is Advent?'

'You are indeed.'

'Then why are we eating meat?'

'It is not against the word of the Lord: only Catholics maintain the old ways now.' Then he pauses. 'You are not, I hope, from a Catholic household?' He glances at the other men.

'It depends what you mean by that word "Catholic",' I reply.

'Well, very simply, do you acknowledge the supremacy of Rome?'

'I follow the word of God, the guidance of my priest, and the direction of our bishop. But that is not the point. There was a time when there were no such divisions and all Englishmen acknowledged the overlordship of the king in temporal matters and the guidance of Rome in spiritual ones. Nowadays all society is divided. But why? How does a man determine God's will? I think that a man knows God no more than a cat knows its own grandfather.'

'The will of the people reflects the will of God,' says the older man.

William nods and says, 'That is true,' as he reaches forward to help himself to some of the venison pie.

'Mister Perkins is right,' replies Mistress Parlebone. 'God made mankind in His own image. It follows that the will He gave to Man is in accordance with His divine will.'

'If that is the case,' I reply, helping myself to some carrots, 'then God is as fickle as Man, and as greedy, disloyal, selfish, cruel and pompous. That is a terrible thing to say.'

'Wherefore do you speak in this strange archaic manner?' asks the younger man.

'We've been travelling a long while,' William replies, draining the wine from his glass.

'What happened to you? Were you captured by Turks?'

'No, thanks be to God,' I reply.

'It is truly dreadful, the Turkish horror,' says the older man, whom Mistress Parlebone described as Mister Perkins. 'I heard of a Dartmouth woman whose husband went to sea three years ago and never returned. Had he drowned, she could have remarried, but the ship was taken by pirates; boys from the vessel later were sold in the slave markets of Tunis. Not until seven years have passed can she be allowed to presume her husband dead and then remarry. Until then she has neither money nor food but three children to feed and rent to pay. She pleaded with the churchwardens for relief and they gave but fourpence a week. It is a sad lookout for a woman in such a plight, at the beckoning of any man with a sixpence.'

'How can that be God's will?' I ask. 'Has God deserted the people? Has not the wrongful interpretation of God's law caused Him to shut his eyes to the suffering of the great flock?'

'I do not understand your meaning,' says Mister Parlebone.

'Even if God's law has changed rightfully from generation to generation, how do you know that by following the will of the people you are not deviating from God's will, and not bringing damnation upon all your souls?'

'That is why we are fighting this war,' says Mistress Parlebone. 'God shall express His will through victory. The Royalists hold that King Charles is king by the grace of God, and that he is God's representative among us, and that the king's will is to be obeyed as if it were that of God Himself. Others believe the king to be a weak and foolish man who should be deposed and replaced by a council for the common wealth of men. If the Royalists are right, then God will ensure that the Parliamentarians shall be vanquished. But that is highly unlikely. Few major strongholds are left to the king – the town of Oxford and the city of Exeter being the only important ones.'

'It is not only a military question,' adds Mister Parlebone. 'God does not restrict His judgement to battlefields. He sends it in the form of the plague as well. Leeds has been sorely affected this year. So have Worcester, Winchester and Bristol.'

'Exeter has been hit hard too,' says Mister Perkins. 'They've banned pigs from roaming the streets in the hope of limiting the disease.'

I finish the carrots on my platter, and leave the cauliflower, the taste of which is disagreeable to me. I sip my wine, and reflect that here I am eating exotic vegetables while people are still dying from the plague.

My uneaten cauliflower catches the attention of young Thomas opposite me, who is kicking his legs to and fro under the table. He has a pleasant demeanour and an impish smile. 'You should eat your cauliflower, Goodman Drayman. It nourishes the blood.'

His elder sister nods in agreement. 'Alone of all the cole-worts it is good and nourishing when boiled in vinegar.' She looks across at the younger man. 'Uncle Edward used to tell us, everything else that is green is of small nourishment and agitating to the melancholy humours.'

'Is that so?' says William. 'In that case I'll have more veni-son pie, if I may.'

'Have you visited the Americas?' asks Thomas. 'Have you shot any Indians?'

'The Americas?' I ask, still feeling anxious on account of the food. 'No, we've not ventured there. Have you?'

'No, silly,' answers his sister. 'It is too far. And I would get sea-sick.'

'But we do have turkey fowl,' adds Thomas.

'From the sight of your turkey fowl, the Americas are strange islands indeed.'

'They are not islands,' says Sarah. 'They are one great country, a hundred times larger than England.'

'There are so many Indians there,' says Thomas. 'They hide in the forests and have bows and arrows, spears and clubs, and they attack all the Christians in the night, and cut the top of your head off. So you have to shoot them.'

'Thomas, that's enough,' says his mother.

Mister Perkins speaks. 'If I may return to Mistress Parlebone's statement about the two opposing viewpoints, that is to say Man's will against God's will, I would suggest that in the graciousness of her words she gives both sides more credit than they deserve. Against the king you could hold up the case of Giles Mompesson.' There is a nodding of agreement by Mister Parlebone and the younger man at the mention of this name. 'Mompesson is living proof that when kings appoint ministers, it is not with God's guidance. The people should choose their ministers – and by "people" I mean the prosperous landowners and employers of the nation – the stalwart backbone of England, from the Justice of the Peace to the tax-paying householder.'

'I like carrots,' says Thomas. 'Master John Gerard says that they give you wind in the gut, like turnips do.' Saying this he grins guiltily and looks at his mother.

'That is enough,' she says sternly.

'Who is this Giles Mompesson?' I ask.

Mister Perkins explains. 'A rogue. He took control of the king's forests and sold all the wood for his own profit. He forced innholders throughout England to buy licences for their inns from him, at five or ten pounds a time. On one notorious occasion he sheltered from the rain at an alehouse. It did not stop raining all night. In the morning he paid his host a token for his trouble, and when the money was accepted, he accused his host of running an unlicensed inn and had the poor man clapped in irons until he purchased a licence. Mompesson was found guilty of more than three thousand cases of extortion against innholders.'

'There were dozens of others like him,' says the younger man. 'Royal appointees who lined their own pockets at the expense of others. I would that I could meet him and his ilk on the road to Exeter. It would be a good deed that I'd do with my sword.'

'There are bad men under Fairfax's command too,' says Mistress Parlebone. 'Those who took our horses were none of the kindest. To teach *them* a lesson would be also a good deed.'

'I myself wish for nothing more than to spend the rest of my days engaged in good deeds,' I say. 'But how can I tell what a good deed is in this day and age? What is "good" and "bad" if God's law is constantly changing? How can we do good if the meaning of "good" and "bad" are dependent on who wins the war? How can a man go through this world in sure knowledge that he is doing the right and proper thing?'

'Those are difficult questions,' replies Mister Parlebone. 'And my chief answer is that you must search within your own heart for what you yourself know to be right. And take direction from the Good Book, of course. Especially the Ten Commandments.'

'But therein lies my point. One of the Commandments tells us not to make any graven images – and yet I am a sculptor. I've made many such images over the years. The Ten Commandments also say that we should not commit adultery – but did not the kings of the Old Testament have many wives, and so commit adultery many times over?'

'Goodman Drayman, your heart is earnest but your theology wrong. It is not a sin for a sculptor to carve a design or even the figure of a man for a secular purpose. And if a king in days long past took many wives, it was not a sin. You must balance the law as you know it with the law that applied then, the law of Deuteronomy. A king who was victorious in battle could take the women and cattle of his enemies as his spoil. That of course is no longer God's will and has become sinful. When our side have won this war, our Parliament will reinforce the morality of the common wealth by making it a statute law that women who are found to have fornicated outside wedlock will be hanged.'

William chokes on his pie. When he has recovered, he looks at Mister Parlebone. '*Women* who fornicate? Mister Parlebone, I don't know how much you know about for-nication but I cannot help but think men are at least partly responsible. If not, I'm the Pope's pardoner.'

'Not in front of the children,' says Mistress Parlebone, looking severely at William. 'We do not tolerate that word in this house.'

'What word?' I ask.

'Pope,' Sarah says, with a barely suppressed smile.

'Hear, hear,' answers the younger of the two other guests. 'No one should refer to the Antichrist in the presence of minors.'

'Master Christopher!' exclaims Mistress Parlebone, 'that's enough. You two children, it is time to leave.'

'So much for keeping your names secret,' mutters Mister Parlebone as his wife ushers the children from the hall. 'It's a good thing we are here at the far-flung corner of England

and not in Oxford or Exeter. Or – God forbid – London. All those eavesdroppers, I'd never have a night's sleep.'

Mister Perkins looks at me straight across the table. 'So what good works are you intending to perform after leaving this house?'

'I do not know,' I reply. 'But I worry that I might do something that I believe is good only to find that the law has changed, with the result that I find that I've sinned.'

'Maybe your role is not to do the good act yourself but to let others do it for you,' says Mistress Parlebone, returning to her seat and laying her napkin across her lap. 'Maybe it is because I am merely a woman but I do believe that sometimes there is merit in holding back and letting others take the glory.'

I shake my head. 'Mistress Parlebone, I know that my soul is in need of redemption. And that cannot be a matter of standing back. I must do the good act myself. I was a sculptor of stone once. Now it's my destiny that I need to shape.'

I think back across the centuries. I remember the babe, Lazarus, and the cold night outside the walls of Exeter listening to a whole city lamenting its dead. I recall my own terrible deed in taking the infected child into the house of the blacksmith, and repaying his and his daughter's kindness with cruel death. And I reflect on how little I have been able to do since. I remember my family, who died without me. Perhaps they died cursing my memory.

'It is a small thing we can offer you but a good deed,' says Mistress Parlebone. 'If successful, you would save a man's life.' Her face is most solemn. She places her hands on the table.

'No one would recognise them,' says Mister Perkins, looking at Mister Parlebone.

Mister Parlebone nods. He thinks for a moment, and then speaks to us. 'Do you know Fulford, in Dunsford parish?'

'We know it,' I reply.

'Major Fulford, who first defended it, has long since been driven from the place but a desperate group of Royalists still hold out there, headed by Captain Edward Trevelyan. From there he and his men mount damaging attacks on the Parliamentary army, stationed near Crediton. They stand in the way of a protracted siege of Exeter. The two colonels for Parliament, Thomas Fairfax and Oliver Cromwell, have already set the plans. These two gentlemen on my left inform me that before the attack on Exeter is set in motion, Colonel Fairfax will deal with the king's men at Fulford. In the meantime, Cromwell will prevent any relief of the place by Lord Wentworth's Royalists, who are currently stationed in Bovey Tracey. In short, Fairfax intends to attack Fulford in two days' time, and to burn the house, and to execute every last man therein as an example to others.'

'Edward Trevelyan is my brother,' explains Mistress Parlebone. 'He is a good man. At the start of the war he was commissioned to serve in the king's army. But his cause is not the king's but his own sense of duty and loyalty to his fellow men.'

'What do you want us to do?' asks William.

Mister Parlebone answers. 'Captain Trevelyan will not give up Fulford House at our say-so. But it is certain death that he faces now, and we feel we must tell him. The time has come for him to surrender his sword, with honour undiminished.'

'But that means informing the enemy, a Royalist captain, of Colonel Fairfax's plans in advance,' adds Master Christopher.

'So none of us can be seen to do it,' says Mister Perkins. 'It would be treason.'

'We have been considering how to send him a message,' says Mistress Parlebone. 'Your arrival is most propitious. You could go to my brother at Fulford to tell him about the colonels' plans. We believe the attack will begin in two days' time – early in the morning of Friday the nineteenth.'

'We have stabled a good riding horse in the barn of the mill at Clifford,' says Master Christopher. 'Captain Trevelyan is to flee from the house to Clifford on foot. He is then to ride here, under cover of darkness, if he can get through the snow.'

'Why will he trust us?' I ask.

'Because you will know the signal,' Mistress Parlebone replies, 'which is to wave a black cape above your head three times within sight of the front gate of the house. In addition we will give you a letter of safe passage in case you are stopped by the Parliamentarian troops.'

'And what if he refuses to leave?' William asks.

'That is not your worry,' says Mistress Parlebone. 'As long as he knows, that is all.'

I turn to William. 'It cannot be a bad thing to save a man's life. We should deliver this news.'

'Even in war,' says Mister Parlebone, 'we must find it in our hearts to do the acts of common decency and respect that our fellow men and women expect of us. But you'll need less conspicuous clothing than those reds.'

'No, husband,' says Mistress Parlebone. 'Who would suspect men wearing such garments? A black cape for William will be sufficient; John, you can wear that old cloak you were wearing on your arrival. But be discreet. Take the lane from this house to the bridge over Blackaton Brook, then proceed through Rushford Woods to Sandy Park, and then take the paths through the woods on the north side of the river. Do not go by the south side, through Cranbrook, for there are many Parliamentarian troops billeted in and around Moretonhampstead.'

'Well,' I say, with a deep breath, 'I am ready.'

'As am I,' adds William.

'In that case,' says Mister Parlebone, 'my good Arthurian knights, you have a quest.'

The next hour is spent preparing to set out for Fulford. Mistress Parlebone gives us instructions as to what to say to her brother. Master Christopher and Mister Perkins both tell us how to avoid the Parliamentarian forces, and what to do if accosted by armed men of either side. In the chamber upstairs I repack my sack of things, and fasten my old eating knife on my belt. Then I hold up my old tunic. It is filthy and torn.

'It will be extra weight,' says William, knowing my mind.

'Like so much of the past,' I respond.

'No, brother. We'd be nothing if we did not carry the past with us. We'd be ignorant of good and evil, of changing circumstances and unchanging virtues.'

'Unchanging virtues? There's no such thing.'

'Without the past, there'd be no understanding of virtue at all. We'd be no more than cattle.'

I look at my chisels. With them to hand, I am a sculptor. I can draw on a lifetime of experience. Without them, I would be – what? A pilgrim without a shrine. A man leaping from the cliff of time. I put them too in my travelling sack, though I leave the tunic.

We say farewell to our hosts in the hall. William gallantly kisses the hand of Mistress Parlebone. She gives him a letter of safe conduct, signed by her husband, who is a Justice of the Peace, and he places that also in my travelling sack. Mister Perkins hands William his black cape, and the men wish us well, and take our hands in theirs and shake them, which seems to be the common way of expressing goodwill among these people. I don my travelling cloak and shoulder my sack, and the two of us set out into the bright air.

The snow crunches under our feet as we walk away from the house.

'You have got what you wanted – a quest,' says William, his breath billowing about his beard.

'And you, you've had what you wanted – a meal.'

'But you did not grant my last request.'

'What? To aid your seduction of Mistress Parlebone? Forget her, William. You did a good thing by not trying your luck.'

He says nothing but looks at the snow-covered branches of the trees and kicks the ice in the road. And thus we trudge on through the snow in silence, sometimes in the wheel ruts of a wagon that has passed this way, and then over the bridge and through the woods, where the snow is not so deep.

'It still confuses me,' I say, thinking aloud, 'that, with all the luxuries of this age, men are fighting among themselves.'

'I am sure that not everyone is as comfortable as Mister Parlebone.'

'But even that churl who approached us with a pitchfork, Caleb, lived in a stone-built house with a fireplace.'

William says nothing.

'Perhaps that's why there's fighting now between the king and Parliament. The ordinary folk, now that they live like lords, want to command like lords too. They no longer accept the rule of a king.'

Still William says nothing.

'In fact, that's not the half of it. This king they're fighting now must be a true tyrant if his liege subjects want to do away with kings altogether.'

William stops. 'It's not our war, John.'

'What do you mean by that?'

'We know nothing of current times. We know only the rule of a good king, Edward the Third, of blessed memory. Even his father, Edward the Second, was not all so bad, by my reckoning. He was pious, and true to his friends.'

'It sounds to me that this present king has been more than just true to his friends. He has enriched them at the expense of others.'

'Maybe so. But you do not kill the goose for the laying of a bad egg, still less do you do away with geese altogether.

Should we help do away with kingship itself when we know kings can be good as well as bad? What justice would we be doing to the memory of good King Edward if we were to help depose his lawful heir?'

'The last king of which we heard, King Henry the Eighth – who destroyed all the monasteries – sounded no better. Maybe the people are just sick and tired of bad kings. If you've had too many bad eggs, one after the other, you'd surely kill the goose and eat her,' I say.

'And what if a sculptor was to produce a bad carving? Then would you abolish all sculpture?'

'But back at Mister Parlebone's house you said that you would help with this mission.'

'I said what I said because I'd had enough. I wanted to leave.'

We walk on, striding over the sticks and smattering of snow under the canopy of the trees.

'William, tell me. Why are you so melancholy? We've got our quest.'

'We've got nothing, John. They were kind to us – but without good reason. They trusted us – again, without any reason. They gave us a quest – but do you believe in it?'

'They gave us a letter of safe conduct.'

'It is probably worth nothing.'

We say little for the next hour. After that we come to the edge of the wood. Before us there is the way along the north bank of the river through the thickly wooded steep valley. To our right is a mill, and the bridge over the River Teign. William stops and I do too.

'It is time to decide,' he says.

'Decide what?'

'Whether you wish to follow that path along the north of the river, to Fulford, as Mistress Parlebone instructed us, or come with me along the south side.'

'You mean, back to Moreton? But she said there were many Parliament men stationed that way. And if we return to Moreton . . . Well, we were none too welcome last time.'

'I mean to Cranbrook, John. I want to see Cranbrook again. I want to see where we grew up, the old fort where we played together as boys, the old house where our father and mother lived and died. I want to see what I still think of as home, just one last time.'

'Why? Why now?'

'We were told a pack of lies back there. And you, who used to be so perceptive, you can't see it.'

'William, what do you mean?'

He throws his hands in the air. 'Nothing can change fate.' He puts his hands on his forehead.

'William, there is no question of me leaving you. Not for any cause. You are not only my brother, you are everything I've got in the whole world. I can no more leave you than walk away from my own heart.'

'Do you want to see me die?'

'No, of course not.'

'Then go your own way. Go, and do your good deed.' With that he reaches out and clasps me to his chest, and hugs me, and holds me.

'William, don't be a cut farthing. You did not desert me

when I'd lifted up that baby, so I'll not leave you. I'll be your brother until the end of time. Until the *end* of time, William – not just until the end is in sight.'

'You will not go your own way?'

'No. Never.'

'Then give me your fardel.'

'What?'

'Give it to me. I need to be carrying the letter of safe conduct.'

'Why?'

'Either give it to me or go your separate way from me.'

We look at each other. 'Not until you tell me the truth of your mind.'

He takes a deep breath. 'Back there, those people were all too keen to entrust us with their secret message. I've been thinking over the matter. You raised their ire by talking of the changing nature of God's will. They thought we were Catholics. And yet they still told us all those things about Fulford.'

'So?'

'No one is that trusting with strangers, especially those who differ from them in religious matters. Would you trust a heretic with your secrets?'

'Mistress Parlebone said it does not matter whether we persuade her brother – as long as the message is delivered.'

'Exactly. All they care about is that he receives the message. And do you know why?'

'No.'

'Because they want him to fight on.'

I stare at him, trying to understand their duplicity, hardly believing it. And then I remember Mister Parlebone's words when the name of the younger man was mentioned. He referred to the dangers of living in Oxford or Exeter – the last two Royalist strongholds.

'Give me your fardel.'

I hand it to him. He opens it and takes out the letter of safe conduct. It is written on white material that is like vellum but much thinner. He reads it.

'What does it say?'

'The script is unlike that of our time but, as far as I can make out, it asks that whoever receives the letter give us safe passage.'

'Is that all?'

'Apart from a few niceties and greetings, yes,' he replies, putting the letter back in the sack and shouldering it. 'Let us go up to Cranbrook.'

We start walking towards the bridge. The snow is between two and three feet deep, and in places deeper still. The road is completely covered – no one else has been this way all day. Birds call to our left and right and fly between the bare branches of the trees, no doubt in fear that the snow will leave them starving, with the sparrowhawks avid for prey. We try climbing the snow-laden granite walls that run alongside the road, in the hope that the snow on top will have settled less thickly, but we are slowed even more by the hidden brambles, holly and bracken, not to mention the crevices in the stone. The temperature is falling already, our clouds of breath catching the odd ray of sun behind us.

We walk through Whiddon Park and find the old lane from Chagford to Cranbrook that we know so well. But here we are tracing a path that others have taken – and not so long ago. Deep imprints in the snow indicate that a number of men have come this way. I know we have three days left to live but still I worry that we might be caught by soldiers. I glance up at the old fort, its ramparts covered in snow; I half expect to see people up there watching us. It is not just the cold that makes me shiver. It is the awareness of how obvious we are, two dark-clothed figures stumbling through this white landscape.

William notices. 'It troubles you?'

'If we meet with a company of soldiers, I don't know what we'll say.'

A few minutes later we see a group of men at the cross-roads. They are wearing breastplates, back plates and round helmets, and bearing long pikes. As we get closer, we see that more men are coming up the valley to this point, and mustering here.

'I presume these are all Parliamentarians,' I say under my breath.

'If they were the king's men, they'd be less easy in their manner.'

They do not appear grimly determined, as men are when they know their lives depend on the outcome of a forthcoming battle. But nor are they kindly.

We walk past.

Just before Cranbrook itself the road twists to the right and then slightly descends into the small valley where the mill stands. Here the road has been cleared. There are piles of snow flecked with twigs and dead leaves on either side. Holly grows from the top of the hedgerows, and beech and oak trees shield the old mill from the worst of the weather. There are more men standing at the small ford, where the road goes through the brook that runs down from the mill. On our right, I see a low wall where once there stood that stone barn in which we slept our first night after visiting the stones. Behind, remnants of the old house seem to have been incorporated into a newer one. On the other side of the road are new barns, set around a yard. As we draw nearer to the brook it is clear that there are several dozen men in the yard too.

We walk on.

Three rooks in the branches of the oak trees flap their way from perch to perch, watching us. I remember the bird on the dead man soaking into the earth of that field near Honyton, all those years ago. Maybe one of these will alight on my corpse.

No, I have three days.

The door to the mill opens and a tall man strides out, catching our attention. His clothing is much the same as his fellow soldiers' but his movements betray his power of command. Out of the corner of my eye, I see two men from the yard move to block our way, levelling their long pikes before us.

'Where you going?' one of them says.

'To Exeter, by way of Dunsford,' William answers confidently, turning to make sure all the men around us can hear.

'Should you wish to see it, we've a safe conduct, signed by a Justice of the Peace.'

The man who challenged us glances at the approaching commanding figure, and then back at William. 'You sound strange.' He looks from William to me. 'What's your business in coming this way?'

'We were born here, in Cranbrook,' I reply as William pulls out the safe-conduct pass. 'This is our usual route.'

I turn to see the commanding officer right behind me. He is about thirty, clean-shaven, dark-haired and with curiously deep-set eyes. 'Who are they, Goodman Tozer?'

'They claim to be from this place, Captain Baring. But they speak most strangely.'

'And where is your destination?' asks the captain, taking the letter from William.

William was so fast with his answer last time that I leave him to respond. But now words fail him. 'We are heading . . . to the church.'

The lie falls flat, like a stone dropped in the snow.

The captain points to another man. 'Fetch the miller,' he says, keeping an eye on us. 'He'll know if these men are local or not.' He starts to scrutinise the document. He pauses for a moment, then looks William in the eye. 'What's your business in Dunsford? It must be important to warrant a safe-conduct.'

William pulls a couple of chisels out of my travelling sack. 'We are masons, carvers of stone. We've completed our contract at Mister Parlebone's house, where there was some damage to his porch, and now we're heading to see the rector of Dunsford, who has told Mister Parlebone that he too requires our services.'

Three men approach: the first is an old man with wisps of grey hair on his domed head, rough working clothes and milky blue eyes. The two men behind him both carry long *gonnes*, similar to the one we saw at Master Hodge's house in Moreton. These must be what Mistress Parlebone called muskets.

'Miller White,' says Captain Baring, 'do you know these men?'

The old man shakes his head. 'Not seen 'em before – never in my life.' He spits into the snow.

'They claim to have been born here, at Cranbrook.'

'Can't remember their faces. Don't know their names.'

The captain gestures for the miller to leave. 'We are looking out for two men travelling together, one of whom is bearded. They were stopped by a patrol on the road north from Bovey last night. These two men had pistols. One opened fire on our patrol, killing a man. They both got away but one was wounded – at least, he screamed in pain when the patrol fired back.'

Captain Baring looks me in the eye. 'Do you know where these men might be?'

I shake my head.

The captain then stands before William. 'Royalists travelling north from Bovey are heading only in one direction. Is that not true?'

William says nothing.

The captain turns to me. 'If you are from these parts you'll know the answer.'

He turns back to William. 'Does it not seem unusual for a Justice of the Peace to grant a letter of safe conduct for someone merely doing masonry work?'

I think frantically, trying to remain calm. I plan to tell the captain that the lord of the manor has died and we are to produce a funeral effigy; however, I realise I don't know who the lord of the manor is these days.

William suddenly launches himself away from us and runs across the lane and through the yard. Immediately a pike is levelled in front of me and a musket pointed at my chest. 'Stay where you are!' snaps Captain Baring, quickly turning from me to shout several orders to the men. I watch my brother hurry past the new barns, and into the snow-filled field. Then he runs down the hill, through the snow.

A mighty explosion booms across the land, and another. The rooks all fly from the trees. Another two deafening musket explosions ring out in quick succession, and another two. Several men are kneeling in the snow and shooting. More shots are fired. Smoke rises from their muskets and obscures my brother.

Captain Baring shouts, 'Cease fire!'

I look for William, all over the snow-covered field. No one is running any more. Instead a dozen or so men are trampling over the snow towards a motionless figure lying darkly against the snow.

'Let me go to him,' I plead.

'Lock him up,' says Captain Baring to the men nearby, not even looking at me. He heads into the field.

'Let me speak to my brother,' I shout, as three men seize

hold of me and push me towards the barnyard. Over my shoulder I see two men dragging William over the snow. I hear him screaming in agony, as if his nerves were being rent with a rusty blade.

'William!' I yell. 'William!' The men bundle me through the snow. 'Go with God, William!'

They shut me in a dark barn near the mill pond and leave me there on the earthen floor.

I have wanted to scream ever since the plague started; now, there is no will to yell left in me. I whisper my brother's name again, and then again. I sound like Lazarus crying – imploring help yet expressing such disappointment and outrage with the world.

There are noises outside: men moving to and fro, shouts, orders and horses whinnying. I look through the chinks in the barn door. But I do not see William.

I kneel down and feel the tears welling.

After about an hour a latch on the outside of the barn is unfastened and the door swings wide. The light dazzles me, even though it is fading. A voice commands me to get to my feet. I am manhandled across the barnyard to the old house. Two men drag me into the hall. Although it is my childhood home, I barely recognise it. It has a fireplace now. There is a table at one end where Captain Baring is seated with several loose papers in front of him. There are three other men standing around the room, all of them armed.

Then I see William.

He is barely alive, with bandages around his head, right

arm and left leg. He is lying slumped on a chair, mouth open, eyes staring at the light coming in through the window. His shirt is stiff with dried blood from his arm. His beard is crusted with blood too. Some blood is trickling still from a wound under the bandage around his head.

'Why did you run?' I ask him.

He lifts a hand, weakly, but says nothing.

'Do not speak to the prisoner,' says Captain Baring sternly. 'Do not say anything without being spoken to. What is your name?'

I turn to him. 'John of Wrayment.'

'Is this man your brother?'

'I am proud that he is.'

'Why does he call himself by a different name from you?'

'Because of his beard. They called me after Wrayment because that was my home.'

'Your brother is a traitor to the people of this country. He was carrying a traitorous message sewn into the collar of his cape, and has confessed he knew its contents. He shot one of our soldiers last night . . .'

'He did not. He was with me.'

'And where was that?'

'In a tinner's hut, out on the moor.'

'Then he must have made his way there after the deed. Today, when challenged, he resisted arrest. In his bag he was carrying coins that are marked with the figure and motto of a pope. He had a crucifix and rosary on him, contrary to the law.'

'The sack was mine. If he is guilty then I am too.'

'Are you also a Catholic spy?'

'I was taught to cross myself when the name of the Lord was uttered and I pray to Him for His blessing to be on us all. Your Protestantism corrupts everything. Everyone thinks only of himself, not of the common good.'

'We all think of the common good. And the extirpation of the Catholic superstition and the destruction of the Antichrist is part of that common good.'

I shake my head, and laugh at the ludicrousness of it all. 'What do you know?'

Baring just looks at me. Then he says, 'Fortunately for you, I am not here to hang Catholics. However, it *is* my duty to hang Royalist soldiers, collaborators, spies and messengers. The document sewn into your brother's collar is unambiguous, and by his confession on that score he has convicted himself.'

'If you hang him, you will have to hang me also. We are guilty of the same crime. The sack was mine.'

'Do not play games with me, John of Wrayment. It will cost us nothing to use the same rope twice.'

'That cape was not William's, it belongs to Mister Perkins.'

'Where did you meet this Mister Perkins?'

'At the house of Mister Parlebone, in Gidleigh.'

'So, not at a tinner's house on the moor.' He pushes a piece of paper forward. It has writing on it. 'Read it.'

I shake my head. 'I cannot.'

Captain Baring beckons me with his finger. I go nearer until I am within an arm's length of the table. He stabs down with his finger on the unfolded letter. 'Read it.'

I stare at the black marks. 'I cannot.'

'Then write the name of the man who is in command of the Royalist forces at Bovey.'

I shake my head. 'I never learned how.'

'Do you know his name?'

'Lord Wentford.'

'Wentworth. Write it down.'

'I do not know how.'

'To save your brother's life.'

I shout, 'I do not know how!'

I turn to William. He looks dead.

'Spare him, please,' I say, turning again to face Captain Baring. 'He is a good man.'

Captain Baring gets to his feet. He comes around the table and faces me. 'Do you want to die?'

'No, but—'

'We will hang William Beard at the old fort on top of the hill,' he says, addressing the others in the room. 'I am satisfied that this prisoner is ignorant of the plot. He did not shoot our man last night and I do not believe he even knew what message his brother was carrying to Fulford. He could not have written it or read it. Nevertheless, he assisted the traitor, and so his punishment will be to act as William Beard's executioner.'

'No!'

Captain Baring looks at me. 'If you perform the duty, we will bury your brother in the churchyard, and you may walk free. If you refuse, you will both be shot and buried here, in unconsecrated ground.'

'Why? Oh, Mother of Christ. Hang me too!'

Captain Baring clicks his fingers at two of the guards. 'Take these men out of here. Let this one help carry his brother to the fort. He can go when he has done what is necessary.'

'You heard the captain,' says one of the men, pointing his musket at me.

I look down at my poor brother. 'In Christ's name, William, we should have embraced the plague. We should have accepted death then.'

Tears come painfully, as if so many are welling up within me they are pressing on my eyes from behind, trying to burst out of me. I wipe them away, and blink, but they keep coming. I put his arm around my shoulders and try to lift him. He is heavy, and when he is on his one good leg, he cannot put weight on the other. The musket ball did not just lacerate the skin; it pulverised the flesh inside and broke the bone. I wince at the thought of him being dragged across the snow. Between my lifting him and him reaching out for the wall to steady himself, we manage to get him to the door.

When we are outside, William gestures to one of the men to pass him a long stick on which to put his weight when he shifts his good leg, and thus we move through the snow, at a snail's pace.

'Fear not,' I say in the lane. 'We still have three more days.'

'No,' he says in a parched voice. 'No, not for me.'

'William, the voice at the stones said we had six days. You were there too.'

'The voice told me three.'

'No, William. It said six! You are saying three now to calm me.'

'It said six to you. It said three to me.'

'No!'

'Listen, John. You asked me once, three hundred years ago, as we walked towards Exeter, what have I ever done to save my soul? Well, I am doing that thing now. When you said that you had heard that you had six days left to live, I knew that we were not hearing one voice but two. And knowing that there is but one Lord God, and that He speaks with one voice, I felt I had to help you. That was why I changed my mind, and decided not to go back home but to join you on this quest.'

'I heard six days, William. Clearly. You must have heard wrongly.'

'John, do you not understand? There were two voices, one in each of our heads. Your voice spoke differently from mine.'

'Keep going,' comes a voice from behind.

'Brother, I know this is the end. But I know too that there is something good in it. I must die now because you must go on. Not just for the sake of your own soul – for mine too. I know I am a sinner. I've fornicated with many women, and to tell you the truth, I find it a struggle to be sorry. Lying with the ugliest of them was still a pleasure. How then can I truly repent? I'll be saying so only in order to obtain my selfish desire, as Master Ley said. So I need you to go on and do that great act for which you've been preserved . . .'

'No, William.'

'When you see Saint Peter, seated at the right hand of God, you can say to him that you had a brother once, and he was not all good, but nor was he all bad. And call as witness good King Edward, and tell him that, although William Beard had many faults, they were all faults of love. He never abandoned a woman that had blessed him with her affection, and he was never a traitor to his king, nor to his country, nor his family.'

It is difficult shuffling through the snow in the dimming light. We have only made half the distance to the old fort.

'You understand me, John? Only through you can my soul be redeemed.' He stops again, to regain his breath. He looks back to our house, and pauses for a moment. He looks down and rests his stick against his side and fumbles with his hands. I cannot see what he is doing but then he passes something to me.

I take it and look at it. It is his garnet and gold ring.

'No, William, I cannot accept this.'

'And who else will I give it to?'

I put the ring on my finger and then we start again on the slow, painful struggle up the hill to the old fort.

I can see the ramparts now. At one point I slip on the snow-covered grass, and William falls with me, crying out in pain. The guards shout at us, and I lift him to his feet, and start once more to help him.

'You asked me why I ran,' William says. 'It was because I knew that I was going to die today. And it was a good thing to know. For this way I could make something of my death.

Maybe you too will be able to do the same thing for someone else, when your time comes.'

'I cannot understand this world,' I reply. 'In our time, we struggled to get by and life was hard but we lived well. We worked long days and had straightforward pleasures. But now, so many things are easier – yet what does the world do? It revels in causing suffering and killing.'

We reach the top of the hill and pass between the white mounds where the gate once stood. Before us, the whole of the moor appears: miles and miles of undulating white hills. Over to one side of the fort I can see a man fixing a noose around a bough of a lone oak tree, testing its strength. A horse has been brought forward, and waits there.

William falls silent, looking at the last red gleams of the sunset in the clouds above the moor. After a while he says, 'You were right. The wilderness *is* God's Creation unchanged. But it is not God with whom you must now deal. It is not God who stops men from going to Heaven. God welcomes all those who escape the clutches of the Devil, and it is the Devil with whom you must parley next. Go with God, John, my brother. Go with God.'

Then he turns to me, and I feel his arm around my shoulder squeeze me tight in an embrace, and he rests his head against mine for a moment.

Then the men come for him, and take him away from me. They take him to the tree. Another guard gestures for me to follow.

William cries out with pain as they drag his bad leg over the horse's back. The noose is placed over his head and fastened around his neck. The horse is steadied, and then one of the men beckons me. I step forward, hardly knowing what I am doing, and take the reins of the horse.

'Forgive me, brother,' I say, looking up at him. He has raised his eyes to Heaven and does not look down. My voice is so thick with emotion I do not know that he has heard me. So I say again, in a louder voice, 'Forgive me, William, blessed and best of all brothers. My heart goes with you, always. We'll be brothers until the end of time.' And closing my eyes, I lead the horse forward, saying the words of the benediction we learned as children, '*Benedicat vos omnipotens Deus Pater et Filius et Spiritus Sanctus.* Amen.'

After I stop speaking all I can hear are the horse's hooves crunching on the snow.

A man takes the reins from me. I stare at the white moor.

I hear a voice, that of the man who relieved me of the reins. 'You may break his neck if you wish.'

I turn.

'Clutch his body and let yourself fall suddenly. He'll die more easily.'

I look at William's twisting body. I walk over and place my arms around his jolting waist. I shudder at the thought that my next move will end my brother's life. But his body is struggling to leave this world, like a fly caught in a web. I jump, letting my full weight fall with his body. I hear a muffled snap, and see his neck suddenly much elongated, distorted with our combined weight. I put a foot to the ground and slip, and fall, and lie there, staring at the muddied snow.

I see all the tears that have ever fallen frozen beneath me, stretching away, across the moor. That is us. We are living on the frozen tears of our ancestors.

I look up to see William turning slowly, his eyes staring towards Heaven. He is no longer out of time. He is no longer of this world.

'Go, now,' commands one of the soldiers. 'We will take his corpse down the hill to the churchyard in the morning.'

I get to my feet, and start walking slowly across the fort. I descend the far side of the hill, climbing over snow-covered hedgerows. I am soaked. I am so tired. After an hour, it is dark. I no longer know where I am. I yearn to lie down, and I resent my body's weakness. I start to hate my feebleness of mind too. When I fall in the snow, and lie there, I despise myself. I should die of cold, and be eaten by foxes and wild pigs.

But I have not yet fulfilled my promise to William. *Get up! Get up, John. You have no right to lie here longer, nor to resent yourself. To hate yourself is to squander the privilege of being alive.*

I struggle back to my feet and stumble on through the darkness, lurching from hedgerow to hedgerow. After two hours I come to a river and wade into its cold water, hoping I will be swept away. It is deep, and the blackness covers me, so that I cannot breathe. I struggle to the surface, just as I did this morning, and emerge into darkness and feel a rock. I gasp for air, and the grief washes over me like another river, for when I struggled out of the snow this morning I called for William and he was there. Now I know he is gone forever.

I have lost everything – all I have now of my own time is my old boots and his ring.

I climb out of the water and, shivering, climb up a hill through some woods. The cold is painful – I cannot rest. So I walk on, and on. After what seems like an age I find a lane, and some time after that I hear a lowing sound, and it seems gentle. Hands outstretched, I feel a wall, then a wooden door and the bolt. I enter the warm darkness of a byre, and sink down on the straw, listening to the cows breathing and chewing in the darkness, gratefully letting the river of sleep wash me away.

Chapter Six

I am woken by the sound of the barn door opening. An arc of light cuts across my eyes. I look around. Half a dozen cows are eating from a manger, and a bushy-eyebrowed farmer is staring at me. He is wearing a round straw hat and a sleeveless jerkin over his shirt, and brown breeches that start high above his waist and end at the tops of his muddy leather boots.

'What are you doing in my barn?'

I get to my feet and walk slowly towards the door. I pause, blinking in the light. I feel dizzy. The view spins around me and, unsteady on my feet, I slump to my knees. I reach out and put a hand on the wall.

'Forgive me,' I say.

'Where've you come from?'

'Moreton.'

'You're dressed in mighty strange clothes. Even for Moreton.'

'They're from my grandfather.'

'You're hungry?'

I nod.

'I'll not turn away a starving man reduced to wearing his grandaddy's clothes. Go on inside the house and ask the wench for some breakfast. You'll find her in the kitchen.'

I nod my thanks, get to my feet and take a step to the barn door. I see thatched farm buildings, fields and trees. Although sunny, it has clearly been raining recently as the barnyard is a quagmire of mud. 'Where is this place?'

'This here's Halstow, in Dunsford parish.'

I look at the house, sunken into the landscape. Even the chimney stack looks old.

'Through the front door, turn left. She's called Kitty,' says the farmer. 'Go on, she won't bite you. Long as you don't lay a finger on her.'

I go to the house: the door is open. Inside is a flagstone-floored passage and a doorway that leads through to a whitewashed kitchen. It is light and airy; the large windows are filled with many small rectangular panes of glass. There is a fire on the hearth burning gently, smoke twisting its way up the chimney. A young woman in a long apron and a bonnet of thin white fabric is busy kneading dough. A wisp of dark hair is loose on one side of her face. I can almost hear William commenting on her pretty features. Thinking about him overwhelms me for a moment, and I cannot say anything.

She looks up at me. 'And who might you be?'

'John – from Moreton.'

'Well, I'm none the wiser for that. What do you want?'

'Your master said that I might ask you for some breakfast.'

'That's a crooked tongue in your mouth. Are you sure you're from Moreton?'

'I've been travelling for many years.'

She resumes working. 'He's a soft-hearted one, is that George Hodges. Always letting strangers sup and stay or break their fast. Next thing, he'll be having a bell put in so that any passing ragrowsterer can call to be waited on. So, what'll you be wanting? Bread and butter with sage? Or bread fried in dripping?'

'I will be more than content with a little bread and butter. Thank you.'

'Sit yourself down over there by the window. I'll be seeing to your breakfast just as soon as I get these loaves in the oven.'

I sit where she directs me, and look around the room. On a shelf above a large table against the far wall there are four copper pans of various sizes with long handles. A wooden salting tub is to my right. To my left there are working surfaces with milk dishes, dripping pans and pots piled on them. Flitches of bacon and strings of onions hang from a rail below the ceiling. In the fireplace is a spit, several gridirons and two brass kettles. A tall wooden piece of furniture – a sort of chest on legs with four open shelves above, displaying metal platters – is on the far left-hand side of the room. Near it is a tall machine in a wooden case. There is a clicking sound coming from it.

My gaze returns to the young woman. I watch the movement of her breasts as she leans over, kneading the dough. William would not have been able to take his eyes off her. She goes over to the fireplace, picks up a metal implement, and then steps around the hearth to open the wooden door to the oven. She places her loaves on a griddle inside and closes the door quickly, sealing it with clay from a wooden pail, kept beneath.

'Now,' she says, wiping her hands on her apron. 'Bread and butter.'

As she takes a loaf and a knife and starts to cut a couple of thick slices, someone rings a small bell. She pays it no attention. After four or five rings I realise it is the wood-cased machine, ringing by itself, like the clock in Chagford. It chimes eight times in all, the last dying away slowly. Then it continues with its slow clicking noise.

'Tell me,' I say, 'does every house around here have one of those in its kitchen?'

'Aw, he's a one, isn't he? Most men would've placed a thing like that in the parlour for all the gentlefolk to see. But not old George. "We country folk live in the kitchen," he says, "so that's where I'll be putting my clock."'

She hands me two slices of bread, spread thickly with butter, on a smooth metal platter. The bread is made with wheat – far from the husk-flecked brown rye loaves we used to eat.

'Well, are you going to take it or what?' she asks. 'I haven't got all day. It's eight o'clock already, and I've yet to collect the eggs, and clean Mister Hodges' daughters' room.'

I take the platter from her. 'I'm sorry for my slowness.'

'It's just Mister Hodges' other maid, Polly, left to be married three weeks ago,' she says, 'so the housework's all down to me now.' And with that she marches out of the kitchen, leaving me to gaze at this world of copper pots, white bread and light.

I eat the bread and butter very slowly.

When I finish, I sit listening to the click, click, click of the clock.

What now? There is nothing for me out on the moor. Nor here, in this comfortable house. It is poor people that need me, and whom I need.

Still I do not move from the seat. Only when the clock strikes its little bell once more do I get up. I walk over to it. I see a circle of engraved marks, which must be numbers. I see a 'ɪ', a 'ɪɪ' and a 'ɪɪɪ' in succession. I follow the remaining numbers, noting the 'v' mark for a five. I see an 'x' as two 'v's, one on top of the other.

My curiosity shifts to the window, which is of a type I have not seen before. The glass is contained in two wooden frames, both painted white. These frames each have six rectangular panes and are held in a larger, outer frame. When one frame is pushed up and the other down, as they are now, a single catch holds them in place and thus secures the whole aperture. I cannot help but think that it would be easy for someone wanting to break into this house to smash one of the small panes and undo that catch. Is there really so little crime in this country now that farmers do not need to guard against housebreakers and thieves?

Through the window I watch a pair of birds flying over the barn. Sheep graze in the small square fields beyond. A sprig of ivy just outside flutters in the breeze.

Still Kitty has not returned. And so I walk back across the

kitchen and make my departure without saying goodbye. Outside, I see Farmer Hodges walking from an outhouse with a spade over his shoulder. 'Thank you, Mister Hodges,' I call to him. He raises a finger to his hat in acknowledgement and disappears behind a linney.

I head east, towards Exeter. The lanes here have hedgerows covered in weeds, thorns and brambles. I suspect they are the remnants of the earth banks that folk created in our day – a ditch four feet wide and four feet deep, with a bank of the same dimensions. But the ditches have largely been left to silt up and fall in on themselves, so they are grass-filled dints in the ground, running alongside the lanes. The road itself between these shallow ditches has a familiar trampled strip of grass down the middle, where horses pulling carts add their manure. The edges are rutted with wheels, which crush the few weeds or grasses that try to grow there.

I recognise the twists in the lane at the next turning: from here it is just over two miles into Exeter. Occasionally I catch sight of some of the people of this time, which must be the year seventeen forty-four. Most of them are riding horses, or driving small carts. They wear front-fastening long tunics of green, blue, grey and red. The men wear black hats and white shirts, and their shoes have buckles. The women have long dresses with big skirts, and coats that cover their bodies from neck to foot. Their hats sit perched atop their strangely coiffured hair. Many wear long, elegant gloves. But a country lass who passes me hurriedly on foot, carrying a pail of fresh milk in each hand, looks very different. She is wearing a straw hat, like Farmer Hodges' one, and her shirt sleeves are rolled up, exposing her naked arms beyond the elbow. Her light-brown skirt is very high, with a belt not far below her breasts. A lad of perhaps fifteen running after her shouts out the word 'Charity', which seems to be her name, for she looks around and waits for him. I study his clothes too: a short blue jacket and brown breeches which extend to the knee, with grey hosen below that. Yet again, my clothes are obviously out of date.

About two hours after leaving the farm I arrive at the top of Dunsford Hill and look down on Exeter. There, before me, stands the old cathedral: two crenellated defenders of my time and my art. One of the two great towers has lost its low spire but otherwise the old building seems unchanged. The city around it, however, has spread out considerably. It used to be defined by its high surrounding walls. Now those walls have disappeared behind taller buildings. There are fewer gardens. There are too many houses in the suburbs to be able to see the bridge, let alone the river. It seems as if the whole city has risen within the walls like a loaf of bread, and spilled out.

I walk down the hill and pass beneath the eaves of thatched houses with tall chimneys and glazed windows. Everybody looks at me. I smile nervously at some of them. No one smiles back. Some are haughty. One man strides by with no more than the briefest glance in my direction. He looks less than thirty but he has silver-white hair in tight curls falling down either side of his head. He carries no sword – indeed, no one seems to be wearing a sword – but he wields a long, very straight stick, with a golden head on it, swinging its tip out in front of him and striking the ground with it.

When I come to the end of the street and see the bridge, I experience a snatch of joyful recognition: it is the same old bridge across the Exe that I used to take in my day, with the church of Saint Edmund at the far end. Houses have been built along its length. Clothes left hanging out to dry from the upper windows above detract from its grandeur; the stonework looks as though it is crumbling into the river. Nevertheless, it has lasted. There are still piles of rubbish on the marshy riverbank where I saw the rats nearly four hundred years ago. On the far side of the bridge I turn left down Frog Lane and see old timber-framed buildings – but even the oldest of them now have glass in their windows. There is a strong smell of woodsmoke in the air. At the end of the street there are gardens through which a wide leat runs. The waters slosh and swirl through it. I look up and see the sandstone city wall on the hill above me. I am glad I have returned; my only regret is that I am alone.

I head to the quay where several large sea-going vessels are moored. You'd not have seen such a sight in my day for, in the year I was born, Lord Courtenay blocked up the river with a weir. After that, all goods had to be unloaded at Topsham, so he could profit from the lading tolls. The citizens must have opened up the old way again. But these vessels are far removed from the single-masted hulks and cogs on which William and I sailed to France. Most have two or three masts. As for the quay itself, it is considerably longer and wider than it was, with open-fronted warehouses. Many men are busy carrying barrels and crates on wheeled transporters from the sides of the ships.

At the near end of the quay is an elegant new building. It is two storeys high, with glass windows on the upper floor and a white-painted pediment above. Crates and bound-up goods are stacked under the open arches on the ground floor. But the most remarkable thing about it is that its walls are built of small rectangular reddish blocks. These are new to me. They look like sandstone but they are harder. I wonder where they were quarried, and why such a rare and fine stone should be used for a structure down here, where only the workers and shipmen will see it.

I walk back to the West Gate, pass under the old stone arch, and climb the steep lane that leads into the heart of the city. Every building here has changed: every angle is square; every roof that was tiled is now slated; every building that was two storeys is now three or four. The filth of the place, however, has not altered at all. The streets still stink of cesspits and rotting refuse. Nor have the lines of the roads moved. They remain timeless casts of ancient paths and directions. They are the true estate of the people.

The main streets, which are cobbled or covered in gravel, are crowded with horses, wagons, carriages and small carts. The smaller carriages without roofs are mostly drawn by a single animal, the larger ones with roofs are mostly pulled by a pair. Many more people are riding than in my day, and those on foot have to pick their way carefully between the animals and vehicles to avoid injury, at the same time avoiding the piles of dung in the street. Every so often a carter has to call out to warn someone that he or she is stepping into his path, or a horseman shouts to let him past. There is clearly an etiquette as to who should make way for whom, and this applies to those on foot as well as those riding. Always it is the best-dressed people who maintain their line. One young man with white hair raises his long stick and uses the point of it to guide other people gently out of his way.

The old South Gate has been extended, with huge drum towers projecting beyond the walls; that work was obviously done in the distant past as the stonework is in a poor state of repair. The street itself is narrower and more cramped. Whereas in my day each of the hall houses was sixty or seventy feet wide, with a great arch leading to the courtyard behind, now very few have a frontage of more than twenty feet and they all have narrow doors, not gates. Every one of them is taller, rubbing shoulders with its neighbour. They each have a gabled roof, peering down on passers-by. I get the impression that they are all holding out their palms imploringly to passing customers, shuffling forward like a row of mitred beggars.

On the north side of the street, where the Bear Inn used to stand, there is a painted board hanging down from a projecting iron frame. I have noticed many of these signs in the street leading to the South Gate but this one gives me a special thrill. It shows a picture of a bear.

It is a salutary thought that something as insubstantial as a name can endure so long. I have seen that towns sometimes do change their names – as Moreton has become Moretonhampstead – but on the whole, people returning to a place years after their own time can rely on it being called the same thing. Tradition, like a centuries-old creeper of ivy, slowly winds its way into the crevices of our conversations and fastens itself on to such words, holding them firmly in place. You'd have thought that it was the private property, kept away from prying eyes and jealous fingers, which would endure. But all the houses from my time have been replaced. As for possessions, fires consume them, thieves steal them, and time erodes them. But common things, like names and roads, last for centuries.

Sunlight is reflected into my eyes from the square windows at the front of the Bear Inn. Somewhere a great bell rings – and before it has finished its twelfth call, others around the city have started to chime too. I close my eyes and try to recall how the inn appeared in my day. I remember an arch here, and the way through to a courtyard beyond. The stables were at the back of the yard, the hall on the left, and a chapel on the right – for the inn was owned by the abbots of Tavistock. There was a goodly hearth in the middle of the hall, and a staircase up to a solar wing at the back where wealthy guests could stay. Those of us who paid less bedded down on straw-filled mattresses in the hall, sometimes having a mug of ale beside our log headrests. Normally just two candles were left burning – two spots of golden light in the great darkness – so that heading over to piss in the buckets in the corner was an awkward business. Sometimes you'd hear people fornicating, as the inn's whores plied their trade. In the morning, when we all roused ourselves, the people travelling a long way would call for ale for their breakfast. Then it was a case of finding the leather-aproned innkeeper, sorting out the silver pennies, retrieving the weapons you'd left with him, and summoning the stable lads to bring your horse.

A man calls out and a covered carriage speeds past. For an instant, I catch a glimpse through the window of the tall-hatted occupant: he seems bored. A moment later he has gone, rattling down towards the South Gate, his driver cracking a long whip on the backsides of two black horses, their harnesses rattling. I watch the carriage go, pondering on the fact that these days even vehicles have glass in their windows, and those who can afford to travel in such luxury can also afford to regard the experience as tedious.

I enter the inn. There are several small rooms at the front, with low beams. Each one is occupied by an individual group. In the first, I see two men in long tunics with white, combed-back hair. One has his back to the window and is leaning across a table stirring a steaming drink that looks like mud. His companion is holding up a huge piece of white vellum-like material and talking about the loss of a warship off the Channel Islands. Apparently the *Victory* has sunk with all hands. More than nine hundred men have perished and a hundred cannon have been lost. The boat cost more than thirty-eight thousand pounds to build, he says, reading from the large sheet of vellum. I want to stay and listen to more but the man stirring the mud looks at me in an unfriendly way. So I move on, my mind reeling with the thought of a ship so large it could contain nearly a thousand men, and which cost more than the annual wages of six thousand masons like me. Think what you could build with just a quarter of that number! Vessels like that must be the cathedrals of this new age.

There is a small table set into an opening where a cheery-looking man and his female companion are being served. I watch the maidservant lay a white linen cloth across the table and set down two polished platters, and a dish of bread and butter with some cheese, and then a meat pie with a pastry top. In the next room a young man in white silk breeches and silver-coloured tunic is sprawled across a chair, and the remains of a feast are spread over the table. There are two flouncy women with him, their cheeks made very red with powder. On the table are several dark, bell-shaped bottles: he pours wine from one of them – except that he is already drunk and he spills some of it on the tablecloth. Both of the women laugh at the sight. They have no shirts on under their tightly laced robes, so they expose their cleavage to his view. He is wearing a thin sword, although he does not look as if he would know what to do with it even if he were sober.

I cross a passageway, which leads from a backstreet on my left to the inn yard on my right. Many people are talking on the other side of the door ahead. Opening it, I find myself in a lofty panelled hall with high windows on both sides, and about twenty tables. Six or seven three-cornered hats have been hung on a line of hooks to my left. There are silver-haired men sitting at one table, discussing something earnestly with glass goblets of wine in front of them. Two men seated together have white sticks in their mouths. These sticks have small bowls at the end, from which wisps of smoke are rising. I sniff the air and catch the scent of a burning herb of some sort. They seem quite at ease with this fire in their faces.

'Can I get you something, lovey?'

I turn to face the woman who has addressed me. She has a white apron and a linen bonnet. There is a pile of metal plates in her hands.

'No. I'm waiting to meet someone.'

'Well and good,' she replies, moving away. 'Let me know when you're ready.'

I walk around the hall. In the far right corner there are four women drinking some colourless liquid and laughing a lot. A man is reading a book at the table in the far left corner, using round eye-windows like those worn by the canon precentor, except these have arms that fasten them to his ears. The woman with him is drinking from a glass in little sips and watching the goings-on. In the space between these two groups, in front of an elaborate painted-stone fireplace where a good pile of logs is burning, is a table occupied by four people. They must be respectable folk, I think, as everyone else has allowed them to occupy the best space in front of the fire. On the right is a woman wearing a crimson tunic and a three-cornered hat. She has long black hair, looks about thirty and is wearing white gloves. Over these gloves are four gold rings, two on each hand, containing four different-coloured jewels. Her companions are men of various ages: a silver-haired young man with a very gaunt face; an older man with brown hair and a paunch that wants to explode from his tightly fastened tunic; and a blue-eyed, freckled, red-headed lad of about twenty. The men are not talking to each other but taking it in turns to lay down small pieces of vellum, which have red and black emblems on them. Suddenly they start laughing and pointing, the gaunt-faced man waving one of the pieces of vellum in the air triumphantly. Silver coins are shoved across the table towards him. I turn, and make my way back towards the door.

As I am crossing the hall I catch the eye of the serving woman who called me 'lovey'. She nods back in the direction of the game players. 'Clara's calling you.'

'Who?'

'Clara Coldstream. Better known as Clara Cold Dreams. I'd not turn my back on her, if I were you.'

I look round and see the four card players looking at me. I return to their table.

'You're new in town, aren't you?' asks the woman. Her two older companions take a taper from a man at a neighbouring table and set light to their white sticks with herb-filled bowls.

'I am,' I reply.

'What's your name?'

'John of Wrayment.'

'Well, Johnno. Why don't you sit down? Peter here will sit this one out so you can join us.'

She points to an unused stool at a nearby table. I draw it closer and sit down.

'What'll you be having, gin or brandy?'

I do not know either of these things. I prefer the word *brandy*, so I ask for that.

'The good stuff,' says Clara to her companions. They syco-phantically nod at her and smile.

'A man of taste and discernment,' says the man with the paunch, puffing on his white stick.

'As you can see by his clothes,' says the gaunt-faced man. There is laughter all around the table.

'They are not mine,' I say, as Clara leans forward and pinches the fabric of my sleeve, examining it.

The serving woman is suddenly at my side.

'Pint of each, Meg, my dear, if you please,' says Clara, letting go of my sleeve.

'So, what brings you to Exeter, Johnno?'

'I've come back here to do good works. I need to save my soul.'

Clara snorts. 'You don't sound like much of a cards man, neither in what you say nor in your way of saying it.'

'What?'

'Playing cards, dear. You know.' She lifts up a pile of the pieces of vellum they were playing with earlier. 'These things. Recognise them?'

'I am sorry, I've been travelling . . .'

'Where did you say you're from?'

'Moreton.'

'And they all speak like you, do they, in Moreton?' This causes a trickle of mirth around the table.

'They did once,' I reply.

'And how long ago was that? The Middle Ages?'

Everyone laughs. I smile nervously, having no idea what she means.

Meg puts two silver jugs down on the table. They are polished so much I can see my reflection in the metal. Clara fills a glass with a dark-brown liquid and pushes it towards me. I take it, sniff it, and realise it is strong, even more so than wine. Then, aware of being watched, I drink it, pouring it down my neck as if it was ale. It burns my throat, and I gasp.

'Well, at least he can drink,' Clara says to the others. 'So, are you going to play or what?'

Only slowly does it dawn on me that they expect me to play the gambling game with them. I shake my head. 'Truth be told, I'm unsure of the rules.'

She refills my glass with a weary expression. 'It's whist, dumbcluck. Everyone knows whist. Some people call it trumps.' She picks up the cards, and holds them at the ready. 'A shilling, if you please.'

I feel the brandy warming my body, making me bold, and I raise my glass a second time, and down it. 'I've no money,' I say, gasping again, setting the glass back on the table.

Clara slams the cards down. 'Then what the bloody hell did you just sit down for? Jesus! What've you got? That coat ain't worth tuppence.'

I look down at my clothes. I have no purse or valuables. I shrug.

'Then how are you going to pay for your bloody drink?'

'Me? You ordered it.'

She looks at the man with the paunch. He just grins at her. She turns back to me.

'Your ring,' she says, looking at my right hand.

'He's got a knife and all,' says the gaunt-looking man, nodding to my belt.

'Not any more he hasn't,' says the freckled lad, leaning forward and drawing my eating knife from its scabbard.

I sense the coldness of a hatred of strangers. 'Give it back.'

Clara holds out her hand and takes the knife from the lad. 'You don't seem to catch on, Johnno. No one sits down at a table with me, and gets a bloody drink out of me for nothing. So now if you haven't got any money, you're gonna have to give me your ring. Dick, hold his arms while I make myself clear.'

The freckled lad gets up and grabs my left hand, bending my arm behind the back of my chair. I do not stop him, only going so far as to draw my right hand close to my chest. I don't suppose this youth has done more than rough up a few drunken sots. But Clara deserves her nickname. Only now, as she pushes the knife in my face, does she smile.

It is like watching a tree being struck by lightning.

Three days ago I woke in a barn and was facing a blade before noon. Today the same thing has happened. But three days ago I was facing Baldwin Fulford.

'Why are you smirking?' she asks.

'The more things change, the more they stay the same.'

'Yeah, yeah, dearie. Give me the ring.'

I wait for my moment, holding her gaze, then spring to my left, swinging behind the freckled lad, using his firm grip on my left arm to turn him and push him backwards into Clara. The two of them fall into the table, sending the silver jugs of drink and the glasses flying. The boy lets go of my arm to break his fall. Furious, he comes at me again. But I step to one side and pick up the chair on which I was sitting, holding it out before me in defence.

The whole room is suddenly silent. Clara is still holding

the knife. The man with the paunch looks from her to me and back again, and takes the white stick out of his mouth.

I watch their eyes for any indication of movement behind me. 'I did not fight for the king in France only to be taken advantage of by a clutch of drunken cheats, whose church is an inn and whose communion wine this strong drink.' I look from face to face. 'As I was telling you, I came into the city to do good deeds. So, I am going to do a good deed now. I am going to leave you all in peace. Keep the knife in payment for the brandy.'

I back away, and glance again over my shoulder, and carry on backing away until I am halfway across the hall. People scrape their chairs on the flagstones as they move out of my path. No one says anything. Had this been a squabble in my own time, they would have resumed talking by now. The moment would have been over. But these people stay silent, as if the final part of this drama is yet to be played out.

'Get out, quickly. Go,' says the serving woman, beneath her breath.

I hear someone else nearby say in a low voice, 'Some have ended up in the river with their throats slit for less.'

I put the chair down and walk out of the hall. Outside, I weave in and out of the long-coated pedestrians and make my way briskly to the water conduit at the bottom of the High Street, where there is a small crowd of people waiting to fill large black-leather jugs and wooden pails. The sun has gone behind the clouds, and the air has turned colder. I hurry down Fore Street, then take a right turn towards the priory of Saint Nicholas, passing not far from where

Richard the blacksmith used to live. The houses and lanes here are totally unfamiliar. The priory church has gone. Disorientated, I take a muddy path but it is a dead end. I retrace my steps and head down another lane, turn a corner, and find myself in another small passage beneath an old sandstone-fronted house. My head swirling, I feel I am walking through a narrow gorge.

The next alley I walk down ends in a courtyard of dilapidated houses. I feel raindrops on me. I come across an old woman standing in a doorway, who stares at me as I pass, turning her head as if her eyes were fixed immovably in her skull. I see three young urchins playing in a puddle with a stick, and two old women sitting and making cloth by twisting needles and thread together in the light of an open door. For all its outward smartness and pride, the city has as many pits of desperation as it ever had. For every haughty man with a silver-headed cane there's a trio of children squatting in the gutter. The new houses on the main streets look handsome but, behind them, there are intersecting alleys of old buildings and crumbling halls, with windows that have no glass in them but which are blocked by planks of wood. A timber-framed wall shows great holes where the cob has fallen out and not been replaced: I can see straight through to the staircase in the dimness within. In one sad courtyard of mud and gravel, I see a stinking well which has moss growing over the lip of the shaft. I cannot find my way out of this chaos of dereliction, and I turn and turn, seeing decay, roughly patched walls and doors, and sheer neglect everywhere. The houses lean on their own decrepitude.

And then I find myself on a road I know: North Street. There is the old gate where William and I entered that night, when I was carrying Lazarus.

I walk purposefully back to the High Street. When I reach it, I see nothing familiar except the line of the street itself. There are buildings five storeys high with painted frontages, carved woodwork, balustrades and balconies. Most of the people here are gathered around the last few pens of unsold cows and sheep. As I watch a couple of bullocks being led up and down, I see a smiling fat woman distracting a man flirtatiously. She raises her hand to his cheek and a girl, who can be no more than nine, creeps up behind him. I presume this is the woman's daughter. While the mother smiles and draws him closer to kiss, the daughter removes the purse from the pocket of the man's coat. But the child is still learning her immoral craft. He notices the movement, breaks away from the mother, feels for the purse, then looks around and shouts in outrage as he sees the girl running away. He runs after her, dodging the other pedestrians, and catches her by the collar. He snatches back his purse and twists her ear before cuffing her. Then he shoves her hard, sending her sprawling across the mud of the street, and kicks her. A few people turn to watch and then they shift their attention back to the cattle auction.

Everyone here is fumbling his or her way through life. There seems to be no overarching design – no elegance to society. What good work could I do for them? They are all divided from each other, snatching, pilfering and deceiving. Even the houses are jostling for attention – those that are not are decaying into the mud. Haughty men with silvery hair – their vanity cries out from afar. The brandy has made my judgement poor – but not so poor that I cannot see the ugly side of life.

I walk under the arch of Broadgate, into the cathedral precinct.

The incompleteness of the recognition is painful. The cathedral yard has been fenced off, grassed, and made to look like a rich man's garden. All the old canons' houses of my time have gone, replaced by wide sandstone-fronted mansions. As for the cathedral, it feels as if I am looking at the corpse of a dear old friend who has been stripped of all her skin. The tracery of the windows is broken in places. The cloisters, where I carved that portrait of William with oversized ears, have gone. So much for my promise to William that he would always be remembered here. Now the space is filled by a line of tall buildings with walls of those small, rectangular stones that I first saw at the quay. Houses have been built right up against the north tower, dividing the cathedral green in two. The great screen of carved kings has lost all its paint. All the old stonework has decayed. My sculpture of Henry the Third has broken off at the chest. The angel beneath him, with her wing outstretched protecting the columns on which he stands, has had her eyes and nose obliterated, leaving her looking more like a ghoul from the underworld than an angel. My portrait of the kind canon treasurer has similarly had the features wiped smooth, so that his head resembles a worm with a horse's mane. I had hoped to preserve his face forever, but all this new age has received from me is a mangled lump of rock, returned almost to its natural form.

The great west door of the cathedral is closed. But a lesser door just to the right is open. I cross myself as I walk inside and meet a man in a black cassock. He is young and clean-shaven but not tonsured as a priest should be. I try to step past him but he bars my way. I try to go the other side of him but he moves.

'Tuppence, if you please,' he says.

'For what?'

'For the glory of God.' He gives me a smile, and waves at the roof.

'Does everyone in this city put money before everything else?'

'Two pence,' he says firmly.

I shake my head.

'Then you will have to leave.'

'It is not right that you should deny a pilgrim access for want of a couple of coins.'

'Your breath shows you are no pilgrim. You are drunk. Leave – or I will call the city beadles.'

I step forward and push him. 'No. God has promised me that I will not die today – nor tomorrow either.'

'You cannot enter!'

'You are wrong. Most evidently, I can.'

I walk past him and turn left to the chapel of Saint Edmund. I go up to the wooden screen separating it from the body of the church. The gate is locked. I look through the opening, hoping to see the altarpiece containing my carving of William's face. It has gone – the whole altarpiece has been removed. There is nothing there – not even an altar.

It is a chapel no longer. It is a stone box.

I hit the screen with my hand in anger, and stride up the nave. The area is now filled with wooden seats, as if people today were too weak to stand to listen to the word of God. I look up: almost every carved figure has gone. Altarpieces have been torn out and the altars removed. Effigies of the dead have been desecrated with graffiti. A beautiful female head carved by William Joy has had its jaw smashed off, leaving her face broken-lipped and ugly. The rood has gone from above the chancel screen, replaced with a huge block of timber and metal flutes. In the side chapels all the altars and all the paintings have gone, and the windows have been filled with plain clear glass.

They have pulled the teeth from the cathedral's sweet smile, leaving blackened hollows.

'You! You must leave,' shouts a priest behind me. 'You cannot enter. This is a holy place.'

'It is no longer that,' I reply, walking beneath the screen. Two more men in cassocks catch up with me. One tries to pull my hand away from the door through to the quire but I shake him off. The other tries to restrain me by grabbing my shoulder; I turn and push him away too.

'Do not presume to interfere with my calling,' I say. 'The spittle of the Devil's kiss lingers in my mouth and you would not wish it to taint you too.'

Immediately I turn and start walking through the quire. My anxiety grows ever greater as I see so much destruction about the place. The paint has gone from the walls. The altarpiece is no longer behind the high altar; it has been replaced by plain wooden panels. The great east window of the cathedral has lost its rose of blue and red light: smaller arches have been put in its place. Even Bishop Stapledon's huge throne resembles the unpainted timbers of a wrecked ship.

Then I turn and enter the chapel of Saints Andrew and Catherine.

The first face I see is William's. It no longer looks like a face, let alone that of my brother. It looks as if it has been rinsed away by the tides and is now just a vague shape. Next I turn to look at the face of my wife, by Saint Catherine's altar. She is still there, a little damaged and stripped of her paint. Bird lime cascades down her wimple, as if someone had broken a dozen eggs over her head, and left them to rot. The face opposite, which William Joy modelled on my own features, shows a little crumbling of the jaw – and another dozen eggs.

This is all that is left of us. This is all that will be left of anyone: small fragments, mutilated by people who do not care for the past nor understand what its relics signify.

It feels as though the whole building has been tossed, like a huge stone, into a deep pool. Now the small fish of mute priests swim in and out of the wreckage, blindly passing the figures of my life, not seeing them. A pike in a cassock flashes in the bright light of the stained-glass windows; bubbles rise up past the intricate beauty of a carved arch. The pike does not notice them, its cold eye is searching only for the silver gleam of another coin that might come tumbling down through the water, thrown by a visitor.

My eye shifts to a small carved head at the springing of a

vault. I carved it in my twentieth year. It was a tiny thing, the head of a bald deacon, but it gained me the praise of my fellow workers. Now the deacon's lips have been chiselled away, so there is a deep gash in the middle of his face and up one side of his cheek. It looks like a skull shrieking at eternity.

I turn to the chapel door. The three priests who pursued me are there. 'You are heathens,' I shout. 'Would you chisel your mothers' faces from their heads? Because that is what you've done to this place.' I gesture to the walls around me and the vault above. 'Every one of these stones was carved by a man. Every one of those men had fears and passions, and all of that feeling went into these stones. This cathedral was built to bring men and women together in the eyes of God, and thus to bring us all closer to Him. But your ungodly priest-hood has turned it into a faceless pile of rubble – and all for the sake of devilish profit.'

'Have you now said your piece?' says one.

'No,' I reply. 'Where are the beautiful sculptures that once graced this place? Where is the colour, the light? Where is the love?'

'You must leave, now!'

'Enough of this,' snaps the oldest and most portly priest. 'This man is going to the cells. Timothy, fetch the beadles. I want him up before the magistrates before sundown, and the skin lashed off his back.'

One of the younger men departs.

'Your charity, priest, must flow out of your arse – for nothing charitable comes out of your mouth.' The two remaining priests both advance on me and try to grab me but I kick the older one in the back of his lower leg and he sprawls forward. His companion tries to grab hold of my tunic but I beat his hand off, and give him a sharp punch on the nose. I run around the ambulatory, my footsteps echoing against the stone walls and vaulting. I pass the faces of the familiar long-dead: bishops staring up at their Creator; knights lying motionless on their sides, forever drawing their swords.

I hear shouts from somewhere in the nave and slip through into the quire to avoid my pursuers, running quickly past the bishop's throne. But more men have entered and are spreading out, trying to trap me between the seats. I dodge the first, climb over a row of benches, push another man away by thrusting my palm in his face, and run hard for the door. Beadles or constables appear there too. I slow down, trying to evade them, and am seized from behind.

My hands are tied behind my back and I am marched out of the cathedral and across the city to the Guildhall, where they lock me in a cold, windowless cell. For over an hour I wait in the darkness, sitting on the floor with my hands still tied. I hear drips from the damp walls. I smell the dank air. I hear the great bell of the cathedral ring out the second hour of the afternoon. I feel I am losing the cathedral too, on top of losing my wife and family and my brother. It is being stolen from me, sculpture by sculpture.

Before the third hour can ring, the door opens. Once again, my eyes are squinting at the sudden onset of light.

Two beadles are standing there. One of them speaks. 'This is Mister Birch. My name is William Green. We come on behalf of the mayor. He has heard the reports of your church-breaking at the cathedral, your striking of the priest, and your violent affray at the Bear Inn. He has decided that, because no damage was done to any property, no charges will be pressed. However, on account of the affray and the insult to the cathedral and its staff, you are to be taken to the workhouse at Heavitree and given twenty lashes. Afterwards you may stay in the workhouse for up to three days, on condition that you pay your way by working. After you leave you may not return to the city, on pain of further whipping and imprisonment in the castle.'

There are lines of houses now outside the East Gate, where once the town ditch lay filled with stagnant water and stinking rubbish. They are very regular in their proportions, built of the same red rectangular stones I first saw at the quay. On my right, adjacent to the area I know as Crulditch, is a flat green space where men in three-cornered hats are playing a game on a square of well-kept grass, rolling large black balls carefully towards a small white ball. There is a sense of order, and decency, as if nothing should disturb the equanimity of those that come here. I distrust it. If you look at one street of these new buildings, it looks elegant; if you look at all the rows of them, they look oppressive – for they are without curves. Here, the only concept of architectural flow is the straight line. Everything is calculated, squared off, measured and exact. The rules are cold, as if they were laid down by unimaginative men, not master masons hoping to please God.

Not long afterwards I see ahead a huge palace, set around

three sides of a large quadrangle, with a garden and orchards on the near side and fields on the other. It is about twenty bays wide along the front and ten wide along each wing, and it is built of the same rectangular red stones. As we draw closer, I see a low wall running around the perimeter of the grounds, and an elaborate ironwork gate at the front of an impressive wide approach road. Two young men are racing their horses towards us; they pass and turn off to the north, disappearing with a splattering of mud and thundering hooves. An old farm cart trundles past. A woman and her children, carrying baskets covered with cloths, make their way into the quadrangle.

'What stone is that palace made from?' I ask.

'That ain't a palace,' says one of the beadles, with a smirk. 'That's the workhouse. And it is not made out of stone but brick.'

The very word *workhouse* is hideous. It says that it doesn't matter where you come from, or how kind you are; all that matters is your labour. You are nothing more than a draught animal. If you are a vagrant, then this is where you will be brought. The old God of forgiveness has given up and shut the gates of Heaven, directing the gatekeeper to tell all those seeking clemency to go to the workhouse. Yet is not poverty a virtue? If Christ were living in this day and age, would He not have ended up in a workhouse? Yes, even He would be treated as a draught animal in this godless age.

This realisation is crushing. What good can I possibly do in a world in which 'goodness' is something shunned by the majority? I cannot support this persecution of mankind with its absolutes, its straight lines, and its lack of tolerance of human weakness. I see no beauty in a world without curves, innocence and natural grace. And yet what I think should be a natural right – freely entering the cathedral – is abhorrent to these people. In the last century, at the house of Mister Parlebone, I was troubled by the changing nature of good and evil. Now I have to confront the possibility that there is no common ground between my sense of good and these people's. What positive act can I do in this world if it will only be seen as sin?

My fear of the workhouse is not lessened by my entrance. Standing before the barred teeth of its front door, with the high roof towering over me like giant eyes, and its great wings enveloping me like those of an immense dragon, I feel its hunger to consume embodied souls and turn them into soulless bodies. Above the door is a giant version of one of those dials that formed the face of the clock in Farmer Hodges' kitchen. One of the beadles knocks on the great door. I hear several locks being undone, and eventually it swings open. All the incremental horrors of control seem to be here in attendance. And as I pass into the building – into a stone-floored hall with corridors leading off on either side – I become another body to be controlled.

The door closes behind me with a heavy thud and the fastening of the locks by a tired-looking, fat-faced man of about fifty in a black overtunic and white shirt. 'Mister Birch, Mister Green, it is good to see you both,' he says, taking up his position at a writing pedestal nearby. He has eye-windows like those worn by the man reading a book at the Bear Inn.

'Mister Pethybridge, likewise,' replies Mister Green.

'Mayor's orders, this one. A vagrant and church-breaker, found guilty of causing a violent affray and striking the cathedral choirmaster. The mayor wants him taught a lesson – twenty lashes. Following the punishment, he may stay for three nights, provided he works to reimburse the corporation. After which he is banished for life.'

Mister Pethybridge looks me up and down, and takes off his eye-windows. 'It is all very well for the mayor to show clemency but you need to understand that it makes for extra work for all of us here. This man will have to be inspected for diseases, and disinfected in a bath. We'll have to find him workhouse clothes for three days – and then wash them again at the time of his departure. We'll have to have his clothes laundered in the meantime. We'll have to feed him and find him somewhere to sleep. I've already got forty too many here as it is, and Mister Turner is not with me today. Nor is Mister Evans. I have an onerous duty as it is, sorting out the women who give notice and leave the institution one day only to play the squirrel all night at a bawdy house and beg to be readmitted the following morning. That means more clothes, more washing, more food and more paperwork. If the mayor wishes to reprimand men and women, he should just send them to prison or to the gallows, not here.'

'I will certainly pass on your candid report,' replies Mister Green. 'You could not have made your position clearer.'

Mister Pethybridge sighs. 'Doctor Hallett has not yet left, so at least the inmate can be examined. But there are only three of us here at present, so for punishment he'll have to wait until Mister Kinner arrives.'

'Then so be it, Mister Pethybridge,' answers Mister Green.

Mister Pethybridge puts his eye-windows back on, shuffles some pieces of paper on the writing pedestal, and picks up his quill. He dips the nib in the ink and looks at me. 'Name?'

'Your *name*,' says Mister Birch, kicking me in the shin with the side of his foot.

'John of Wrayment,' I say.

'What is your surname?'

'I don't have one.'

Mister Pethybridge looks at me as if I were a spider. 'What was your father's name?'

'Simon,' I say.

'John Simonson, then,' says Mister Pethybridge. 'Age?'

'Four hundred and thirty-three years.'

He looks at me over the rim of his eye-windows. 'I can easily give you ten times as many lashes. When were you born?'

'The Wednesday after Whitsun in the fifth year of the king's reign.'

'Which reign? King George the First? You're older than twenty-five.'

'King Edward the Second.'

He shakes his head. 'If you mean the reign of Queen Anne, then you're thirty-eight. If you mean King William the Third, then you're fifty-one. Which one is it?

I shrug.

'You look nearer thirty-eight. Parish of origin?'

'Moreton.'

'You mean Moretonhampstead?'

'That is what they call it now.'

'Occupation?'

'What is that?'

'What do you do for a living?'

'Stonemason.'

'Married?'

'Yes.'

'Children?'

'Yes.'

'How many?'

'Three.'

'Ages?'

'They'll all be dead by now.'

'So, no children then. Can you read and write?'

I shake my head.

'Arithmetic?'

I shrug.

He puts the quill down, and holds up the piece of paper, checking it. He sets it down again. 'In a minute you'll see the doctor, who will examine you and bleed you. But first, these are the rules. Remember them well. You will rise each morning with the bell at six. Breakfast is three ounces of bread and an ounce of cheese, with half a pint of beer. Dinner is eight ounces of beef, four ounces of bread, a pint of beer and coleworts, peas or beans. Supper: bread, cheese and beer. You will work at spinning worsted until six each day, and attend chapel on Sundays – except in your case, you will have left by Sunday. No singing at any time. No dancing at any time. No running or shouting at any time. No indecent exposure of your body at any time. Any failure to obey an order from a warden will result in whipping and loss of food. Interference with female inmates will result in one hundred lashes and incarceration in the dark house for two weeks, on half-rations, followed by permanent expulsion from the workhouse. Sodomy will result in your being handed over to the city authorities for trial and hanging. Acts of violence against other inmates will result in whipping and an appropriate period in the dark house. Do you have any questions?'

I shake my head.

Mister Pethybridge picks up the paper on which he has been writing and says, 'Follow me.' He walks across the hall, opens a door and goes through.

Mister Green unties the rope binding my hands and pushes me forward. 'Follow the warden.'

I walk across the stone floor to the door and look down a long corridor. Mister Pethybridge emerges again from the right and gestures for me to enter the room. 'Doctor Hallett will see you straight away.'

The doctor's room is high-ceilinged and glazed, with a fire burning low in the hearth. There is a thick woven fabric on the floorboards, which reminds me of the one I saw covering a chest in Master Hodge's house in Moreton two days ago. Painted pictures hang on the walls in black frames, and a small clock stands on the shelf above the fireplace. At a table, writing in a book, sits a man of about sixty. He has a small round head, grey hair turned in curls at the bottom, a white scarf tied around his neck, and a long black overtunic, which is buttoned up over his chest. He does not look up.

The movements of his hands are very precise, despite his age. A bench stands against the wall on my right; on my left is a large cabinet full of drawers.

I look out through the window. The whipping post stands in the yard at the back of the building.

Doctor Hallett glances at the piece of paper. 'John Simonson?'

'Yes.'

'I see you are a stonemason. Any history of injury?'

'I have some scars from past battles. A few more from slipped chisels and careless hammering.'

'Any severe illnesses?'

'What?'

'Have you ever experienced any bouts of a serious illness? Smallpox, for example, or syphilis?'

'I was plague-stricken once.'

He shakes his head. 'That was probably malaria. Were you living near water when you suffered this affliction?'

'It was the plague.'

'There haven't been any outbreaks of plague in this country for over seventy years.'

'None? No plague at all?' I think of the disease as a dragon preying on the people for so many years, at last being killed by Saint George.

'Not since the reign of King Charles the Second . . .'

My mind spins again. 'The second? What happened to King Charles the First?'

'I beg your pardon?'

'You said "Charles the Second". What happened to Charles

the First? I want to know what happened to the Royalist cause. They were all set to lose – they only had Exeter and Oxford left to them.'

'Charles the First was beheaded, as every child in this country knows. But the Commonwealth government fell apart after Cromwell's death ten years later, and General Monck recalled the prince to reign as Charles the Second in sixteen-sixty. Is that good enough for you?'

I think of Mister and Mistress Parlebone and wonder if they lived to see their monarch's son crowned. Or maybe they accepted the government of Cromwell and were later found to be disloyal. I have no way of knowing.

He looks back down at his book. 'You are illiterate. No knowledge of arithmetic.'

'I've never heard of it.'

'Can you count?'

'Yes.'

'Can you add up? Subtract?'

'Yes.'

'What is one thousand less one hundred and fifty-three?'

'Eight hundred and forty-seven.'

Doctor Hallett raises an eyebrow. 'And seven times seven?'

'Forty-nine.'

'Fifteen times fifteen?'

'Two hundred and twenty-five.'

He sits back and looks at me. 'Thirty-five times thirty-five?'

I see Doctor Hallett making a note on the side of the book in front of him. 'One thousand two hundred and twenty-five,' I say while he is still writing.

He looks up at me and says nothing. He crosses something out and then writes something else down. 'Where did you go to school?'

'I never went to school, Mister Hallett.'

'*Doctor* Hallett,' he corrects me.

'I am sorry, Doctor Hallett. I was never schooled.'

'And yet you can multiply faster than I can.'

He gets out of his chair and comes and stands in front of me. He looks me up and down. 'Hold out your hands,' he orders.

I do so.

'The ring: is it yours?'

'It belonged to my late brother, and before him, to our father.'

He examines my arms, my neck, my hair and inside my mouth. 'Will you please lower your breeches,' he says.

I do as I am told. The doctor looks at my private parts. 'No sores? Itchiness?'

'No, Doctor Hallett.'

'Good.' He returns to his table and takes a glass flask. He hands it to me. 'Could you urinate in this for me, please?'

'What?'

'Piss into it. If clear, it will assure Mister Pethybridge and Mister Kinner that you are not carrying a disease, which may in turn save your life.'

He passes me the flask, and looks out of the window. I have great difficulty producing anything: I have not drunk enough recently. Eventually a small trickle comes out. 'That is all I can do.'

He takes the flask from me and holds it up to the light. 'Brackish but otherwise clear.' He sets the flask on the table. 'You are lousy and flea-bitten and have a number of historic wounds but that's all. No smallpox scars. You'll be washed in the morning. Your hair will be cut then, and so will your nails. I strongly recommend you hide that ring – do not let the wardens see it. Are you otherwise well in yourself now?'

'I am,' I reply, turning the garnet of William's ring inwards.

'Turds solid and free from blood and blackness?'

'As far as I remember.'

'Good. In that case, I will just draw a modicum of blood now.'

He goes over to the cabinet and gets out a silver basin and a knife. He gestures for me to sit on the bench. Having rolled up my sleeve, he gently turns my arm, trying to catch some light from the north-facing window. There is the cut from my self-adminstered bloodletting.

'How recent is that one?' he asks.

'Four days ago,' I reply.

He says nothing but makes a small incision on the inside of my lower arm, just beside the last cut. Holding the basin ready, he releases the blood but lets it run gradually.

'Take the basin, please.'

I do so.

'You are aware, they intend to flay the skin off your back,' he says, returning to the cabinet.

'The mayor has ordered twenty lashes.'

'Such is the hypocrisy of this place.' He pulls a bandage out of a drawer.

I am surprised. 'Do you find it so?'

'Look at this building: it was designed to shield the observer from the horrors that lie within. It shows the outside world that everything is in order while containing a living Hell in which people are locked up and beaten, whipped and sometimes killed. I have been called to attend to boys who have had their limbs broken in here and young girls whose bodies have been irreparably damaged through lustful violence. Many of those whom we call idiots have no option but to come here, where they are at least fed and tolerated. You will see many lost souls staring into space within these walls. In here too are men and women who have more insidious diseases of the mind: who behave normally for the most part but cannot deal with some aspect of life, so they fight, or commit unspeakable acts, or foul themselves regularly. It is appalling that they are allowed to bring up their children in here: what sort of impression does that leave on the little ones? Yes, of course it is a place of hypocrisy.'

'But why does the king allow it? Why do you not petition His Highness and tell him what injustices are perpetrated in his name?'

'Let me put it like this, Simonson,' he begins – but then he pauses. He reaches up and pulls off all his silver hair, and runs his fingers over the few wisps of real grey hair around the sides and back. His head is actually a dome of blotched skin. He inspects the silver curls of the wig, and brushes off some dust before replacing it. 'As you can see, by nature we are revolting and ugly – or at least most of us are. Think of the old hag with her rouge and whitener; think of me with my wig. We put a brave face on things. Is that a crime? Do you think it offensive to cover up our ugliness? No. A lie is not always a bad thing. So it is with society. There are unattractive corners in our population, which must be corrected or covered up in some way. It is hypocrisy, I grant you, but it is hypocrisy with a brave face. One that makes life easier to bear for the majority.'

He staunches the flow of my blood with a dressing and bids me press on it. Then he starts to bind my arm with the bandage.

'Doctor Hallett, are we still at war with France?'

'Of course. We have been now for about three years. Why do you ask?'

'Three years? Not four hundred?'

'I know it can feel like centuries but in truth we tend to fight the French intermittently, not all the time.'

'We've been fighting every ninety-nine years. Against the French in thirteen forty-eight, fourteen forty-seven and fifteen forty-six, against our fellow Englishmen in sixteen forty-five, and now against the French again in seventeen forty-four.'

'And we'll no doubt still be fighting in eighteen forty-three too. Only this year we started fighting the French in North America, to check their colonial ambitions on that continent.'

'Where is this place, North America?'

'Its east coast is three and a half thousand miles across the Atlantic Ocean. And it stretches for three thousand miles beyond that. Sit on the bench, if you please.'

'And then what is there beyond North America?'

'Six thousand miles of the Pacific Ocean.'

'And then?'

'Eight thousand miles of the Asian continent, until you come to Constantinople.'

'So the world is round?'

'A sphere. Floating around the Sun in the vacuum of space.'

I shake my head. 'No, it is the other way round. The Sun floats around the Earth. You can see it passing across the sky, from the east to the west.'

'You're not a Catholic, are you?'

'Some say I am.'

'I would keep quiet about that too, if I were you. They intend to flog you as it is; if they find out you are a Catholic, they'll enjoy it all the more. However, for your information, the papal teaching on the matter is wrong. There is no doubt that the Sun is at the centre of our solar system. What you see when the Sun appears to go around the Earth is actually due to the rotation of the Earth.'

He picks up the piece of paper and runs his eye down it. 'Unless you have any other burning questions, I believe that is all.'

He picks up a walking stick and follows me out of the room and back into the hall. The beadles who brought me here have gone but two other men are waiting there with Mister Pethybridge. 'This Simonson is a clever man, Pethybridge,' he announces, tapping me with his stick. 'I hope you will not be too hard on him.'

'Noted, Doctor Hallett,' says Mister Pethybridge, unlocking the heavy front door for the doctor. 'I'll see to his care, don't worry.'

Mister Pethybridge closes the door and locks it again. He speaks without looking at me. 'You'll have to keep your own clothes until morning, when you'll be bathed. In the meantime, you will go to the spinning hall where you'll work until six. Your whipping will take place after that, when Mister Kinner arrives.'

I look from Mister Pethybridge's face to those of the men with him. One is a particularly unpleasant-looking fellow of about thirty. His companion is a thin man about ten years older, with blue eyes and unkempt, straw-coloured hair.

'Simonson, you will go with Mister Rogers here. He'll take you to the spinning hall.'

Mister Rogers is the blue-eyed thin man. He leads me down along a corridor on the far wing of the building to the end where there is a long hall, with large windows on one side. It is furnished with three lines of solidly built tables running most of the length of the room, on top of which there are many machines with large wooden wheels. These make a constant 'clackety-clack' rattle as men and women attend them, spinning yarn. At the end is a workshop where people sit on low benches making baskets. Two men are going from table to table, lighting smoking tallow candles on iron candlesticks, as the daylight is fading. Here and there are benches on which old women talk in pairs. Children hang around their skirts, bothering them with questions, or chasing each other.

Mister Rogers leads me to a table where there is an idle machine. He tells me that the women on either side will assist me if I need help. Then he leaves.

I sit and look to my left. The woman there is in her thirties, plain, with long unkempt brown hair, wearing a faded blue tunic with a dirty white apron over the front. She has bags under her eyes and a deep ridge in her forehead which resembles a permanent frown.

'What is your name?' I ask her.

She looks at me briefly and then returns to her work. 'Hettie,' she says.

I stare at the machine in front of me. 'I do not know how this works.'

'Watch Rose and me. You'll soon pick it up.'

I turn to my right – and my heart stops.

It is Catherine.

I stare at her. She is young again, about fourteen. She moves in the same way that my wife did. Her face looks the same, her shoulders too. Her grey skirt is dirty, and she wipes her hands on its hem without looking at it – again, just like Catherine used to do. Her hair has been cut by an inexpert hand and is only partially covered by her thin white head covering. But there is the same beauty to her that I recall from my own time.

'Catherine?'

She does not acknowledge that I have spoken to her. When she briefly glances at me, some moments later, it is due to an awareness that I am looking at her. Her dark eyes have the same beauty. But there is not a flicker of recognition.

I turn to my machine but I cannot use it. My hands are shaking.

I take a deep breath and look back at her. She is feeding her combed wool into a hole, which is twisted by the action of a small wheel on to a long metal spindle. She carefully works it, ensuring the wool remains at an even tension – neither allowing it to get too thin, so it breaks, nor letting it get too fat, so it makes an uneven bulge in the yarn. When she comes to the end of the wool on her distaff, she stops the wheel and goes to a basket against the wall behind us, and fetches some more; this she winds on to the end of the spun yarn.

'Would you help me?' I ask her, tentatively.

'Rose doesn't speak,' says Hettie, who is busy removing a spindle full of yarn from the machine.

When Rose's wheel starts moving again by itself, I look for the cause. Under the table is an artful mechanism: by moving her feet on two platforms she can drive two levers that in turn make the wheel rotate, seemingly of its own accord, leaving her hands free to even out the wool.

She notices my attention, and sees that I need help. She points to the wool basket and holds her hands apart to show me how much wool I need. Taking a piece of her own yarn, she shows me how to tie the wool on to the spindle, demonstrating how to pull the yarn through the hole, and wind the unspun wool around it. She points to the foot mechanism for making the wheel rotate. My first attempt is unsuccessful: I get the tension wrong, and the yarn breaks. She touches my hand and shows me how to twist the wool back in, as if there were no break. After a while she leaves me to continue and returns to her own spinning.

I work badly, half attending to what my clumsy hands are meant to be doing and half looking at her, pretending to be studying her skill. In truth, I am struggling to come to terms with the fact I am sitting next to a ghost who is more alive than I am.

People come and go around us, collecting wool, carrying spindles to the pile at the end of the room. All the time there is a rattling of the foot-levers turning the wheels, and a creaking of the machines. No one talks to us. Neither Hettie nor Rose seeks to communicate with me beyond what is necessary for the work. But Mister Rogers and his colleague walk through the hall, inspecting our diligence.

As the last light fades and we strain our eyes in the candlelight, the yarn on my spindle grows into a swollen bulb of thread. I take it to where Rose and Hettie leave their spindles, take another empty one and return to my seat. Rose shows me how to fit the spindle into the machine. I hardly breathe as her body comes close to mine; if I were to smell the aroma of Catherine's body on her too, I know it would pull hard at my feelings. When I do inhale, her smell is sufficient to confirm and amplify the closeness. She sits back, and once again we start spinning.

My hands fumble, the futility of my task making me a slow learner. I pause regularly. Why am I working for the people who are about to flog me? Where is the goodness in this? Does the acceptance of persecution amount to doing a good work, as I believed it did when I helped break stone at

Watern Tor? One look at Catherine, however, and my heart is touched. There is nowhere else I want to be. Even though she does not recognise me, and even though she is just fourteen, I know her kindness, and I know that her kindness is the only kindness I have come across in this whole city.

Suddenly I hear a voice behind me. 'Why are you dawdling?'

I turn. In the dimness between the glow of the candles I see a man in his early forties, with dark hair, a low forehead and a cold expression. His face is long and his chin even longer, so he reminds me of a horse, and there is an abnormally large gap between his upper lip and his nose, which is covered with hair. His black tunic is like that worn by Mister Pethybridge.

'I said, "Why are you dawdling?" nocky boy.'

I say nothing.

'You're the new one – the one we're going to give twenty lashes to, aren't you?'

I turn back to my machine, repelled by the sight of him. I glance to my right. Rose's shoulders are tensed together, with her arms clasped over her breasts. The wheel of her machine has stopped. She is staring downwards.

'And why have you stopped spinning, my rum-princess?' he says, turning to her. 'Are you cold?' He grabs her shoulders and shakes her, then leans over, and forces her arms apart, so he can clutch her breasts in his hands. 'I'll warm you up handsomely. You're certainly my favourite – because you *never* complain.'

I watch his lank hair falling down over the side of her face as he bends forward to kiss her neck.

He notices, and turns towards me. 'What are you staring at?'

Again, I say nothing.

'Are you as dumb as this doxy?'

And then there is a locking of our eyes on each other, and the acknowledgement of disgust. I stare at the veins in his neck, the slightly flared nostrils and the cruel mouth. One of his front teeth is missing.

He turns back to Rose, and runs his finger slowly down the side of her neck. She flinches again, but does not drive him off.

I feel sickened and angry. But striking him now will not help her.

'Be good, my Rose, be careful with your thorns,' he says, twisting a lock of her hair between his fingers and pulling it, drawing her head back. Then, suddenly, he lets go of her. He is looking at my hand. 'That ring, give it to me.'

I lean forward and start the wheel on my machine revolving.

'I said, "Give it to me."'

I shake my head.

He spits on the floor and wipes his mouth on his sleeve. 'That's it. Keep on spinning, nocky boy,' he says in a different tone of voice. I hear slow footsteps and another man approaching. Rose's molester leans over me and whispers aloud, 'If you don't give it to me when we whip you, I am going to cut it off your bloody finger.'

With those words, he strides away down the hall.

'What is that man's name?' I say, watching him go.

'Michael Kinner,' answers Hettie, as Rose just stares at her lap. 'The way he handles Rose, it makes yer want to shit through yer teeth. He does it to all the young ones. He'll have your ring too. I heard what he said. He doesn't make idle threats.'

'Why does no one report him to Mister Pethybridge?'

'They're all at it. As long as there are enough bobbins in that pile by the door at the end of the day, no one will say the warders are doing anything but a good job.'

'Why not leave?'

Hettie glances at me while she spins. 'I've nowhere else to go. As for Rose, she's an orphan, and stuck here until she's twenty-one – unless her next of kin come to take her away, or the mayor orders it.'

'Then ... is there not something that discourages the wardens?'

'The only thing they're scared of is the pox.'

'The pox?'

'The young ones are less likely to be diseased.'

I see that Rose still has not started working her wheel again. It is not the cold that makes her shiver. I reach out and put my hand on her shoulder, to reassure her. She flinches away.

'I am sorry.'

She does not respond.

I turn back to Hettie. 'Is it common, this pox?'

She gives a mock-laugh. 'Common? Where've you been? If it was any more common we'd all have it. How many of those silver-wigged men have lost their hair because of mercury treatment? How many of the fine ladies you see in the street wearing long gloves and high-necked dresses have hands blotched with red sores and backs pock-marked with the signs of the disease? Every whore in England must be carrying it, and thus every man of wayward enterprise, and thus every wife.'

A bell rings. All through the hall, the wheels stop, the rattling stops, and the tone of a hundred conversations starts to rise. 'That'll be supper,' says Hettie, getting up, letting her machine slow to a standstill.

The workers file out of the hall. Rose nudges me and points to the door. Slowly we all shuffle into the dim corridor. At the foot of a staircase we are joined by another crowd coming down from upstairs. In this larger group we move through to a stone-floored dining hall. It smells of rotten vegetables. There are candles to illuminate the room but no more than two or three on each long table. Children run around their mothers' skirts in the shadows. I cannot see the ceiling: it is lost in the darkness. I follow Rose's example in taking a wooden platter from a pile and queuing up for the small piece of cheese and the hunk of bread that we are allotted, and the mug containing a pint of beer. We sit side by side on a bench, in the darkness between two candles.

As I pick up my mug, two men make their way between the tables.

'On your feet, Simonson. Leave your drink and come with us.'

I take a deep breath and get up, pushing my food and beer in front of Rose. Mister Kinner spins his knife in his hand and catches it by the handle, and then points with it, directing me to follow Mister Pethybridge. 'Good thinking. You're about to lose yer appetite.'

The moon is in its last quarter: a semi-circle of silver light low in the sky. Two flaming torches are set in tall brackets in the ground. Mister Rogers is waiting beside the whipping post, together with his unpleasant-looking colleague. Their faces gleam in the light. Mister Kinner and Mister Pethybridge seize me and manhandle me up to the post, locking my wrists into iron bracelets at the top, so that my arms are forced to hug the wood. One of them threads a lace around my neck and tightens it, drawing my cheek against the oak. How many unfortunates have been forced to kiss this same dull timber. Someone tries to pull William's garnet ring from my finger but I make a fist with my hand and do not let him. I catch a glimpse of Mister Kinner glancing at Mister Pethybridge. Without a word, he takes his knife and stabs the back of my hand. I feel a surge of pain and cry out; I cannot stop him spreading out my fingers, holding my hand flat by pushing the knife against the post. Twisting the ring, he draws it from my finger. Then he pulls the knife out of my hand and uses it to cut the tunic, jacket and shirt off my back, tearing off the sleeves and leaving me half-naked and shivering.

When the first lash strikes my back it feels as though the leather of the whip sticks and lifts the skin away from my body. With the second I hear the breath in my lungs suddenly forced out of me. The third and fourth come so close together that I know there are two men flogging me, one on either side. I bite my lip and close my eyes. Soon the repeated strokes have ripped so much skin that each lash is worse than the one before. And then they start delaying them, so that I fear the stroke as well as feel the pain. After fifteen, each one is beyond agony. At twenty, they pause. I can hear them panting. I taste the blood where I have bitten my lip. And then comes another flesh-ripping lash. And another. I know they want me to complain – so they can punish me more. So I say nothing. But not knowing how many more blows I might receive makes every one of them worse.

I see Michael Kinner's face, mouth open. 'You know what that was for?'

I cannot speak.

'You know what those extra ten lashes were for, nocky boy?'

'What?'

'They were for nothing. So just try something. Next time I'll beat you until there's no skin left.'

There is a moment's pause and I feel a pail of freezing water suddenly thrown over my back. But it is not water, it is brine – and the salt jabs its clawlike sting into my skin as Mister Pethybridge unlocks my wrists. I cry out, gasping, and crouch down, but the tension in my back as I lean over makes the skin tear further.

'Stop your moaning,' he says. 'The woman we beat yesterday took thirty lashes better than you.'

I turn and walk slowly back to the door.

'Pick up your clothes,' shouts Mister Pethybridge.

I return to the whipping post and pick up the torn scraps

of cloth with my left hand. Bundling them together, I carry them inside, my whole back pierced and burning, and my right hand skewered with pain.

In the candlelit dining hall, I see a few people in the shadows. Most have left. I sit on a bench, still holding the clothes, and I stare into space.

Other inmates look at me. No one comes close.

I look at my cut hand, and the empty ring finger. It is like another lash. The worst.

I think of Catherine. The one thing that I treasure, my memory, is what causes me pain. I try to stop remembering and try to think of mercy, but the very idea seems like a delusion.

'Man is a devil to man,' I whisper to myself, rocking to and fro, clutching my cut-up clothes. '*Homo homini daemon.*'

So absorbed am I in this thought that I do not notice the figure approaching. Only when she waves her hand in front of my eyes do I realise there is someone there. I look up, startled. At first I see Catherine's face. Then I realise it is Rose. She is holding some bread and cheese – my supper – and offering it. She kept it for me. I thank her with a smile, and put my old clothes down on the bench. Taking the cheese, I break it and pass half of it back to her. She declines, holding up her hands, but I press it on her, and she accepts.

I put my piece of cheese in my mouth, and savour it. It tastes of kindness. If all the world were to turn bad, and everyone were to be touched by evil, just one good act would restore my hope in mankind.

I let her eat the bread. I have no stomach for it. I am

shivering with cold and the pain of the beating. The only good I can think of is her presence.

I ask her where she is from.

She points at the ground, then holds her hand flat at a low height.

'You've been living here since childhood?'

She nods.

'Will you ever leave?'

She nods, vigorously.

'Is it always as bad here as it seems today?'

Again she nods, slowly, and makes the gesture of the whip. Then, with her right hand, she squeezes her left breast and points back to the door.

'Listen, Rose. In the parish of Dunsford, which is only five miles or so to the west of here, there stands a very out-of-the-way house called Halstow. The farmer there is a good man, as far as I can tell, called Hodges. He has daughters and a maidservant, Kitty, who is kind, but he has need of another maidservant. They'd look after you, if you were to run away and go there.'

She shrugs. Her face is in shadows, staring into the dark corner of the dining hall.

'Do you remember your parents?'

She shrugs again.

'Brother? Sister?'

She shakes her head.

I start to tell her about William, for no other reason than the companionship of talking to her. She watches me as I tell her about how he was caught with a crucifix that had belonged to me, and coins that had the Pope's head on them. I get as far as telling her that my sentence had been to act as his executioner, and how he had given me his ring.

We both look at my cut hand and my bare finger.

With a quick look around to see who is watching, she makes the sign of the cross.

I smile at her. And as I do, she smiles at me. The most beautiful smile.

A bell rings out, and she rests her face on the pillow of her hands.

We leave the dining hall and walk to the stairs. Here there are no candles but many other people, and we merge into the group in darkness. I still have my cut-up tunic, held in a bundle before me. I cry out when someone bumps into my raw back, and thereafter try to walk along near the wall. Soon Rose is lost to me. On the first floor I sense the men moving in the direction of a candle at the end of the corridor, while the women walk up another flight of stairs to the attics. No one speaks. I follow the men into a dormitory. There is a single small light burning in here. I can just make out the mattresses on the floor, and the blankets. Not knowing who is sleeping where, I leave the others to take their places. I finally lay my rags on the floorboards near the door, and lie on top of them, face down.

In the hours that follow I think of William turning his face upwards to God and resigning his life, without saying another word. And of Rose, making the sign of the cross.

I wonder what tomorrow will be like – whether the punishments of the landless and destitute will be even worse, and the haughtiness of the wealthy even greater.

I recall little Lazarus, burning on the fire. I think of the baby, the plague marks, the flames and Susannah's scream. William once said that he was seeing his life passing before his eyes. These last days of my life – I do not wish to see them again.

I drowse, and wake with the pain of my lashed back and the cut in my right hand. But something else has woken me: the sound of a woman's scream. I hear other yells of alarm, upstairs.

People stir uneasily around me but they do not get up, even though there are many women shouting now. I rise and go to the door, but there is no latch, only a handle. It doesn't open.

'Door's locked,' someone says nearby.

'Do you not care what is happening up there?'

'Go back to bed.'

I pull the door again. I hit it with my left hand to see how solid it is. It is hollow, made of two panels set into frame. I tap at one with my boot: it feels solid enough, so I test it with a hard kick. Something cracks but the panel does not give.

'Get back to your bed,' urges a voice in the darkness. 'Do you want Kinner and Pethybridge coming in here with their batons?'

'They'll thrash you for a disturbance,' says another.

There is still more shouting from upstairs, and the sounds of a man yelling at the women, and someone screaming. I give the door another hard kick, and something splinters. I kick it again, harder. The door pane is too strong but the door frame is coming away from the wall, which is not stone but merely a partition. After ten kicks, I lurch forward as it gives way to my boot, and I find myself on the dark landing.

A hurrying lantern appears further along the corridor, throwing a little light against the walls and ceiling. The bearer pauses, as if uncertain about his direction. He decides to go upstairs. I hasten after him, hearing the sound of women crying and shouting.

There are figures in the shadows, flitting this way and that along the corridor. All around there are people speaking hastily in whispers. The lantern enters a dormitory and I follow, pushing past the women, feeling children passing between us, and trampling over mattresses to get to the source of the commotion. There is a second light at the far end. Some women inadvertently touch my back and cause me to flinch with pain, but the agony acts as a sharp reminder of how much I hate the men who run this workhouse.

'What has happened?' I ask. 'Tell me what has happened.'

'Someone's stabbed Mister Kinner,' replies a female voice. 'She stabbed him in the heart with a spindle.'

'Be quiet, or I'll have you all flogged,' shouts a man at the far end of the dormitory. 'Ah, thank goodness, Mister Rogers,' he says when the man I followed approaches him. 'Look what one of the bitches has done.'

'She got that bastard Turner in the throat,' hisses a second woman to my side.

'No more than what he deserved.'

'She'll be hanged, poor mite.'

'It's Kinner, not Turner,' says another woman.

'Deserves it,' says another.

I push forward, hearing more comments.

'Should've known better than to swive with a girl against her will.'

'You hang on to Jenny — don't want her to be having nightmares.'

'Kinner and Turner used to do it to Edith Gosling too. Took it in turns, they did: every night she had to put up with one of them. I used to comfort her afterwards sometimes. It was a blessing for her when she died.'

'Vengeance is always worth it. Kinner had it coming. They all have it coming.'

Then I hear a second man's voice from the end of the room. 'Stand back, for God's sake, give him space. Let him breathe.'

'Shit,' says a woman, 'he's still alive.'

'The worst of both worlds. She'll hang and he'll carry on soiling the next little pearl.'

'Even if the bastard lives, I hope he pays for what he's done. Scarred or something.'

'Pay? They never do. Not his sort.'

'Scars won't make him any uglier.'

I force my way past the last few women and see Mister Pethybridge crouching on the floor, tending a blood-covered body on a mattress. Mister Rogers is beside him, holding the lantern. There is a smear of blood in a quarter-circle on the wall above the bed, where blood-soaked fingers have clutched at the plaster in the act of falling. Mister Kinner is on his back, mouthing incomprehensibly, like a dying fish on land. Mister Pethybridge is holding a candle by his shoulder, trying to control the bleeding. The spindle is still embedded in Kinner's neck.

I think of the desperation of the woman who did this. Or the girl. I wonder if it was Rose.

'Give me the light,' I say in a loud voice.

Mister Pethybridge looks up. 'Who's that?'

'You called me John Simonson when you admitted me this afternoon. But my name is John of Wrayment.'

'What are you doing here? Why aren't you in the dormitory?'

'I have come to do a good deed,' I reply.

'Take this, hold it,' says Mister Rogers to his companion. Then he rises to his feet, pulling his baton from his belt. 'Get back to the men's dormitory. Or you will regret it.'

His silhouette looms before me and I back away slightly, feeling the women around me also retreating. 'Give me back my ring, which Mister Kinner stole from me,' I say, provoking Rogers to step further from the light. 'He stole it when he was flogging me.'

Mister Rogers readies his baton. But he cannot see me as well as I can see his silhouette. I let him come two more paces forward, into the dark. Although my right hand is weak it is easy for me to step forward and seize the baton with my left hand and twist it backwards out of his grasp. I kick his feet out from beneath him as he lunges to grab me, and fall on him. Pushing myself up, I bring the baton down on his head as hard as I can – once, twice. The third time I miss as he writhes on the floor, and I strike his shoulder.

'Mister Rogers!' shouts Pethybridge, who is now also on his feet, holding the lantern. 'Are you hurt?'

'Stay there,' I shout. 'Listen, all of you in here. You all know the woman who did this only did it to protect her virtue. Mister Pethybridge and Mister Rogers know that too, in their hearts. But Mister Kinner is not yet dead. In return for lashing my back, in return for the theft of my brother's ring from me, and in order that no girl or woman might suffer at his hands again, nor be unfairly judged guilty of the crime of killing him, I am going to finish him off now. If they want someone to hang for the death, they can hang me, John Simonson. So, if you'd help me in this, allow Mister Pethybridge and Mister Rogers to leave this dormitory now. Someone relieve Mister Pethybridge of his lantern.'

'You are going to kill Mister Kinner in cold blood?' shouts Mister Pethybridge. 'The man is defenceless ... It is sheer murder!' But then I hear him shout, 'Leave off me! Leave me!' He is dragged to the door, his lantern knocked from his grasp and extinguished.

Now there is just the light burning by Mister Kinner's shoulder.

I walk to the end of the room, the women making way for me. I bend down and look at the blood-soaked mattress and the dying man. His leg is trembling. I can hear his short breaths, his gasping for air. I notice his breeches are not properly up, only drawn up by one of his colleagues to cover his modesty. I see the spindle in his bloodied throat. He raises a hand but I grab it and push it down. With his other hand, however, he makes a sudden lunge for the candle. I go to stop his hand and he knocks the candle over, plunging us into darkness.

'Mister Kinner, you told me those extra ten lashes were for nothing – in case I should "try something", as you put it. Now, this is what I am going to "try" to do. I am going to try to send you to Hell.' I feel his face, and put my finger on the bridge of his nose. He moves his head from side to side. There is a gasping and a gurgling of blood in his throat. I move my fingers across to an eye socket. He continues to move his head but he knows there is no hope. I withdraw the spindle from his throat with my painful right hand and place the point there, in the corner of his eye, and push it into his skull, as far as it will go. His head stops moving. I withdraw it and plunge it in again, at the other corner. His body goes limp beneath me.

Cutting the throats of French soldiers who had fallen on the battlefield was much harder.

I feel for his hand: he is not wearing William's ring. I search his clothes and find it in a small pocket inside his over-tunic. I replace it on the ring finger of my wounded right hand, and get to my feet.

Three lights are burning beside the door. They are waiting for me.

I take up the baton in my left hand and walk slowly in that direction. In the near-darkness I am once more engulfed in the mass of women. But then someone stands in my path and does not move aside. In the silhouette of the flames I see the shape of her head. She embraces me. I cannot see her face, for the candles are too far away. But the smell of her is familiar. I know it is Rose. When I try to move past her, she holds me more firmly. Without a word, she kisses me on the cheek, and continues to hold me. She lingers there for a long moment. And then hands silently draw her away from me.

I see the men's faces in the candlelight: Mister Pethybridge, Mister Rogers and the unpleasant-looking man whose name I do not know.

'Well? Have you carried out your cowardly threat?'

'He deserved to die. This house was built to take care of the poor, and orphaned children, not to ruin them.'

'Give me that baton,' Mister Pethybridge replies.

'Let him go,' shouts a woman behind me.

'Let him make a run for it.'

'Kinner had it coming to him.'

Mister Pethybridge shouts with fury in his voice, 'Give me that baton, damn you!'

'Hit them with it, the bastards!'

I stand still. 'I'll not give it to you. I am sure you will beat me if I am defenceless.'

'Oh, you *are* going to be beaten, make no mistake.'

'You might outnumber me,' I say calmly, 'but in the dark, I'll cause all three of you to regret lifting a finger against me. I've nothing to lose.'

'Very well,' replies Mister Pethybridge. 'Have it your way. Mister Rogers, Mister Fley, we are going to take this man down to the lock-up. We will deal afterwards with the late Mister Kinner.' Turning to the women, he says, 'All of you, stay in the dormitory. Anyone who leaves will be flogged a hundred times. We will be back to remove Mister Kinner later.'

I am marched along the corridor, down the stairs and along another corridor. Suddenly I feel something whip across my back and a heavy blow on my head. The next moment I am on the ground. Their violence is severe – all the more so as they are hitting me out of guilt. I try to strike at their lights, so they cannot aim at me. But I cannot get off the floor, and have to endure the onslaught. Curled up, with my right arm protecting my head, and my back in so much pain, I hit blindly with the baton in my left hand. Only when I finally connect with a man's kneecap, and there is a yell of pain, do the other two make a last concerted effort to kick me in the chest and head. They force the baton from my grip and drag me down some stone steps into a dark cellar. There they leave me.

Breathing heavily, chilled to the bone, I turn so I am on my knees, bent over, with my forehead on the stone floor. I take stock of my pains. My back is burning, my right hand stinging, my head ringing. I am covered in blood – both my own and Mister Kinner's.

The sound of my panting is loud. But gradually it calms down, and returns to normal.

There is someone else in here, breathing too.

'Who is there?'

There is a long pause before I hear the voice that sounds like my own. It sings.

> *Ei! Alas!*
> *This night is long.*
> *And I, most unjustly wronged,*
> *sorrow and mourn fast.*

'Never has that song sounded so bitter,' I reply.

'You killed a man, John. Now the gates of Heaven are swinging in the breeze, as if the locks were broken, the hinges creaking. Fire has burned through the halls of your Lord, and all is a desolate waste.'

'What do you mean?'

'You broke the Commandment. Again. Your place in Heaven is wasted by the vengeance of the Devil.'

'You are the Devil.'

'I am your conscience, John.'

'Then are you on your knees also?'

'You know I am, as I know you are. You put me here.'

'It was no worse than what we did on the battlefields in France.'

'You did not kill that man in the name of your king or the Lord but on your own behalf.'

'I did it for the girl, Rose. Do you suppose it was an idle indulgence?'

'Nothing was supposed. You were trying to do a good act.'

'Yes, I was. And that *was* one.'

'You do not know what a good act is.'

I think of George Beddoes, who killed Richard Townsend out on the moor that cold night. Was that killing as justified as mine?

'You think of morality as something certain,' continues the voice. 'Even now you think of it as a rock on which you can rest your arm and say, "What I have done is good." But, in truth, morality is like a long ribbon trailed along in the breeze by a happy child. It floats up and down; it flickers and twists. You may take aim. Your deeds might or might not hit the difficult mark. Only of this can you be certain: morality is not something you can own.'

Over the course of this day I have seen all the seven deadly sins displayed. There was the pride of the haughty man with the long walking stick in Cowick Street; the gluttony of those at the Bear Inn, particularly the man dining with the wenches; the sloth of those idling their time away drinking; the greed of the gamblers; the envy and the lust of Michael Kinner and, finally, the wrath of whoever tried to kill him, whether it was Rose or someone else. And then there was my own wrath. I too am as guilty as the rest.

'It is the city that makes us sinful,' I say. 'Too many people. Does that not lessen our guilt?'

'It is easy for a hermit in the wilderness to think of himself as a good man. For there is no one there to challenge his declaration that all his works are good. But in the city, the judgement of a man's soul lies with others. If your fellow citizens damn you, then you are damned indeed.'

'The will of the folk is the will of God,' I say, remembering Mister Perkins.

'That is the great illusion.'

'What do you mean?'

'You will see.'

Chapter Seven

As I wake there is a bell ringing. It sounds as if a boy is running along the corridors upstairs wakening the institution. He calls out something every so often and then runs on, the slowing clapper telling me that the bell is heavy in his hands. He fits into the routine of this world like I do not. For this must now be the seventeenth of December in the year one thousand eight hundred and forty-three. I am even further from home. And even further from Heaven.

I hear many footsteps, thundering on the stairs and scurrying along passageways. I feel a piece of smooth round wood, which I realise is the baton from last night, ninety-nine years ago. What other things do I have? Apart from William's ring, and Mister Parlebone's old breeches, my boots are my only possessions.

I could remain here, in this cellar, safely for my last two days. Yet I know I will not. I have a curiosity that will not be satisfied by hiding in the shadows. I suspect that it is an instinct we all share – to know where and how we will die. Will death find me curled up on the side of a road, freezing? Or will a musket ball flying through the air lodge in my heart? Or will the demon of the plague that I know lurks within me reach up with its gnarled black hands from the pit of my stomach and push its fingers through my throat, clawing at my mind and the backs of my eyeballs, and force me into a frenzy?

I wonder what time I will die tomorrow. Will it be at night, or as the dusk comes on at five? Or in the morning? Every day of my life I have breathed easily through the hour of my death and never given it a second thought. And yet, quite soon, that time of day will be the moment of my very last thought.

I wonder what happened to Rose? Did she grow up? Did she leave the workhouse? Did she ever know the joy of love? If she did, was it because of me? I do not know if I stand to be credited with even that much goodness.

I pick myself up off the floor, and feel for the door. I touch what seems to be a handle and turn it. It is not locked.

I walk slowly up the stone stairs and into the grey light of the morning, like some ghost of a shipwreck victim returning to haunt the mariners who survived. No one sees me until I step into the main entrance hall of the building, where there are two wardens talking and a third taking delivery of a wooden crate. They are all taller than me – as tall as William was. They do not have grey curly wigs but are wearing tall black hats. Their grey breeches are long, their black overtunics cut away above their waists. Their expressions are of astonishment as they see me come from within the work-house, baton in hand, half-naked, in my old knee-length brown breeches, covered in blood, bruises, cuts and lashes, with a length of stubble now that could be fairly called a beard and my hair as wild as a furze bush.

'Who the devil is that?' says one.

'No one I know,' says another.

'You!' shouts the first man. 'Whence in God's name have you come?'

I stare at them. 'Forget you saw me. I was never here.'

'He isn't one of ours,' says the third man.

The lashes on my back still hurt. So do the bruises from last night. I leave the building and walk into the bright light of the morning. No one follows me.

The immediate approach to the workhouse is much as it was, and so are the adjoining fields, but everything else has changed. The cows are much larger than those I saw in the High Street, ninety-nine years ago. There are rows of houses of brick around the centre of town. The last spire on the cathedral has disappeared. Clouds of black smoke are billowing up from an immense chimney above a build-ing on the south side of town. There are many people on the roads: some in black two-wheeled carriages drawn by a single horse; others in carriages with four wheels; others riding horses. People are walking strangely coloured small dogs, which they have tethered on short ropes. Rich-looking women are strolling side by side, their coats covering their dresses and their hair trimmed with intricately woven thin tracery. The menfolk have elaborate beards and moustaches. They swing silver-topped sticks as they stride along or lean forward in their carriages to give directions to their drivers. And all of these people are tall. I, who used to think of myself as being of normal height for a man, now see women who are taller than me. Only a few people are shorter, and they all seem to be poor or children. A woman with an old cap on her head and a heavy basket on her back stares at the muddy gravel of the road, bent double as she hauls her load into Exeter. Also shorter than me is the water carrier, with a bright-red undertunic, a grey overgarment and a straw hat, puffing on one of those long smoking tubes as he forces his emaciated nag forward, hauling his cart and its heavy barrel up the hill.

Everywhere I look, I see something has changed. On the ground are iron bars sealing the light wells to underground cellars. Large flagstones now line the streets, so men and women are raised above the dung-smitten dust. Even the road is cleaner than it was. You cannot imagine a herd of cattle being auctioned in the High Street now: there are too many carts and carriages. The gates to the city have disappeared. Narrow, brick-fronted traders' houses seem ubiquitous, with tall windows at ground-floor level, each one filled with many rectangular panes of glass. Inside they show what they have for sale, in packets and boxes with writing on them. The more I look, the more I see words all around me. The shops have scripts above their doors, and there is writing on the doors of some of the carriages and on the clock faces that project out into the street above large buildings or on church towers. Some buildings have large words painted across them.

There is a greyness to the air and the acrid smell of something like charcoal burning. The smell is horrible, as if the whole city were a blacksmith's forge. It is as undesirable as the bowls of congealing blood that barber surgeons used to put outside their shops to advertise their services back in my day.

If the look and the smell of the city do not make me feel at home, the expressions of the people are even less inviting. I see curled lips, turned heads and expressions of shock at my appearance. If I draw near to someone, he or she walks quickly away. Children playing in the street stop their games and stare as I walk past. These people are not my folk; they are strangers from a world of words and metal. Iron-framed signs hang down from metal hangers. Every house has iron pipes leading down from its iron guttering. There are iron railings in front of many buildings, lamps and lanterns in the streets, and metal scrapers for people to clean their feet set into walls. I come across two bridges made purely out of iron – in particular, one very large one at the bottom of North Street, where the North Gate once stood.

I cross this bridge and walk up Saint David's Hill. I do not recognise the building where the old church used to stand. What is there now does not look like a church: it has a line of plain columns along its front. It seems to me that the citizens have become so beholden to straight lines that they have even started to worship them. They have started to worship words too. All around the church are many engraved stones. I stop and wonder whether people today worship God or the word of God. But then I ask myself: have they been worshipping words all these centuries, without truly knowing?

I walk down the hill to the river. Bless the river. It flows by, strong and silent, the one and only unchanging thing in this country. I can see why my namesake John the Baptist chose to baptise people in a river. It is a sort of embodiment of God: both life-giving and unstoppable. The weeds waft in its muscular flow. I run the baton through the water, creating ripples. Then I put my hand under the surface, feeling the icy purity of Creation. This is what I know and trust. Everything back there in the city – the tall, unfriendly people and the bridges of iron, the writing and the tyranny of straight lines – none of it is for me.

I step into the river, feeling the freezing cold around my lower legs, and let the baton gently slip out of my fingers. It drifts downstream.

'Excuse me,' says a voice behind me. 'Can I help you?'

I turn quickly and, in doing so, lose my balance and tumble, and I am suddenly immersed in the cold water. I put my hands out to break my fall and the pain of the wound shoots through my right hand when it hits the stones of the riverbed.

As I get to my feet, dripping, I see a round-faced man with spectacles. He looks to be about the same age as me, and not as tall as most people in this new time. He has a high forehead and his thick hair is strangely pushed all over to one side of his face. His beard is bushy and a little grey on one side. His clothes are all black, including his coat, except for a little white collar and white gloves. He is holding a very tall black hat in one hand and a silver-headed stick in the other.

'I've seen men with scars like those before.'

He has kind eyes. They give the impression that he is always smiling.

'I mean to say,' he continues, 'that such is the chilliness of the season that I do not believe you are here for a pleasure-dip.'

I look down the river; the baton is disappearing from view. 'I've lost everything. Everyone I ever knew is dead. My home is in ruins. Everything I ever owned has gone. I've lost my faith – for that was taken away from me by King Henry the Eighth. Most of all, I've lost my place in time. I know I will die tomorrow – and yet tomorrow cannot come soon enough.' I look at the man. 'Did the voice from the stones send you?'

'I beg your pardon?'

'You have no need of my pardon. It is rather that I have need of yours. I want to die, to slip under the water and join my kin, but ... Ah, now I see – the voice has told you to rescue me.'

He looks at the water, composing his thoughts. 'Do you remember the cholera outbreak of thirty-two?'

I shake my head. I do not know what cholera is.

'One morning I came down here, as I often do on my morning walks, and I found a pretty woman. She had two young children with her. She had drowned both of them, in that very spot in the river where you are now, because her husband had left her and her mother had died. She explained to me, most matter-of-factly, that she did not want them to die of cholera too. She was laying them out on the bank as she spoke to me, and singing. I have no doubt she intended to drown herself as well.'

'And you stopped her?'

'I did. Later, when the story broke, the city authorities wanted to hang her for murder but I successfully persuaded them that the woman was out of her wits and was better off in the lunatic hospital at Exminster.'

'If you would truly help me, you would hold my head under.'

'Now, come, my friend. Things are never as bad as all that. Why, even in the darkest night, you can see something, if only a silhouette of a rooftop or a branch.'

'Who told you that?'

'It is just something my mother used to say to me when I was a boy.'

I look up at the trees. 'When I was young, I understood it like that. In fact, I used to say that very thing to my sons — that it is never truly dark. But I was wrong. There is darkness: it exists, and sometimes it can be overwhelming, even when the daylight streams through the leaves.'

'If there is light and you see only darkness, then either there is a deficiency in your sight. Or you need to open your eyes.'

He holds his right hand out to me. 'I am Father Edward Harington, curate of the parish of Saint David's.'

I do not take his hand.

He leans a little further forward. 'Please? You do not look like a man who wants to drown himself.'

'I've nowhere to go.'

'Then why not spend some of your day with me.' He still holds his hand out.

'Every day now I find myself further and further from home, and lonelier, and lonelier – and there is no hope of me performing a good deed and saving my soul. Every day is composed of . . . of an unpredictable horror – no, of a horrific unpredictability. I know no one. No one knows me. No one needs me, and yet I need someone. Every day I wake and it's the seventeenth of December yet again, and another ninety-nine years have passed and I feel in pain and lost. I know I've but two days to live – and, truthfully, I'd rather not live them.'

'That is indeed lamentable. But I would point out that today is not the seventeenth of December. It is the twenty-ninth.'

'You are kind to pretend. But I know.'

He withdraws his hand. 'I do not believe it! There you are, half-naked, standing in the freezing river, telling me I do not know the date . . . Which of us is closer to his wits' end, eh? My good fellow, four days ago I shared our Christmas feast with my mother and sister. They are at home now, in Southernhay: you can ask them the date, if you so wish. You can ask anyone. Why not ask those labourers working on the site of the railway station, or the men building the new inn at the foot of the hill? Oh, there is no doubt about it: today is Friday the twenty-ninth of December in the year of our Lord one thousand eight hundred and forty-three.'

I feel deceived, ignorant and ashamed. At least yesterday I

was able to console myself that I knew what the date was, and would be ninety-nine years hence on the morrow.

Father Harington gestures at my back. 'I can see that you have been beaten and that your mind is in despair. I discern both angels and devils dancing about your soul. But it is my belief that no one is beyond recovery on Earth, just as no one's soul is beyond redemption in Heaven. So I have a proposition for you. Will you grant me this one day of your time, so I might try to convince you that life is worth living? If I fail, you can come back here and throw yourself in the water tomorrow, if you must.'

'Why?'

'Because I do not wish to see a soul in such distress.'

'Where are you planning to take me?'

'How does the idea of a nice warm bath appeal? A soothing medication for your back and a clean shirt? Maybe when we have seen to those injuries we can eat a hearty lunch. I believe cook is producing a hake and oyster pie for the three of us – that is, my mother, my sister and myself – but I am sure it will go round four. Do you know the engravings of Bartlett, the paintings of Northcote, or the music of Schubert? Have you ever drunk the juice of oranges? There are so many good things happening in the world that I am sure, were you to give me just one day of your time – one day that you say you do not want to live and so which, I assume, is free in your schedule – I could turn it into an excellent day, and one that you will be glad to have lived, even if you choose not to live another.'

I reflect on my duty to live all six days allotted to me – and my obligation to William to do what I can to save both our souls. I have no choice. I wade to the bank and climb out of the water.

He holds his right hand out again, even though I am no longer in danger of drowning. I take it in my left, and we shake. The completion of this small act seems to make him happy, for he smiles. 'I am glad. Now, I have told you my name, what is yours?'

'They call me John of Wrayment.'

'Ah,' he says, 'an ancient and noble name, "Offremont". I seem to recall reading about a Gerard d'Offremont who witnessed charters in twelfth-century Normandy.' He holds up a finger as if to stop himself talking. 'Oh, but excuse me. I'm sure that medieval history is of no interest to you. I apologise. Let me show you the way up to my house; it's near the theatre. The sooner we can get back there the sooner I can have Eliza prepare a hot bath.'

We set off in silence towards the city. As we pass a building site, he points to the rising walls. 'The first train should arrive in four months' time. Then we'll be able to travel to London or Manchester in just a few hours. I was composing a sermon on that very theme for next Sunday. For it appears to me that the inventions of the modern world are connecting us and thereby binding us all together as one people, breaking down our regional boundaries. The whole world is becoming united through God's great gift of steam power.'

'A train?' I ask. 'A wagon train? Pulled by packhorses?'

He looks at me. 'Where are you from?'

'I told you. Wrayment, in the parish of Moreton. Or Moretonhampstead as it is now called.'

'Well, Moretonhampstead's not such an out-of-the-way place.'

'But what is it, this train?'

'You see those chimneys over there?'

'Yes.'

'Do you understand what goes on inside them?'

As we walk along, I see people staring at the sight of this finely dressed man walking side by side with me, a half-naked, lacerated beggar.

'The steam engines, John,' he repeats. 'Do you understand how they work?'

'They carry smoke away.'

He stops and takes a silver round object with a glass front out of a pocket. He looks at it. 'We have time. Can you bear a short detour? The water will be just as hot when we get home.'

I am cold and ashamed of my near-nakedness, but I have just one day left to live after today. A bath and cloak means less to me than whatever it is Father Harington wants to show me. I simply nod.

As we walk, he talks about his parish. The local people, he tells me, want this 'railway station' to be called 'Red Cow Station', as this is apparently the name of the area, but he is adamant that it should be named 'Saint David's Station'. 'That,' he says, 'sounds like a place in which established and decent people might meet their fellows coming from afar. What will gentlemen and ladies from London think if they have to alight at a stop called "Red Cow"? They will assume they will step off the train to be met by fellows with straw in their hair and women exposing their breasts and bare arms, perhaps with milk pails swinging from their shoulders and an infant clinging to their skirts. It will not do. We must build for a better future, not the way things are today.'

I start to grasp that a 'railway station' is where people from London might come – like a quay. On carts called 'trains'.

The new bridge into the city is much lighter and more graceful than the old one, and free from all the houses that used to line its way. Further on, the old quay is larger than ever, and busier too. Edward Harington tells me of an artificial channel for ships called a 'ship canal' that circumvents the weir downstream. He tells me too about the brick structure at the quay that caught my attention ninety-nine years ago. It is a customs house, for a Crown officer to charge duty on imported wares. Behind it there are several tall chimneys in which 'steam engines' are housed. He tries to tell me how they work. I do not follow the explanation but I do understand the principle of the expanding steam driving a piston. Nowadays, I gather, you do not have to build your mill near a river: you may build a steam-driven mill anywhere, and it will be just as powerful as a water mill, if not more so. 'One day,' he says, 'water mills will no longer be required. Everything will be powered by steam.'

Shortly afterwards we see a wooden boat, with two masts, fore and aft, and a large waterwheel on each side. A tall metal chimney in the middle of the vessel rises almost as high as the masts.

'There,' he says, as proudly as if he had just built the ship himself. 'What do you make of that?'

I struggle to see why this boat is such a thing of amazement. She is not much larger than the single-masted vessel in which I sailed to France with the king's army, and a fraction of the size of the *Victory*, which sank ninety-nine years ago, with its nine hundred men and one hundred cannon. And I can't see how the waterwheels will work, even if the boat is blown along. In fact, if she has to tack into the wind, they'll be useless. I guess the smoking metal chimney is the key to the remarkable nature of this ship.

'Is there a mill on the ship?'

'John, my good man, no! That chimney, or funnel, as they call it, is attached to a steam engine in the hull of the boat, and that drives those two great wheels, forcing the ship through the water. This here is a boat that is driven by the power of coal! How about that – no more getting caught in a lull, when there is no breeze. No more having to tack this way and that as you sail into a contrary wind.'

I stare at the boat and then put the two together – the steam-driven mill, which needs no water power, and the boat. This vessel *does* have a steam mill inside it – one that drives the waterwheels that push the boat along. My mind tumbles at the very thought of using a waterwheel to *drive* water. This is like having a cart in which you drive horses around. It seems so wrong, so contrary to the way God intended things to be. And yet, if it works, why should it be anything other than a gift from God? Even so, I am suspicious. For if people still trust God, why do people no longer trust Him to direct the wind?

I turn and look downstream, at the placid water, and then

back to the boat. 'Folk will use it to no good purpose, I can tell you that for sure.'

'Why on earth do you say such a thing? Is it not a marvel? Do you not see how it – and the many ships like it yet to be built – will change the world?'

'Oh, I see that,' I reply. 'But I see also what changes will come of it. Men are starting to direct things that rightly only God should control. And when men break down the barriers that God has given us, there are no safe places.'

'I do not follow you, John.'

'Back in the day when the city gates were guarded, and the night watchmen were on the lookout, then a traveller was a man to be held in high esteem, and listened to earnestly. And the poor were such folk as one wanted to look after and nurture – for the good service they could render. Now all the walls of the world have been thrown down, and the world is a colder, harsher, more frightening place, in which only the rich thrive. Money has taken the place of our safe walls.'

'Most curious. But who has been telling you these things? Can you read?'

'Father Harington, I've seen it with my own eyes.'

'What have you seen?'

'I've seen all the past paraded before me, since the days of our good king, Edward the Third. One day from every ninety-nine years, one after the other. I've seen the gates of the city of Exeter standing ninety-nine years ago, albeit in dilapidation, and I've seen them at their great height, and I've seen them as they were before that. I've seen the folk of this city when they were stout enough to give their lives in fighting for King Edward and when they were so weak and poor in spirit they would charge a man tuppence just to enter the cathedral. I've seen the butchery of those that supported Colonel Fairfax, and the hypocrisy of a canon precentor, and the exploitation of tinners like the Periams. Father Harington, ask me not the whys and the wherefores, for I do not understand them, but I've seen all Christian life laid out, as on a table at a feast – and I've dipped my fingers into the sauces and I've tasted the soul of mankind in its many forms, and at the end of the day, I've got to say, it has left a bitter taste in my mouth.'

Father Harington stares at me. He starts to speak but stops himself and looks away over the boats moored at the quay. Then he seems to make up his mind about something and turns back to face me. 'You have had a vision, an extraordinary experience. No, no, that does not quite do it justice. *God* has given you a vision. That is what has happened.'

I shake my head. 'I have had no vision. I only wanted to explain ...'

'But I have to correct you,' he adds. 'Edward the Third was not a good king. He started a war with France that lasted for more than a hundred years. He taxed his people mercilessly, hated peace, and was a vile seducer of women. He was not the sort of man who encouraged free trade or free thinking, or freedom of any sort, except freedom for himself. He was, in short, a dilettante, a frivolous thing and damned lucky not to die on the battlefield.'

'No! What do you know of him? He was a man of the most noble disposition, an embodiment of kindness to his folk, and a fearsome enemy to the warriors of France. All kings have taxed their people but if a man could not afford to pay eightpence to King Edward, then he paid nothing. He loved his wife, Queen Philippa, her and no other – never another – at least, not while I lived. And it was through the love of God and his own genius, he won every battle. They say that Alexander the Great's men followed him as far as India; well I can tell you that if Edward had set out to conquer India, we'd've been there right behind him, all the way. And nothing in all the years I've seen since has led me to believe we've yet seen his like in England. Would our present army follow our king to India?'

Father Harington replies, 'Today we do not have a king. We have a queen. And she *rules* over India.'

This amazes me. Once we wondered about women reading and writing; it has never occurred to me that a woman might reign. 'But if we now have a queen in England, and she is queen of India as good King Edward was rightly king of France, it is because long ago he showed us the true spirit of an Englishman. You've forgotten him, and now you besmirch his good name. Nowadays the truth is changed. Everyone here is a stranger. And your puffing boat – I'll tell you why it'll be used to no good purpose: it is because man is a devil to man, that's why. *Homo homini daemon.* Ever since the great plague men've strived to compete and outdo one another, as if nothing is the will of God and everything is the will of man. And the cleverer that man has become – what with all his clocks and spinning machines, blowing houses and steaming ships – the more he's used all such innovation against his fellow man. Click, click, click goes the clock, and ting, ting, ting rings the bell – and it's "Do this now!" says the rich man. That boat will be used to fight and kill. It might not be this year or next, but one day, steam boats will be used to kill people. There's a great girdle drawn tight around the world, and it's being drawn tighter and tighter, and while it's bringing our bodies closer together, it's driving our souls further apart.'

Father Harington bows to me. 'Sir, I had not expected such an erudite sermon from one who seemed not half an hour ago ready to end his life. May I enquire, noting that your breeches are of an antiquated variety, if perchance you are an actor? Such rhetoric I would expect of someone who had drunk deeply of the works of the Bard. I am myself descended in a direct line from the Elizabethan poet and courtier Sir John Harington, and am familiar with many of the works of the period; thus I have had occasion to meet very fine actors who could not read a word of Shakespeare but performed his works with such facility that I could have believed them capable of penning the very words themselves.'

'I do not understand you, Father Harington.'

'Which bit did you not understand?'

'What's an "actor"?'

Father Harington shakes his head. For a long time he says nothing. Then, with curiosity in his voice, he says, 'You said that there's a great girdle drawn tight around the world, and it's bringing our bodies closer together but driving our souls further apart. Well, if that were correct, it would make this boat a sad object – a symbol of a great striving for improvement but in truth marking just another station of the cross towards our mutual dissent and eventual destruction as a species.' He looks at me. 'But I do not believe that. I cannot. Indeed, even if it were true, we *should* deny it. The progress of the human spirit is dependent on the progress of the human mind – that is undeniable. How else are we to relieve the suffering of the poor? How else might we defend ourselves against the vitriol of our enemies? Or bring the word of God to the hot-blooded tribesmen murdering wayfarers and living in sin in the hills of Africa? Yea, you stand here now, half-naked, impoverished and scourged – appearing for all the world like Christ Himself come down from the cross – yet it behoves me to say unto you that the Lord God has vouch-safed mankind with great intelligence, and it would not be a Christian thing for us to deny it or fail in any way to do good with it.'

'Then you would tighten the girdle still further.'

'No!' says Father Harington. 'I would bring countries closer together to bring men's souls closer to the Lord. I would have boats built that could cross oceans and take the grain of the wide American plains to the poor and starving. I would have boatloads of good missionary men and women teach the word of the Lord unto the African, the Chinaman, the Indian, the Eskimo, the Aborigine and the Maori. I would have the fruits of the West Indies shipped to England for the factory workers to taste and enjoy, as if they were living in Eden. I would make life better for *everyone*.'

I look down and see a stone at my foot. I pick it up and hurl it into the open water. The ripples spread out in rings.

When I can no longer see them, I turn back to the priest. 'Father Harington, I am uncertain as to what the Americas are, or even what one America is. A man did try to explain to me yesterday, and a boy told me about it the day before that, so I do not doubt that they exist. But I cannot be sure whether God made them, or whether He likes what we've done with them, if He did. Nor do I know what an esquimo is, or an aboriginey. But I do know this: tomorrow I shall see what life in Exeter will be like in ninety-nine years' time. Perhaps men will not always be so cruel to one another. Perhaps God will steer us to a peaceful and more blessed occupation of the Earth than hitherto I've seen. I hope so.'

'John, I can see that you are a godly fellow, and that is what matters most. Now, I promised you a hot bath – and I shall not fail in that promise. Come, this way. To Southernhay!'

Thus we leave the quay in a wholly different manner from the way in which we arrived. Rather than being ashamed of walking beside this priest, I walk with dignity, despite my broken flesh and near-nakedness. And we talk as we walk. Or rather, he talks. He tells me about the poor – and how it is his lifelong ambition to see that every family has enough to eat and every child has an education, and every mother has the attendance of a physician at the time of her confinement, as well as a midwife who has been trained for the purpose. He tells me about how the slum buildings that have been developed in these days of cheap labour should all be cleared away and replaced with houses that have drains and their own running water supply. He tells me about a man called

Chadwick in London who is similarly seeking to eradicate the
noxious smells that are killing the poor in cities and towns all
over England. And he talks about the cathedral, and what a
pivotal role it plays in people's lives, even though it was created in a time of 'Catholic superstition', as he calls it, and how
it has become the irreplaceable heart of the city.

'But when you entered the cathedral in the distant past,' I
tell him, 'there was a wonderful light and deep colour and the
smell of incense. There was a feeling that this was the very
antechamber to everlasting bliss. And there was a corner of
the chapel of Saint Andrew and Saint Catherine that was very
special to me, for there I carved the likeness of my wife, so
that men and women could gaze on her for eternity.'

'Then we must go and visit the cathedral later,' he says,
as we arrive at a wide door in a line of brick buildings overlooking a long thin garden, where Crulditch once was.

He knocks. A pretty young maidservant with dark hair
in a long plait down her back opens it, curtseying on seeing
him. Then she sees me – and puts her hand over her mouth
in shock.

'Fear not, Eliza, this is John Offremont: a most remarkable man who has come to us for the day. He is in need of
our assistance. Be kind to him. Is Mother Harington not at
home?

Eliza closes the door behind us. 'Sir, your mother and Miss
Harington have gone to pay a visit to the Misses Jenkins.
They asked me to reassure you they had not forgotten that
they would be dining with you here at one o'clock.'

'Good.' He turns to me. 'We shan't have to worry about

tedious introductions while you're in a state of semi-nudity that would both agitate my sister, who is of a slightly nervous disposition, and excite my aged mother to a sermon over lunch.' Turning back to the servant, he says, 'Eliza, tell cook we are now four for lunch, and ask Charlotte to help you prepare a bathtub in my dressing room, and lay out some clothes for our guest – the black suit at the left-hand end of my wardrobe, the shirt that Doctor Hibbert left when he stayed here in October, which he no longer wants. John can try on the pair of shoes that belonged to my father and which I used to wear.'

My eye is drawn up, down and everywhere. This house is opulent. The floor is made of polished wooden boards; over them lie what look to me like tapestries. The walls are not just painted a light blue; they have a white board at floor level, a rail painted white at a height of about three feet and another rail at a height of about nine feet. The ceiling is a good two feet higher than that and, up there, I can see decorative moulded white plasterwork. Huge paintings of intricate detail and colourful beauty hang on the walls in ornate gilt carved frames. There is a handsome staircase, which elegantly sweeps up to the second and third storeys, and a polished wooden handrail flows alongside it, with a glass window at the top. That strikes me as very clever: no one in my day ever imagined having a glass roof.

'Father Harington,' I begin, 'I never compassed such grace and riches behind the straight lines of these houses. I thought they were all cold and geometrical. This is beautiful.'

'Thank you, John. But you are just looking at the hallway.

First, put this on.' He hands me a dark-blue overgarment. 'Come this way, into the drawing room.'

I follow him into a chamber which makes my jaw drop. The air is warm, heated by a coal fire set in a decorated iron fireplace. The walls seem to be lined with a red silk, which shows off the paintings in the gilt frames particularly well. On the floor there is another huge tapestry of woven coloured wool, on to which Father Harington blithely steps as if it were just scattered rushes. The late-morning light streams in through a window at an angle, picking out the inlay on a round table nearby. Books are piled on its surface. There is not a wooden bench in sight: instead there are delicate chairs around this table, all of which have brightly embroidered cushions fastened to their frames. In one corner there is a polished wooden object on legs, like the coffin-shaped instrument at Mister Parlebone's house. In a large wooden bookcase along one wall are several hundred books with leather covers and gold writing on the spines. There is a clock atop a ledge above the fireplace surround, made of a sort of marble. Besides this clock are two heads carved in white alabaster, and above it there is a large looking glass, which makes the room seem bigger than it is.

Whoever carved the marble clock did so expertly. Its edges are absolutely straight, its cornices decorated with scallop-shell designs. I am in no less awe when I look at the paintings. One, in which a man in armour is shown astride a wide-eyed horse, leaping over a great chasm with a dark background, has such liveliness to it that I realise that the painters of my day did not know a fraction of what there was to be learned about depicting motion and emotion in paint. But it is not just the quality of this piece or that one; *everything* here is precious. In my hall I had few luxuries – most of the things I had were practical, for dressing and carving stone, working the land, storing things or cooking. Apart from a table board, two trestles and three benches, most of our possessions were made of earthenware, including the bowls we ate and drank out of and the vessels in which we cooked our pottage.

'Have you read all these books?' I ask.

'These aren't for reading, as such. This is just a selection of medical texts, which I collect. If you want to see my library, it is this way.'

I follow Mister Harington along a corridor to another room, the window of which looks out of the back of the house and over a small garden. The walls are covered to the height of about ten feet in dark wooden bookcases containing thousands of leather-bound volumes. Only the fireplace and the wall above it, where a large view of a wooded valley hangs, are not covered by books. The air is still and sacred – like the inside of an hourglass after the sand has run out.

'Untold riches,' I say in amazement.

'Especially if you have the time to read,' he replies. 'Alas, these days, I have too few idle hours.'

'It is the fault of your clocks.'

He takes a book from one of the shelves. Leafing through it, he finds what he is looking for, and pushes it towards me.

'I cannot read,' I reply.

'You do not need to. Look at the engraving.'

I look at the book he is holding out to me. It contains a coloured picture so close to nature that I half expect the scene to move. It does not look like a painting. It shows a large brick bridge and a series of straight lines leading through a steeply sided brick valley to a series of three fine stone bridges, under which a carriage with a funnel is passing, with white smoke.

'This is a railway?' I ask him.

'Indeed. That train can travel forty miles in an hour. If it were travelling from Plymouth to Exeter, it would take only one hour to complete the journey.'

It would take me two days to walk to Plymouth.

'This is not the Exeter to Plymouth line,' he continues. 'That, as you have seen, is still under construction. This is the London and Birmingham Railway. But do you know who built it?'

'I'd have thought it would have taken a good many people to build that brick valley alone.'

'No, no, I mean who designed it. Two men: Robert Stephenson and George Parker Bidder.'

He pauses to see my reaction.

I shake my head.

'Robert Stephenson is the son of the great George Stephenson, the father of our railways, and you'll know all about George Parker Bidder.'

Again I shake my head.

'The famous Calculating Boy, from your home town of Moretonhampstead. He's about the same age as you – surely you knew each other?'

'I think I must have left town some time before he became famous.'

'Well, then, you should know this. Long before he could read and write, he taught himself how to do advanced calculations, lying awake in bed listening to his elder brother's lessons. At the age of seven he corrected the local people on their sums, even though he could not read a single written number. Then his father, a stonemason, saw the chance to make money; he started exhibiting him in all the fairs of Devon as "The Calculating Boy". At the age of nine he was displayed before various dukes and earls, and eventually the queen, Queen Charlotte, who asked him a number of very difficult mathematical questions, most of which he answered in less than half a minute.'

Father Harington puts down the open book on a nearby table. He searches along a bookcase, withdraws a thin volume and opens it. 'Listen to this. If a coach wheel is five feet ten inches in circumference, how many times will it revolve in running eight hundred million miles?'

I stare at him.

'Bidder replied, at the age of *nine*, "Seven hundred and twenty-four billion, one hundred and fourteen million, two hundred and eighty-five thousand, seven hundred and four – with twenty inches remaining." All done in his head, in fifty seconds. *That* is why they called him the Mozart of mathematics.'

'What is a motesart?'

'Heaven's above, John! You'll be asking me who Shakespeare was next.'

'What is that round thing in that picture – above the train?'

'What? Oh, in the engraving of the London and Birmingham Line?' Father Harington lifts up the book. 'That is a hot-air balloon.'

'A what?'

'A flying machine.'

'With people in it?'

'Yes.'

'MEN CAN FLY?' I shout in alarm.

I look out of the window. Even though I see no flying objects, my confidence that I understand this world lies suddenly in tatters. Past centuries of doubt troubled me, in that I did not know what people *believed*; but this is even more disturbing for I no longer know what is physically possible. Trains can sweep between cities two days apart in the space of an hour. Men can fly up into the sky. Oh Lord! If we had had balloons during the siege of Calais we would not have sweated for eleven months before those walls. Either the French would have attacked us from the sky, where our longbows would have had little effect, or we would have flown over the walls of the citadel and dropped Greek fire on the defenders.

Eliza knocks and comes into the room. 'Bath's ready, Father Harington, as you asked, and the clothes all laid out.'

'Thank you, Eliza.' Then he says to me, 'John, I'll see you at lunch. I hope you enjoy your bath.'

I follow Eliza up the stairs to a room on the first floor. Every step of the way I stare at paintings, floor-tapestries,

panelling and rich drapery. Even the dressing room is lav-
ishly appointed, with a pale-green paint on the walls, edged
around with a light brown. There are two large highly
polished upright chests, one of which contains a number of
garments on metal hanging frames. There is a painting of
a young fair-haired knight kneeling and praying, earnestly
looking up at a light from above an altar while an older
knight looks on from the shadows. The centrepiece of the
room is an elongated copper vat, with a curved lip all the
way around. This is full of warm water, which steams gently
in the cold morning air.

Eliza tours the room, pointing out everything I'll need.
'Towels are here,' she says, pointing to a stand near the bath,
'and soap, pumice stones and sponges. Lemon juice and lye, if
you need them, and a flannel. There's a looking glass, shaving
soap and a razor, if you're accustomed to shaving yourself;
hairbrush; comb. Toothpowder, if you use it, and tooth cloths
are by the sink in the corner. Clean clothes are on that table
over there; your old ones can go in the buck basket beside it.
I think that's all. Enjoy your soak, Mister Offremont.'

When Eliza has gone I take off the coat I was given downstairs, shed the clothes I have been wearing for days, and stand
naked in front of the looking glass. I look at the growth of
hair on my chin and think of William. I decide to keep it, in
his honour.

I turn and get into the bath tub, slowly, and painfully.
The scars on my back and my hand sting as I enter the warm
water. Once in, I sit there, unmoving. I glance at the picture
of the old knight watching the young one taking his vows.

It is curious: I did not notice any knights in the streets of Exeter. But this does not look like a knight from my era. After a while I wonder if it is a modern reflection on a previous age – like someone trying to portray a scene from my own time, in the way that I carved kings and prophets from the Old Testament. Perhaps this new time of flying balloons and trains and everything travelling frighteningly fast and far has made people yearn for things from the past.

I wash myself as best as I can, using everything that looks as if it is intended to clean the body, and scrubbing myself all over, saving my back and my hand. When I have rinsed myself adequately I step out and towel myself down and set about inspecting the clothes. I wonder which goes on first. The decorative garment that men tie around their necks baffles me: how should I even begin to knot it? I leave that aside and wear the clothes that will keep me warm. I look at myself in the looking glass – unshaven, and lacking the neckpiece and hat, but otherwise, superficially, the complete man of eighteen forty-three.

I descend the stairs and find Father Harington still in his library. 'My word, John, a bath and a shirt make a world of difference. You look quite the part.'

'You are a most generous host, Father Harington. I am deeply grateful.'

'Well, that is kind of you to say so, John, but think nothing of it. So, now that you are ready, we can ring the bell for lunch and go through to the dining room to meet my sister and mother.'

'One thing first, Father Harington. I need to relieve myself.'

'Of course. Down the steps, past the door to the kitchen, through the back door and you'll see our chamber of office on the right-hand side of the garden.'

I follow his directions and find the earthen closet very smart and clean. There are two seats, side by side, of different heights. Both are of polished wood boards with a hole in the middle and a hinged wooden cover blocking the hole. There are neat piles of this white vellum-like material on the side. I reckon that I understand what they are to be used for. Apart from the materials with which one should wipe, I cannot help but feel that this is one of the few aspects of daily life that will never change, like sleep and hunger. Sitting there, I almost feel at home.

Back indoors, the dining room is decorated every bit as opulently as the drawing room I saw earlier. There are eight upholstered seats of the most elegant polished wood, and four places set. The centre is adorned with silver candlesticks, already lit. There are covered dishes there made of glazed white pottery painted with blue figures. Each place has two glasses and three bone-handled knives, two silver tools with prongs, and two silver spoons. The glass drinking goblets are of such fineness I cannot imagine that King Edward himself drank out of such elegant vessels. But what are the tools with prongs for? And how does one eat when both knives have rounded ends? It seems to me that the only thing unchanged from my day is the whiteness of the table linen.

Father Harington's sister, who is seated opposite me at the table, has three names: Mary Georgiana Harington. Fortunately, I do not have to use all three every time I address her.

I understand her to be seven years younger than her brother but she appears younger still, with very pale skin. Her hair is parted in the middle and combed straight down the sides of her head, and as she moves, it follows her around with a moment's delay. Her light-blue tunic is decorated with pictures of red roses. The sleeves are short, exposing her bare forearms. In the lobes of her ears there are pieces of gold containing dark-blue jewels.

Father Harington's mother, Frances, is old. Her long-sleeved tunic is black. Her dark hair is parted in the centre, like her daughter's, but whereas Georgiana's hair hangs down the sides of her face, Frances's is tied back behind her head. It gives her an austere look, and every time she turns towards me I feel as if I am being judged.

Father Harington says grace, in a brief manner. Then I open my eyes and stare at the array of implements.

'What is it you do for a living, Mister Offremont?' asks Frances as she puts some butter on her bread.

This question, coming on top of my current confusion, almost passes me by. I see that the old lady is using her small knife for the buttering and so I do likewise. 'I am a stone-mason,' I reply.

'How useful. Do you build churches?'

'I shape figures and pinnacles, as well as cutting the stone for the vaulting and tracery.'

'I hear from my cousin in London that they have finally put Nelson on top of his column in Trafalgar Square. Now *that* would have been a figure to work on, do you not agree, Mister Offrement?'

'My lady, my name is just John of Wrayment. I am no "mister".'

'Well, you don't need to refer to me as "my lady" either. I am not a baroness. But what about this column for Admiral Nelson? If you are good with figures, how is it that you don't move to London and work on our other heroes – I'm sure Lord Melbourne's not long for this world.'

'Or the Duke of Wellington,' says Georgiana. 'Just think how high they'll make his column when he goes.'

'For my part,' says Father Harington, 'I think Trafalgar Square is a travesty of the virtues of our age. We live in the most enlightened decade that mankind has ever known, and yet many poor men's houses were destroyed by the government to make space for that monument to military vanity. I find it quite depressing that the progressive, reforming administration of the Whigs should have swept so many homes away. Especially when it is to celebrate a man of war and an adulterer who abandoned his own spouse to live in sin with another man's wife.'

'Oh, Edward,' Frances replies, 'the people need heroes too. It is not all about finding homes and improving the living conditions of the poor. You're beginning to sound like Mister Chadwick.'

'We've got enough heroes,' says Georgiana. 'The problem is they're all men. I can read and write, discuss and dispute as well as any man – yet I am not permitted to study . . .'

'We know, Georgie,' says Father Harington. 'But there are more pressing—'

'You say you know but you never speak up for us. For you,

it's all about the poor, as if only the poor matter. Let me tell you, even rich women can be made poor by unthinking and uncaring men.'

A serving woman whom I have not previously seen enters with Eliza. They are each carrying two white ceramic circular platters. Eliza sets hers down in front of Father Harington and myself; the other woman sets hers down in front of Frances and Georgiana.

'Oh, that does look delicious,' exclaims Georgiana.

'There are only so many fights one can take on,' explains Father Harington to his sister. 'I agree, it is a profound injustice that young women from a good home are not able to attend a university. But you are not destitute, and many intelligent women are quite capable of finding ways of pursuing their interests without the burden of having to attend a college. It is an even greater injustice that the poor daughters of this city cannot get a decent education. But you say you want me to speak on your behalf. So, what should I say? That the poor families who depend on their sons' and daughters' wages should give up that income and spend more money sending them to school? They would be twice as badly off. Change must happen gradually, and first we must improve the living conditions of the poor and the income their households receive, and *then* we may be able to reform their education.'

'But you won't improve their lot until you give them decent schooling,' insists Georgiana.

'How do you find your pie, Mister Offremont?' asks Frances.

A piece of pastry falls off my round-ended knife and on to my plate. Unable to spear it, I have been trying to steady it on the flat blade while I move it to my mouth. 'It is very wholesome,' I reply, seeing Father Harington raise a segment to his mouth on his pronged implement.

'What is this tool called?' I ask.

'A fork,' replies Georgiana. 'Do they not have them where you come from?'

'We could never have afforded silver,' I say.

'Have you seen what the theatre is showing tonight?' asks Frances. 'A play by *that* playwright.'

'I've already bought tickets,' replies Father Harington.

Frances chokes.

There is silence for a long moment, broken only by the clink of cutlery against the platters. Everyone looks at Frances.

'I beg your pardon,' she says at last, drinking some water. 'I thought you said you had bought some tickets.'

'I have indeed. For the three of us to see the Marlowe play.'

'Edward!' Frances has stopped eating.

'Mother, the man was almost as clever as Shakespeare.'

'You may keep such opinions to yourself. I know the truth.'

'Oh, really?' exclaims Father Harington. 'Pray, what makes your opinion better?'

'We gave you a good education so you would not embarrass me by asking such foolish questions,' says Frances. 'In case you do not remember, I am the widow of a clergyman, and the mother of a clergyman, and it would be wrong for a woman in my position to see a play written by a man who openly denied that God existed and then made matters worse by consenting to acts of . . . of sodomy!'

'He did not consent to them, Mother,' says Georgiana. 'He wanted them to happen. Is this *Doctor Faustus* we are talking about?'

'Daughter of mine, you are NOT going to see that play!' says Frances, putting her knife and fork on the table.

'But why not?' she replies. 'Edward has bought tickets.'

'Because you are the daughter of a clergyman, and the sister of a clergyman, and I do hope that one day you will be the wife of a clergyman and thus the mother of clergymen. And any self-respecting man of the cloth who hears that you stepped into a place where that man's shameful words were uttered will hastily revise any good opinion of your virtue that you had managed to instil in him.'

'And for that I am to be chained up at home? How is it Edward can go?'

'He is a gentleman and may do what he likes. But he will face dire consequences if he does.'

'You see, sister dearest, what would happen if I spoke up for the rights of well-brought-up young women? I would not get far. Not even as far as the other end of the table.'

'Well,' says Georgiana, 'I do not see what is so terrible about a man kissing men.'

'It isn't about the kissing,' says Frances.

'I understand that,' says Georgiana, straightening her back. 'I just don't think that his playing with boys was as immoral as what a lot of men do to their wives. How is it that a man can take everything his wife owns, and beat her – even to the point of breaking her limbs – and *that* is not against the law, whereas a man making love to another man is a hanging offence? Frankly I think we should be hanging the wife-beaters, not the love-makers.'

'My dear,' says Frances, 'I thought you were campaigning for women's rights, not the freedom of sodomites.'

'I am, Mother, but you were talking about Marlowe.'

'Don't you dare say his name,' says Frances.

Georgiana continues. 'If people of your generation object so strongly to the principle that men might give other men *pleasure*, then I am hardly surprised that you have done nothing to object to the principle that they may cause women pain.'

'Mister Offremont,' asks Frances, 'do you have quiet, peaceful dinners at home? Or do you also have a family?'

'Sssh,' says Father Harington, looking at his mother warningly.

'I had a family,' I say, swallowing my last piece of pie, which did taste good. I put my knife and fork back on the tablecloth. 'I had a beautiful wife called Catherine. We had three sons, called William, John and James. But they all perished many years ago, her and them.'

There is silence.

'I am sorry,' says Frances at length. 'That is truly awful.'

'That is indeed terrible,' says Georgiana. 'But, Mister Offremont, do you think women like me should be allowed to attend a university and do things men do, such as practise as a physician or a surgeon, and vote for a Member of Parliament?'

'I really do not think our guest—' begins Frances.

But Father Harington holds up his hand. 'No, Mother, Mister Offremont is most eloquent. It would be interesting to hear what he says on the matter. Should men and women be equals?'

I clear my throat. 'With respect, Father Harington, those are different questions. What your sister asked me was whether women should be allowed to do certain things that men do today. Your question about equality – that is quite a different thing. That is about whether they should do *everything* men do today.'

'I am not sure I follow you,' replies Father Harington, who has finished his food and is setting his knife and fork together in the middle of his plate. 'But let us know your opinion.'

'I've seen many men and women in different times and places, and some men treat their women in one way and some in another. To say that one is correct and another wrong is just to pick and choose: there is no rightness in the act of choosing. But it seems to me a fair question, should women be allowed to be physicians? In my day they could be, albeit not doctors of medicine, and many of us sought the help of women when suffering a disease. These days folk have clearly decided that women should not perform medical treatments, at least not publicly. Far be it from me to say they are wrong in deciding that. But in the future, women physicians could be allowed to practise freely, as they could in the time of good King Edward. And the queen could allow women to enter schools and do learning. But that won't make them equal. Being allowed to do something does not make you the equal of all the others that do the same thing.'

'Hear, hear,' says Georgiana. 'We'll make the best doctors.'

'My lady,' I add, 'you must justify bringing this change about. You need to convince all of society that it is in everyone's interests, not just your own.'

'Piffle,' replies Georgiana. 'It is simply a matter of fairness. And the good we will do, of course.'

'My lady, I have lived many long years and I can tell you that fairness is to society what water is to a duck's back. Society does not change because of fairness: it changes because it sees an advantage. And it won't change if most people do not see an advantage. What if rich women have the vote for Parliament – and are physicians and so forth – and poor men do not? Some hard-working men might feel aggrieved if they are passed over for rich women.'

'Here comes the pudding,' says Frances. 'Now one thing I want to make exactly clear. When it comes to second helpings of bread and butter pudding, we are all equals.'

'You do find fairness in society,' says Father Harington. 'Take the telegraph, for instance. Women are just as free as men to send a telegram ...' He looks at me, and sees my blank expression. 'You don't know what a telegram is, do you, John?'

I shake my head.

'It is a message sent by pulses of electrical energy along long wires set out besides the railway lines. It arrives at its destination almost immediately. The telegraph will change the world, as surely as railways have done. People will be able to send messages at a moment's notice telling policemen to apprehend criminals.'

'Policemen?' I ask.

'Special constables,' replies Father Harington, starting to eat his pudding with a spoon and fork.

I pick up my spoon and follow his example. 'I've known some women that did not need the law to protect them. They took their advantages and disadvantages and beat them together into something that could be called fair retribution, if not equality. Women have always been able to get their husbands to do their bidding: it is an art almost as old as love itself. And women don't always need to use love. Even if you could bring about equality in law, it would not be the same as equality in life. And I reckon women get much more benefit from the latter than they do from the former.'

'I still want to see the play,' says Georgiana.

'No,' Frances replies.

'Mother, I am twenty-five years of age.'

'Then you are old enough to know better.'

There is silence.

At length, Father Harington sets his spoon down. 'Dearest sister, I will take you to the play – in spite of our mother's protestations – if you will play the pianoforte for us. Perhaps that piece of music by Mozart that I love?'

'Edward, she is *my* daughter!' says Frances.

'The Fantasy in D Minor?' asks Georgiana.

'John told me earlier that he is not familiar with the works of the great Wolfgang Amadeus.'

'Edward!'

'Mother, she is my sister. She is under my roof. She is under my protection. And when she marries her clergyman, I will be the one who gives her away at the altar, not you. Besides, the play we are going to see features neither sodomy nor atheism.'

'You mean, you have read it?' asks Frances, aghast.

'I have.'

'Devils! I don't know what to make of you two. Your father will be turning in his grave.'

'If he wakes, he'll hear his daughter playing Mozart, and that is enough to soothe any troubled soul.'

At the end of the meal, Father Harington gives thanks for the food and we leave the servants to clear away our dirty dishes. We make our way back to the drawing room. Georgiana opens up the huge musical instrument that Father Harington called a pianoforte. We settle on the soft chairs to listen.

And then she plays a few slow notes.

The music is like nothing I have ever heard. This is what people who live in the lap of luxury think is heavenly. And how right they are. It is a pure blessing. It is like the sound of reminiscence itself. As she plays, Georgiana is not looking at us; for her, the music is about divine inspiration, not about her and us. She closes her eyes. We are just bystanders while she performs the miracle on the instrument with her fingers.

I wish Catherine could hear this. William, I know, would rather run his hands over Georgiana's breasts than listen to her run her fingers over the instrument. But Catherine would love it. And she never knew such a thing. She never knew such beauty could come out of musical notes. This is why there are tears in my eyes when Georgiana stops playing.

There is a long silence, which is only broken when Father Harington says, 'That was special. Thank you.'

'It has made everything special,' I say.

'I don't know why you want to corrupt yourself by going to see a filthy play,' says Frances.

'Oh, Mother, let it be,' says Georgiana, shutting the cover of the piano forte with a bang.

'John, do you fancy going for a walk?' asks Father Harington.

We take our leave. Father Harington lends me a coat. Soon we are out, walking along Southernhay, him swinging his cane and pointing to various buildings. The sun has gone in and it is a cold, grey day now. People are out doing business. The wind is sharper than it was.

'Where are you from, really?' he asks.

'I am from the past. As I told you before.'

'Do you know where you are going?'

'The future. I have one more day to live. Ninety-nine years from now.'

'And thereafter?'

'What do you think? I suspect I will go to Purgatory. It is the length of time I must spend there that worries me.'

'John, there is no such place as Purgatory. It's just an old Catholic superstition. No amount of prayer after your death can change the course of your soul.'

I look at him. But he smiles and says, 'Who knows what the afterlife is like? Sometimes I think it is the biggest confidence trick in the history of the world. For two thousand years we've been telling people what tortures are done to you in Hell and never once have we explained exactly what is so attractive about Heaven.'

Father Harington begins his tour of the city by walking me up and down both sides of Southernhay. Opposite his house there is a wide building fronted by tall columns: this is the Public Bath House, he tells me, where there are hot and cold baths for the public to enjoy. He points out the theatre to which we will head later. A huge brick building at the other end of the street is the Devon and Exeter Hospital. As we tour the precincts of the cathedral he shows me the Royal Clarence Hotel, which is like an inn, he explains: a place for food, drink, accommodation and entertainment. One of the houses nearby is full of books: he takes me inside so I can see the leather bindings that line the walls from floor to balcony, and then, above the balcony, up to the ceiling. Old men sit at polished wooden tables reading huge pieces of vellum which Father Harington calls 'news-papers'. These, he explains, are produced anew every day, and thus readers learn about what is happening in different places. All those words need not be written by hand but can be 'printed' by a machine in a matter of seconds. And the 'paper' on which they are printed, he tells me, is not very thin vellum but a product of linen.

Of all the times I have seen, this is by far the most civilised. The carriages are elegant, the clothes tasteful as well as elab-orate. The library is a veritable palace of learning. The city's buildings have grace and light and few draughts, because they all have glass. Life, in all its aspects, seems beautifully lived. This strikes me most when Father Harington tells me he has a letter to post, and so he takes me to the post office on the High Street. Here we enter a high-ceilinged hall and, at a counter, he pays a penny for a small piece of red paper that he calls a stamp. The man behind the counter cuts the stamp from a sheet with a pair of scissors and pastes it on to the front of the letter. And so it joins many others being delivered around the country. I marvel at this. 'It won't last long,' he says to me, when we are outside. 'Soon the telegraph will connect the whole nation. Then we won't need to send letters.'

Father Harington explains many of the changes to the city. The last of the gatehouses, he tells me, was taken down about twenty-five years ago, to allow coaches and carriages to pass more easily through the streets. The great iron bridge was brought here in pieces along the ship canal from a foundry in the north of the county. He shows me the Royal Public Rooms at the top of the High Street, where the old East Gate once stood: these days, there is a hall here for 'balls', which are huge dances for well-dressed citizens. At the place where the Dominican Friary stood in my day there now stands a great ring of fine brick buildings, called Bedford Circus; the curving frontages of the houses on this oval street seem to embrace you, bringing a touch of gentleness to the straight lines of this tall architecture.

We walk down a grand street that has recently been laid out and named Queen Street in honour of the present monarch. The size and prestigious proportions of the buildings say much for the ambitions of the mayor and corporation. Next we walk up through the grounds of the castle, whose ancient walls and gatehouse I recognise. The old moat around the castle is laid out as a pleasure garden, and the law courts stand within the castle walls. So many public works have been completed that it feels as if the city has been turned inside out: what once was private now is public. Gentlemen's houses and the old monasteries have been demolished to make way for public halls, churches, libraries and hospitals, opening up spaces in the city for the people.

He takes me to a new cottage in his parish — one of five in a row. This is lived in by Patience Mudge and her daughter, Mary. 'Patience is a poor woman of ninety-three years of age,' he tells me on the way there. 'Think of that, John, *ninety-three*. Think of all the things that have happened in her lifetime! When she was born we were still using the old Julian calendar — which, incidentally, is why you thought the date was the seventeenth of December when we first met. In her youth, the Americas were ruled by the British; we transported our prisoners there. Captain Cook had not sailed across the Pacific Ocean. No one had dreamed of using a steam engine to propel a train or a ship; now you have Brunel's SS *Great Western*, which crosses the Atlantic Ocean in less than fifteen days. When Patience was born, the French Revolution had not yet happened. The Great Reform Act had not been passed. Almost all industrial power was derived from waterwheels. The population of England was less than half what it is today. Australia and New Zealand were unsettled except by their Aboriginal inhabitants. No one had ever taken a photograph or sent a telegram . . . England had barely stepped out of the Middle Ages.'

'Father Harington, I saw Exeter ninety-nine years ago, and it was just as strange as this. Everyone thinks their own time the most different.'

When we come to Patience's cottage we go up two steps and through the front door into her parlour. This room has a metal fireplace in its brick hearth, three wooden chairs, a table and a bed, with blankets and clean sheets. It has glass in the windows and the walls are plastered. The floor is bare brick. There is a wooden-framed black-and-white picture on the wall. There is a pot beneath the bed. And there are cracks in the plasterwork, and cobwebs up in the corners. The old woman is with her daughter in the back room, which is a kitchen. The daughter Mary is old herself, chopping leeks and onions on a table top for their supper, and clearly worn down by the workload of tending for two at the age of seventy. She offers us a hot drink called 'tea' as we talk to the old woman, who is sitting close to the hearth, with a blanket over her lap. I say little, holding my tea on account of it being served to me too hot. I presume the heat of the drink is to kill off the impurities in the water. As I look about the place, I am left with two lasting thoughts. The first is that, for women like Patience and Mary, life is very much as it was for everyone in my day. There may be coal on the fire rather than wood or peat, and they may drink tea rather than ale — but the routines and frustrations of life are the same. And the second is that, when I ask Patience what has been the biggest change she has seen in her life, presuming she would pick one from Father Harington's list, she replies without hesitation that it was the death of her husband. 'Because that was the day I had to stop worrying about his drunkenness and swearing, and had to start worrying about money.'

I remember talking to William, when we were out on the moor, and reflecting that kings always live in luxury. 'Time stands still in the palaces of kings,' I said that day. But here it is quite the reverse. The life of the poor is not changing half as much as that of those with money, who can go to the Bath House or to the post office. If your only family is your daughter, and she lives with you, what use is the post office?

The last thing we do before returning to Southernhay is to enter a bookshop. Inside, as it is growing dark, the proprietor lights lamps: two enclosed lanterns, two suspended oil lamps and several candles in hanging frames behind glass. The glow gives the bookshop a haloed atmosphere. Father Harington pulls volumes off the shelves and nods appreciatively at what he reads by the light of one of the oil lamps. He reads a passage aloud to me from a book by a friend of his, Doctor Forrester, which is entitled *A brief inquiry into the eternal soul of mankind*.

> In the underworld of the past, the sun does not shine and the wind does not blow. Those who attempt to write about this place can only see things very dimly, and hear the vaguest sounds, as if they were coming across an immense distance. Only the learned scholar, who dwells on an intricate detail for many years, can hope to

understand a single fact in all its complexity. But herein
lies a question: is it better to have a blurred vision of all of
the human past, or a clear one of a tiny particle of mankind's experience? The learned scholar, peering at you
over his spectacles and a pile of dusty tomes, will assert
that just a little certain knowledge is worth a ton of mere
fable. The man in the street, who puts a higher value on
a little love than the greatest victory of a dead king, will
reply that the years spent searching for an arcane truth are
time wasted.

He stops and holds the book solemnly.
'Why have you ceased reading?' I ask.
'I am sure you must find this most tedious.'
'No. I agree with your friend. The man who has no know-
ledge of the past has no wisdom. Read to me what follows.'
He looks at me. 'What did you say?'
'The man who has no knowledge of the past has no
wisdom.'
'Yes, that is what I thought you said.'
He looks at me for a moment longer, and then resumes.

How then should we regard the past? Indeed, why
should we study it at all but to prove to our fellow men
that we can, and for the skill of disputation? The answer
lies not in preferring the blurred, grand vision to the
scrupulous detail, nor does it lie in the opposite prejudice:
neither contains sufficient truth. Instead, we must find our
own way, in the sure knowledge that we too will enter that

underworld, where the sun does not shine and the wind does not blow. If we wish to understand our own place on earth, we must seek to understand those who have gone on before us. We must look beyond the present moment and see ourselves reflected in the deep pool of time as individual elements of a greater humanity, and not as the passing shapes that we may glimpse every day in a looking glass, which then are gone forever.

He gently shuts the book, replaces it on the shelf and pauses for a few moments. When he has finished thinking, he looks at me and says, 'Let us go.'

Night has fallen. But the streets are far from dark. Metal posts with glass lamps on top illuminate them. Not only can you see your way, you can see who is approaching. Father Harington explains that the lighting is powered by something called 'gas', which is like burnable air, and that every evening a team of men go through the streets of the city with a light and a ladder, setting each lamp going. It is a far cry from when I groped my way around this city in the darkness and rain, all those lifetimes ago.

Back at Father Harington's house the mood is sombre. His mother does not talk to him at supper except in the most clipped tones. 'Pass the breaded ham, if you would be so kind, Edward.' His sister seems a little regretful that she was so eager to defy her mother earlier but she does not want to admit she was wrong, so now she tries too hard to engage in pleasant conversation with her. Her efforts do not yield rewards.

After the meal, Father Harington, his sister and I set out for the theatre. This building too is lit with gas, both outside and within. We leave our coats with a cloakroom attendant, just as men visiting a manor house used to leave their swords with the gatekeeper. I follow Father Harington up a cloth-covered staircase to our seats, which are in the gallery. A pair of enormous curtains covers the stage. There is an excited chatter all around. And then the lights in the seating area dim and go out, and the curtains are drawn back.

There is a dais before us. Doctor Faustus is there in a huge library, like the one I saw earlier. One figure comes forward out of the darkness and offers him the works of Aristotle. Another emerges and offers him medical knowledge; another, jurisprudence. He scorns them all and, instead of these sciences, he holds up a Bible. 'Divinity is best,' he says. But then, torn by some inner frustration, he declares, 'The reward of sin is death: that's hard. If we say that we have no sin, we deceive ourselves, and there is no truth in us.'

I am transfixed. I feel my fingertips are just touching a truth about sinfulness, and why we must all do good works. Then Doctor Faustus says that, if we sin, 'We must die an everlasting death. What doctrine call you this? *Que sera sera* – what will be, will be?' At that I hear Master Ley's voice again: 'The thing you seek to do can only come from you naturally. You cannot make it happen.' I feel that I am on stage myself, in the drama of my own sinfulness.

Doctor Faustus is lectured by two angels, one good and one bad. Despite the warnings of the good angel, he goes to a solitary grove at night. There, using the works of Roger

Bacon and Albertus, he utters an incantation in Latin and summons up a devil, Mephostophilis, to attend on him. As he speaks to Mephostophilis, the lights around him dim to an eerie thin light. I remember the night on the moor, and the mysterious starlight in the stone just outside the stone circle: my skin is cold, trembling with the anticipation of real mysteries and deep truths.

Mephostophilis steps forward and speaks, in the form of a Franciscan friar: 'I am a servant to great Lucifer, and may not follow you without his leave.'

'Was not that Lucifer an angel once?'

'Yes, Faustus, and most dearly loved of God.'

'How comes it, then, that he is prince of devils?'

'O, by aspiring pride and insolence, for which God threw him from the face of Heaven.'

'And what are you that live with Lucifer?'

'Unhappy spirits that fell with Lucifer, conspired against our God with Lucifer, and are forever damned with Lucifer.'

'Where are you damned?' asks Faustus.

'In Hell,' Mephostophilis replies.

'How comes it, then, that you are out of Hell?'

'Why, this is Hell, nor am I out of it. Do you think that I, who saw the face of God, and tasted the eternal joys of Heaven, am not tormented with ten thousand hells, in being deprived of everlasting bliss?'

I cannot help but let out a gasp of alarm. Could *this* place be Hell? Are these people around me here not in Hell with me? Perhaps they, with their luxurious dining rooms and forks and pianoforte music and baths and paintings, are being prepared for Hell – being shown the treasures of eternity only to lose them all.

Georgiana prods me in the ribs. 'John, you must keep quiet. And do lean back. People behind you cannot see.'

The next time we meet Faustus he is in his library again, asking himself 'Must you needs be damned – can you not be saved?' Mephostophilis tells him that Lucifer is offering him an agreement. For twenty-four years Faustus may have whatever he wants – money, power, knowledge and magic – but after those twenty-four years are up, Lucifer will come for his soul, and he will be damned forever. To agree the compact he must bequeath his soul to Lucifer in a deed, signed with his own blood.

From the moment that Faustus stabs his arm and signs the bond, all is a descending spiral of mayhem. Giant dark devils appear on the stage, with Lucifer among them, and Lucifer declares to the wavering Faustus, 'Christ cannot save your soul for He is just!' Where does that leave me, I wonder? Have I sinned so much that Christ can no longer save me? Oh Lord! And what about William? Faustus summons Helen of Troy from the ancient world to satiate his lust, and he kisses her – at which Lucifer reappears with Mephostophilis and Beelzebub with him, to take him down to Hell.

This is my fate and William's being played out before me by some unknown, terrible power, written in an ancient book, long ago. I see the evil angel step forward to take the stage but I hear the voice that I heard at the cathedral, at Scorhill and in the cellar of the workhouse. The voice of my fate is addressing me as if I am Faustus. 'Let your eyes with horror stare into that vast perpetual torture-house. There are the Furies tossing damned souls on burning forks; there bodies boil in lead; there are live quarters broiling on the coals, that never can die . . .'

'I have seen enough!' I cry. 'I have seen enough to torture me!'

The evil angel looks up at me in the gallery and says, pointing at me, 'Nay, you must feel them, taste the smart of all. He that loves pleasure must for pleasure fall. And so I leave you, Faustus, till anon; then will you tumble in confusion.'

Suddenly there is silence.

'John,' whispers Father Harington, 'are you unwell? Do you need to leave?'

I am shaking, trembling. And I want to answer yes, I will leave now, but before I can say anything I hear the voice of my conscience coming from the stage, addressing me.

'Now you have but one bare hour to live, and then you must be damned perpetually!'

A clock strikes eleven times.

'What can I do?' I say. 'How might I repent?'

People around me tell me to be quiet.

But Faustus speaks again in the voice of my conscience. 'O, half the hour is past! It will all be past anon. May you live in Hell a thousand years, a hundred thousand! No end is limited to damned souls.'

'I repent!' I shout, standing up and being pulled back and hearing hissing and shouting all around me. 'I repent! I repent!'

But Faustus is not satisfied. 'This soul should fly from you, and you be changed into some brutish beast! All beasts are happy, for, when they die, their souls are soon dissolved in elements. But you must live still to be plagued in Hell. Cursed be the parents that engendered you!'

'No, Faustus, curse Lucifer,' I cry, as people shout all around me. 'It is he who has deprived me of the joys of Heaven.'

And over the tumult I hear a clock chiming once, twice – all of twelve times. As it rings out I stare at those in the seats around me and see they are all snakes and bears, wolves and killing animals. From them I hear the verdict. 'It strikes, it strikes! Now, body, turn to air, or Lucifer will bear thee quick to Hell! O soul, be changed into small water-drops, and fall into the ocean, never be found!'

They seize me, from all sides. I hear myself crying, 'O mercy, Heaven! Look not so fierce on me! Adders and serpents, let me breathe a while! Ugly Hell, gape not! Come not, Lucifer! Come not, Lucifer! Come not, Lucifer!'

The next thing I know is that I am lying, painfully, on my back. I can hear the clicking of a clock, the crackle of a fire. And the voice of Frances Harington on the far side of the room.

'I told you that nothing good would come of taking him to see a play by an atheist.'

'No you did not, Mother,' replies Georgiana. 'It was me you told not to go.'

'I think it was a case of the impact when he fell,' says the voice of a man whom I do not know. 'It can affect the brain in the most extraordinary ways.'

'Well,' replies Frances, 'I have to say that I am ashamed that he should have been so overcome and my own good Christian children should prove inured to naked heresies and bestiality. It was not the way they were brought up.'

'There was no bestiality!' exclaims Georgiana.

'In that case, no doubt you were mightily disappointed,' says Frances.

'Thank you, Doctor,' says Father Harington. 'Please add this evening's call to my bill.'

'Thank you, Father, I will. And now if I may have my coat and hat, I'll wish you an easy night.'

I blink. I seem to be on some sort of narrow bed in the drawing room of Father Harington's house. They have taken off my overtunic but otherwise I am fully clothed. There are several blankets draped over me.

I turn my head and see Father Harington. 'The hour is drawing near,' I whisper.

'I am sorry the play upset you.'

'It was a warning. It is a most moral play. You should take your mother to see it.'

'Is our guest pulling through?' asks Frances, in a politely loud voice from the doorway.

'He is, Mother. He will be fine.'

'Good. In that case I will retire for the night. Come on, Georgiana, you too. Goodnight, Mister Offremont, I hope your condition improves before morning. Just ring the bell for Eliza if you want anything in the night.'

'Goodnight, Mister Offremont,' says Georgiana.

I hear the door close.

Father Harington takes my left hand in his hands. 'Tell me, John, what was it that so affected you?'

I make the sign of the cross on my breast. 'Just as Doctor Faustus could not step aside from the pact he made with the Devil, so it is with me. I've but one day to live.'

'John, do not say that.'

'It is true. I made a pact once. And the spirit with whom I made it was there tonight. I heard him.'

'Then he is your evil angel and I am your good one. Give up this pact.'

I look up at the ceiling. 'It is not so easy, Father. The only reason why I am here is because of it. To give it up would be to die now.'

'John, promise me that you will not try to take your own life again.'

'You have been very good to me, Father Harington. But I once undertook a quest, and I am still engaged upon it. I did it in the hope of being good to others. I've failed every step of the way.'

'John ...'

'Father Harington. There are precious few men who are truly sent from God. But I believe you are one of them. Where I was last, I saw all around me the Seven Deadly Sins, in the flesh. They all spoke to me. Tonight, I saw them all again, on the stage. And I thought to myself, where are the Seven Cardinal Virtues? Now I see. They are in you: chastity, temperance, liberality, diligence, patience, kindness and humility. I've no doubt that, on account of your virtues, the next and final stage of my journey will be the best. The world will be a better place in ninety-nine years on account of men such as you, I've no doubt now. But still I am afraid – more afraid than ever.'

I hear the clock chime. It rings twelve times.

'Leave me now,' I say. 'I do not want you to see me depart.'

Father Harington nods gently. 'I hope you sleep well, John. Is there anything else you need? There are more blankets here. The bell rope is by the door, if you need to call the servants in the night. Ask them to wake me.'

'Goodnight, Father Harington. And thank you.'

'I will pray for you,' he says, laying a hand on my breast, and leaving it there a moment. Then, getting to his feet, he says, 'We never went to the cathedral, did we? I never saw the sculpture of your wife.'

'You can see her tomorrow,' I reply. 'I pray that I will too. In Paradise.'

Chapter Eight

I hear Hell long before I see it. A huge droning sound, as if a hundred thousand knives are being sharpened on a hundred thousand granite boulders, which are in turn rolling across a rocky landscape with such crushing force that no obstacle can stop them. And yet this immense noise is not without a tone. It contains the low hum of a bow drawn slowly across the strings that bind Heaven and Earth.

There are crosses in the sky. A dozen droning crosses, flying westwards.

Nothing in all the ages could have prepared me for this. The voices I heard at the stones were not so unnerving. Even the plague itself was easier to understand than this array of black flying crucifixes. I lie still, hating the noise, fearing it. And then it dies away.

Father Harington's house is gone. Around me there is splintered painted wood and broken slates, pieces of mangled ironwork and huge amounts of shattered pottery and glass. There is no ceiling or roof above me; there are no walls except the one that looks out over the street. All the neighbouring houses have gone too – I can see for a hundred yards in each direction. All that is left is the façade of the row of eight houses. Here and there is a small relic in the rubble to show that this was someone's home: a white leather baby's shoe, a clock face without a clock. I can see a fragment of a gilt picture frame, the front of a wooden drawer with a blackened brass handle, and a scorched book. A dented and discoloured copper saucepan. The arm of a small sculpted figure.

It would have taken many men several days to destroy the houses like this, and everything in them, ripping off the roof and pulling down all the walls and floors. Why, if they were prepared to go to such an extent, did they not finish the job and pull down the façade too? This destruction can only have been the work of men with siege engines or a great cannon.

Stepping through the rubble I see more signs of a home rent apart. In a small wooden frame, with glass across the front, is a picture of a young husband and wife. It is a black-and-white picture, but otherwise so detailed in its portrayal of their features and moods that one might have thought that Nature herself had frozen within the frame. The young woman holds a small bunch of flowers and is wearing a long white tunic, and has a veil lifted up over her head. The young man looks very proud, wearing a black upper tunic and breeches, with a tall shiny hat. They are standing outside a

church, and smiling. But the glass across the front of the picture is cracked. And what of the couple themselves? Do they
lie now beneath this debris?

I am still wearing the suit of clothes and black shoes
that Father Harington lent to me. Nothing I have is my
own; the only thing that has lasted from my own time is
William's ring. I raise this to my lips and kiss it, in memory
of him.

Leaving the house, I climb past the wooden barricade outside the front door, and feel unsteady and sick. The air stinks
of things burning. The road looks and smells strange. There
are boards down over the grass on Southernhay; the buildings
on the other side of the road lie in ruins. But in the centre
of this scene is a monstrous covered wagon, with large black
wheels and a chamber made of dark-red iron. This chamber
has glass windows and doors in its sides, and an enormous
carrying space at the back. Surely no beast could possibly pull
such a vehicle? How much larger could horses and bullocks
have grown to draw this?

Suddenly the wagon gives a huge burst of noise, like that
of the flying crosses, and a cloud of stinking smoke billows
from the back. The throbbing cacophony increases still further in volume. I can't hear anything but its terrible roaring
and raging. And then, just when I am about to run, it moves
away – without anything dragging, pushing or pulling it.

Astonished, I watch it disappearing down the road, leaving
a stinking trail of smoke, sickened in my mind and by the
taste the smoke has left behind.

Roger Bacon foresaw this. If only I could go back and tell

Master Ley. What were his words? 'Friar Bacon wrote of chariots that could move at the most incredible speeds without a single draught animal.' But it leaves no delight in me. Rather, it is as if I have stumbled into some vast cathedral of unsuspected knowledge. Its vaults look like sky to my eyes – and yet across them crucifixes fly, and beneath them great roaring wagons grind their way at huge speed. Is there a window of divine light that shines on these things equally as it shines on me? Is there an altar or a pulpit that commands the humanity of such things? If there is, I fear it. Because I do not see it.

Directly opposite Father Harington's house, where the Public Bath House once stood, is a pile of rubble. The last building on this site was clearly a church, for an isolated steeple rises high into the overcast sky. Huge chunks of cemented brick, carved window mouldings and glass have been left in piles. The next site along the street is similar, and so is the next. The plots of the houses are heaped with wreckage. Only the road surface itself is clear.

I walk, watching the people come and go. There is a sense of urgency in their movements that is unfamiliar. Or, rather, it is familiar – but the last time I saw it was when we were in France, with the king's army, on our way to Crécy. Then, everything that needed doing was done positively. War is like that. And very clearly, Exeter is at war.

In the middle of Bedford Circus I come across another of these self-moving metal wagons. It is painted dark green and many young men in matching long green breeches and woollen upper tunics are unpacking shovels, pails, crowbars and other implements. Several of them are laughing in a way that looks so free and easy, their laughter could have come from my own time. But that is the only sign I recognise, and it is not reassuring, for it makes me think that men can be at ease with all these deafening sounds and signs of violent destruction around them. Two young women pause briefly to watch them: they are both dressed in dark-blue tunics with short skirts, revealing not just their ankles but the lower part of their legs too – something I have never seen women do in public. It seems they are inviting men to think lustful thoughts about them amid the blasted remains of the build-ings. More women in the same dark-blue clothes are walking together on the other side of the street. I turn away from the sight, reeling with the image of so many females dressed in a lewd manner, like armies of prostitutes marching towards war: a ruthless coupling with the enemy.

And then I turn the corner.

No destructive army in all my experience ever wrought such damage as this, not even one that had *gonnes*. In France, in the *chevauchées*, when we had to destroy every building we came to, we did not manage to lay waste so comprehensively. We did not have the time. When we put French houses and churches to the torch, those that were timber and thatch burned completely but many churches, merchants' houses and municipal buildings were made of stone. We left them as burned-out ruins. Here, between me and the High Street, one or two broken houses remain, seemingly hanging precariously in mid-air, but almost everything has been thrown down to ground level and now is a pile of splintered wood, smashed glass, fragmented pottery and rusting metal.

The people appear calm, however. They seem hardly to notice the devastation all around them. Men in long coats and soft hats are walking along stone pathways as if the huge wasteland of brick and twisted metal beside them is a flower garden. Here and there a building pokes its head up above the rubble, screaming in grief at its own destruction – its window frames empty, thin curtains blowing in the breeze – but people nonchalantly lean against it, reading newspapers. Pieces of sculpture and wall lie fallen by the ruins of the church of Saint Lawrence, and women sit on the rubble, eating pies and stuffed slices of bread, seemingly unaware of the tragedy of the smashed roofs behind them. Huge metal trusses, which once supported the roof of a wide building, stick up like giant bones into the sky – and yet a man steers one of those grinding metal carriages into the space beneath them. A large building on the High Street still stands to first-floor level but it looks as though a great pair of jaws has reached down and taken a huge bite out of it, leaving its jagged brickwork bearing the impression of enormous teeth marks. Two women stand in the doorway, sucking on small white cylinders of the fragrant weed whose smoke people like to inhale – again, oblivious to the diabolical sight above them.

At first glance, the cathedral looks as if it has survived unscathed. A more prolonged inspection reveals that all the windows are broken. Up close, the old building is a ruin. I look at the screen. I see that the carefully sculpted hands of one figure have been worn away entirely: they were images of my own hands, and were carved with the hands they showed. Faces have cracked. Arms have broken off. Some figures have been replaced entirely with clumsily carved modern versions. Inside the building, piles of glass remain in the nave and there are puddles of water on the floor. The Great East Window has gone entirely. The great throne of Bishop Stapledon has disappeared. Light floods through a ghastly void on the south side of the quire. The whole of the chapel of Saint James has been destroyed.

I climb over the barrier to have a closer look at the ruins of the chapel, ignoring the warnings of an onlooker. There are piles of carved stone here and there, in tidied lines. The buttresses have gone. Two adjacent ones have been shattered. The remaining supports on either side are vulnerable, doing twice the work they were intended to do; they will fail before long. The vault above me hangs precariously: I can feel its weight, like a colossal tear about to drop from God's eye.

I return to the nave and sit on one of the wooden seats, dazed. Once war was a matter for brave soldiers, fighting hand to hand. Then it became a bloodthirsty zone of deadly musket balls. And now it is everywhere. War has infected everything, so that even the most precious things in our lives are vulnerable. The last day I was here, in eighteen forty-three, was the only time since the plague when we were not at war. The people who build weapons must have made use of that peace to design more effective means of destroying and killing. But who could have been so soulless as to attack this glorious building? This cannot be the result of a civil war – no Englishman would harm a cathedral, surely? The blame must lie with the accursed French.

I walk to the chapel of Saint Andrew and Saint Catherine, fearing the worst. But the chapel is intact. Catherine's face too is intact. I feel relief: the screw of my anguish has not been given another twist. I look at her stone image, and am glad that the stone does not have eyes with which to look at me. The past is only there to be seen, it cannot see. But then I wonder. Is this destruction around me not due to the fact that we can only look back in time? Would the people of today have caused such destruction if those of Father Harington's day had been able to look forward? Or would they have made different mistakes?

I leave the cathedral. At the top of the street that leads to the South Gate I see further devastation in the form of a row of burned-out buildings. Here and there a blackened wall, relieved of its plaster, shows that it is ancient, with an old window and an arch. But such antiquities are just awaiting their turn to be pulled down, along with the rest of the wrecked walls, and left in piles of rubble.

I walk down the hill past more bombed buildings towards the river, needing the reassurance of something that will not have changed. Even before I arrive, I can see that the elegant bridge of Father Harington's day has gone: a single-arch span of iron and stone now stands there, with balustrades on either side of the roadway. As I draw nearer, I see that this bridge is nowhere near as long as its predecessors. The river is not as wide as it once was. It runs through a channel, and the marshes on either side where so much rubbish was habitually dumped have gone. No rats are to be seen scampering over the piles of offal and bone thrown down amid the washed-down sticks and earth mounds of the river bank. This new century seems to have pushed away everything that went before, even the river.

I walk back up into the town feeling as if I have lost another old friend.

On a street corner I watch a large self-moved carriage stop and many young men in grim green garb get out, carrying heavy bags over their shoulders. They all look at me in my old clothes. A few other people watch them. Most get on with their business. A shop here that seems to sell sweetmeats is doing a brisk business: the door rings every time someone opens or closes it. On a table beside the road two women in overalls attend large cauldrons, handing out steaming brown drinks to a number of men and women waiting in a row. One woman catches my eye as she sips her drink. She does not look away from me. She is tall and has black curly hair, and olive skin, and beautiful brown eyes. She must be in her early twenties. Her coat, which is open at the front, is a light brown with a fur trim around the hood, and beneath she is wearing a tunic of blue-coloured fabric, not unlike the lewd uniforms I saw earlier.

She is looking at me intently. I want to continue to watch her face as I turn away. Reluctantly, my attention is dragged to the woman beside her, who has just started to scream. My gaze does not remain on her for long, however, for my ears are filled with a screeching sound. And something strikes me with a sudden and tremendous weight.

*

It is late, almost dark, when I get home. I lift the latch and open the door. Catherine is sitting on a bench, sewing a boy's tunic by the light of a rushlight on the table. I close the door behind me, noticing that since I left it has started to drag on its hinge. Have all these other centuries and days been a dream, which is now over? Am I well again, in my own time?

Catherine puts down the needle and comes over. I back away instantly, cautious of infecting her.

'Are you all right, John?'

I put a hand to my brow. I am not feverish. 'I think so. Yes.'

I let her give me a hug and a kiss. 'How fare the angels in Salisbury?'

'They are fine. And how fare the angels here?'

'All well. All in bed.'

I sit down on a stool and look at the window which one day I will see ruined. I try to put the experience of the future out of my mind. 'Things are bad across the county. The roads and fields are littered with the dead, and haunted by townsmen fleeing the plague. The markets are desolate spaces now – a few upended and broken trestles.'

'Moreton market is flourishing and cheaper than ever. Buyers are scarce so the sellers are only too glad to see customers. I bought serge enough for all the children to have a new tunic for fourteen pence.'

'And what about you? Did you find something for yourself?'

She smiles and looks at me with raised eyebrows. 'I bought pepper.'

'Pepper?'

'Only a little. Isolda from Wreycombe and I were talking about it, and there it was in the market. The trader knew Isolda and as there were so few folk about, he gave us three ounces for elevenpence.'

'That's more than a fair price. Does this mean my wife will be coming to me all hot and vigorously spiced?' I ask, putting my arms around her and kissing her.

'I'm a meal you fancy, then,' she replies, kissing me back.

'You can hold me to that.'

She kisses me longer, and I try to pull her down on to the straw by the fire. But she breaks away. 'Let me make sure that the boys are asleep.'

She goes through to the sleeping chamber. I sit on the bench and look into the fire, thinking about the vision I have had of the future, of what is to come, and how lucky we have been to escape the plague. I think of the closing of the monasteries and the beating of the tin beam house, the carriages with glass windows and the rich paintings. I think of the troops who hanged William and of Rose in the workhouse. All this knowledge, it is too much. I just want to wash it from my mind, and the only way I know of doing that is to lose myself in her. In my Catherine. The smell of her hair, the feel of her body, the joy of our lovemaking, the sounds of her delight – my satisfaction in her happiness, her satisfaction in mine.

I look in the direction of the sleeping chamber.

I hear nothing. There is just a dark space.

I get up and walk over. Even in the doorway, I hear nothing.

'Catherine?'

She does not answer. Perhaps she lay down to sleep too? In the dimness I can see hardly anything, and so I head back to the hall, and pick up the rushlight. Taking it back to the sleeping chamber, I raise it to see where she is.

Our three boys are laid out, on the mattress. Just like Elizabeth Tapper's two sons. Catherine is hanging from a rope in the corner.

I scream her name – 'Catherine!' – and with it feel all hope flood out into the void of death. Grief slices through my body, and I cry. I strike the walls and the door, yelling to the far side of existence.

Then I see the light.

'So, you're alive then?' says a female voice.

I am in a long yellowish hall, in which there are two rows of metal beds. My wounded back feels tender, my hand still hurts, but neither of them compares to the pain in my head, and the feeling of grief that has pierced my heart. I turn my head from side to side to try to dislodge it but the pain is fixed within me, hardening by the minute.

My eyes slowly focus on the shape that is talking to me. It is the face of the woman with the curly black hair and the beautiful eyes, from near the cauldrons.

'That was quite some knock you took from the transporter,' she says. 'You stepped right out in front of it, you silly ha'p'orth. It is a miracle that you aren't seriously injured.'

'Are you an angel? Is this Heaven?'

She laughs. 'No, I am Celia and this is Devon.' She adjusts

a bandage which is wrapped around my head. 'Oldest joke in the world, rhyming Devon and Heaven. Sorry about that. Actually, this is the Royal Devon and Exeter Hospital. I came with you in the ambulance.'

'In what?'

'The ambulance. Big van, bed in the back, siren, red cross on the side. I'm helping out here with the nurses. I had just finished my shift and was on my way home when you saw me at the tea stall. I mean, it's all very flattering when strange men stop in the street and stare at you – but personally I prefer it if they don't then get themselves run over. It's a bit embarrassing. Anyway, I suspect you're suffering from concussion. The doctors will probably want to keep you in here for a while. They've asked me to fill out a form with your details. What's your name?'

'John of Wrayment.'

'John . . . ?' she asks, holding a board with a piece of white paper on it and a writing stylus. 'I find it hard to understand your accent. Ovreeman? Averyman? Everyman?'

'Of Wrayment.'

'Can you spell that for me, please?'

I close my eyes. 'I am sorry.'

'Very well. I'll put down "Everyman" and we'll come back to that one if we need to. Next of kin?'

'What do you mean?'

'Are you married?'

'Yes.'

'And your wife's name is?'

'Catherine.'

'And how old are you, Mister Everyman?'

I shake my head.

'When were you born?'

I look at her. Her brown eyes invite honesty and I have no reason to lie. 'The Wednesday after Whitsun in the fifth year of the reign of King Edward the Second.'

'You mean Edward the *Seventh*? Nineteen-o-five? So you are thirty-seven years old?'

'If you say so. When were you born?'

'Me? Oh, the eighth of May, nineteen eighteen.'

'And who is your husband?'

'That's very forward of you, Mister Everyman. I'm not married, actually, although I do have a boyfriend. He's an American, called Ron. He is about the only good thing to have happened to me since the war began.'

'Why are the French trying to destroy our city?'

'You mean the Germans. The French are on our side – at least, the resistance fighters are. When our chaps bombed Lübeck in March, the whole city was destroyed by a fire-storm. So Hitler ordered that all the equivalent English cities should be obliterated. He started with Exeter.'

I hold up my hand to stop her. 'I am an ignorant man, Mistress Celia . . .'

'Just call me Celia.'

'I do not know this man, Hitler.'

'Goodness me. How can anyone not know who Hitler is? Your concussion must be bad. He's the Chancellor of Germany – the leader of the German Third Reich, and he has invaded most of Europe.'

'What are the crosses in the sky called?'

She stops, leans forward and looks at me. 'How many fingers am I holding up?'

I see two fingers. 'Two.'

'I'm going to have a word with someone. Back in a tick.'

I close my eyes. Oh, Catherine, I pray that that was not your fate. Of all the bad dreams, the worst is the one that could be true. Catherine, please, I pray, through tears and on the day of my death, please, don't have done that. Even though all our beautiful boys be dead, don't give in to the shadows. Live – remarry, try to be happy.

'And then, will *you* try to live, John?' I hear her say in reply.

And what can I say to that?

'I repent. Though it be too late, I repent of the moment I chose to leave our own time.'

I look at the ceiling and its strange round lights hanging from thin black ropes, feeling myself shivering in the bed. This is no place to spend my last hours. I have to do the good work that I must attempt, for William's sake as well as my own. I lean on my elbow and look along the room. There are many men in here, some with their limbs in bandages. A few are accompanied by their womenfolk. Some are young lads. If I am set to die, and the flying crosses are the agents of my destruction, then these men are liable to be killed. The Germans will destroy this whole hospital, killing everyone within it. My presence here is a silent death knell for these people.

I throw back the covers and, slowly, swing my legs out of

the bed. I find my shoes and put them on, my hands shaking even more than they were this morning. I cannot tie the shoes either, even when I have hold of them. I am still trying to tie my second shoe when Celia returns.

'John, what are you doing? You're suffering from concussion. Get back into bed, you need rest.'

'Mistress Celia,' I gasp, my pulse beating fast. 'Did you discover what those crosses in the sky are?'

'They are called aeroplanes. But, John, you need . . .'

'Mistress Celia, I must go now. No one here is safe. Not you, not these poor people – no one can come near me. I am doomed to die today, and if anyone is with me when an aeroplane strikes me, they'll not be spared. I've seen the damage they wreak.'

I try to step past her but she grabs my arm. 'John, what do you mean? We're all in danger, every day and every night. We just have to keep calm and maintain the order of our ordinary lives, and stay optimistic.'

'Where's my overtunic?'

'Your jacket? It's here,' she says, pointing to where it is hanging up behind her coat. 'I had them take it off you . . .'

I put it on.

'John, what are you doing? You are in no fit state to leave. Your head's in bandages because you've cracked your skull. You've lost a lot of blood . . .'

'I am sorry, Mistress Celia. But I cannot have the deaths of all these people resting on my conscience. I need to go to Heaven to plead for my brother's soul, and to discover what happened to my wife and children.'

I lurch towards the door. Celia picks up her coat and comes after me. 'John, listen. You need rest. You need to recuperate. No aeroplanes are going to attack you in here, it is quite safe.'

I leave the room and start to go down the stairs.

'Do you even know where you are going?' says Celia as she descends behind me. 'Listen to me, John!'

The note of anguish in her voice forces me to stop. I look up at her. 'Mistress Celia, you are most kind, and I could not bear it if you were to be struck by an aeroplane aiming to kill me.'

'You silly man. The Germans only drop bombs after dark, when the gunners on the ground can't see the planes to shoot them.' She looks at me. 'Do you have anywhere to go?'

I shake my head. 'I'll go to the cathedral.' Then I think this through a little further. 'No, no. I cannot go to the cathedral, for if the crosses in the sky see me, they'll attack the cathedral and all it will take is the slightest knock and that whole vault will fall, and all the stonework on the south of the quire by Saint James's chapel.'

Celia descends the last steps to join me. 'John, listen. You are hurt. You were knocked over by a lorry, for Heaven's sake. You need looking after.'

'This is my last day on Earth,' I say, shutting my eyes.

I feel her put her arm around my shoulders. 'In that case, you are coming back to have a nice cup of tea at my flat. And then, when you're ready, we'll find you somewhere to stay until we can get in touch with your wife and let her know you are safe. There are hostels around the city for people who have been made homeless by the bombing.'

Celia takes my arm firmly and leads me out of the hospital, across Southernhay and through the cathedral precinct to the remains of the High Street, and eastwards, through the midst of the devastation I saw earlier. We walk past the building that I thought looked as if it had been bitten open by some mighty jaws from the sky. 'That's such a shame,' she says. 'Everyone loved Deller's. My father bought me my first glass of wine there on my twenty-first birthday. There was a string quartet playing Mozart, and waiters with bow ties, and all my family and friends were there. The quartet all stopped playing their piece to play "Happy Birthday to You", and everyone in the café started singing along. It was frightfully funny. And now look at it. So sad.'

It is impossible to tell where the East Gate was. Nothing stands there now – not even the building that Father Harington told me was where they held dances. Everything is piles of smashed brick and metal on the other side of the street too – until we reach a huge modern building. Celia tells me it is called the Odeon, and they show 'pictures' there. We pause outside and she surveys some large colourful images with writing on them, one of which depicts a metal boat with giant muskets attached to its deck. 'I want to see that,' she mutters. 'They say Noel Coward is brilliant. He wrote the script and the music, and stars in it. I was hoping to go with Ron this afternoon.'

I am about to ask what she means by 'stars' but I feel defeated by new meanings. I despair of understanding this age. I just turn and look back to the city. The cathedral rises over it, dominating it more than ever. A little sunlight is breaking through the clouds, and striking the twisted metal in the wasteland between it and us, and it seems to me that we are on the edge of a preci-pice. The cathedral might have lost its spires, and it might have a gash in the side that could give way at any moment, but still it stands, defiant, as if there was some truth that we who built her knew, and which will always be true.

'They want it blown up,' says Celia, turning and following my gaze. 'Some of the councillors say that the German pilots are using the cathedral as a guide to line up on the houses in the east of the city, so we should blow it up ourselves, to save our houses. Madness, isn't it? Like throwing a priceless heir-loom on the fire to stop it being stolen.'

Celia and I resume walking. Ten minutes later, we arrive at her house. It is one in a row: three storeys high and built of red brick. There is a protruding bay of windows at the ground floor and the floors above. Unlike the glazing I saw at Father Harington's house, which was made up of many small panes in a sliding frame, these windows are made of large single sheets of glass.

'I'm at the top,' explains Celia, 'but first we've got to get past Missus Harbottle. She's about ninety and lives on the ground floor. She owns the place. She doesn't approve of women living by themselves. So, after she realises I've come home accompanied, she'll prop her door open and wait until you've gone, and then tell me off, knowing exactly how much time you've been here.'

'She sounds a most moral woman.'

'Ssshh.'

Celia unlocks the white-painted door and I slip inside after her. The hallway is covered with a plain cream-coloured

THE OUTCASTS OF TIME

fabric, and so is the staircase, which is on our left. To the right
is an open door. Seated in a large brown cloth-covered chair
in the corner of the room, and looking out through menacing
black-framed eye windows, is an ancient-looking woman.
Skin sags from her face. Her lips, however, look unnaturally
red, as if she had painted them.

'Is that a man with you, Veronica?' she asks.

'It's Celia, Missus Harbottle. This is John Everyman. He
has been wounded.'

'House rules, my girl. Not under my roof.'

'Mister Everyman is only coming in for a cup of tea,' says
Celia. 'He was run over this morning. He has only just come
out of hospital – as you can see from his bandages. You would
not refuse an injured man, would you?'

Missus Harbottle peers in my direction. 'Tell him to come
closer.'

Celia nods at me, and I walk closer. I stand directly at the
foot of the chair, looking down at the old woman. There is a
fine sweet-smelling dust on her face.

'How old is he?'

'Thirty-seven. And he is married.'

'So you've got to know him quite well already then?'

'Missus Harbottle, I drew up his notes in the hospital.'

The old woman nods. 'Very well. He may come in for a
cup of tea. But I expect him to be out within the hour.'

'Thank you, Missus Harbottle,' replies Celia.

We ascend a flight of stairs past various doors on the land-
ings and the first floor. At the top there are two more doors:
Celia opens the right-hand one. The room beyond has a

sloping ceiling on one side, where there is an alcove with a window set into it, facing the back of the house. A small table with two seats is against the wall on my right; there is a fireplace in the wall opposite with a container full of coal. Against the wall to my left is a large cream-coloured metal object which has various levers and numbers on the front, and beside that, a deep white sink with taps over it. In front of the fireplace, hanging from the ceiling, is a frame supported on a rope, with several garments draped over it, drying. There is also one of those round white lights on a thin rope, like the ones I saw at the hospital.

'I'm sorry about Missus Harbottle,' says Celia, taking off her coat. 'She is a terrible bore. And if she had any sense she'd realise it's futile her trying to prevent Veronica and me ever taking our knickers off.'

'Knickers?' I ask.

She makes a strange expression at me, widening her eyes. 'Are you sure you're married?'

'Yes.'

She reaches up to the rack above her fireplace, pulls down a white garment with lace around the hems, and tosses it to me. I catch it and fumble with it until, holding it up by the sides of the largest aperture, I understand. Hurriedly, I hand it back to her.

'Why, Mister Everyman,' she says with a smile as she places it on a shelf, 'I do believe I've made you go red. There's no need to be embarrassed. I recommend you tell Catherine to buy a pair.' She claps her hands together. 'I promised you a cup of tea. That's the next thing on the agenda.' She walks over to the door and moves a tiny black lever set in a round black box in the wall, and the light in the middle of the room turns itself on.

'How does that work?' I ask. I go to the box, and turn the lever back, and the light goes off. I turn it again, and the light goes on.

I turn it off again. And on again, marvelling at it.

And off again, and on again.

'That's enough, John,' she says, filling a kettle of water from the tap at the sink and putting it on the large metal machine. She takes a small piece of wood from a box nearby and strikes it against the side, and it instantly produces a flame. She then ignites the air moving through the large metal machine and it produces flames directly beneath the kettle. Soon the kettle starts whistling and she pours the water into a pot with a spout, and stirs it. 'Why don't you go through to the front room?' she says. 'It's more comfortable in there. I'll be through in a minute with the tea.'

I return to the landing and go through the other door. This large room runs the whole width of the house. To the left of the window, which faces the street, is a bed with a purple woollen blanket and a white linen-covered pillow. A chest containing four drawers is beside the bed. On the other side of the room, there are two cloth-covered chairs with arms and a cloth-covered padded bench. In the middle of the room, in front of the cloth-covered bench, is a low table with various books on it, and a newspaper. There are pictures in here too. There's a painting of a castle and some trees by a lake, another of a dog, and there is a collection of small black-and-white pictures of people, all hung together. There are about two dozen of them, some of individuals and some of groups: old and young, men and women, and several children too.

'You've met my family, I see,' says Celia as she comes into the room bearing a tray on which the pot stands with some cups. 'Could you be a darling and move those books for me,' she asks, nodding in the direction of the table.

I pile the books on the floor, and toss the newspaper on to the cloth-covered bench. She sets the tray down, and sits on one of the chairs.

'Have you read all these?' I ask.

'Most of them. I was reading English here at the University College in Exeter ...'

'Women are allowed to study there?'

'Of course. This isn't the Dark Ages, you know. I was reading English literature until the war came along. Daddy was forced to come out of retirement and re-join the army, running a training camp. And I was told that the university courses would reconvene when peace resumed. Unfortunately they couldn't tell me when that would be. So I had to get a job – and they were crying out for nurses. I keep my hand in with my studies, reading poetry, in between nursing shifts.'

She pours the tea.

'Do you have an earth closet?' I ask, feeling the urge.

'I beg your pardon?'

'A chamber of office?'

'Oh,' and she laughs. 'A WC. Yes. Just down the first flight of stairs, and through the door straight ahead of you.'

I go down the stairs, wondering if she understood what I meant by an 'earth closet'. We are on the second floor: how can anyone have such a thing between the first and second floors of their house? Nevertheless, I follow her directions and find the door to which she referred. Inside is a small room which has a single large white bowl with a small amount of water in it. It has another metal cistern above it connected by a pipe, with a chain hanging down. I am confused. Is this where she washes? I can see that by pulling the cord, one can fill the lower cistern – but I don't want to go where she and others might wash their faces.

I see the roll of paper. Does this serve the same function as the pile of papers at Father Harington's earth closet? Or is this for drying your face?

I decide to hang on and urinate in the gardens outside after I leave.

She is sipping her tea and reading the newspaper when I return. 'They've started bombing again. Eastbourne and Fulham were hit yesterday.'

I say nothing.

'I don't know if it's madness or cruelty, or both, this idea of blitzing places,' she mutters. 'Why do people fight when they have so much to gain from peace?'

'Because people need a common enemy. War is one of those things that bind us together. You could say that men need someone to oppose – otherwise we start fighting among ourselves.'

'You men. It's always you men.'

'But if there were no men in England, the women would have to do what the men do.'

'I don't blame men generally. I blame those men who started this war in the first place. Like Hitler.'

'I know nothing about this Hitler but I'll hold you that he started this war in the belief that he was doing a service for his people, bringing them together and making them stronger. If that was not so, they'd not be fighting for him.'

I sip my tea. It has a mild and pleasing flavour, better than that I was served by Patience Mudge, but I cannot say that I think it better than the ale I used to drink every day in my own time. My eyes rest on the volumes on the floor. 'What are all these here books?'

'I told you. English literature. Poetry. The classics – Byron, Shelley, Keats. A few more modern writers – that one on top is Yeats. I have a couple of recent things too. It is good to keep abreast of what my contemporaries are publishing.'

I lift the topmost volume, and look at the incomprehensible words. The volume beneath it is bound in leather. Three gold letters appear on the front cover, smartly arranged as if chiselled carefully. I put the first book down and lift this other one: inside it is full of blue-coloured figures.

'Is this in your hand?'

'It is.'

'These letters on the cover – what do they mean?'

'C.R.B. They stand for Celia Rose Baring.'

'Rose?'

'It's an old family name, on my mother's side. Not sure where it comes from.'

'What do you write about?'

'I write poems.'

I hand the book to her. 'Will you read them to me?'

She frowns at me. 'No, they're private.'

'Please. Just one.'

She thinks for a moment. 'Very well, I'll read you one. And then I'm going to have a bath.'

At that moment an aeroplane flies over us, issuing that horrible low grinding tone. She pauses, seemingly holding her breath, and looks at me. The noise passes away. But still she does not say anything. She sits there waiting, listening, in fear.

She looks at her page. 'This is called "Despite Everything". I wrote it for my mother. Here goes.'

> It is never truly dark. You can still see
> something, if only a shadow of a tree
> which spreads its twigs like torn lace
> against the sky. Silence too is never
> absolute. Even in the quietest night
> you can still hear an owl or a train
> beyond the trees; you can always hear
> something stir on this side of the stars.
>
> Take heart from this when you lie awake
> and dream of what may never come to pass.
> Not even the wind can blow utterly cold.
> No one is ever forgotten. I think of you
> and the great crescendo of another day
> lifts its arms to pray that we in turn
> might still have hope. So make a wish;
> it will, in some small way, come true.

I am silent when she finishes. It is such a sad sweetness that fills my mind.

She is looking at me, expecting me to say something.

'That is most touching. I am moved. You are a most skilful woman.'

'Thank you. I'm hoping to publish it soon. I had an acceptance from an editor but he was not sure when it would appear – what with the current difficulties obtaining paper.'

Another aeroplane passes overhead, and I see her shudder again.

We are silent.

'Now,' she says, suddenly getting up. 'I'm going to have a quick bath. There's some bread and corned beef in the kitchen if you want to make yourself a sandwich. I'm sorry, I don't have any butter. Rationing, you know.' She goes over to a wooden box beside her bed. 'I'll leave you with the wireless for company. I won't be long.'

As she gathers up some robes and clothes, noises come from the box. It is a man's voice. After she has left the room, I go over and pick it up. It has a tiny metal grating at the front, where the noise comes out, but it has no connection to anything else. It is as if a sort of magic powers it. The man's voice tells me about new tactics being introduced in bombing German sites in France, and the positive effects they are having on the war effort. Next I hear about the development of operations in the Mediterranean. I hear the name 'El Alamein' a great deal, and other words that have no meaning to me, such as 'tanks', 'Russians' and 'Stalingrad'. An aeroplane pilot has now flown over the Atlantic one hundred times. In India, a group of people called 'the Japanese' have started bombing Calcutta. As I listen I cannot help but think back to Father Harington's great hope that the world would come closer together. It seems evident that the world has indeed drawn closer to one another – but only in order to fight.

The man speaking on the radio comes to the end of his speech and announces that there will now be some music.

The longer I stay here, the more likely it is that the bombs will destroy this young woman's home. But I cannot leave without saying goodbye.

As the radio plays a lively tune I get up, and walk anxiously. There is a large looking glass on a chest in the corner of the room, in which I see my bandaged head. There are all manner of ointments and pastels on the surface, too many for me even to guess at their various purposes. I see books with paper covers that have pictures on the front. A small metal clock is beside her bed. A flower in a large pot with earth stands in the window. And then I wander over to look at the two dozen or so family portraits on the wall. Among them is a picture of an old man. He is reading a book by a window in a library, with a jar containing flowers next to him. His face is familiar. It is Father Edward Harington.

I hear the door open and feel Celia standing beside me. She is dressed in a grey woollen upper tunic and a black lower tunic, and drying her hair on a white towel.

'What does that say?' I ask her, pointing at some words beneath Father Harington's picture.

She bends down and reads. '"The man who has no

knowledge of the past has no wisdom." That's my great-great-uncle.'

'What happened to him?'

'He was chancellor of the cathedral, and spent his days doing good works for the poor – that and attending the opening of every blessed railway line in the whole country.'

'The Lord bless you, Father Harington.'

'How do you know his name?'

'He was a good man, if ever there was one,' I say, looking at each of the pictures.

I spot an image of his sister. In fact, I see two: one of her with her brother as a younger woman and another when she is about seventy, holding a baby, with an infant standing beside her. 'That'll be where you get your spirit from,' I say, pointing. 'Mary Georgiana.'

'John!' she exclaims, drawing away from me. 'How do you know them?'

I raise my hand in apology. 'Oh, no, Mistress Celia! I do not want to worry you. I am sorry. Forgive me.'

'How do you know them?'

There is fear in her face. I don't know what to say.

'Tell me.'

'I met them. At their house.'

'But that is impossible.'

'I stayed at their house in Southernhay. This morning, when I woke up there, it was a ruin. Those crosses in the sky are to blame, I'll warrant.'

Celia looks as if she is about to scream. But she says nothing.

'Your great-great-uncle was very good to me.' I look down at what I am wearing. 'These are his clothes.'

'It must be your knock on the head.'

'It was not my fault, Mistress Celia. Father Harington told me not to drown myself in the river. He showed me his library and his books, and all the paintings in his house in Southernhay, including one with a horse and a rider making a great leap over a chasm . . .'

'No! That is in my parents' bedroom, in Cornwall.'

'And I heard your great-grandmother play a piece of music by Mozart on an instrument they called a pianoforte. In Father Harington's dressing room was a painting of a knight and a boy—'

'Please, please stop. Just go. Now. I don't know who you are or how you know all these things, but I don't want to hear them.'

I look around the room. 'He was a good man, Father Harington. I just wanted to say that.'

'Leave now. Please.'

I walk to the door and glance back. This is not the way I wanted to part from this kind soul. Her head is down, not wanting to look at me. I hear the low rumble of another of the aeroplanes. I turn and go down the stairs as quickly as I can. I bow to Missus Harbottle, and struggle to let myself out of the door, as it is not clear to me how these new latches work. In the street, the aeroplane overhead makes a huge noise, and I glimpse it for a moment, flying over the houses towards the east.

I head in the direction of the centre of the city, not

knowing where to go or what to do. The clouds are breaking here and there, allowing occasional shafts of light to fall on me. I recall that the weather was doing the same thing when I walked along this road all those years ago with William, when we last returned to Exeter. Just a little further from here was the burial pit. Houses now cover the place where so many people were laid to rest. And now it is time for my own death. The only question left is how it will actually happen. In what position will I die? Or will one of these thunderbolts from an aeroplane strike me, so that nothing is left of me at all?

I go into a garden down the street and relieve myself against a bush.

As I walk on, I curse myself. Ultimately, this moment is the result of all my decisions. Even scaring poor Celia like that was the consequence of a decision, all those years ago. And what now? I cannot walk back to the cathedral, and risk its destruction. Must I walk out into some distant field, where no one can be hurt, and wait for the end?

Several noisy wagons and carriages pass me by. To my surprise, one stops not far from me. A door opens, and Celia steps out. 'John, I'm sorry,' she says, walking towards me. 'That was not fair of me, throwing you out like that. Especially with you having concussion and all. I know you're delirious, and you're not in control. I'd feel simply awful if something happened to you. I was just . . . I don't know, scared.'

I do not know what to say.

She looks into my eyes, then glances back over her shoulder. 'Ron and I are going to go to the cinema. Will you come with us?'

The driver of the self-moving carriage comes towards us. He is very tall, clean-shaven and has black hair. His clothes are very smart, a matching upper and lower tunic, with very shiny black shoes. He has one of the white tubes of pungent herbs burning in his mouth.

'Ron,' says Celia, 'this is John Everyman. John, this is Ron, who is from New York but employed by the British government.'

Ron holds his hand out. I take it with my left hand and shake it. 'Maybe you can tell me a thing or two about my folk in the old days,' says Ron. 'Family legend says that the Whites came from round these parts, back when the *Mayflower* was still afloat.'

I smile at him, not understanding a word.

'We're going to watch the Noel Coward film, *In Which We Serve*,' says Celia. 'Do you remember? We saw the posters earlier.'

'Mistress Celia, there will be a bomb that falls on me today, that I know for certain. You must go and live a long and happy life, like Father Harington, and thus you must be nowhere near me when that bomb hits me.'

'Mister Everyman,' says Ron, 'the Germans can't afford to throw their planes away merely on having a poke at our morale. They'll wait until after dark.'

'You speak most strangely,' I say. 'Is that the usual manner of speaking in York these days?'

'*I* speak strangely?' says Ron, with a laugh. 'Oh boy. Now I've heard them all. *New* York, sir, is in the good old United States of America.'

'Where the turkey fowl are from?'

'Yes, sir. Every Thanksgiving there's a turkey on the table. Why, do you like turkey?'

'I don't know. But I do know that I am going to die.'

Ron glances at Celia. 'We are all going to die, John.'

'But there is a difference. It's going to happen to me today.'

'Well, it's your call, bud,' says Ron. 'I can give you a lift down to the Odeon in my car – and you don't need to worry about the elevenpence entry – or you can go your own way. But we need to get moving now. The projectionist won't wait for us. What is it to be?'

I look both ways up and down the road. I cannot hear any aeroplanes. I weigh up whether to trust their assurances that the Germans never attack in the daylight.

'I'll come,' I say.

'Bravo,' says Celia. 'You won't regret it.'

We walk back to Ron's carriage. He looks down the street, purposely drops his white tube of burning herbs, treads it into the road, and gets in. Leaning back over his chair, he opens the door at the back of the carriage for me. Celia sits in the front beside him.

The machine is noisy and very fast – faster than galloping on a horse. I close my eyes but the motion of the vehicle then makes me feel sick. I look at my hand grabbing the back of Celia's seat and realise my knuckles are white. I relax my grip, telling myself that we will be at our destination soon.

Ron stops the machine near the bombed remains of Saint Sativola's church and we walk through the desolation to the enormous building that towers over the neighbourhood.

After queuing along with many other people, we enter. Ron pays for us and I follow him and Celia up some fabric-covered stairs to 'Screen One' as it is called. Inside are rows and rows of seats. If the bombs come for me here, they will destroy not only me and this picture house but also hundreds of lives.

'Don't look so worried,' says Celia, as she sits between us. 'If anything happens, the air-raid siren will sound. We'll leave this place and go to the nearest shelter.'

All of the lights around Screen One go out and we are in darkness for a moment. A huge black-and-white picture appears on the white wall in front of us. It shows people in a street in amazing detail. And they are *moving*.

How can the image itself move? It has to be the very thing itself I am seeing, not a picture. But how can you pipe a view to the wall like that?

What follows is a moving, talking newspaper. I see pictures of large metal wagons with cannon on top of them, speeding across the African desert, where a British army is fighting a German one. I do not know which is which: the armies do not carry coats of arms, banners or standards as in my day. I see pictures of bombed and wrecked buildings in Germany, damaged by the king's air force. The sound is loud – much louder than listening to someone speaking in person. Images of destruction and sad people walking in long lines shock me, and fill me with despair for all mankind.

When the news has finished, the 'film' starts. There is a moment of darkness before we hear stirring music played by many instruments from some hidden place.

'This is the story of a ship,' says a voice. I watch images

of how they build modern ships out of metal. I wonder how they can possibly float. I want to ask Celia but there are so many other things I want to ask. I wish there were windows so I could tell if it was growing dark outside, so I could see if there were aeroplanes coming.

A newspaper is seen drifting on muddy water. Celia leans over and says to me, 'The headline reads: "No war this year – Berlin emphatic, Hitler is not ready."' I watch as this ship, the *Torrin*, is built and goes to sea. Her captain is a man with a strange accent called Kinross, who speaks so fast I cannot understand more than a few words. He loves his wife, called Alix, very much, and well he might, for she is beautiful. Soon the aeroplanes of the enemy are shooting at the *Torrin* and dropping fish-shaped objects on her deck, which explode. After a few of these aeroplanes have been shot by men on the deck with cannon, two of these exploding objects hit the *Torrin*, and she starts to sink. Men throw themselves overboard and hang on to a float in the sea. But the aeroplanes return to shoot them in the water with rapidly firing muskets, even though they are defenceless.

As the surviving men wait in the water, they all think back to their wives. Captain Kinross remembers talking to Alix about whether there will be a war, and I realise that that particular discussion must have taken place before the war started. Captain Kinross drinks tea and smokes what they call 'cigarettes' while overlooking the sea. His wife drinks tea, and so do all the other wives and families of the other sailors who think back on their earlier days as they cling to the float. I see many images of trains arriving at 'stations', as Father Harington called them, and people chatting as they travel very fast on them through the countryside, even at night.

Gradually, I am brought closer to the reality of this war. Aeroplanes drop explosives on ordinary houses, not knowing if there are women and children below. Ships like the *Torrin* carry great long exploding pipes, called 'torpedoes', which can blow up another ship and leave all its men diving into the sea, whereupon the *Torrin's* men shoot them with their muskets. I watch many men listening intently as a disembodied voice says, 'At eleven fifteen the prime minister will broadcast to the nation. Please stand by.' Shortly after that we all hear a sombre voice say, 'I am speaking to you from the cabinet room in Ten Downing Street. This morning the British ambassador in Berlin handed the German government a final note stating that, unless we heard from them by eleven o'clock that they were prepared at once to withdraw their troops from Poland, a state of war would exist between us. I have to tell you now that no such undertaking has been received, and that consequently this country is at war with Germany.'

This is when I notice that Celia is crying.

The people of today might not live in the luxury of the people of ninety-nine years ago. They might be squeezed together in portions of houses and have the tiniest amounts of land allocated to them by their manorial lords for gardens. They might be incapable of sculpting figures as well as me. But they can create a picture that surpasses any experience from any other time. She is moved by this film. I too am moved. If the cathedral speaks for the achievements of my age, and the hammers of the tin workings speak for Master

Periam's time, and the hundred-cannon ships of seventeen forty-four prove that greatness was possible in that century too, and the railways stand for the ingenuity of Father Harington's contemporaries, then surely these moving pictures are the proof of the genius of nineteen forty-two. For in this film the feelings of people and their grief are shown as powerfully as in any sculpture – even more so. What does this war mean? Not that some men in flying crosses can destroy something but that some people can create something – an uplifting story, full of ideals and sympathy – even though they live constantly in fear.

At the end of the day, all art is a matter of stirring the emotions, in the hope of touching the soul of mankind. I am struck by these people's feelings on hearing that a loved one is well, or that a husband or wife is not coming home. I am with them when a heartfelt departure is made. I am impressed by their fortitude and honesty. I realise that so many of the things that have impressed me down the years are unimportant. It is not that women can now read the Bible and tell their husbands to be more merciful or kind; it is not that they can read the telegram that says 'your husband is safe and well' or 'your husband is dead'. What is important is what does not change – that mothers and wives are so happy when they hear that their sons and husbands are alive that they run around the house yelling for joy; that men do their duty in the face of great danger not purely for themselves but for all their community. I am touched by these people's strength of spirit, which is as great as ever it was in my day.

Finally, Captain Kinross and a few of his shipmates are

rescued. He gives a short speech to say farewell to those who have survived. He pays tribute to his ship, and to its crew, over half of whom have been killed. He says, 'If they had to die, what a grand way to go.' Those words ring in my ears and resound in my body, in my mind and in my soul. It is as if I have been waiting five hundred and ninety-four years to hear them.

The lights come up in Screen One, and I see that many other people have also been moved by this picture. Some are holding pieces of white cloth to their faces, some are just staring at the screen, and some are looking down as they wait in the queue to leave.

Ron is the first of us to speak, when we are outside. 'When I saw the poster, proclaiming that this was the greatest film of our time, I was sceptical. I mean, come on. Noel Coward only did it to keep the British chin up. I'm sure he'd rather have spent the war in a bar in the Caribbean. But I have to say, that was the best movie I've seen for years – and the best one about the war, full stop.'

Celia clears her nose on a white cloth and pushes it up her sleeve. 'Well, now that we've watched so many people drinking cups of tea, shall we go and have one ourselves?'

'Capital idea, as you Brits say,' says Ron. 'But as Deller's is out of action – albeit only temporarily, we hope – let's go to that little place in North Street. John, are you coming with us?'

I stop. 'No,' I say, and my voice is barely a whisper. I clear my throat. 'No, I'll be leaving you now.'

'John, are you feeling unwell?' asks Celia.

'No.'

'Is it your head?' asks Ron.

'No.'

I look up into the sky. I cannot see or hear any aeroplanes.

'Come and have some tea, you'll feel better,' says Celia.

'Mistress Celia,' I say, taking her hand, 'you know that all is not normal with me. You know that I've skipped across time like a stone skips on water. Six times, to be truthful.'

'And I want to quiz you all about my great-grand . . .'

At that moment, the siren starts to sound, with its wailing crescendo of foreboding.

I keep looking at Celia.

'That's a cheek,' she says, looking up briefly. 'They're not meant to drop bombs by daylight.'

'This is not planned,' says Ron gravely. 'It's a tip-and-run raid. They'll be aiming for the centre of the city. We must go to the nearest shelter, now.'

'Look after her, Mister Ron.'

'John, don't be daft,' says Celia, reaching for my hand. 'You have to come too.'

I pull away from her. 'Lovely, kind Celia, I need to be as far away from you as possible. Look after one another, both of you, not just now but always.'

'Well, if that's the way you want to play it,' Ron replies. 'But we must be off.'

I hold out my left hand to him. He shakes it.

'Thank you for taking me to the picture, Ron.' Then I turn to Celia. 'Go with God. Praise and please your husband, and be as good a friend to him as my wife Catherine was to me. And he'll praise and please you in return. And when you look on your picture of Father Harington, remember he was a good man, and his goodness runs in you.' And with that I bow to her, and walk quickly away.

I hear the approaching sounds of the first aeroplane. The walls around me here are all echoing with the steady grinding note. I pause on a corner, wondering where I should go, and am standing in the street when the sound becomes deafening. There is a huge flash of light and I hear the most almighty boom of an explosion and the immense shock in the air as the whole city quakes. A huge aeroplane appears above a building and goes over the street. There are shouts of defiance from some pedestrians but the noise of a collapsing building and the screams of people drowns them out.

That one will be just the first of many, I know. Within seconds I hear the next. It is flying up the estuary towards the city. It is followed by the noise of Hell.

There is only one thing for me to do now. I go to the rubble-strewn space near what used to be Market Street, and here I kneel down. When the bomb falls on me, it will hurt no one else. It will be nowhere near the cathedral. My hopes of performing a good act have gone. All I can hope for is a quick death, and for no one else to suffer, nothing else precious to be destroyed.

I cross myself and start to pray for the souls of the departed – Catherine, my sons, my brothers and my parents. I pray too for the souls of Master Ley, Rose in the workhouse, and Father Harington and his sister. And I pray for Celia and Ron. I yearn for them to be safe and happy.

Aeroplane after aeroplane mangles the air above my head, some dropping their deadly cargo in the southwest corner of the city, some in the east. The ground reverberates with every blast and the sounds of crashing masonry resonate around me as I kneel. The wailing siren continues. But although I know that the time has come for my soul to depart from this world, to be reunited with that of my wife, the bomb destined to kill me does not come.

I look up at the dark clouds. 'Have you forgotten me? You said you would come for me on the sixth day. Leave me not to endure a seventh.'

The only answer is another explosion and the sounds of more sirens as self-moving carriages race through the streets. I can hear shouting, growing more and more urgent, and screams as another house collapses.

'I am ready!' I shout, with my arms outstretched. 'Receive me now.'

'Oi, you, what the blazes do you think you're doing?'

I look up. A man in a dark tunic is standing over me. He has a round metal hat on his head and a short hand-held musket in his belt. 'Get yourself to a bloody shelter, now.'

I can barely speak. 'I am destined to die tonight,' I say, 'and I will not attract the falling bombs to the shelter. It is all the goodness I can do.'

'Well, mate, get up off your arse and go and help out with the blaze at Holloway Street. There's a dozen people unaccounted for down there.'

The old hollow way was just outside the South Gate. In that direction, a huge column of black smoke is rising against the grey clouds. I thank the man, get to my feet and hurry down to where the gate once stood, hearing people crying and yelling, and the shouting of orders. I make my way past one burning building, where there is a corpse on the steps. Further on, there is another body lying in a pool of blood by the side of the road. Men in uniforms with helmets and a long hose from a large wagon are running as they fight the deafening blaze inside a nearby house. I hear more sirens ringing out and run on, past rubble in the street where a building has collapsed. Two more self-moved carriages come past me but they have to turn off down a side road, unable to proceed past the collapsed building.

When I reach Holloway Street there is so much thick smoke billowing from the burning line of houses that the flames themselves are hardly noticeable amid the blackness, mere tongues of orange here and there. Men in uniform with hoses are forcing a stream of water up on to the roof, which is ablaze. Many people are standing around watching, and I see too there are men on the roof of an adjacent building, beating at the flames. Those on the ground are shouting at them to come down; others are just looking on in horror.

I continue walking towards the houses, seeing one doorway in particular with smoke billowing out of it. A man emerges from it with a tunic wrapped around his head.

'Has anyone seen Missus Brown?' I overhear someone say. 'I think she is still in there.'

'Oh Lord, I pray not. She is looking after two of her grandchildren this week, Christopher and Frederick.'

An upstairs window explodes with the heat inside. Then another. There is a huge noise from the burning – of roaring flames and crashing glass.

I hear my brother's voice: 'I knew that I was going to die today. It was a good thing to know. For this way I knew I could make something of my death.' And I hear too Captain Kinross: 'If they had to die, what a grand way to go.' I answer them both in speaking to God. 'Lord, I am ready. Just let me do this one good deed to help the folk of this city.'

I take off Father Harington's old upper tunic and hold it in my right hand, ready to put it over my mouth. People are shouting around me. I feel a hand on my shoulder and I just shrug it off, I do not even turn. A moment later, I run forward and enter the smoke-filled building, crouched low.

The heat is intense. My eyes sting; I can see next to nothing. There is a terrible noise of wind rushing through the structure and the crackle of flames burning furiously, and the heat of the fires below and above. In several places in the darkness are roaring pockets of flame that, as the billowing smoke swirls, suddenly burn brightly. I look into rooms and see them in just white, yellow, red and orange, coughing and choking on the eye-cutting smoke. Upstairs, balls of fire emerge suddenly out of the darkness and lick across the ceiling. I recall the houses we set alight in France, and how they roared into infernos as we watched them.

On the first floor I can find no one, and so proceed up to the second floor. I inch my way forward on my knees in the scorching darkness. The smoke here is angry and the flames, when they appear, move so fast. On the second landing I come to a door, which is shut: I reach up and feel for the handle. The heat of it immediately burns my hand. With my eyes shut, I try to open it using my tunic. But still it does not open: it is locked. I get to my feet and use my shoulder. Still it does not open. Choking and spluttering, I draw back and kick it hard, repeatedly, until it gives way.

Inside the room is aglow. Part of the roof has collapsed, and the brightness of the flames shows me that this is where the old woman and her grandchildren were. She is dead, flames swarming all across on her clothes and hair. One of the children, an infant, is also dead, lying alongside her. The other child, who is about nine years of age, is on the far side of the room. He is alive, crying, trapped beneath a fallen beam, which is itself burning. He holds his arms out to me as if I can pull him out from the disaster. I go to him and hold his blood-covered hands, and look into his eyes. I have seen that expression of pleading terror before, in Lazarus.

'I am here to help you. What is your name?'

He cannot hear me. His crying turns to screaming. Still he holds his hands out to me.

I try to lift the beam off him but it is far too heavy. I shout to him to stay still, and that I will have him out of here soon, but the smoke gets to me and my coughing and blindness make me flounder as I search frantically. I see a chair in the smoke and, smashing it against the floor, I draw from it a length of wood about three feet long; I jam this under the heavy timber in the hope of lifting it off him but it barely moves more than an inch or two. Then the lever snaps, leaving the timber to fall back on him, forcing a cry of agony from him.

And his eyes close.

This is what it means to sell your soul. You want to empty your bones of time. What does that mean? It's not that you want to die. You want never to have lived.

'Why could you not let me save this one poor boy?' I look up at the rolling flames. 'Why, in all these centuries of struggling and suffering – why have you not let me do one good act? Why have you denied me?'

The heat now is unbearable. I scream with the pain of it scorching my skin. I remember the story of the Protestant martyr, Anne Askew, burning for her faith. Endurance, everything in life is about endurance. Through the door I can see the whole stairwell alight, and high flames rushing through, striving to reach Heaven faster than me.

I fall to my knees, and cough again as the smoke and flames rise in a furious black and orange rage all around me. I lie on the floorboards beside the dead boy. I take his hand in mine, hoping he will lead me safely into whatever death holds for us.

My sleeves are on fire.

And now I hear the voice. The voice of Faustus. The voice of my conscience.

'Do you still believe the will of man is the will of God?'

It is steady amid the heat and fear. I try to reply with an equal calm. 'This cannot be the will of God. This is the will of man – they are not the same.' But my hair is burning, my skin weeping with my own fat. 'What more do you want from me?'

'If this be the will of man,' says the voice, 'and you are a man, is this not your will?'

'This is no will of mine,' I gasp. 'Man is a devil to man, that I've learned.'

'And is that all you've learned?'

The pain of the burning rips another layer of skin from me. 'I . . . understand that everything has a dark side and a good. Not even a good man can make the world a better place for everyone. Even if all the men and women in the world were kind to one another, it would not last. It would be merely a moment, and that moment of perfection would pass as surely as the hand on a clock passing the hour, moving onward towards strife and war.'

I feel strangely apart from my body, as it lies there on the floorboards in the smoke and fire. I see the flames on my arms now, I do not feel them. But I cannot move.

'And what else have you learned?'

'That men and women have a limited capacity for happiness and suffering. If you were to make their lives more luxurious, and to remove their pain, they would find other ways in which to be discontented. And if you were to make their lives miserable, they would find joy in the slightest delights.'

'Tell me more.'

'I know nothing, please.'

'You know the secret of life. You saw it when the girl gave you something that was yours.'

The girl? Celia? Rose? Then I remember. 'If all the world were to turn bad and everyone were to be touched by evil, just one good act would restore my hope in mankind.'

'Your six days are now over,' says the voice. 'Is there anything else you wish to say before judgement is passed upon you?'

I look at the burning bodies in the orange-lit room. 'I . . . I wish I could have helped more. I wanted to help people but I never could. I was weak, ignorant and useless. The only good that touched my life was what other people did for me.'

'Stand up, John,' says the voice.

I slowly get to my feet. There is no effort or pain now. I close my eyes.

'What you have just said to me, say to God.'

'To God?'

'Yes, to God.'

'Lord, Father Almighty, Maker of Heaven and Earth, I so wanted to help others, but I must be an unworthy beast, as You must know, for I never could. The only good that touched my life was what others did for me – and I am so sorry. For I know that it is not enough not to sin but rather I should have done a truly good act. So cast me out now – do away with my soul forever, but I pray, listen to me as I speak of my brother, William. He was not always chaste. He ate red meat on the fast days and often did not go to church. But he was true to us, and true to himself, and true to all those that he loved. And do not forget the soul of my good wife Catherine, who always loved me, from the day she first danced a cartwheel for me. Without her, I would've been a most sad and lonely man.'

'Open your eyes,' says the voice.

I do. And I see that the flames around me are not orange

and red but blue and green. They are the blue of the sky and the green of the hills.

'Do you see now?'

'See what?' I ask.

'You are the most blessed of men.'

'Blessed? In what way? I failed in everything.'

'John, you did the greatest good a man can do.'

'Jest not, please, I can suffer no more.'

'You did the greatest good a man can do – only you do not see it, for you are looking only at yourself. You must see what you mean to others to know your true worth.'

'But I was nothing. I wore rags, I begged. I killed a man. I failed even to save this boy.'

'No, John. You saved them all. Without you, none of them would have lived.'

'I beg you . . .'

'At the stones on Scorhill, you chose not to return to your home. Had you chosen otherwise, your family would have all perished from the pestilence.'

'But that is what happened – I saw the ruined house.'

'No, John, they all lived. Everyone you have met since then has lived because of you. Every one of them is your descendant.'

I cannot speak.

'Your sons became prosperous and sired children, remembering you in all goodness. And your twelve grandchildren did likewise, and your great-grandchildren. None of the people you have met in other ages would have lived if it had not been for your decision. And if among such people you've glimpsed some goodness, then that goodness arises from you. You are right in thinking that people in themselves are not good or bad; it is what they do for others that matters. You gave life to millions. They do not know your name but your good action remains forever, and cannot be undone.

'A beast could have done as much.'

'No, John. You gave them strength. Your three sons all remembered how, when they were downhearted, you would take them outside the house and show them the night sky and say, "Look! It is never truly dark, you can always see something, even if it is just the shape of a tree." And each one of them was so moved by that that in turn he said the same thing to his sons and daughters, and they to theirs, so that comfort passed down the centuries. Some forgot those words; others remembered. But they all understood from you what it was to want to live and to battle with adversity.'

And as I hear those words, with the blue and the green flames all around me, and the burning of the sun itself inside me, I finally understand the beautiful secret of dying. It is that one may, at last, escape the tyranny of time. I do not know, in truth, where my body lies. I do not know if it remained on the top of the cathedral screen all those years ago, or rotted away at the stones on the moor. I do not know if I drowned in the Exe, or burned in the fire in Holloway Street. It doesn't matter. These blue flames are not just the blue of the sky, they are the blue of the sky above Wrayment on a spring day. The green of those flames is the grass of the hills above the Wray Valley. I know this place. I can see my house – I am walking towards it, taking the old familiar bend in the lane and seeing the thatched roof. As I approach, I see the door open, and Catherine appears. No sculpted memento in the cathedral: she is there in the flesh. She looks towards me, recognises me, and then starts running, holding her skirts up to aid her speed. Our eyes meet, and I hold her again – I *hold* her. I hold her as if our lives are blessed by our being forever conjoined. And that is what matters. And nothing else. For in that embrace, which is our ending and our beginning, I know that, whatever happened to me, before I died, I did one small but truly great thing.